I0576695

James H. Graff, Edmund Hodgson Yates

The Forlorn Hope

a novel

James H. Graff, Edmund Hodgson Yates

The Forlorn Hope
a novel

ISBN/EAN: 9783337349370

Printed in Europe, USA, Canada, Australia, Japan

Cover: Foto ©Andreas Hilbeck / pixelio.de

More available books at **www.hansebooks.com**

THE FORLORN HOPE.

A Novel.

BY

EDMUND YATES,

AUTHOR OF

"KISSING THE ROD," "BLACK SHEEP," "LAND AT LAST," ETC., ETC

FOURTH EDITION.

LONDON:
CHAPMAN AND HALL, 193, PICCADILLY.
1868.

[*The right of Translation is reserved.*]

TO

CHARLES FECHTER

CONTENTS.

CONTENTS.

THE FORLORN HOPE.

CHAPTER I.

"SOUND AN ALARM."

THE half-hour dressing-bell rung out as Sir Duncan Forbes jumped from the hired carriage which had borne him the last stage of his journey to Kilsyth, and immediately followed his servant, who had put in a pantomimically abrupt appearance at the carriage-door, to his room. The steaming horses shook their sides, and rattled their harness dismally, in the dreary autumnal evening; but a host of gillies and understrappers had hurried out at the noise of the approaching wheels, and so quickly despoiled the carriage of its luggage, that within a very few minutes its driver—comforted by something over his fare, in addition to a stiff glass of the incomparable Kilsyth whisky—was slowly wending his way back, over a road which to any one but a Highlander would have seemed impassable in the fog that had begun to cloud the neighbouring mountains in an almost impenetrable shroud of misty gray. From the cold, chilly, damp mountain air, from the long solitary ride, for the last twenty miles of which he had not met a human creature, to the airy bedroom with its French paper, the

B

bright wood-fire burning on its hearth, the wax candles on
the dressing-table, the drawn chintz curtains, the neat
writing-table, the little shelf of prettily-bound well-chosen
books, was a transition indeed for Duncan Forbes. One
glance around sufficed to show him all these things, and to
show him in addition the steaming bath, the warmed linen,
the other various arrangements for his comfort which the
forethought of Dixon his servant had prepared for him.
He was used to luxuries, and thoroughly accustomed to
rough it; he was not an impressionable young man; but
there are times, even if we be only eight-and-twenty, good-
looking, and in the Household Brigade, when we feel a
kind of sympathy with the working-man who declared that
"life was not all beer and skittles," and are disposed to
look rather more seriously than usual upon our own condition and our surroundings. The journey from Glenlaggan
—it is, it must be confessed, an awful road—had had its
effect on Duncan Forbes. Why he should have permitted
himself to be worked upon either by a sense of solitude, or
by an involuntary tribute to the wildness of the scenery,
or perhaps by dyspepsia, arising from a recent change of
living, to fall temporarily into a low state of mind; to
think about his duns, debts, and difficulties; to wonder
why he was not at that moment staying with his mother in
Norfolk, instead of plunging into the depths of the Highlands; to think of his cousin Ethel Spalding, and to clench
his fists violently and mutter strong expressions as the
image of a certain Dundas Adair, commonly called Lord
Adair, rose before him simultaneously with that of his said
cousin; why he then fell into a state which was half lachrymose and half morose, impelling him to refresh himself
from a silver flask, and to make many mental resolutions
as to his future life,—why he did all this is utterly immaterial to us, as Sir Duncan Forbes is by no manner of
means our hero, in fact, has very little to do with our story.

But the journey had its effect upon him, and rendered the comfort and luxury of Kilysth doubly precious in his eyes. So that when he had had his bath, and, well advanced in his dressing, was luxuriating in the comfort of cleanliness and fresh linen, and the prospect of an excellent dinner, he had sufficiently returned to his normal condition to ask Dixon—who had preceded him by a couple of days—whether the house was full, and who were there.

"House quite full, sir," replied Dixon. "Colonel Jefferson, sir, of the First Life-guards; Capting Severn, sir, of the Second Life-guards, and his lady; Markis Towcester, as have jist jined the Blues; Honble Capting Shaddock, of the Eighteenth 'Ussars; Lord Roderick Douglas, of the Scots Fusiliers; and—"

"Drop the Army List, Dixon," growled his master, at that moment performing heavily on his head with a pair of hair-brushes; "who else is here?"

"There's the Danish Minister, sir—which I won't try to pronounce his name—and his lady; and there's the Dook and Duchess of Northallerton—which the Dook has the gout that bad, his man told me—used to be in our ridgment, Sir Duncan, and was bought out by his mother on his father's death—as to be past bearin' sometimes; and Lady Fairfax, sir; and Lady Dunkeld, as is Lady Muriel's cousin, sir; and a Mr Pitcairn, as is a distant relation of the family's; and a Mr Fletcher, as is, I'm told, a hartist, or something of that kind, sir—he hasn't brought a man here, sir; so I'm unable to say; but he seems to be well thought of, sir; quite at his ease, as they say, among the company, sir."

"Dear me!" said Duncan Forbes, suspending the action of the hair-brushes for a moment, while he grinned grimly; "you seem to be a great observer, Dixon."

"Well, sir, one can't keep one's hears shut entirely, nor one's eyes, and I noticed this gentleman took a kind of leading part in the talk at dinner sir, yesterday. Oh, I forgot, sir; Miss Kilsyth have not been well for the last two or three days, sir; kep' her room, havin' caught cold returnin' from a luncheon-party up at what they call a shealing—kind of 'ut, sir, in the 'ills, where they put up when stalkin', as I make out, sir—and her maid says is uncommon low and bad."

"Ill, is she?—Miss Kilsyth? Jove, that's bad! Haven't they sent for a doctor, or that kind of thing?"

"Yes, sir, they have sent for a doctor; and he's been, sir; leastways when I say doctor, sir, I mean to say the 'pothecary from the village, sir. Comes on a shady kind of a cob, sir, and I shouldn't say knew much about it. Beg your pardon, sir—dinner gong!"

Sir Duncan Forbes' toilette is happily complete at the time of this announcement, and he sallies downstairs towards the drawing-room. Entering, he finds most of the company already assembled; and in the careless glance which he throws around as the door closes behind him, he recognizes a bevy of London friends, looking, with perhaps the addition of a little bronze in the men, and a little plumpness in the ladies, exactly as he left them at the concluding ball of the season two months ago. Some he has not seen for a longer period, his host among them. Kilsyth of Kilsyth, keen sportsman, whether with rod or gun; landlord exercising influence over his tenants, not by his position alone, but by the real indubitable interest which he takes in their well-being; lord-lieutenant of his county, first patron and best judge at its agricultural meetings, chairman of the bench of magistrates, prime mover in the herring fishery,—what does Kilsyth of Kilsyth do in London? Little enough, truth to tell; gives a very perfunctory attendance at the House of Commons, meets old friends at Brookes's, dines at a few of the earlier meetings of the Fox Club, and does his utmost to keep out of the way of the Liberal whip, who dare not offend him, and yet grieves most lamentably over his shortcomings at St Stephen's. See him now as he stands on the hearth-rug, with his back to the drawing-room fire, a hale hearty man, whose fifty years of life have never bent his form nor scarcely dimmed the fire in his bright blue eye. Life, indeed, has been pretty smooth and pleasant to Kilsyth since, when a younger son, he was gazetted to the 42nd; and after a slight sojourn in that distinguished regiment, was sent for by his father to take the place of his elder brother, killed by the bursting of a gun when out on a stalk. A shadow—deep enough at the moment, but now mercifully lightened by Time, the grim yet kindly consoler—had fallen across his path when his wife, whom he loved so well, and whom he had taken from her quiet English home, where, a simple parson's daughter, she had captivated the young Highland officer, had died in giving birth to a second child. But he had survived the shock; and long afterwards, when he had succeeded to the family title and estates, and was, indeed, himself well on the way to middle age, had married again. Kilsyth's second wife was the sister of a Scottish earl of old family and small estate, a high-bred woman, much younger than her husband, who had borne him two children (little children at the time our story opens), and who, not merely in her Highland neighbourhood, but in the best society of London, in which she was ungrudgingly received, was looked upon as a pattern wife. With the name of Lady Muriel Kilsyth the most inveterate scandalmongers had never ventured to make free. The mere fact of her being more than twenty years younger than her husband had given them the greatest hope of onslaught when the marriage was first announced; but Lady Muriel had calmly faced her foes, and not the most observant of them had as yet espied the smallest flaw in her harness. Her behaviour to her husband, without being in the least degree gushing, was so thoroughly circumspect, they lived together on such excellent terms of something that was evidently more than amity, though it never pretended to devotion, that the scandalmongers were utterly defeated. Balked in one direction, they launched out in another; they could not degrade the husband by their pity, but they could mildly annoy the wife with reflections on her conduct to her step-children. "Poor little things," they said, "with such an ambitious woman for step-mother, and children of her own to think of! Ronald may struggle on; but as for poor Madeleine—" and uplifted eyebrows and shrugged shoulders completed the sentence. It is needless to say that Kilsyth himself heard none of these idle babblings, or that if he had, he would have treated them with scorn. "My lady" was to him the incarnation of everything that was right and proper, that was clever and far-seeing; he trusted her implicitly in every matter; he looked up to and respected her; he suffered himself to be ruled by her, and she ruled him very gently and with the greatest talent and tact in every matter of his life save one. Lady Muriel was all-powerful with her husband, except when, as he thought, her views were in the least harsh or despotic towards his daughter Madeleine; and then he quietly but calmly held his own way. Madeleine was his idol, and no one, not even his wife, could shake him in his adoration of her. As he stands on the hearth-rug, there is a shadow on his bright cheery face, for he has had bad news of his darling since he came in from shooting,—has been forbidden to go to her room lest he should disturb her; and at each opening of the door he looks anxiously in that direction, half wishing, half fearing Lady Muriel's advent with the doctor's latest verdict on the invalid.

The thin slight wiry man talking to Kilsyth, and rattling on garrulously in spite of his friend's obvious preoccupation, is Captain Severn, perhaps the best steeple-chase rider in England, and untouchable at billiards by any amateur. He is a slangy, turfy, raffish person, hating ladies' society, and using a singular vocabulary full of *Bell's-Life* idioms. He is, however, well connected, and has a charming wife, for whose sake he is tolerated; a lovely little fairy of a woman, whose heart is as big as her body; the merriest, most cheerful, best-tempered creature, trolling out her little French *chansons* in a clear bird-like voice; acting in charades with infinite character and piquancy; and withal the idol of the poor in the neighbourhood of their hunting-box in Leicestershire; and the quickest, softest, and most attentive nurse in sickness, as a dozen of her friends could testify.

That bald head which you can just see over the top of the *Morning Post* belongs to the Duke of Northallerton, who has been all his life more or less engaged in politics; who has, when his party has been in office, held respectively the important positions of Postmaster-General and Privy Seal; and who was never so well described as by one of his private secretaries, who declared tersely that his grace was a "kind old pump." Outwardly he is a tall man of about fifty-five, with a high forehead, which has stood his friend through life, and obtained him credit for gifts which he never possessed, a boiled-gooseberry eye, a straight nose, and projecting buck-teeth. As becomes an old English gentleman, he wears a very high white cravat and a large white waistcoat; indeed it is only within the last few years that he has relinquished his blue coat and gold buttons, and very tight pantaloons. He is reading the paper airily through his double glasses, and uttering an occasional "Ha!" and "Dear me!" as he wades through the movements of the travelling aristocracy; but from time to time he removes the glasses from his nose, and looks up with a half-peevish glance at his neighbour, Colonel Jefferson. Charley Jefferson (no one ever called him anything else) has a large photograph album before him, at which he is not looking in the least; on the contrary, his glance is directed straight in front of him; and as he stands six feet four, his eyes, when he is sitting, would be about on a level with a short man's head; and he is tugging at his great sweeping grizzled moustache, and fidgeting with his leg, and muttering between his clinched teeth at intervals short phrases, which sound like "Little brute! break his neck! beastly little cad!" and such-like.

The individual thus objurgated by the Colonel is highly thought of by Sir Bernard Burke, and known to Debrett as John Ulick Delatribe, Marquis of Towcester, eldest son of the Duke of Plymouth, who has just been gazetted to the Blues, after some years at Eton and eighteen months' wandering on the Continent. Though he is barely twenty, a more depraved young person is rarely to be found; his tutor, the Rev. Merton Sandford, who devoted the last few years of his life to him, and who has retired to his well-earned preferment of the largest living in the duke's gift, lifts up his eyes and shakes his head when, over a quiet bottle of claret with an old college friend, he speaks of Lord Towcester. The boy's reputation had preceded him to London; a story from the Viennese Embassy, of which he was the hero, came across in a private note to Blather-wick of the F. O., enclosed in the official white sheep-skin despatch-bag, and before night was discussed in half the smoking-rooms in Pall-Mall. The youngsters laughed at the anecdote and envied its hero; but older men looked grave; and Charley Jefferson, standing in the middle of a knot of men on the steps of the Rag, said he was deuced glad that the lad wasn't coming into his regiment; for if that story were true, the service would be none the better for such an accession to it, as, if it were his business, he should take an early opportunity of pointing out; and the listeners, who knew that Colonel Jefferson was the best soldier and the strictest martinet throughout the household cavalry, and who marked the expression of his face as he pulled his moustache and strode away after delivering his dictum, thought that perhaps it was better for Towcester that his lot was cast in a different corps. You would not have thought there was much harm in the boy, though, from his appearance. Look at him now, as he bends over Lady Fairfax, until his face almost touches her soft glossy hair. It is a round, boyish, ingenuous face, though the eyes are rather deeply set, and there is something cruel about the mouth which the thin downy moustache utterly fails to hide. As Lady Fairfax turns her large dark eyes on her interlocutor, and looks up at him, her brilliant white teeth flashing in an irrepressible smile, the Colonel's growls become more frequent, and he tugs at his moustache more savagely than ever. Why? If you know anything about these people, you will remember that ten years ago, when Emily Fairfax was Emily Ponsonby, and lived with her old aunt, Lady Mary, in the dull rambling old house at Kew, Charley Jefferson, a penniless cornet in what were then the 13th Light Dragoons, was quartered at Hounslow; danced, rode, and flirted with her; carried off a lock of her hair when the regiment was ordered to India; and far away up country, in utter ignorance of all that was happening in England, used to gaze at it and kiss it, long after Miss Ponsonby had married old Lord Fairfax, and had become the reigning belle of the London season. Old Lord Fairfax is dead now, and Charley Jefferson has come into his uncle's fortune; and there is no cause or impediment why these twain should not become one flesh, save that Emily is still coquettish, and Charley is horribly jealous; and so matters are still in the balance.

The little old gentleman in the palpable flaxen wig and gold spectacles, who is poring over that case of Flaxman's cameos in genuine admiration, is Count Bulow, the Danish

Ambassador; and the little old lady whose face is so
wrinkled as to suggest an idea of gratitude that she is a
lady, and consequently is not compelled to shave, is his
wife. They are charming old people, childless themselves,
but the cause of constant matchmaking in others. More
flirtations come to a successful issue in the embassy at
Eaton-place than in any other house in town; and the old
couple, who have for years worthily represented their
sovereign, are sponsors to half the children in Belgravia.
They are both art-lovers, and their house is crammed with
good things—pictures from Munich and Düsseldorf, choice
bits of Thorwaldsen, big elk-horns, and quaint old Scan-
dinavian drinking-cups. Old Lady Potiphar, who has the
worst reputation and the bitterest tongue in London, says
you meet " odd people " at the Bulows'; said " odd people "
being artists and authors, English and foreign. Mr Fletcher, R.A., who is just now talking to the Countess, is one
of the most favoured guests at the embassy, but he is not
an "odd person," even to Lady Potiphar, for he goes into
what she calls " sassiety," and has been " actially asked to
Mar'bro' House "—where Lady Potiphar is not invited. A
quiet, unpretending, gentlemanly, middle-aged man, Mr
Fletcher; wearing his artistic honours with easy dignity,
and by no means oblivious of the early days when he gave
drawing-lessons at per hour to many of the nobility who
now call him their friend.

There are three or four young ladies present, who need
no particular description, and who are dividing the homage
of Captain Shaddock; while Lord Roderick Douglas, a young
nobleman to whom Nature has been more bountiful in nose
than in forehead, and Mr Pitcairn, a fresh-coloured, freckled,
blue-eyed gentleman, lithe and active as a greyhound, are
muttering in a corner, making arrangements for the next
day's shooting.

The entrance of Sir Duncan Forbes caused a slight

commotion in the party; and every one had a look or a word of welcome for the new comer, for he was a general favourite. He moved easily from group to group, shaking hands and chatting pleasantly. Kilsyth, who was specially fond of him, grasped his hand warmly; the Duke laid aside the *Morning Post* in the midst of a most interesting leader, in which Mr Bright was depicted as a pleasant compound of Catiline and Judas Iscariot; Count Bulow gave up his cameos; and even grim Charley Jefferson relaxed in his feverish supervision of Lord Towcester.

As for the ladies, they unanimously voted Duncan charming, quite charming, and could not make too much of him.

"And where have you come from, Duncan?" asked Kilsyth, when the buzz consequent on his entrance had subsided.

"Last, from Burnside," said Duncan.

"Burnside!—where's Burnside?" asked Captain Severn shortly.

"Burnside is on the Tay, the prettiest house in all Scotland, if I may venture to say so, being at Kilsyth; of course it don't pretend to anything of this kind. It's a mere doll's-house of a place, nothing but a shooting-box; but in its way it's a perfect paradise."

"Are you speaking by the card, Duncan?" said Count Bulow, with the slightest foreign accent; "or was there some Peri in this paradise that gave it such fascination in your eyes?"

"Peri! No indeed, Count," replied Duncan, laughing; "Burnside is a bachelor establishment,—rigidly proper, quite monastic, and all that kind of thing. It belongs to old Sir Saville Rowe, who was a swell doctor in London—oh, ages ago!"

"Sir Saville Rowe!" exclaimed the Duke; "I know him very well. He was physician to the late King, and was knighted just before his Majesty's death. I haven't seen him for years, and thought he was dead."

"He's anything but that, Duke. A remarkably healthy old man, and as jolly as possible; capital company still, though he's long over seventy. And his place is really lovely; the worst of it is, it's such a tremendous distance from here. I've been travelling all day; and as it is I thought I was late for dinner. The gong sounded as I left my room."

"You were late, Duncan; you always are," said Kilsyth, with a smile. "But the Duchess is keeping you in countenance to-night, and Lady Muriel has not shown yet. She is up with Madeleine, who is ill, poor child."

"Ah, so I was sorry to hear. What is it? Nothing serious, I hope?"

"No, please God, no. But she caught cold, and is a little feverish to-night; the doctor is with her now, and we shall soon have his report. Ah, here is the Duchess."

The Duchess of Northallerton, a tall portly woman, with a heavy ruminating expression of face, like a sedate cow, entered as he spoke, and advancing said a few gracious nothings to Duncan Forbes. She was closely followed by a servant, who, addressing his master, said that Lady Muriel would be engaged for a few minutes longer with the doctor, and had ordered dinner to be served.

The conversation at dinner, falling into its recent channel, was resumed by Lord Towcester, who said, "Who had you at this doctor's, Duncan? Queer sort of people, I suppose?"

"Some of his patients, perhaps," said Lady Fairfax, showing all her teeth.

"Black draught and that sort of thing to drink, and cold compresses on the sideboard," said Captain Severn, who was nothing if not objectionable.

"I never had better living, and never met pleasanter people," said Duncan Forbes pointedly. "They wouldn't have suited you, perhaps, Severn, for they all talked sense; and none of them knew the odds on anything—though that might have suited you perhaps, as you'd have been able to win their money."

"Any of Sir Saville's profession?" cut in the Duke, diplomatically anxious to soften matters.

"Only one—a Dr Wilmot; the great man of the day, as I understand."

"Oh, everybody has heard of Wilmot," said half-a-dozen voices.

"He's the great authority on fever, and that kind of thing," said Jefferson. "Saved Broadwater's boy in typhus last year when all the rest of them had given him up."

"Dr Wilmot remains there," said Duncan; "our party broke up yesterday, but Wilmot stays on. He and I had a tremendous chat last night, and I never met a more delightful fellow."

At this moment Lady Muriel entered the room, and as she passed her husband's chair laid a small slip of paper on the table by his plate; then went up to Duncan Forbes, who had risen to receive her, and gave him a hearty welcome. Kilsyth took an opportunity of opening the paper, and the healthy colour left his cheeks as he read:

"*M. is much worse to-night. Dr Joyce now pronounces it undoubted scarlet-fever.*"

The old man rose from the table, asking permission to absent himself for a few moments; and as he moved, whispered to Duncan, who was sitting at his right hand, "You said Dr Wilmot was still at Burnside?"

Receiving an answer in the affirmative, he hurried into the hall, wrote a few hasty lines, and gave them to the butler, saying, "Tell Donald to ride off at once to Acray, and telegraph this message. Tell him to gallop all the way."

CHAPTER II.

MASTER AND PUPIL.

DUNCAN FORBES was given to exaggeration, as is the fashion of the day ; but he had scarcely exaggerated the beauty of Burnside, even in the rapturous terms which he chose to employ in speaking of it. It was, indeed, a most lovely spot, standing on the summit of a high hill, wooded from base to crest, and with the silver Tay—now rushing over a hard pebbly bed, now softly flowing in a scarcely fathomable depth of still water through a deep ravine with towering rocks on either side—bubbling at its feet. From the higher windows —notably from the turret ; and it was a queer rambling turreted house, without any preponderating style of architecture, but embracing, and that not unpicturesquely, a great many —you looked down upon the pretty little town of Dunkeld, with its broad bridge spanning the flood, and the grey old tower of its cathedral rearing itself aloft like a hoary giant athwart the horizon, and the trim lawn of the ducal residence in the distance—an oasis of culture in a desert of wildness, yet harmonizing sufficiently with its surroundings. Sloping down the steep bank on which the house was placed, and overhanging the brawling river beneath, ran a broad gravel path, winding between the trees, which at certain points had had been cut away to give the best views of the neighbouring scenery ; and on this path, at an early hour on the morning succeeding the night on which Duncan Forbes had arrived at Kilsyth, two men were walking, engaged in earnest conversation. An old man one of them, but in the enjoyment of a vigorous old age ; his back is bowed, and he uses a stick ; but if you remark, he does not use it as a crutch, lifting it now and again to point his remark, or striking it on the ground to emphasize his decision. A tall old man, with long

white hair flowing away from under the brim of his wide-
awake hat, with bright blue eyes and well-cut features, and
a high forehead and white hands, with long, lithe, clever-
looking fingers. Those eyes and fingers have done their
work in their day, professionally and socially. Those eyes
have looked into the eyes of youth and loveliness, and have
read in them that in a few months their light would be
quenched for ever; those fingers have clasped the beating
pulses of seemingly full and vigorous manhood, and have
recognized that the axe was laid at the root of the apparently
tall and flourishing tree, and that in a little time it would
topple headlong down. Those eyes "looked love to eyes
that spake again;" those hands clasped hands that returned
their clasp, and that trembled fondly and confidingly within
them; that voice, professionally modulated to babble of
sympathy, compassion, and hope, trembled with passion and
whispered all its human aspirations into the trellised ear of
beauty, once and once only. Looking at the old gentleman,
so mild and gentle and benevolent, with his shirt-front
sprinkled with snuff, and his old-fashioned black gaiters and
his gouty shoes, you could hardly imagine that he was the
hero of a scandal which five-and-thirty years before had rung
through society, and given the *Satirist,* and other scurrilous
publications of the time, matter for weeks and weeks of filthy
comment. And yet it was so. Sir Saville Rowe (then Dr
Rowe), physician to one of the principal London hospitals,
and even then a man of mark in his profession, was called in
to attend a young lady who represented herself as a widow,
and with whom, after a time, he fell desperately in love.
For months he attended her through a trying illness, from
which, under his care, she recovered. Then, when her recovery was complete, he confessed his passion, and they were
engaged to be married. One night, within a very short time
of the intended wedding, he called at her lodgings and found
a man there, a coarse slangy blackguard, who, after a few

words, abruptly proclaimed himself to be the lady's husband,
and demanded compensation for his outraged honour.
Words ensued; and more than words; the man—half-drunk,
all bully—struck the doctor; and Rowe, who was a powerful
man, and who was mad with rage at what he imagined was a
conspiracy, returned the blows with interest. The police
were summoned, and Rowe was hauled off to the station-
house; but on the following day the prosecutor was not
forthcoming, and the doctor was liberated. The scandal
spread, and ruffians battened on it, as they ever will; but
Dr Rowe's courage and professional skill enabled him to
live it down; and when, two years after, in going round a
hospital ward with his pupils, he came upon his old love at
the verge of death, his heart, which he thought had been
sufficiently steeled, gave way within him, and once more he
set himself to the task of curing her. He did all that could
be done; had her removed to a quiet suburban cottage,
tended by the most experienced nurses, never grudged one
moment of his time to visit her constantly; but it was too
late: hard living and brutal treatment had done their work;
and Dr Rowe's only love died in his arms, imploring Heaven's
blessings on him. That wound in his life, deep as it was,
has long since cicatrized and healed over, leaving a scar
which was noticeable to very few long before he attained to
the first rank in his profession and received the titular reward of his services to royalty. He has for some time retired
from active practice, though he will still meet in consultation
some old pupil or former colleague; but he takes life easily
now, passing the season in London, the autumn in Scotland,
and the winter at Torquay; in all of which places he finds
old friends chattable and kindly, who help him to while away
the pleasant autumn of his life.

The other man is about eight-and-thirty, with keen bright
brown eyes, a broad brow, straight nose, thin lips, and heavy
jaw, indicative of firmness, not to say obstinacy; a tall man

with stooping shoulders, and a look of quiet, placid attention in his face; with a slim figure, a jerky walk, and a habit of clasping his hands behind his back, and leaning forward as though listening; a man likely to invite notice at first sight from his unmistakable earnestness and intellect, otherwise a quiet gentlemanly man, whose profession it was impossible to assign, yet who was obviously a man of mark in his way This was Chudleigh Wilmot, who was looked upon by those who ought to know as *the* coming man in the London medical profession; whose lectures were to be attended before those of any other professor at St Vitus's Hospital; whose contributions on fever cases to the *Scalpel* had given the *Times* subject-matter for a leader, in which he had been most honourably mentioned; and who was commencing to reap the harvest of honour and profit which accrues to the fortunate few. He is an old pupil of Sir Saville Rowe's, and there is no one in whose company the old gentleman has greater delight.

"Smoke, Chudleigh, smoke! Light up at once. I know you're dying to have your cigar, and daren't out of deference to me. Fancy I'm your master still, don't you?"

"Not a bit of it, old friend. I have given up after-breakfast smoking as a rule, because, you see, that delightful bell in Charles-street begins to ring about a quarter to ten, and—"

"So much the better. Let them ring. They were knockers in my day, and I recollect how delighted I used to be at every rap. But there's no one to ring or knock here; so you may take your cigar quietly. I've been longing for this time; longing to have what the people about here call a 'crack' with you—impossible while those other men were here; but now I've got you all to myself."

"Yes," said Wilmot, who by this time had lighted his cigar—"yes, and you'll have me all to yourself for the next four days: that is to say, if you will."

"If I will! Is there anything in the world could give me greater pleasure? I get young again, talking to you, Chudleigh. I mind me of the time when you used to come to lecture, a great raw boy, with, I should say, the dirtiest hands and the biggest note-book in the whole hospital." And the old gentleman chuckled at his reminiscence.

"Well, I've managed to wash the first, and to profit by the manner in which I filled the second from your lectures," said Wilmot, not without a blush.

"Not a bit, not a bit," interposed Sir Saville; "you would have done well enough without any lectures of mine, though I'm glad to think that in that celebrated question of anæsthetics you stuck by me, and enabled me triumphantly to defeat Macpherson of Edinburgh. That was a great triumph for us, that was! Dear me, when I think of the charlatans! Eh, well, never mind; I'm out of all that now. So you have a few days more, you were saying, and you're going to give them up to me."

"Nothing will please me so much. Because, you see, I shall make it a combination of pleasure and business. There are several things on which I want to consult you,—points which I have reserved from time to time, and on which I can get no such opinion as yours. I'm not due in town until the 3rd of next month. Whittaker, who has taken my practice, doesn't leave until the 5th, which is a Sunday, and even then only goes as far as Guildford, to a place he's taken for some pheasant-shooting; a nice, close, handy place, where Mrs Whittaker can accompany him. She thinks he's so fascinating, that she does not like to let him out of her sight."

"Whittaker! Whittaker!" said Sir Saville; "is it a bald man with a cock-eye?—used to be at Bartholomew's."

"That's the man! He's in first-rate practice now, and deservedly, for he's thoroughly clever and reliable; but his beauty has not improved by time. However, Mrs Whittaker doesn't see that; and it's with the greatest difficulty he ever gets permission to attend a lady's case."

" You must be thankful Mrs Wilmot isn't like that."

" Oh, I am indeed," replied Wilmot shortly.

" By the way, I've never had an opportunity of talking to you about your marriage, and about your wife, Chudleigh. I got your wedding cards, of course: but that's—ah, that must be three years ago."

" Four."

"Four! Is it indeed so long? Tut, tut! how time flies! I've called at your house in London, but your wife has not been at home; and as I don't entertain ladies, you see, of course I've missed an opportunity of cultivating her acquaintance."

" Ye-es. I've heard Mrs Wilmot say that she had seen your cards, and that she was very sorry to have been out when you called," said Dr Wilmot with, in him, a most unnatural hesitation.

" Yes, of course," said old Sir Saville, with a comical look out of the corners of his eyes, which fell unheeded on his companion. " Well, now, as I've never seen her, and as I'm not likely to see her now,—for I'm an old man, and I've given up ceremony visits at my time of life,—tell me about your wife, Chudleigh; you know the interest I take in you; and that, perhaps, may excuse my asking about her. Does she suit you? Are you happy with her?"

Wilmot looked hard for an instant at his friend with a sudden quick glance of suspicion, then relaxed his brows, and laughed outright.

" Certainly, my dear Sir Saville, you are the most original of men. Who on earth else would have dreamt of asking a man such a home-question? It's worse than the queries put in the proposal papers of insurance-offices. However, I'm glad to be able to give a satisfactory answer. I *am* happy with my wife, and she *does* suit me."

" Yes; but what I mean is, are you in love with her ? "

" Am I what ? "

" In love with her. I mean, are you always thinking of her when you are away from her ? Are you always longing to get back to her ? Does her face come between you and the book you are reading ? When you are thinking-out an intricate case, and puzzling your brains as to how you shall deal with it, do you sometimes let the whole subject slip out of your mind, to ponder over the last words she said to you, the last look she gave you ? "

" God bless your soul, my dear old friend ! You might as well ask me if I didn't play leap-frog with the house-surgeon of St Vitus's, or challenge any member of the College of Physicians to a single-wicket match. Those are the *délassements* of youth, my dear sir, that you are talking about ; of very much youth indeed."

" I know one who wasn't ' very much youth ' when he carried out the doctrine religiously," said the old gentleman in reply.

" Ah, then perhaps the lady wasn't his wife," said Wilmot, without the smallest notion of the dangerous ground on which he was treading. " No, the fact is simply this : I am, as you know, a man absorbed in my profession. I have no leisure for nonsense of the kind you describe, nor for any other kind of nonsense. My wife recognizes that perfectly ; she does all the calling and visiting which society prescribes. I go to a few old friends' to dinner in the season, and some-times show up for a few minutes at the house of a patient where Mrs Wilmot thinks it necessary for me to be seen. We each fulfil our duties perfectly, and we are in the evening excellent friends."

" Ye-es," said Sir Saville doubtfully ; " that's all delightful, and—"

" As to longing to get back to her, and face coming between you and your book, and always thinking, and that kind of thing," pursued Wilmot, not heeding him, "I recollect, when I was a dresser at the hospital, long before I passed the College, I had all those feelings for a little cousin of mine who was then living at Knightsbridge with her father, who was a clerk in the Bank of England. But then he died, and she married—not the barber, but another clerk in the Bank of England, and I never thought any more about it. Believe me, my dear friend, except to such perpetual evergreens as yourself, those ideas die off at twenty years of age."

"Well, perhaps so, perhaps so," said the old gentleman; "and I daresay it's quite right, only—well, never mind. Well, Chudleigh, it's a pleasant thing for me, remembering you, as I said, a great hulking lad when you first came to lecture, to see you now carrying away everything before you. I don't know that you're quite wise in giving Whittaker your practice, for he's a deep designing dog; and you can tell as well as I do how a word dropped deftly here and there may steal away a patient before the doctor knows where he is, especially with old ladies and creatures of that sort. But, however, it's the slack time of year,—that's one thing to be said,—when everybody that's anybody is safe to be out of town. Ah, by the way, that reminds me! I was glad to see by the *Morning Post* that you had had some very good cases last season."

"The *Morning Post!*—some very good cases! What do you mean?"

"I mean, I saw your name as attending several of the nobility : 'His lordship's physician, Dr Wilmot, of Charles Street,' et cetera ; that kind of thing, you know."

"Oh, do you congratulate me on those? I certainly pulled young Lord Coniston, Lord Broadwater's son, through a stiff attack of typhus; but as I would have done the same for his lordship's porter's child, I don't see the value of the paragraph. By the way, I shouldn't wonder if I were indebted to the porter for the paragraph."

"Never mind, my dear Chudleigh, whence the paragraph comes, but be thankful you got it. 'Sweet,' as Shakespeare says,—'sweet are the uses of advertisement;' and our profession is almost the only one to which they are not open. The inferior members of it, to be sure, do a little in the way of the red lamp and the vaccination gratis; but when you arrive at any eminence you must not attempt anything more glaring than galloping about town in your carriage, and getting your name announced in the best society."

"The best society!" echoed Wilmot with an undisguised sneer. "My dear Sir Saville, you seem to have taken a craze for Youth, Beauty, and High Life, and to exalt them as gods for your idolatry."

"For *my* idolatry! No, my boy, for yours. I don't deny that when I was in the ring, I did my best to gain the approbation of all three, and that I succeeded I may say without vanity. But I'm out of it now, and I can only give counsel to my juniors. But that my counsel is good worldly wisdom, Chudleigh, you may take the word of an old man who has—well, who has, he flatters himself, made his mark in life."

The old gentleman was so evidently sincere in this exposition of his philosophy, that Wilmot repressed the smile that was rising to his lips, and said:

"We can all of us only judge by our own feelings, old friend; and mine, I must own, don't chime in with yours. As to Youth—well, I'm now old for my age, and I only look upon it as developing more available resources and more available material to work upon; as to Beauty, its influence died out with me when Maria Strutt married the clerk in the Bank of England; and as to High Life, I swear to you it would give me as much pleasure to save the life of one of your gillies' daughters, as it would to be able to patch up an old marquis, or to pull the heir to a dukedom through his teething convulsions."

The old man looked at his friend for a moment and smiled sardonically, then said:

"You're young yet, Chudleigh; very young—much younger than your years of London life should permit you to be. However, that's a malady that Time will cure you of. Saving lives of gillies' daughters is all very well in the abstract, and no one can value more than I do the power which Providence, under Him, has given to us; but—Well, what is it?"

This last remark was addressed to a servant who was approaching them.

"A telegram, sir, for Dr Wilmot," said the man, handing an envelope to Wilmot as he spoke: "just arrived from the station."

Wilmot tore open the envelope and read its enclosure—read it twice with frowning brow and sneering mouth; then handed it to his host, saying:

"A little too strong, that, eh? Is one never to be free from such intrusions? Do these people imagine that because I am a professional man I am to be always at their beck and call? Who is this Mr Kilsyth, I wonder, who hails me as though I were a cabman on the rank?"

"*Mr* Kilsyth, my dear fellow!" said Sir Saville, laughing; "I should like to see the face of any Highlander who heard you say that. Kilsyth of Kilsyth is the head of one of the oldest and most powerful clans in Aberdeenshire."

"I suppose he won't be powerful enough to have me shot, or speared, or 'hangit on a tree,' for putting his telegram into my pocket, and taking no further notice of it, for all that," said Wilmot.

"Do you mean to say that you intend to refuse his request, Chudleigh?"

"Most positively and decidedly, if request you call it. I confess it looks to me more like a command; and that's a style of thing I don't particularly affect, old friend."

" But do you see the facts? Miss Kilsyth is down with scarlet-fever—"

" Exactly. I'm very sorry, I'm sure, so far as one can be sorry for any one of whose existence one was a moment ago in ignorance; and I trust Miss Kilsyth will speedily recover; but it won't be through any aid of mine."

" My dear Chudleigh," said the old man gently, " you are all wrong about this. It's not a pleasant thing for me. as your host, to bid you go away; more especially as I had been looking forward with such pleasure to these few days' quiet with you. But I know it is the right thing for you to do; and why you should refuse, I cannot conceive. You seem to have taken umbrage at the style of the message; but even if one could be polite in a telegram, a father whose pet daughter is dangerously ill seldom stops to pick his words."

" But suppose I hadn't been here? "

" My dear friend, I decline to suppose anything of the sort. Suppose I had not been in the way when Sir Astley advised his late Majesty to call me in; I should still have been a successful man, it's true; but I should not have had the honour or the position I have, nor the wealth which enables me now to enjoy my ease, instead of slaving away still like— like some whom we know. No, no; drop your radicalism, I beseech you. You would go miles to attend a sick gillie or a shepherd's orphan. Do the same for a very charming young girl, as I'm told,—Forbes knows her very well,—and for one of the best men in Scotland."

" Well, I suppose you're right, and I must go. It's an awful journey, isn't it? "

" Horses to the break, Donald; and tell George to get ready to drive Dr Wilmot.—I'll send you the first stage. Awful journey you call it, through the loveliest scenery in the Highlands! I don't know what causes the notion, but I have an impression that this will be a memorable day in your career, Chudleigh."

"Have you, old friend?" said Wilmot, with a shoulder-shrug. "One doesn't know how it may end, but, so far, it has been anything but a pleasant one. Nor does a fifty-mile journey over hills inspire me with much pleasant anticipation. But, as you seem so determined about it being my duty, I'll go."

"Depend on it, I am giving you good advice, as some day you shall acknowledge to me."

And within half-an-hour Chudleigh Wilmot had started for Kilsyth, on a journey which was to influence the whole of his future life.

CHAPTER III.

WATCHING AND WAITING.

THE news which she had learned from Doctor Joyce, and had in her brief pencil-note communicated to her husband, was horribly annoying to Lady Muriel Kilsyth. To have her party broken up—and there was no doubt that, as soon as the actual condition of affairs was known, many would at once take to flight—was bad enough; but to have an infectious disorder in the house, and to be necessarily compelled to keep up a semblance of sympathy with the patient labouring under that disorder, even if she were not required to visit and tend her, was to Lady Muriel specially galling; more specially galling as she happened not to possess the smallest affection for the individual in question, indeed to regard her rather with dislike than otherwise. When Lady Muriel Inchgarvie married Kilsyth of Kilsyth, —the Inchgarvie estates being heavily involved, and her brother the Earl, who had recently succeeded to the title, strongly counselling the match,—she agreed to love,

honour, and obey the doughty chieftain whom she espoused ;
but she by no means undertook any responsibilities with
regard to the two children by his former marriage. The
elder of these, Ronald, was just leaving Eton when his step-
mother appeared upon the scene ; and as he had since been
at once gazetted to the Life-guards, and but rarely showed
in his father's house, he had caused Lady Muriel very
little anxiety. But it was a very different affair with
Madeleine. She had the disadvantage of being perpetually
en évidence ; of being very pretty; of causing blundering
new acqaintances to say, "Impossible, Lady Muriel, that
this can be your daughter!" of riling her step-mother in
every possible way—notably by her perfect high-breeding,
her calm, quiet ignoring of intended slights, her deter-
minate persistence in keeping up the proper relations with
her father, and her invariable politeness—nothing but
politeness—to her step-mother. One is necessarily cautious of using strong terms in these days of persistent
repression of all emotions; but it is scarcely too much to
say that Lady Muriel hated her step-daughter very cordially. They were too nearly of an age for the girl to look
up to the matron, or for the matron to feel a maternal
interest in the girl. They were too nearly of an age for
the elder not to feel jealous of the younger—of her personal attractions, and of the influence which she undoubtedly exercised over her father.

Not that Lady Muriel either laid herself out for
attraction, or was so devotedly attached to her husband as
to desire the monopoly of his affection. By nature she was
hard, cold, self-contained, and very proud. Portionless as
she had been, and desirable as it was that she should
marry a rich man, she had refused several offers from men.
more coeval with her than the husband she at last accepted,
simply because they were made by men who were wealthy,
and nothing else. Either birth or talent would, in con-

junction with wealth, have won her; but Mr Burton, the great pale-ale brewer, and Sir Coke Only, the great railway carrier, proffered their suits in vain, and retired in the deepest confusion after Lady Muriel's very ladylike, but thoroughly unmistakable, rejection of their offers. Sho married Kilsyth because he was a man of ancient family, large income, warm heart, and good repute. At no period, either immediately before or after her marriage, had she professed herself to be what is called "in love" with the worthy Scotch gentleman. She respected, humoured, and ruled him. But not for one instant did she forget her duty, or give a chance for scandal-mongers to babble of her name over their five-o'clock tea. No woman married to a man considerably her senior need be at any loss for what, as Byron tells us, used to be called a *cicisbeo*, and was in his time called a *cortejo*, if she be the least attractive. And Lady Muriel Kilsyth was considerably more than that. She had a perfectly-formed, classical little head, round which her dark hair was always tightly bound, cul· minating in a thick knot behind, large, deep, liquid brown eyes, an impertinent *retroussé* nose, a pretty mouth, an excellent complexion, and a ripe melting figure. You might have searched the drawing-rooms of London through and through without finding a woman better calculated to fascinate everybody save the youngest boys, and there were many even of them who would gladly have boasted of a kind look or word from Lady Muriel. When her marriage was announced, they discussed it at the clubs, as they will discuss such things, the dear genial old prosers, the bibulous captains, the lip-smacking Bardolphs of St James's-street; and they prophesied all kinds of unhappiness and woe to Kilsyth. But that topic of conversation had long since died out for want of fuel to feed it. Lady Muriel had visited London during the season; had gone everywhere; had been reported as perfectly adoring her two little

children; and had no man's name invidiously coupled with
hers. Peace reigned at Kilsyth, and the intimates of the
house vied with each other in attention and courtesy to its
new mistress; while the gossips of the outside world had
never a word to say against her.

I don't say that Lady Muriel Kilsyth was thoroughly
happy, any more than that Kilsyth himself was in that
beatific state; because I simply don't believe that such a
state of things is compatible with the ordinary conditions
of human life. It is not because the old stories of our
none of us being better than we should be, of our all having
some skeleton in our cupboards, and some ulcerated sores
beneath our flannel waistcoats, have been so much harped
upon, that I am going to throw my little pebble on the
great cairn, and add my testimony to the doctrine of *vanitas
vanitatum*. It would be very strange indeed, if, as life is
now-a-days constituted, we had not our skeleton, and a time
when we could confront him; when we could calmly un-
twist the button on the door and let him out, and pat his
skull, and look at his articulated ribs and notice how deftly
his wire-hooked thigh-bones jointed on to the rest of his
carcass; and see whether there were no means of ridding
ourselves of him,—say by flinging him out of window, when
the police would find him, or of stowing him away in the
dust-bin, when he would be noticed by the contractor; and
of finally putting him back, and acknowledging ourselves
compelled to suffer him even unto the end. I do not say
that in the broad-shouldered, kind-hearted, jovial sportsman Lady Muriel had found exactly what she dreamed
upon when, in the terraced garden at Inchgarvie, she used
to read Walter Scott, and, looking over the flashing stream
that wound through her father's domain, fancy herself the
Lady of the Lake, and await the arrival of Fitzjames. I
do not say that Kilsyth himself might not, in the few
moments of his daily life which he ever spared to reflection,

and which were generally when he was shaving himself in
the morning,—I do not say that Kilsyth himself might not
have occasionally thought that his elegant and stately wife
might have been a little kinder to Madeleine, a little more
recognisant of the girl's charms, a little more thoughtful of
her wants, and a little more tender towards her girlish
vagaries. But neither of them, however they may have
thought the other suspected them, ever spoke of their
secret thoughts; and to the outer world there was no more
well-assorted couple than the Kilsyths.

It was a great thing for the comfort of the entire party
that Lady Muriel was a woman of nerve, and that Kilsyth
took his cue from her, backed up by the fact that it was
his darling Madeleine who was ill, and that any inconvenience that might accrue to any of the party in consequence
of her illness would be set down to her account. Lady
Muriel gave a good general answer, delivered with a glance
round the table, and was inclusive of everybody, so as to
prevent any further questioning. Dr Joyce had said that
Madeleine was not so well that night; but that was to be
expected; her cold was very bad, she was slightly feverish:
any one—and Lady Muriel turned deftly to the Duchess of
Northallerton—who knew anything, would have expected
that, would they not? The Duchess, who knew nothing,
but who didn't like to say so, declared that of course they
would; and then Lady Muriel, feeling it necessary *that*
conversation should be balked, turned to Sir Duncan
Forbes, and began to ask him questions as to his doings
since the end of the season. Forbes replied briskly,—there
was no better man in London to follow a lead, whether
in talk or at cards,—and so turned the talk that most of
those present were immediately interested. The names
which Duncan Forbes mentioned were known to all present; all were interested in their movements; all had something to say about them; so that the conversation speedily

became general, and so remained until the ladies quitted
the table. When they had retired, Kilsyth ordered in the
tumblers; and it was nearly eleven o'clock before the gentlemen appeared in the drawing-room. Then Lady Fairfax, with one single wave of her fan, beckoned Charley
Jefferson into an empty seat on the ottoman by her side,—
a seat which little Lord Towcester, immediately on entering
the door, had surveyed with vinous eyes,—and, while one
of the anonymous young ladies was playing endless variations on the "Harmonious Blacksmith," commenced and
continued a most vivid one-sided conversation, to all of
which the infatuated Colonel only replied by shrugs of his
shoulders and tugs at his heavy moustache. Then the
Duchess pursued the Duke into a corner; and rescuing
from him the *Morning Post*, which his grace had pounced
upon on entering the room with the hope of further iden-
tifying Mr Bright with Judas Iscariot, began addressing
him in a low monotone, like the moaning of the sea; now
rising into a little hum, now falling into a long sweeping
hiss, but in each variety evidently confounding the Duke,
who pulled at his cravat and rubbed his right ear in the
height of nervous dubiety In the behaviour of the other
guests there was nothing pronounced, save occasional and
unwonted restlessness. The Danish Minister and his wife
played their usual game at backgammon; and the customary
talk, music, and flirtation were carried on by the remainder of
the company; but Lady Muriel knew that some suspicion
of the actual truth had leaked out, and determined on her
plan of action.

So that night, when the men had gone to the smoking-
room, and the ladies were some of them talking in each
other's bed-rooms, and others digesting and thinking over, as
is the feminine manner, under the influence of hair-brush,
the events of the day; when Kilsyth had made a tip-toe visit
to his darling's chamber, and had shaken his head sadly over

a whispered statement from her little German maid that she was "*bien malade,*" and had returned to his room and dismissed his man, and was kicking nervously at the logs on the hearth, and mixing his tumbler preparatory to taking his narcotic instalment of *Blackwood,*—he heard a tap at his door, and Lady Muriel, in a most becoming dressing-gown of rose-coloured flannel, entered the room. The tumbler was put down, the *Blackwood* was thrown aside, and in a minute Kilsyth had wheeled an easy-chair round to the hearth, and handed his wife to it.

" You're tired, Alick, I know, and I wouldn't have disturbed you now had there not been sufficient reason—"

"Madeleine's not worse, Muriel ?   I was there this minute, and Gretchen said that—"

" O no, she's no worse ! I was in her room too just now,—though I think it is a little absurd my going,—and there does not seem to be much change in her since I saw her, just before dinner.   She is asleep just now."

" Thank God for that !" said Kilsyth heartily.   " After all, it may be a fright this doctor is giving us.   I don't think so very much of his opinion, and—"

" I could not say that.   Joyce is very highly thought of at Glasgow, and was selected from among all the competitors to take charge of this district, and that, in these days of competition, is no ordinary distinction.   And it is on this very point I came to speak to you.   You got my pencil-note at dinner ?   Very well.   Just now you contented yourself with asking a question of Gretchen—"

" She said Madeleine was asleep, and would not let me into the room."

" And quite rightly; but I went in to the bed-side. Madeleine is asleep certainly; but her sleep is restless, broken, and decidedly feverish.   There is not the smallest doubt that Dr Joyce is right in his opinion, and that she is attacked with scarlet-fever."

"You think so, Muriel?" said Kilsyth anxiously. "I mean not blindly following Joyce's opinion; but do you think so yourself?"

"I do; and not I alone, but half the house thinks so too. How do they know it? Heaven knows how these things ever get known, but they get wind somehow; and you will see that by to-morrow there will be a general flight. It is on this point that I have come to speak to you, if you will give me five minutes."

"Of course, Muriel; of course, my lady. But I think I've done the best that could be done; at all events, the first thing that occurred to me after you wrote me that note. Duncan Forbes had been saying in the drawing-room before dinner, before you came in, that the great London fever-physician, Dr Wilmot, was staying at Burnside, away from here about fifty miles, with old Sir Saville Rowe, whom I recollect when I was a boy. Duncan had left him this morning, and he was going to stay at Burnside just a day or two longer; and I sent one of the men with a telegram to the station, to ask Dr Wilmot to come over at once, and see Maddy."

Lady Muriel was so astonished at this evidence of prompt action on her husband's part that she remained silent for a minute. Then she said,

"That was quite right, quite right so far as Madeleine was concerned; but my visit related rather to other people. You see, so soon as it is actually known that there is an infectious disorder in the house, the house will be deserted. Now my question is this: will it not be better to announce it to our guests, making the best and the lightest of it, as of course one naturally would, rather than let them—"

"Ye-es, I see what you mean, my lady," said Kilsyth slowly; "and of course it would not do to keep people here under false pretences, and when we knew there was actual danger. Still I think as this story of scarlet-fever is only

Joyce's opinion, and as I have telegraphed for Dr Wilmot,
who will be here to-morrow; and as it seems strange, you
know, to think that poor darling Maddy should be the
cause of any one's leaving Kilsyth, perhaps, eh? one might
put off making the announcement until Joyce's opinion
were corroborated by Dr Wilmot."

"I am afraid the mischief is already done, Alick, and
that its results will be apparent long before Dr Wilmot
can reach here," said Lady Muriel. "However, let us sleep
upon it. I am sure to hear whether the news has spread
in the house long before breakfast, and we can consult
again." And Lady Muriel took leave of her husband, and
retired to her room.

Trust a woman for observation. Lady Muriel was perfectly right. The nods and shoulder-shrugs and whisper-
ings which she had observed in the drawing-room had already borne fruit. On her return to her own room she
saw a little note lying on her table—a little note which, as
she learned from Pinner, her attendant, had just been
brought by Lady Fairfax's maid. It ran thus:

"DEAREST LADY MURIEL,—A *frightful* attack of neuralgia (*my* neuralgia)—which, as you know, is so *awful*—has
been hanging over me for the last three days, and now has
come upon me in its *fullest force.* I am quite out of my
mind with it. I have striven—oh, how I have striven!—to
keep up and try to forget it, when surrounded by your
pleasant circle, and when looking at your *dear self.* But it
is all in vain. I am in *agonies.* The torture of the rack
itself can be *nothing* to what I am suffering to-night.

"Poor dear Sir Benjamin Brodie used to say that I
should never be well in a *northern* climate. I fear he was
right. I fear that the air of this darling Kilsyth, earthly
Paradise though it is—and I am sure that I have found it
so during three weeks of bliss; oh, such *happiness!*—is

D

too bracing, too invigorating for poor me. But I should *loathe* myself if I were to make this *an open* confession. So I will steal away, dearest Lady Muriel, without making any formal adieux. When all your dear friends assemble at breakfast to-morrow, I shall be on my *sorrowing* way south, and only regret that my wretched health prevents me longer remaining where I have been so entirely happy.

"With kindest regards to your dear husband, I am, dearest Lady Muriel, ever your loving

"EMILY FAIRFAX.

"P.S.—I have told my maid to beg some of your people to get me horses from the Kilsyth Arms; so that I shall *speed* away early in the morning without disturbing any one. I hope dear Madeleine will soon be *quite herself* again."

Lady Muriel read this letter through twice with great calmness, though a very scornful smile curled her lip during its perusal. She then twisted the note up into a whisp, and was about to burn it in the flame of the candle, when she heard a short solemn tap at her chamber-door. She turned round, bade Pinner open the door, and looked with more displeasure than astonishment at the Duchess of Northallerton, who appeared in the entrance. The Duchess had the credit in society of being a "haughty-looking woman." Her stronghold in life, beyond the fact of her being a duchess, had been in her Roman nose and arched eyebrows. But, somehow, haughty looks became wonderfully modified in *déshabillé*, and Roman noses and arched eyebrows lose a good deal of their potency when taken in conjunction with two tight little curls twisted up in hairpins, and a headdress which, however much fluted and gauffered, is unmistakably a nightcap. The Duchess's nocturnal adornments were unmistakably of this homely character, and her white wrapper was of a hue, which, if she had not been a duchess, would have been pronounced dingy. But her step was undoubtedly tragic, and the expression of her face solemn to a degree. Lady Muriel received her with uplifted eyebrows, and motioned her to a chair. The Duchess dropped stiffly into the appointed haven of rest; but arched her eyebrows at Pinner with great significance.

"You can go, Pinner. I shall not require you any more," said Lady Muriel; adding, "I presume that was what you wished, Duchess?" as the maid left the room.

"Precisely, dear Muriel; but you always were so wonderfully ready to interpret one's thoughts. I remember your dear mother used to say—but I won't worry you with my stories. I came to speak to you about dear Madeleine."

"Ye-es," said Lady Muriel quietly, finding the Duchess paused.

"Well, now, she's worse than any of them suspect. Ah, I can see it by your face. And I know what is the matter with her. Don't start; I won't even ask you; I won't let you commit yourself in any way; but I know that it's measles."

Lady Muriel kept her countenance admirably while the Duchess proceeded. "I know it by a sort of instinct. When Madeleine first complained of her head, I looked narrowly at her, and I said to myself, 'Measles! undoubtedly measles!' Now, you know, Muriel, though there is nothing dangerous in measles to a young person like Madeleine,— and she will shake them off easily, and be all the better afterwards,—they are very dangerous when taken by a person of mature age. And the fact is, the Duke has never had them—never. When Errington was laid up with them, I recollect the Duke wouldn't remain in the house, but went off to the Star and Garter, and stayed there until all trace of the infection was gone. And he's horribly afraid of them. You know what cowards men are in such matters; and he said just now he thought there was a rash on his neck.

Such nonsense! Only where his collar had rubbed him, as I told him. But he's dreadfully frightened; and he has suggested that instead of waiting till the end of the week, as we had intended, we had better go to-morrow."

"I think that perhaps under all circumstances it would be the best course," said Lady Muriel, quite calmly.

"I knew your good sense would see it in the right light, my dear Muriel," said the Duchess, who had been nervously anticipating quite a different answer, and who was overjoyed. "I was perfectly certain of your coincidence in our plan. Now, of course, we shall not say a word as to the real reason of our departure—the Duke, I know, would not have that for the world. We shall not mention it at Redlands either; merely say we—Oh, I shall find some good excuse, for Mrs Murgatroyd is a chattering little woman, as you know, Muriel. And now I won't keep you up any longer, dear. You'll kindly tell some one to get us horses to be ready by—say twelve to-morrow. Stay to luncheon? No, dear. I think we had better go before luncheon. The Duke, you see, is absurd about his ridiculous rash. *Good*-night, dear." And the Duchess stalked off to tell the Duke, who was not the least frightened, and whose rash was entirely fictitious, how well she had sped on her mission.

Lady Muriel accurately obeyed the requests made to her in Lady Fairfax's letter, and verbally by the Duchess; and each of them found their horses ready at the appointed time. Lady Emily departed mysteriously before breakfast; but as the Duchess's horses were not ordered till twelve, and as the post came in at eleven, her grace had time to receive a letter from Mrs Murgatroyd, of Redlands, whither they were next bound, requesting them to postpone their arrival for a day or two, as a German prince, who had by accident shot a stag, had been so elated by the feat, that he had implored to be allowed to stay on, with the chance of repeating it; and as he occupied the rooms intended for the Duke and Duchess, it was impossible to receive them until he left. After reading this letter, the Duchess went to Lady Muriel, and expressed her opinion that she had been too precipitate; that, after all, nothing positive had been pronounced; that there were no symptoms of the Duke's rash that morning, which had been undoubtedly caused, as she had said last night, by his collar, and which was no rash at all; and that perhaps, after all, their real duty was to stay and help their dear Muriel to nurse her dear invalid. But they had miscalculated the possibility of deceiving their dear Muriel. Lady Muriel at once replied that it was impossible that they could remain at Kilsyth; that immediately on the Duchess's quitting her on the previous night she had made arrangements as to the future disposition of the rooms which they occupied; that she would not for the world take upon herself the responsibility which would necessarily accrue to her if any of them caught the disease; and that she knew the Duchess's own feelings would tell her that she, Lady Muriel, however ungracious it might seem, was in the right in advising their immediate departure. The Duchess tried to argue the point, but in vain; and so she and the Duke, and their servants and baggage, departed, and passed the next three days at a third-rate roadside inn between Kilsyth and Redlands, where the Duke got lumbago, and the Duchess got bored; and where they passed their time alternately wishing that they had not left Kilsyth, or that the people at Redlands were ready to receive them.

Very little difference was made by the other guests at Kilsyth in the disposition of their day. If they were surprised at the sudden defection of the Northallertons and Lady Fairfax, they were too well-bred to show it. Charley Jefferson mooned about the house and grounds, a thought more disconsolate than ever; but he was the only member of the party who at all bemoaned the departure of the de-

parted.   Lady Dunkeld congratulated her cousin Muriel on
being rid of "those awful wet blankets," the Northallertons.
Captain Severn, in whispered colloquy with his wife, "hoped
to heaven Charley Jefferson would see what a stuck-up
selfish brute that Emily Fairfax was."   Lord Roderick
Douglas and Mr Pitcairn went out for their stalk; and all
the rest of the company betook themselves to their usual
occupations.

"Where's her ladyship?"

"In the boudoir, sir, waiting for the doctor."

"What doctor?   Dr Joyce?"

"And the strange gentleman, sir.   They're both together
in Miss Madeleine's room."

"Ah, Muriel!   So Dr Wilmot has arrived?"

"Yes, and gone off straight with Joyce to Madeleine.
You see I was right in recommending you to go out as usual.
Your fine London physician never asked for you, never
mentioned your name."

"Well, perhaps you were right.   I should have worried
myself into a fever here; not that I've done any good out—
missed every shot.   What's he like?"

"He!   Who?   Dr Wilmot?   I had scarcely an opportunity of observing, but I should say *brusque* and self-
sufficient.   He and Joyce went off at once.   I thanked him
for coming, and welcomed him in your name and my own;
but he did not seem much impressed."

"Full of his case, no doubt; these men never think of
anything but—Ah, here he is!—Dr Wilmot, a thousand
thanks for this prompt reply to my hasty summons.   Seeing
the urgency, you'll forgive the apparent freedom of my tele-
graphing to you."

"My dear sir," said Wilmot, "I am only too happy to be
here; not that, if you could have engrossed the attention of
this gentleman, there would have been any necessity for the

summous. Dr Joyce has done everything that could possibly be done for Miss Kilsyth up to this point."

"*A laudato viro laudari*," murmured Dr Joyce.

" But, fortunately or unfortunately, as I learn from him, a district of thirty miles in circumference looks to him for its health. Now I am, for the next few days at least, a free man, and at liberty to devote myself to Miss Kilsyth."

"And you will do so ? "

" With the very greatest pleasure. In two words let me corroborate the opinion already given. I understand by my friend here Miss Kilsyth has an attack, more or less serious, of scarlet-fever. She must be kept completely isolated from every one, and must be watched with unremitting attention. Dr Joyce will send to Aberdeen for a skilled nurse, upon whom he can depend; until her arrival I will take up my position in the sick-room."

" Ten thousand thanks; but—is there any danger ? "

" So far all is progressing favourably. We must look to Providence and our own unremitting attention for the result."

" I'm so hot and so thirsty, and these pillows are so uncomfortable! Thanks! Ah, is that you, Dr Wilmot ? I was afraid you had gone. You won't leave me—at least not just yet—will you ? "

" Not I, my dear. There—that's better, isn't it ? The pillow is cooler, and the lemonade—"

" Ah, so many thanks I'm very weak to-night; but your voice is so kind, and your manner, and—"

" There ; now try and sleep.—Good heavens, how lovely she is ! What a mass of golden hair falling over her pillow, and what a soft, innocent, childish manner! And to think that only this morning I—ah, you must never hear the details of this case, my dear old master. When I get back to town I will tell you the result: but the details—never."

CHAPTER IV.

MRS WILMOT.

"I WONDER what sort of woman Chudleigh Wilmot's
wife is," was a phrase very often used by his acquaintances;
and the sentiment it expressed was not unnatural or inex-
cusable. There are some men concerning whom people instinctively feel that there is something peculiar in their
domestic history, that their every-day life is not like the
every-day life of other people. Sometimes this impression
is positive and defined; it takes the shape of certain conviction that things are wrong in that quarter; that So-and-so's
marriage is a mistake, a misfortune, or a calamity, just as
the grade of the blunder makes itself felt by his manner, or
even by the expression of the countenance. Sometimes the
impression is quite vague, and the questioner is conscious
only that there must be something of interest to be known.
The man's wife may be dear to him, with a special dearness
and nearness, too sacred, too much a part of his inmost being,
to be betrayed to even the friendliest eyes; or there may be
an estrangement, which pride and rectitude combine to conceal. At all events—and whichever of these may be the
true condition of affairs, or whatever modification of them
may be true—the man's acquaintance feel that there is
something in his domestic story different from that of other
men, and they regard him with a livelier curiosity, if he be
a man of social or intellectual mark, in consequence.

It was in the vaguest form that the question "What
sort of a woman is Chudleigh Wilmot's wife?" suggested
itself to his acquaintances. Naturally, and necessarily,
the greater number of those to whom the rising man became known knew him only in his professional capacity;
but that capacity involved a good deal of knowledge, and

not a little social intercourse; and there was hardly one among their number who did not say, sooner or later, to himself, or to other people, "I wonder what sort of woman Chudleigh Wilmot's wife is?"

This question had been asked mentally, and of each other, by several of the inmates of the old mansion of Kilsyth; while the grave, pre-occupied, and absorbed physician dwelt within its walls, devoting all his energies of mind and body to the battle with disease, in which he was resolved to conquer. But no one who was there, or likely to be there, could have answered the question, strange to say—not even Wilmot himself.

Chudleigh Wilmot's marriage had come about after a fashion in which there was nothing very novel, remarkable, or interesting. Mabel Darlington was a pretty girl, who came of a good family, with which Wilmot's mother had been connected; had a small fortune, which was very acceptable to the young man just starting in his arduous profession; and was as attractive to him as any woman could have been at that stage of his life. Partly inclination, partly convenience, and in some measure persuasion, were the promoters of the match. Wilmot knew that a medical man had a better chance of success as a married than as a single man; and as this was a fixed, active, and predominant idea among his relatives and friends—in fact, an article of faith, and a perpetual text of continual discourses—he had everything to encourage him in the design which had formed itself, though somewhat faintly, in his mind, when he renewed his acquaintance with Miss Darlington, on the occasion of her appearance at his mother's house in the character of a "come out" young lady. He had often seen her as a child and a little girl, being himself at the time a somewhat older child and a much bigger boy; but he had never entertained for her that disinterested, ardent, wretchedness-producing passion known as "calf love;" so that the impression she made upon him at a later period owed nothing to earlier recollection. His mother liked the girl, and praised her eloquently and persistently to Chudleigh; so eloquently and persistently indeed, that if he had not happened to be of her opinion from the beginning, she would probably have inspired him with a powerful dislike to Miss Darlington, by placing that young lady in his catalogue of bores. He was not by any means the sort of man to marry a woman for whom he did not care at all, to please his mother, or secure his own prosperity; but he was just the sort of man to care all the more for a girl because his mother liked her, and to make up his mind to marry her, if she would have him, the more quickly on that account.

The courtship was a short one; and even in its brief duration Chudleigh Wilmot never felt, never tried to persuade himself, that Mabel was his first object in life. He knew that his profession had his heart, his brain, his ambition in its grasp; that he loved it, and thought of it, and lived for it in a way, and to a degree, which no other object could ever compete with. It never occurred to him for a moment that there was any injustice to Mabel in this. He would be an affectionate and faithful husband; but he was a practical man—not an enthusiast, not a dreamer. If he succeeded—and he was determined to succeed—she would share his success, the realization of his ambition, and would secure all its advantages to herself. A man to do real work in the world, and to do it as a man ought—as alone he could feel the answer of a good conscience in doing anything he should undertake—must put his work above and before everything. He would do this; he would be an eminent physician, a celebrated and rich man; a good husband too; and his wife should never have reason to find fault with him, or to envy the wives of other men—men who might indeed be more sentimental

and demonstrative, but who could not have a stronger sense
of duty than he. Thus thought, thus resolved Mabel
Darlington's lover; and very good thoughts, very admirable
resolves his were. They had only one defect, but he never
suspected its existence. It was a rather radical defect too,
being this: that they were not those of a lover at all.

They were married, and all went very well with the
modest and exemplary household. At first the Wilmot
ménage was not so fashionably located as afterwards; but
Mrs Wilmot's house was always a model of neatness, propriety, and the precise degree of elegance which the rising
man's income justified at each level which he attained.
Wilmot's mother continued to like her daughter-in-law,
and to regard her son's marriage as most propitious, though
she had sometimes a doubt whether she really did understand his wife quite so thoroughly as she had understood
Mabel Darlington. But Wilmot's mother had now been
dead some years. Mrs Wilmot had no near relatives, and
she was a woman of few intimacies; her life was placid,
prosperous, conventional. She had, at the period with
which this story deals, a handsome house, a good income,
an agreeable and eminently respectable social circle; a
handsome, irreproachable husband, rapidly rising into
distinction; one intimate friend, and—a broken heart.

Chudleigh Wilmot's wife was young; if not beautiful,
at least very attractive, accomplished, lady-like, and
"amiable," in the generally accepted interpretation of
that unsatisfactory word. What better or what worse
description could possibly be given? It describes a
thousand women in a breath, and it designates not one in
particular. There was only one person in existence who
could have given a more clear, intelligible, and distinct
description of Mrs Wilmot than this stereotyped one.
This person was her friend Mrs Prendergast—a lady somewhat older than herself, and whose natural and remarkable

quickness and penetration were aided in this instance by
close acquaintance and sleepless jealousy. If Mrs Prendergast had been an ordinary woman, as silly as her sisterhood and no sillier, the fact that she was extremely jealous
of Mrs Wilmot would have so obscured and perverted her
judgment, that her opinion would not have been worth
having. But Mrs Prendergast was very unlike her sisterhood. Not only was she negatively less silly, but she was
positively clever; and being severe, suspicious, and · im-
placable as well, if not precisely a pleasant, she was at
least a remarkable woman. Nothing obscured or perverted
Mrs Prendergast's judgment; neither did anything touch
her heart. She had mind, and a good deal of it; she had
experience and tact, insight, foresight, and caution. She
was a woman who might possibly be a very valuable friend,
but who could not fail to be a very dangerous enemy. In
such a nature the power of enmity would probably be
greater than the power of friendship, and the one would
be likely to crush the other if ever they came into collision.
Mrs Prendergast was Mrs Wilmot's friend. Whether she
was the friend of Mrs Wilmot's husband remains to be
seen. If she had been asked to say what manner of woman
the rising man's wife was, and had thought proper to
satisfy the inquirer, her portraiture might have been relied
upon as implicitly for its truthfulness as that of the most
impartial observer, which is saying at once that Mrs Prendergast was a woman of exceptional mental qualities, and
of a temperament rare among those charming creatures to
whom injustice is easy and natural.

The two women were habitually much together. Mrs
Prendergast was a childless widow. Mrs Wilmot was a
childless wife. Neither had absorbing domestic occupations to employ her,—each had a good deal of time at the
other's disposal; hence it happened that few days passed
without their meeting, and enjoying that desultory kind of

companionship which is so puzzling to the male observer
of the habits and manners of womankind. Their respective
abodes were within easy distance of each other. Mrs
Prendergast lived in Cadogan-place, and Mrs Wilmot lived
in Charles-street, St James's. When they did not see one
another, they exchanged notes; and in short they kept up
all the ceremonial of warm feminine friendship; and each
really did like the other better than any one else in the
world, with one exception. In Mrs Wilmot's case the
exception was her husband; in Mrs Prendergast's, the
exception was herself. There was a good deal of sincerity
and warmth in their friendship, but in one point there was
a decided inequality. Mrs Prendergast understood Mrs
Wilmot thoroughly; she read her through and through, she
knew her off by heart; but Mrs Wilmot knew very little
of her friend—only just as much as her friend chose she
should know. Which was a convenient state of things,
and tended to preserve their pleasant and salutary relations
unbroken. Mrs Prendergast had played Eleanor Galligaï
to Mrs Wilmot's Marie de' Medicis for a considerable
time, and with uninterrupted success, when Chudleigh
Wilmot was sent for, in the perplexity and distress at
Kilsyth; and as a matter of course she had heard from his
wife about his prolonged visit to Sir Saville Rowe, whom
she was well aware Mrs Wilmot disliked with the quiet,
rooted, persistent aversion so frequently inspired in the
breasts of even the very best and most conscientious of
women by their husbands' intimate friends. Wilmot was
utterly unconscious that his wife entertained any such
feeling; and Sir Saville Rowe himself would have been
hardly more astonished than Wilmot, if it had been revealed
to him that the confidence and regard which existed between the former master and pupil were counted a
grievance, and Wilmot's visit to Burnside resented,
silently indeed, in grief rather than anger, as an injury.

In this fact may be found the key-note to Mrs Wilmot's character; a key-note often struck by her friend's hand, and never with an erring, a faltering, or a rough touch.

There was not much of the tragic element in Henrietta Prendergast's jealousy of Mabel Wilmot, but there was a great deal of the mean. When Mabel was a young girl, Henrietta was a not much older widow. She was Mabel's cousin; had married, when very young, a man who had survived their marriage only one year. She had more money than Mabel; their connections were the same; she had as much education, and even better manners. She met Chudleigh Wilmot on the occasion of his renewing his acquaintance with Mabel Darlington, and she was as much, though differently, fascinated with him as Mabel herself. She compared her qualifications with those of her cousin; and she arrived at the not unnatural conclusion that their charms were equal, supposing him incapable of discerning how much cleverer a woman than Mabel she was,—and hers very superior, should he prove capable of understanding and appreciating her intellectual superiority. She forgot one simple element in the calculation, and it made all the difference—she forgot Mabel's prettiness. Henrietta Prendergast made very few mistakes, but she did constantly make one blunder; she forgot her plain face, she under-estimated the power of beauty. Perhaps no plain woman ever does understand that power, ever does make sufficient allowance for it, when arrayed against her in any kind of combat; it is certain that Henrietta did not in this instance. It is certain that though Chudleigh Wilmot thought of marrying Mabel Darlington without being very much in love with her, he never thought of marrying Henrietta Prendergast at all.

And now, when she had come to the conclusion that Chudleigh Wilmot had not loved Mabel Darlington, and did not love his wife,—was, in short, a man to whom love was unknown, by whom it was unvalued, undesired,—she was still steadily, sleeplessly jealous of Mabel Wilmot. "I would have made him love *me*," she would say to herself, as she read the thoughts of her friend; "I would have been as ambitious for him as he is for himself; I would have shown him that his aim was the highest and the worthiest. I would have loved him, and sympathized with him too. She only loves him; she does not understand him. Why did she come in between him and me?" For this very clever woman had actually deluded herself into the belief that, but for Mabel, Chudleigh Wilmot would have loved, or at least have married her. She would have made him love her afterwards, as she said. So for a long time she disliked her cousin, and hankered after her cousin's husband, and believed that she would have been the best, the most suitable, and the happiest of wives to the man who evidently had not a wife of that pattern in Mabel, but who somehow did not seem to perceive the fact. That time had come to an end long before people at Kilsyth asked themselves and each other what sort of woman Chudleigh Wilmot's wife was. But though Mrs Prendergast no longer hankered after her cousin's husband, though the love, in which her active imagination had a large share, had given place to a much more real and genuine hatred, she was jealous of Mabel still. This woman's brain was larger than her heart; her intellectual was higher than her moral nature; and a lofty feeling would be more transient than a low one. She pitied Mabel Wilmot too, however contradictory such an assertion may seem to shallow perceptions, which do not recognize in life that nothing is so reasonably to be expected, so invariably to be found, as contradictions in character. She liked her, she understood her, but she was jealous of her—jealous because Mabel had the position she had vainly desired. If she had had her husband's love, Mrs Prendergast would have been still more jealous of her, and would not have liked, because she could not have pitied her. But she knew she had not

that ; she had made the discovery as soon as Mabel, who had
made it fatally soon.

What had the girl's ideal been? was a question none
could answer, and which it is certain her husband never
asked. He was very kind to her; she had every comfort,
every luxury that he could give her; but she lived in a world
of which he knew nothing, and he in and for his profession.
He could not have been brought to recognize the possibility
of over devotion to the business of his life. He would not
have listened to the advance of any claims upon his time,
attention, or interest, beyond those which he fulfilled with
enthusiasm in the interests of his work, and the courteous
observance which he never denied to the rules of his well-
regulated household. Chudleigh Wilmot was a clever man
in many ways beside that one way in which he was eminently
so; but one study had long lain near his hand, and he had
never given time or thought to it; one book was close to
him, and he had never turned its leaves—the study of his
wife's character, the book of his wife's heart.

Mabel Wilmot was inveterately, incurably shy, extremely
reserved and reticent by nature, and rather sullen. The
latter fault of temper had made itself apparent to her husband very early in their married life; and having rebuked it
without effect, he made the great mistake of treating it with
disregard. He never noticed it now; the symptoms escaped
him, the disease did not interest him, and it grew and grew.
Proud, cold in manner, distant; scrupulously deferential
and dutiful in externals; silent, except where speech was
necessary to the management of such affairs as lay within
her sphere; calmly indifferent, to all appearance, to all that
did not absolutely concern her individually in the course of
their life, her shyness and her sullenness were not perceptible to others now—never to him. He did not know that it
was so much the worse; he did not understand that it had
been better to know and feel her faults than to be ignorant

of her and them, unconscious of their growth, or their yielding, or their transformation into others, uglier, worse, harder
of eradication, more hopeless of cure. He did not love her.
The whole story was in that one sentence.

And she ? She loved him; certainly not wisely, all things
considered, and much too well for her own peace. She had
outgrown her girlhood since her marriage; and her character had hardened, darkened, deepened, everything but
strengthened, with her advance into womanhood. The girl
Chudleigh Wilmot had married, and the graceful languid
woman who appeared barely conscious of, and not at all interested in, the fact of his existence, were widely different
beings. Mabel had shrunk from the knowledge of the thraldom in which her love for her husband—her calm, cold,
generous, irreproachable husband—held her when she had
first realized its strength, when the growth of her own love
had revealed to her that his was but a puny changeling, with
all the sensitiveness of a shy, sullen, and reticent nature.
She could not deny, but she could conceal, the bondage in
which it held her. The qualities of her heart and the defects
of her temper had a fight for the mastery, and temper won.
Chudleigh Wilmot, if he had been obliged to think about
the matter, would have unhesitatingly declared that his wife's
temper had improved considerably since the early days of
their marriage : the truth was, it had only lost impulsiveness,
and acquired sulk and secretiveness.

All this, and the terrible pain at the young woman's un-
satisfied heart,—the pain which devoured her the more ruthlessly as success waited more closely upon the devotion to
his profession of the man she loved, and in whose life she
had but a nominal share,—was well known to Henrietta
Prendergast. It had been long in coming, that burst of
agonized confidence, which had made her friend officially
aware of all that her acute mind had long believed; but it
had come, and like all the confidences of very shy people, it

E

had been complete and expansive. All restraint was over. Mabel might yield to any mood now in Henrietta's presence; she might talk of him with pride, with love, with anger, with questioning wonder, with despair; she, whose armour of pride and silence no other hand, not even the hand of the husband she loved, had ever pierced, was defenceless, unarmed, at the mercy of her friend, who fancied she had supplanted her, who was jealous of her.

Chudleigh Wilmot had been nearly a week at Kilsyth, when Mrs Prendergast, entering her cousin's drawing-room rather earlier than usual, found her agitated, and in a state of perplexity.

"I am so glad you have come, Henrietta," said Mrs Wilmot, as she kissed her visitor. "I have been in such anxiety to see you. A messenger was sent early this morning from Mr Foljambe—you know Wilmot's friend, Mr Foljambe the banker, of Portland-place—requesting that he would go to him at once. The poor old man has the gout again very badly. Since then a note has come; written by himself too, and hardly legible. Poor creature! I'm sure he is in horrid pain. Here it is. You see he says, 'the enemy is advancing on the citadel'—he means his heart or his stomach, I suppose—and he entreats Wilmot to go to him at once. What ought I to do, Henrietta?"

"You must tell him, of course, that Mr Wilmot is out of town. I should not say he was so far away as Scotland; I think the mere idea is enough to terrify a nervous old man with a superstition in favour of a particular doctor."

"Yes, yes, you are right; so it is. But about Wilmot. Of course he will not like to leave Sir Saville's friends. He thinks more of Sir Saville than of any one in the world, I do believe."

"Hardly more, Mabel, than of his reputation and Mr Foljambe, I should think. Why, this Mr Foljambe is the oldest friend he has in the world—his godfather, his father's friend,—a childless old man, without kith or kin in the world, who may leave him a fortune any day, and is certain to leave him something very handsome! He would never be so mad or so ungrateful—is he of an ungrateful disposition, Mabel?"

"I don't know exactly," said Mrs Wilmot, as her colour deepened, and tears rose to her dark gray eyes. "If he *has* any feeling, it is certainly for his friends—at least he wastes none of it on *me*."

"You are always brooding over that, Mabel," said her cousin, "and it is labour and sorrow wasted. No man is worth being miserable about, dear, and Wilmot is no more worth it than his neighbours. Besides, this is a matter of business, you know, and we must look at it so. You had better telegraph at once, I think. Put on your bonnet, and come to the office; don't trust to a servant, and don't lose time. The message will take some time to reach him, at the quickest. I fancy Kilsyth is a long way from any station."

Her practical tone had a beneficial effect on Mabel. Besides, she brightened at the hope, the expectation of Wilmot's return before the appointed time. The two ladies drove to Charing-cross, and Mabel telegraphed to Wilmot:

"*Mr Foljambe is dangerously ill. Come at once.*"

CHAPTER V

A RESOLVE, AND ITS RESULTS.

THE illness of Madeleine Kilsyth engrossed the attention and engaged the sympathy of her father so completely, and so entirely blinded him to other considerations, that when he chanced to encounter a servant on his way to Wilmot's room, in whose hand he recognized the ominous yellow cover which indicated a telegraphic despatch, he immediately accompanied the man to the door. He then hardly gave his guest time to peruse the message before he said impetuously :

" Nothing to take you away from us, I trust. Pray tell me ? " and the otherwise polite gentleman did his best to peer at the pencilled characters on the flimsy sheet of paper which Wilmot held in his hand. For a moment his eager question remained unanswered, and his guest stood frowning and uncertain. The next, though the frown remained, the look of uncertainty passed away, and then Wilmot turned frankly to the impatient questioner and said :

"This is a message from an old friend and patient of mine. He wants me very much, and asks me to return at once."

"And—and what will you do ? *Must* you go ? " asked the distressed father in a tone of the keenest anxiety.

" I shall stay here, sir, until your daughter is out of danger. There are many who can replace me in London in Foljambe's case : there is no one who can replace me here in Miss Kilsyth's."

" You are very good, Wilmot. I really can't thank you sufficiently," said Kilsyth, immensely relieved.

" No need to thank me at all, my dear sir," said Wilmot. " And now I will make my report to you, which no doubt you were coming to hear."

The two gentlemen had rather a long talk, and on its completion Wilmot returned to his room to write letters; and Kilsyth went to tell Lady Muriel that they had had a narrow escape of losing Wilmot, but he had determined to disregard the message, and stay by Madeleine. Did she not think Wilmot a very fine fellow ? Had she not perfect confidence in his skill ? and was not the interest he was taking in Madeleine's case extraordinary ? To all these queries the Lady Muriel made answer in the affirmative, with heightened colour and brightened eyes, which, if Kilsyth had happened to notice those phenomena at all, he would have ascribed to an increase of feeling towards Madeleine; to be hailed, on his part, with much gratitude and delight. But Kilsyth did not happen to notice them at all.

Chudleigh Wilmot was a man accustomed to act promptly on a resolution; and perhaps, like many more of similar temperament, likely to act all the more promptly when the motives of that resolution were not quite clear or quite justifiable before his own judgment. In the present instance he certainly did not act with perfect candour towards himself. He made very much to himself of his apprehensions concerning the result of Madeleine's illness, and his absolute want of confidence in the skill of Mr Joyce. He resolutely shut his eyes to the long and substantial claims of Mr Foljambe to paramount consideration on his part, and he determined to "see this matter out," as he phrased it, in his one-sided mental cogitation, by which he meant that he was determined to invest the temptation in his way with the specious name of duty, and to try to persuade himself that he had the assent of his conscience in pursuing a course opposed to his judgment. In pursuance of this determination, Chudleigh Wilmot wrote to his wife the following letter. To any one familiar with the man's habits, it would have been suggestive, that when he had written "Kilsyth," and the date, he paused for several minutes, fidgeted with a stick of sealing-wax, got up and walked about the room, and, finally, began to write with unusual haste :

"My dear Mabel,—Your telegram came all right; but my leaving this is quite impossible for the present. You must tell Foljambe how I am circumstanced. Poor old fellow! I am sorry for him; but he will pull through, as usual; and there is nothing to be done for him which any one else cannot do just as well as myself. He had better see Whittaker; or, if he does not like him for any reason—and the

dear old boy *is* whimsical—let him see Perkins: tell him **I**
recommend either confidently. You had better go and see
him, if your cold is all right again, and cheer him up. As
for me, I am effectually imprisoned here until this case decides itself one way or the other. Miss Kilsyth could not
possibly be left to the care of the country doctor here; and
there is no one within any *possible* distance but Sir Saville,
who would not *stay*, supposing he would *come*, which is
doubtful. The same answer must be given in all cases for
the next week or so. There is no use in any one telegraph-
ing for me. The country about here is beautiful; but of
course I don't see much of it. The Kilsyths are pleasant
people in their way, and full of gratitude to me. Lady
Muriel talks of making your acquaintance when they come
to town. Nothing of consequence at home, I suppose?
Tell Whittaker to look after Foljambe very zealously, if he
will have him.—Yours affectionately,   C. Wilmot.

"P.S. The case is malignant scarlet-fever, and my patient
and I are in quarantine. Kilsyth is in great trouble—devoted to his daughter."

When he had sealed this letter, and left it on the table
for the post, Wilmot once more went to his patient's room.
The suffering girl had fallen into an uneasy slumber; her
face, with the disfiguring flush invading its fairness, was
turned towards the door, the heavy eyes were closed, and
the parched red lips were open. With a skilful noiseless
touch, Wilmot lifted the restless head to an easier attitude
upon the pillow, and moistened the dry mouth. The girl's
golden hair had slipped out of the silken net which had confined it, and a quantity of its thick tresses was caught in one
hot hand. Wilmot released the tangled hair, laid the hand
upon the smooth coverlet, looked long at the young face, and
then, stepping gently to the window where the nurse was
sitting, asked how long the patient had been sleeping. Ever

since he had left her, it seemed. Lady Muriel had been there, "leastways at the dressing-room door," the nurse added, and had wanted to see him particularly, she (the nurse) thought, about sending the children out of the way of infection. Lady Muriel also asked whether they were not going to cut off Miss Kilsyth's hair.

"Which it does seem a pity, poor dear!" said the nurse, speaking in the skilful whisper which does not disturb the patient, and is the most difficult of tones to acquire; and throwing a motherly glance at the sleeping girl, who just then moaned painfully.

"Cut off her hair!" said Wilmot,—as if the mere notion were a horrid barbarism, which he could not contemplate as a possibility; "certainly not—it is entirely unnecessary."

"Well, sir," said the nurse, "it's mostly done in fevers. Wherever I've nursed, I've always done it, first thing."

Wilmot turned red and hot. Why should he shrink from sanctioning or ordering the sacrifice in this case, as he had done in a thousand others without a thought of hesitation or regret, just like any other detail? Why, indeed? if not because those were the *thousand* cases, while this was the *one*. But he did not face the question; he turned aside from it—turned aside, with his eyes piercing the gloom of the shaded room, in search of the gleam of the golden locks. "No, no," he thought, "the 'little head sunning over with curls' shall 'shine on,' if I can manage it." So he told the nurse that was a matter for after consideration, and that she was to have him called when Miss Kilsyth should wake; and he went out for a solitary walk.

Lady Muriel was most grateful to Dr Wilmot for the care and skill which he exercised in Madeleine's case. Scarcely Kilsyth himself was more unremitting in his inquiries after the patient, more anxious as to the result. But husband and wife were actuated by totally different motives. The man feared lest the hope of his life should be quenched, the woman lest the object of her ambition should be frustrated; the man dreaded the loss of his darling, the woman the confusion of her scheme. For Lady Muriel had a scheme in connection with Madeleine Kilsyth, which it may be as well at once to declare.

It is Mr Longfellow who informs us that no one is so accursed by fate, no one so utterly desolate, but some heart, though unknown, responds unto his own. When Lady Muriel Inchgarvie was running her career of two London seasons, waiting for the arrival of the man whom she could persuade herself into marrying, and whom she could persuade into marrying her; while Mr Burton and Sir Coke Only were fluttering like moths round her brilliant light—the world, which thinks it marks everything, and which hugs itself in appreciation of its wonderful sagacity and perspicacity, and which had already supremely settled that Lady Muriel had no heart to lose, little knew that its sentence was a just one—simply because Lady Muriel had lost her heart. There was a connection of the house of Inchgarvie, a tall thin Scotchman, named Stewart Caird, a barrister of Lincoln's-inn, who had been a long time settled in London, and who, in virtue of his aristocratic connections, his perfect gentlemanliness, and his utter harmlessness—for every one knew that poor Stewart merely lived from hand to mouth by the exercise of his profession, and by writing in the law magazines and reviews—was asked into a good deal of society. He was a languid, consumptive-looking man, with a high hectic colour, and deep-violet eyes, and a soft tremulous voice; and after he had claimed kinship with Lady Muriel, and had his claim allowed, he found plenty of opportunities of meeting her constantly, and on every occasion he was to be found by her side. This was the one chance which fortune had bestowed on Muriel Inchgarvie of loving and being simultaneously beloved; and it is but fair to say that she availed

herself of it. Not for one instant did either of them think
of the hopelessness of their passion. Lady Muriel well
knew that a marriage with Stewart Caird was simply
impossible; and Stewart Caird knew it too, possessing at
the same time the additional knowledge, that even if family
affairs could have been squared by his coming into the
immediate heritage of fabulous wealth, there was yet a
slight drawback in the fact that his lungs could not possibly hold out beyond six months. And yet they went on
loving and fooling: to her the mere fact that there could
never be any ties between them was, as it always has been,
an incentive to a quasi-romantic attachment; to him, with
the perfect conviction that he was a doomed man, the love
of a pretty high-bred woman softened the terrors of death,
and prevented him from dwelling on his fate. So they
went on; the world taking little heed of them, and they
ignoring the world; he growing weaker and weaker, but
always disguising his weakness, until one night in the
height of the season, when Lady Muriel, dressed for a ball,
received a short pencil-note, feebly scrawled: "If you
would see me before I die, come at once.—S. C. You
know me well enough to be certain that this is no romantic
figure of speech." The writing, feeble throughout, trailed
off at last into scarcely legible characters. Lady Muriel
wrote one hasty line to the lady who was to be her
chaperon, pleading illness as her excuse for not fetching
her, threw a thick cloak and hood over her ball-dress and
her ivy-wreathed hair, and told the coachman, who was
devoted to her, to drive her to Old-square, Lincoln's-inn.
There, propped up by pillows, and attended by a hired
nurse, who was by no means reluctant to take a hint, and,
accompanied by a spirit-bottle, to betake herself to a further room, she found poor Stewart Caird, with large bistre
rings round his eyes and two flaming red spots on his
hollow cheeks. Between the attacks of a racking cough,

he told her that his end was nigh; that he had long fore-
seen it, but that he could not deny himself the privilege of
winning her love. He acknowledged the selfishness of the
act; but trusted she would pardon him, when he assured
her that the knowledge that she cared for him had inexpressibly lightened the last few months of his earthly
career, and that he should die more happily, knowing that
he left one regretful heart behind him. He said this in a
voice which was tolerably firm at first, but which, touched
by her sobs, grew more and more tremulous, and finally
broke down, when, in an access of emotion, she flung her
arms round him, and clasped him to her heart. How long
they remained thus tranced in love and grief neither ever
knew; it was the first, the last wild access of passion that
ever was to accrue to either. The future, so imminent to
one of them at least, was unthought of, and they lived but
in the then present fleeting moment. But before they
parted Stewart spoke to Muriel of his younger brother
Ramsay, who had been left to his care, and whom he was
now leaving to the mercy of the world. For Muriel there
was, he said he was persuaded, a career in life. When it
fell to her, when she was enjoying it, would she, for the
sake of him who had loved her—ah, so deeply and so
dearly!—whose life she had cheered, and who with his
dying breath would call upon and bless her name—would
she watch over and provide for Ramsay Caird? With the
dying man's hand in hers, with her arm round his neck,
with her eyes looking into his, even then glazed and
wandering, Muriel swore to fulfil his wishes, and to undertake this charge. Within forty-eight hours Stewart Caird
was dead; within six weeks after his death Muriel Inchgarvie was the pledged wife of Kilsyth; and within a fortnight of her betrothal she had hit upon a plan for the
future of her dead lover's brother.

Ramsay Caird's future career in life was, as Lady

Muriel decided, to be one with Madeleine Kilsyth's, and his fortune was to come to him through his wife. Madeleine's godfather, a childless, rich, old Highland proprietor, an old friend and neighbour of Kilsyth's, had at his death left her twenty thousand pounds, to be hers on her coming of age, or on her marrying with her father's consent. A pleasant competence in itself, but a princely fortune for a young man of small ideas like Ramsay Caird, who was earning a very precarious salary, given to him more from kindness than from any desert of his, in the office of the Edinburgh agent to several large estates. Soon after her marriage Lady Muriel sent for the young man to Kilsyth, found him gen-tlemanly and unassuming, sufficiently shrewd to comprehend the extremely delicate hints which she gave him as to the course which she wished him to adopt, and sufficiently deli-cate to prevent his at once plunging *in medias res*. Since then he had been frequently at Kilsyth, and had done his best to make himself agreeable to Madeleine. He was a good-looking, gentlemanly, quiet young man, without very much to say for himself, beyond the ordinary society talk, in which he was fairly glib; he had the names of all the members of all the families for whom his principal was agent at his tongue's end; had seen many of them personally,—even knew the appearance of the rest by photograph; kept himself well posted in their movements, through the me-dium of the fashionable journals; and so could fairly hold his own in the conversation of the people he was thrown amongst. Lady Muriel, who was as clever as she was proud and ambitious, reckoned Ramsay Caird up to a nicety; saw exactly how far he was suitable for her plans, and thought there was little doubt of Madeleine's being cap-tivated by the handsome glib young man who paid her such respectful homage. But for once in her life Lady Muriel was wrong. It is but fair to say that Ramsay Caird never neglected one of the opportunities so frequently thrown in

his way; that he never once committed himself in any pos
sible manner; that he did not on every occasion seek to recommend himself to the girl's favour; but it is certain that
he failed in making the smallest impression on her. Lady
Muriel, watching the progress of affairs with the greatest
interest, soon felt this, and was at first dispirited; afterwards consoling herself by the thought that the girl was
passionless and devoid of feeling, but so docile withal, that
it would be only necessary for her father to suggest her ac-
ceptance of Mr Caird for her at once to fall into the idea.
Thoroughly comforted by this notion, Lady Muriel had of
late given herself no uneasiness in the matter; contenting
herself by asking Ramsay Caird to spend a week or two
now and then at Kilsyth, by throwing him frequently into
Madeleine's society when there, and by keeping up a perpetual gently flowing perennial stream of laudation of her
young *protégé* to her husband.

On Wilmot's return to the house, he inquired whether
it would be convenient to Lady Muriel to receive him.

" My lady " was in her own sitting-room, and would be
very happy to see Dr Wilmot. So he went thither, and
found the mistress of the mansion alone, and looking to
very great advantage in the midst of all the luxuries and
refinements with which wealth—in this instance aided by
good taste—adorns life. Her rich and simple dress, her
finished graceful ease of manner, her sunny beauty, and
the perfect propriety with which she expressed interest and
anxiety concerning her step-daughter, made her a very attractive object to Wilmot. He had not yet discovered that
she did not in the least experience the sentiments which she
glibly expressed in phrases of irreproachable *tournure;* he did
not suspect her of insincerity or want of feeling, or in fact
of any fault. Everything and everybody at Kilsyth wore
the best and fairest of aspects in the eyes of Chudleigh
Wilmot, who was, nevertheless, a very far-seeing and an

eminently practical man. Thus, he only furnished another
proof of the often-proven truth, that his most distinguish-
ing qualities are the first to fail a man, when judgment is
superseded by passion. That is a strong word to use in
such a case as Chudleigh Wilmot's, at least to use so soon;
but the boundary between the feeling which he entertained
knowingly, and the passion which was growing out of it
unconsciously, was very slight, and was destined so soon to
be destroyed that the word may pass unblamed.

The earlier portion of Lady Muriel Kilsyth's conversation with Wilmot was naturally devoted to Madeleine. She
thanked him, with all her own peculiar grace and fluency,
for his attention, his " priceless care," for his resolution,
which Kilsyth had communicated to her, to remain with
them in this great trouble. She asked him to tell her his
" real opinion; " and he told it. He told her Madeleine
was in danger; but that he hoped, and thought, and believed, her life would be saved. He spoke with earnestness
and feeling; and as he dwelt upon the youth, the beauty,
and the sufferings of the girl, upon her exceeding precious-
ness to her father (and gave Lady Muriel credit for sharing
her husband's feelings far beyond what she deserved), the
soft dark eyes fixed themselves upon him with much interest and curiosity. Deep feeling on any subject was unfamiliar to Lady Muriel; it was not the habit of her society,
or included in the scheme of her own organization, and she
liked it for its strangeness. Their conversation lasted
long; for when Wilmot was summoned to see his patient,
Lady Muriel invited him to come again to her sitting-
room; and he did so. The question of sending her children
away was speedily decided in the negative; and then the
talk rambled on over a great variety of subjects, and Lady
Muriel regarded Wilmot with increasing interest and surprise, as she discovered more and more of his originality
and fertility of mind. She was not a remarkably clever

woman; but she had more brains and more cultivation than were at all common among her "set;" and she did occasionally grow very weary of the well-bred vapid talk, which was the only form of social intercourse assumed in her circle. She had sometimes wondered whether something better was not to be found in the limits within which it would be proper for her to seek for it; but she had stopped at wonderment; she had not followed it up by effort; and now the very thing she had wished for had come to her, in the most unexpected form, and through the most unlikely channel. A doctor, a man whose name she had merely casually heard, an outsider, one whom in the ordinary course of events she would have never met, is called in to attend her step-daughter in fever, and all at once a new world opens upon Lady Muriel Kilsyth.

She was quick to receive impressions; and she felt at once that this day marked an epoch in her life. As this fine-looking, keen, intelligent man, in whose deep-set eyes, on whose massive forehead, power was enthroned, bent those dark steady eyes upon her, seeming to read her soul, the frivolity of her life fell away from her, like a flimsy garment discarded, and she felt, she recognized the charm of superiority of intellect and strength of character. She drew him out on the subjects which had the deepest interest for him, as a woman can, who has tact and perfect manners, even when her intellectual powers are in no way remarkable; and he enjoyed the happy social hours of the long, uninterrupted afternoon as much, or nearly as much, as she did. Lady Muriel was too quick and too true an observer to fail in discerning before they had strayed very far into the pleasant paths of their desultory discourse, that there was very little sentimentality in Chudleigh Wilmot. A practical man, full of action, of ambition, of love of knowledge, and resolve to win the highest prizes it could bring him, he yet spoke and looked like a man whose

feelings had been but little tried, and who would be slow
to try them.   Lady Muriel knew that Chudleigh Wilmot
was a married man.   The circumstance had been mentioned
among the people in the house when he had first been
talked of; and she was the first at Kilsyth to ask of herself, for she had no other to whom to address it, that frequent question, "What sort of woman is Chudleigh Wilmot's wife?"   She could not have explained, but she did
not question, the instinct which led her to say, as she went
to her dressing-room, when their long colloquy at length
came to a conclusion, "I am sure he does not care for her.
I am sure it was not a love-match.   I feel convinced he
never was in love in his life, not in any real sense."   And
then, Lady Muriel Kilsyth sighed.   Life was not yet an
old story for either Lady Muriel or Chudleigh.

That evening Wilmot devoted himself to the patient,
whose state was highly precarious; and though he sent
reassuring messages to Kilsyth from time to time, he expressed far more hopefulness than he actually felt.   He was
conscious too of a strange sort of relief—a consciousness
which should have shown him how he had deceived himself—
as the conviction that his presence was indeed in the highest
degree beneficial was confirmed by every passing hour.   The
girl's eyes—now bright and wandering, now dark and weary
—turned in search of him, in every phase of the fever that
was gaining on her, with such innocent trust and belief as
touched him keenly to his conscious heart.   In the stillness
of the night, when the very nurse slept, the physician bent
down over the flushed face, and hushed the murmuring
incoherent voice with the tenderest words, and soothed the
sick girl—little more than a child she looked in her hopelessness and unrest—with all a woman's gentleness.   What did
he feel for the pretty young creature thus thrown on his
skill, his kindness, his mercy!   What revolution was the
silent flight of time, during the hours of that night, working

in Chudleigh Wilmot's life ?   He was learning the reality
of that in which he had never believed ; he was learning the
truth of love.   Now, when it was too late, when every barrier
of honour, of honesty, of duty, and of principle stood between
him and the object of the long-deferred, but terribly real,
passion which took possession of him.

When the dawn was stealing into the sick girl's room,
the change, the chill, which come with that ghastly hour to
sickness and to health alike, in wakefulness, came to Madeleine, and she called in a high querulous tone for her father.
The nurse, then beside her, tried to soothe the girl; but
vainly.   She refused to lie down ; she must, she would see
her father.   Wilmot, who knew that she was quite sensible,
quite coherent, and who had feared to startle her by letting
her see him, now came forward, and gently laid her back
upon her pillow.

"You shall see your father in the morning," he said.
"I am sure you would not have him disturbed now, my
dear ; would you ? "

"No," she said, with a painful smile ; "I would not—
certainly not.   I only wanted to know something ; and you
will tell me."

Her large blue eyes were fixed upon him ; her small
hand was stretched out to him with the frankness of a child.

"Of course, if I can, I will tell you."

"Sit down, then," she said, in the thick difficult voice
peculiar to the disease which had hold of her.

He did not sit down, but knelt upon the floor by the
bedside, and raised the pillows on his arm.   Her innocent
face was close to his.

"Speak as low as you like ; I can hear you," said
Chudleigh Wilmot.

"I will," she whispered.   "I thank you.   I only wanted
to ask my father—and I would rather ask you—if—I am
going to die."

Her lips were trembling. His sight grew dim as he answered:

"No, my dear. You are very ill; but you are not going to die. You are going to get well—not immediately, but before long. You must be patient, you know; and you must do everything you are desired to do."

"I will when I am sensible," she said; "but I am not always sensible, you know."

"I know. You are quite sensible now, and the best patient I ever had. A great deal depends on yourself. I don't mean about not dying; I mean about getting well sooner. Will you try now how long, being quite sensible, you can keep quiet?"

"I will," she answered, looking at him with the strange solemn gaze we see so often in the eyes of a child in mortal sickness. "I am so glad, Dr Wilmot, you are sure I am not going to die."

Not a shade of doubt of him; perfect trust in him, entire calm and serenity in the unruffled feeble voice. Her hand lay loosely in his, undisturbed except by an occasional feverish twitch; her head was supported by his arm, which held the pillows; his serious eyes scanned her face. So he knelt and so she lay as the dawn came; so he knelt and so she lay as the first rays of the sun came glancing in through the closed window-curtains; but they found the patient sleeping, and the steady watch of the physician unrelaxed.

So time passed, and Madeleine's illness took its course, and was met and fought and beaten at every turn by the skill and judgment, the coolness and the experience, of the "rising man." So unwearied a watcher had never been seen in a sick-room; so cheerful a counsellor and consoler had rarely been sent to friends and relatives in anxiety and suspense. He was appreciated at his worth at Kilsyth. As for Kilsyth himself, he reverenced, he esteemed, he next to worshipped Wilmot, holding him as almost superhuman. The nurse "had never seen such a doctor as him in all her born days, never; and not severe neither; but knowing as the best and wakefullest must have their little bit of rest at times." He won golden opinions from all within the old walls of Kilsyth, and more than all from its mistress.

On the whole, and despite his close and devoted attendance on his patient, Chudleigh Wilmot saw a great deal of Lady Muriel, and an infinite number of topics were discussed between them. Each day brought more extended, more appreciative comprehension of her guest to the by no means dull intellect of Lady Muriel; and each day quickened her womanly perception and kindled her already keen and ready jealousy. When many days had gone by, and Lady Muriel would no longer have dreamed of denying to herself how much she admired Wilmot,—how utterly different he was from any other man whom she had ever known; how much more interesting, how much more engrossing; a man to be looked up to and respected; a man to suffice to all a woman's need of reverence and deference,—she would still have been far from acknowledging that she loved him; but her acknowledgment or her denial would have made no difference in the fact. She did love him, in a lofty and reserved kind of way, in which no slur upon her honour, according to the world's code, which takes cognizance only of the letter of the law and ignores its spirit, was implied; but with all her heart she loved him.

So now the situation was this. Chudleigh Wilmot loved one woman within the walls of the old mansion of Kilsyth; and another woman, their inmate, loved him. Would she— the other, the older, the more experienced woman—discover his secret, and overwhelm him with its disgrace? Time alone could tell that—time, of which there was not much to run; for Wilmot had been a fortnight at Kilsyth before he could give its master the joyful intelligence that the fever had relaxed its grip of his child, and—barring the always present danger in scarlet-fever of relapse, or what is technically called " dregs "—Madeleine was safe.

Mabel Wilmot had written to her husband occasionally during the fortnight which had witnessed the rise and the crisis of Miss Kilsyth's illness. In her letters, which were few and sparing of details, she never alluded to the cause of her husband's unprecedented absence ; Wilmot did not notice the omission. She gave him few details concerning herself ; Wilmot did not observe their paucity. The glamour was over him ; the enchanted land held him.

" I am not feeling much better," said Mabel in one of her letters ; " but I daresay—indeed I have no doubt—the weather is against me ; Whittaker thinks so too. I enclose his report. There is nothing new here, or of importance."

Chudleigh Wilmot accepted his wife's account of the state of things at home, and replied to her letters in his usual strain. He had failed to notice that she never alluded to Miss Kilsyth ; or he would hardly have dealt with so much emphasis, or at such length, on the details of a case to which the recipient of his letters manifested such complete indifference.

Dr Whittaker continued to report upon the cases to which he had been called in ; and no more telegrams interrupted the concentration of Chudleigh Wilmot's attention upon the illness and convalescence of Madeleine Kilsyth.

CHAPTER VI.

AT KILSYTH.

THE routine of illness and anxiety, the dull monotony of an absorbing care, had rapidly settled down upon Kilsyth, immensely alleviated, of course, by the confidence imposed

by Wilmot's presence.   The influence of his skill, the insensible support of his calmness and self-reliance, were felt all
through the household by those members of it to whom the
life or death of Madeleine was a matter of infinite importance,
and by those who felt a decent amount of interest, but could
have commanded their feelings readily enough.   As for
Wilmot himself, he would have found it difficult to account
for the absorption of feeling and interest with which he
watched the case, had he been called upon to render any
account of it to others.   In his own mind he shirked the
question, and simply devoted himself day and night to his
patient, leaving the house only once a day for a brief time,
during which he would stride up and down the terrace in
front of the house, gulping-in all the fresh air he could
inhale ; and then his place in the sick-chamber was taken by
an old woman, who had years before been Madeleine's nurse,
and who was now married and settled on the estate.   Not
since the old days of his house-surgeonship at St Vitus's
had Chudleigh Wilmot had such a spell of duty as this : the
fact of his giving up his time in this manner to a girl with
whom he had not exchanged twenty words, with whose friends
he had no previous acquaintance, in whom he could have no
possible interest, came upon him frequently in his enforced
exercise on the terrace, in his long weary vigils in the sick-
room ; and each time that he thought it over he felt or pronounced it to himself to be more and more inexplicable.   In
London he made it an inexorable rule never to leave his bed
at night, unless the person sending for him were a regular
patient, no matter what might be their position in life, or the
exigency of their case ; and even among his own connection
he kept strictly to consultation and prescription ; he undertook no practical work, there were apothecaries and nurses
for that sort of thing.   He had a list of both, whom he could
recommend, but he himself never paid any attention to such
matters.   And here he was acting as a combination of

physician, apothecary, and nurse, dispensing the necessary medicines from the family medicine-chest, sitting up all night, concocting soothing drinks, and smoothing hot and uneasy pillows.

Why? Chudleigh Wilmot had asked himself that question a thousand times, and had not yet found the answer to it. Beauty in distress—and this girl, for all her mass of golden hair and her bright complexion and her blue eyes, could only be called pretty—beauty in distress was no more strange to Chudleigh Wilmot than to the hero of nautical melodrama at a transpontine theatre. He was constantly being called in to cases where he saw girls as young and as pretty as Madeleine Kilsyth "hove down in the bay of sickness," as the said nautical dramatic hero forcibly expresses it. Scarcely a day passed that he was not for some few minutes by the couch of some woman of far superior attractions to this young girl, and yet of whom he had never thought in any but the most thoroughly professional manner, listening to her complaints, marking her symptoms, prescribing his remedies, and entering up the visit in his note-book, as he whirled away in his carriage, as methodically as a City accountant. But he had never felt in his life as he felt one bright afternoon when the wild delirium had spent its rage and died away, and the doctor sat by the girl's bedside, and held her hand, no longer dry and parched with fever, and bent over her to catch the low faint accents of her voice.

"You don't know me, Miss Kilsyth," said he gently, as he saw her dazed by looking up into his face.

"Oh yes," said Madeleine, in ever so low a voice,—"Oh yes; you are Doctor—Doctor—I cannot recollect your name; but I know you were sent for, and I saw you before—before I was—"

"Before you were so ill; quite right, my dear young lady. I am Dr Wilmot, and you have been very ill; but you are better now, and—please God—will soon be well."

"Dr Wilmot! Oh yes, I recollect. But, please, don't think because I could not recall your name that I did not know you. I have known you all through this—this attack. I have had an indefinable sense of your presence about me; always kind and thoughtful and attentive, always soothing, and—"

"Hush, my dear child, hush! you must not talk and excite yourself just yet. You have had, as you probably know, a very sharp attack of illness; and you must keep thoroughly quiet, to enable us to perfect your recovery."

"Then I'll only ask one question and say one thing. The question first—How is papa?"

"Horribly nervous about you, but very well. Constant in his tappings at this door, unremitting in his desire to be admitted; to which requests I have been obdurate. However, when he hears the turn things have taken, he will be reassured."

"That's delightful! Now, then, all I have to say is to thank you, and pray God to bless you for your kindness to me. I've known it, though you mayn't think so, and—and I'm very weak now; but—"

He had his strong arm round her, and managed to lay her back quietly on her pillow, or she would have fainted. As it was, when the bright blue eyes withdrew from his, the light died out of them, and the lids dropped over them, and Madeleine lay thoroughly exhausted after her excitement.

What *was* the reminiscence thus aroused? What ghost with folded hands came stealing out of the dim regions of the past at the sound of this girl's voice, at the glance of this girl's eyes? What bygone memories, so apart from everything else, rose before him as he listened and as he looked? He had not hit the trail yet, but he was close upon it.

The news that the extremity of danger was past was received with great delight by the guests at Kilsyth. With most of them Madeleine was a personal favourite, and all of them felt that a death in the house would have been a serious personal inconvenience. The Northallertons, Lady Fairfax, and Lord Towcester, were the only seceders; the others either had arranged for later visits elsewhere, or found their present quarters far too comfortable to be given up on the mere chance of catching an infectious disorder. Some of them had had it, and laughed securely; others feared that from the mere fact of their having been in the house when the attack took place, they were so "compromised" as to prevent their being received elsewhere; and one or two actually had the charity to think of their host and hostess, and stayed to keep them company, and to be of any service in case they might be required. Charley Jefferson belonged to this class. Emily Fairfax little knew that by her selfish flight from Kilsyth she had entirely thrown away all her hold over the great honest heart that had so long held her image enshrined as its divinity. She never gave a thought to the fact that when the big Guardsman used to hum in a deep baritone voice the refrain of hers—

> " Loyal je serai
> Durant ma vie "—

he was expressing one of the guiding sentiments of his life. Colonel Jefferson was essentially loyal; to shrink from a friend who was in a difficulty, to shuffle out of supporting in purse, person, or any way in which it might be requisite, a comrade who had a claim of old acquaintance or strong intimacy, was in his eyes worse than the majority of crimes for which people stand at the dock of the Old Bailey. In this matter he never swerved for an instant. He never gave the question of infection a thought; he had had scarlet-fever at Eton, and jungle-fever out in India, and he was as case-hardened, he said, as a rhinoceros. He took no credit to himself for being fearless of infection, or indeed for anything else, this brave simple-minded good fellow; but if any one had been able to see the working of his heart, they would

have known what credit he deserved for holding to his grand
old creed of loyalty to his friend, and for ignoring the whispers of the siren, even when she was as fascinating and po-
tential as Emily Fairfax. When some one asked if he were
going, he laughed a great sardonic guffaw, and affected to
treat the question as a joke. When the disease was pronounced to be unmistakably infectious, he at once constituted himself as a means of communication between Dr
Wilmot and the outer world; and his honour and loyalty
enabled him to face the fact that probably little Lord Towcester had followed Lady Fairfax to her next visiting-place,
and was there administering consolation to her with great
equanimity. When Dr Wilmot came out for his half-hour's
stride up and down the terrace, he generally found the
Colonel and Duncan Forbes waiting for him; and these
three would pace away together, the two *militaires* chatting
gaily on light subjects calculated to relieve the tedium of
the doctor, and to turn his thoughts into pleasanter channels,
until it was time for him to go back to his duty. And when
the worst was over, and Chudleigh Wilmot could have longer
and more frequent intervals of absence from the sick-room,
it was Charley Jefferson who proposed that they should
establish a kind of mess in the smoking-room, where the
Doctor, who necessarily debarred himself from communion
with the others at the dinner-table, might yet enjoy the
social converse of such as were not afraid of infection. So
a dinner-table was organized in the smoking-room, and
Jefferson and Duncan Forbes invited themselves to dine
with the Doctor. They were the next day joined by Mrs
Severn, who had all along wished to devote herself to the
invalid, and had with the greatest difficulty been restrained
from establishing herself *en permanence* as nurse in Madeleine's chamber; and Mr Pitcairn asked for and obtained
permission to join the party, and proved to have such a
talent for imitation and such a stock of quaint Scotch stories

as made him a very valuable addition to it. So the "Condemned Cell," as its denizens called it, prospered immensely; and by no means the least enjoyment in the house emanated from it.

Lady Muriel, seeing more and more of Wilmot, as the closeness of his attendance on his patient became relaxed by her advance towards convalescence, and studying him with increased attention, learned to regard him with feelings such as no man of her numerous and varied acquaintance had ever before inspired her with. The impression he had made upon her in the first interview was not removed or weakened, and he presented himself to her mind—which was naturally inquiring, and possessed considerably more intelligence than she had occasion to use, in a general way, in her easy-going, prosperous, and conventional life—in the light of an interesting and remunerative study.

Lady Muriel's faultlessly good manners precluded the indulgence of any perceptible absence of mind; and she possessed the enviable faculty which some women of the world exhibit in such perfection, of carrying, or rather helping, on a conversation to which she was not in reality giving attention, and in which she did not feel the smallest particle of interest. The gallant *militaires*, the dashing sportsmen, the *grands seigneurs*, and the ladies of distinction who were among her associates, and the gentlemen, at least of the number of her admirers, were accustomed to regard Lady Muriel's powers of conversation as something quite out of the common way; and so indeed they were—only these simple-minded and ingenuous individuals did not quite understand the direction taken by their uncommonness. It never occurred to them to calculate how much of her talking Lady Muriel did by means of intelligent acquiescent looks, graceful little bows, sprightly exclamations, a judicious expression of intense interest in the subject under discussion when it chanced to be personal to the other party to the discourse, and sundry other skilful and effective feminine devices. It never dawned upon them that one half the time she did not hear, and during the whole time she did not care, what was said; that her graceful manner was merely manner, and her real state of mind one of complete indifference to themselves and almost every one besides. Not that Lady Muriel was an unhappy woman. Far from it. She was too sensible to be unhappy without just cause; and she certainly had not that. She perfectly appreciated her remarkably comfortable lot in life; she estimated wealth, station, domestic tranquillity and respect, and the unbounded power which she exercised in her household domain, quite as highly as they deserved to be estimated; and though as free from vulgarity of mind as from vulgarity of manner, she was not in the least likely to affect any sentimental humility or mistake about her own social advantages. She could as easily have bragged about them as forgotten them; but just because she held them for what they were worth, and did not exaggerate or depreciate them, Lady Muriel was given to absence of mind; and though neither unhappy, nor imagining herself so, she was occasionally bored, and acknowledged it. Only to herself though. Lady Muriel Kilsyth had no confidantes, no intimacies. Hers was the equable kind of prosperous life which did not require any; and she was the last woman in the world to acknowledge a weakness which her truly admirable manners gave her power most successfully to conceal.

The touch of sorrow or anxiety is a sovereign remedy for *ennui*. It will succeed when all the resources to which the victims of that fell disease are accustomed to have recourse fail ignominiously. If Lady Muriel had loved Madeleine Kilsyth, the girl's illness would have put boredom to flight, with the first flush or shiver of fever, the first dimness of the eyes, the first tone of complaint in the clear young voice. But Lady Muriel did not love Madeleine, and did not pretend to herself that she loved her. Indeed Lady Muriel never pretended to herself. She had seen and understood that to deceive oneself is at once much easier and more dangerous than to deceive other people, and she avoided doing so on principle—on the worldly-wise principle, that is, by which she so admirably regulated her life—and reaped a rich harvest of popularity. She did not dislike the girl at all, and she would have been very sorry if she had died, partly for the sake of Kilsyth, whom she really liked and admired, and who would have broken his stout simple heart for his daughter—"much sooner and more surely than for me," Lady Muriel thought; "but that is quite natural, and as it should be. She is the child of his first love, and I am his second wife, and he is quite as fond of me as I want him to be;" for she was a thoroughly sensible woman, and would much rather not have had more love than she could reciprocate. But she was perfectly equable and composed. Throughout Madeleine's illness it did not cause her sorrow, though her manner conveyed precisely the proper degree of stepmotherly concern which was called or under the circumstances; and she did not suffer from anxiety, being rationally satisfied that all the skill, care, and indulgence demanded by the exigencies of the case were liberally bestowed on Madeleine. Anxiety was quite uncalled for, and therefore did not chase away the brooding spirit of *ennui* from Lady Muriel.

The first thing that struck her particularly with regard to Chudleigh Wilmot was that she did not experience any sense of boredom in his presence. In fact it dissipated that ordinarily prevailing malady; she was really interested in everything he talked about, really charmed by the manner in which he talked, and had no need whatever to draw on the ever-ready resources of her manner and *savoir faire*.

When Wilmot began to make his appearance freely among the small party at Kilsyth, and after the usual inquiries—in which the serious and impressive tone at first observed was gradually discarded—to enter into general conversation, and to exercise all the very considerable powers which he possessed of making himself agreeable, Lady Muriel found out and admitted that this was the pleasantest time of the day. The interval between this discovery and her finding herself longing for the arrival of that time—dwelling upon all its incidents when she was alone, making it a central point in her life, in fact—was very brief.

With this new feeling came all the keen perception, the close observation, and the nascent suspicion which could not fail to accompany it, in such a "thorough" organization as that of Lady Muriel. She began to take notice of everything concerning Wilmot, to observe all his ways, and to watch with jealous scrutiny the degree of interest he displayed in all his surroundings at Kilsyth.

As Madeleine progressed in her recovery, Lady Muriel looked for some decline in the physician's absorption in the interest of her case. He would be less punctual, less constant in his attendance upon her; he would be more susceptible to influences from the outside world; he would be anxious to get away perhaps—at least he would no longer be indifferent to professional duties elsewhere; he would begin to weigh their respective claims, and would recognize the preponderance of those at a distance over that which he had already satisfied more than fully, more than conscientiously, with a fulness and expansion of sympathy and devotion rare indeed.

Wilmot was extremely popular among the little company at Kilsyth. Wonderfully popular, considering how much he was the intellectual superior of every man there; but then he was one of those clever men who never make their talents obnoxious, and are not bent on forcing a perpetual recognition of their superiority from their associates. He allowed the people he was with to enjoy all the originality, wit, knowledge, and good fellowship that was in him, and did not administer the least alloy of mortification to their pride with it. When Lady Muriel forcibly acknowledged to herself, and would as frankly have acknowledged to any one else, if any one else would have asked her a question on the subject, that she held Dr Wilmot to be the cleverest and most agreeable man she had ever met, she did but utter a sentiment which had found general expression among the party assembled at Kilsyth.

As the days went by, Lady Muriel began to feel certain misgivings relative to Wilmot. She did not quite like his look, his manner, when he spoke of Madeleine. She did not consider it altogether natural that he should never weary of Kilsyth's garrulity on the subject of his darling daughter. The physician, taking rest from his long and anxious watch, might well be excused if he had tired a little of questions and replies about every symptom, every variation, and of endless stories of the girl's childhood, and laudation of her beauty, her virtues, and her filial love and duty. But Dr Wilmot never tired of these things; he would, on the contrary, bring back the discourse to them, if it strayed away, as it would do under Lady Muriel's direction; and moreover she noticed, that no circumstances, no social temptation, had power to detain him a moment from his patient, when the time he had set for his return to her side had arrived.

Taking all these things into consideration, and combining them with certain indications which she had noticed about Madeleine herself, Lady Muriel began to think the return of Dr Wilmot to London advisable, and to perceive in its being deferred very serious risk to her scheme for the endowment of her young kinsman with the hand and fortune of her stepdaughter. She was not altogether comfortable about its success, to begin with. Ramsay Caird had not as yet made satisfactory progress in Madeleine's favour. It was not because the girl had no power of loving in her that she had listened without the smallest shadow of emotion to Mr Ramsay Caird, but simply because Mr Ramsay Caird had not had the tact, or the talent, or the requisite qualifications, or the good fortune to arouse the power of loving him in her. Lady Muriel was far too quick an observer, far too learned a student of human nature, not to read at a glance all that her step-daughter's looks revealed; and her knowledge of life at once informed her of the danger to her scheme. What was to be done? Wilmot must be got rid of, must be sent away without loss of time. His business was over, and he must go. That must be treated as a matter of course. He was called in as a professional man to exercise his profession; and the necessity of any further exercise of it having terminated, his visit was necessarily at an end. No possible suspicion of her real reason for wishing to get rid of him could arise. A married man, of excellent reputation, accustomed to being brought into the closest contact with women of all ages in the exercise of his profession— why, people would shout with laughter at the idea of her bringing forward any idea of his flirtation with a girl like Madeleine! And Kilsyth himself—nothing, not even the influence which she possessed over him, would induce him for an instant to believe any such story. It was very ridiculous; it must be her own imagination; and yet— No; there was no mistaking it, that girl's look; she could see it even then. Even if Ramsay Caird were not in question, it was a matter which, for Madeleine's own sake, must be quietly but firmly put an end to. Immensely gratified by this last idea—for there is nothing which so pleases us as the notion that we can gratify our own inclinations and simultaneously do our duty, possibly because the opportunities so rarely arise—Lady Muriel sought her husband, and found him busily inspecting a new rifle which had just arrived from London. After praising his purchase, and talking over a few ordinary matters, Lady Muriel said shortly :

"By the way, Alick, how much longer are we to be honoured by the company of Dr Wilmot?"

The inquiry seemed to take Kilsyth aback, more from the tone in which it was uttered than its purport, and he said hesitatingly,

"Dr Wilmot! Why, my dear? He must stay as long as Madeleine—I mean—but have you any objection to his being here?"

"I! Not the least in the world; only he seems to me to be in an anomalous position. Very likely his social talents are very great, but we get no advantage of them; and as for his professional skill—for which, I suppose, he was called here—there is no longer any need of that. Madeleine is out of all danger, and is on the fair way to health."

"You think so?"

"I'm sure of it. But, at all events, any doubt on that point could be dissipated by asking the Doctor himself."

"My dearest Muriel, wouldn't that be a little *brusque*, eh?"

"My dear Alick, you don't seem to see that very probably this gentleman is wishing himself far away, but does not exactly know how to make his adieux. A man in a practice like Dr Wilmot's, however we may remunerate him for his visit here, and however agreeable it may be to him" (Lady Muriel could not resist giving way in this little bit), "must lose largely while attending on us. He is a gentleman, and consequently too delicate to touch on such a point; but it is one, I think, which should be taken into consideration."

Lady Muriel had had too long experience of her husband not to know the points of his armour. The last thrust was a sure one, and went home.

"I should be very sorry," said Kilsyth with a little additional colour in his bronzed cheeks, "to think that I was the cause of preventing Dr Wilmot's earning more money, or advancing himself in his profession. We owe him a deep debt of gratitude for what he has done; but perhaps now, as you say, Madeleine is out of danger, and may be safely left to the care of Dr Joyce. I'll speak to Dr Wilmot, my dear Muriel, and make it all right on that point."

CHAPTER VII.

BROODING.

The effect of her husband's letter on Mrs Wilmot's mind, strengthened by the view taken of its contents by Henrietta Prendergast, was of the most serious and injurious nature. Hitherto the unhappiness which had possessed her had been negative—had been literally *un*happiness, the absence of joy; but from the hour she read Wilmot's letter, and talked over it with her friend, all that was negative in her state of mind changed to the positive. Hitherto she had been jealous—jealous as only a woman of a thoroughly proud, sensitive, secretive, and sullen nature can be—of an abstraction. Her husband's profession was the *bête noir* of her existence, was the barrier between her and the happiness for which she vainly longed and pined. She had looked around her, and seen other women whose husbands were also working bees in the world's great hive; but their work did not absorb them to the exclusion of home interests, and the deadening of the sweet and blessed sympathies which lent happiness all its glow, and robbed sorrow of half its gloom. Her husband had never spoken an unkind word to her in his life, had never refused her a request, or denied her a pleasure; but he had never spoken a word to her which told her that the first place in his life

was hers; he had never cared to anticipate a request or
to share a pleasure. To a woman like Mabel Wilmot, in
whose character there was a strong though wholly unsus-
pected element of romance, there was an inexhaustible
source of suffering in these facts, combined with her husband's proverbial devotion to his profession. Not a clever
woman, thoroughly conventional in all her ideas, without a
notion of the possibility of altering the routine of her life
to any pattern which might take her fancy, a dreamer, and
incurably shy, especially with him, who never discerned
that there was anything beneath the surface of her placid,
equable, rather cold manner to be understood, she had
ample materials within herself for misery; and she had
always made the most of them.

An incalculable addition had been made to her store by
Wilmot's letter, and Henrietta Prendergast's comments.
Mabel wrote to Mr Foljambe, under the observation and
by the dictation of her friend, merely repeating the words
of her husband's letter; and during that performance, and
the ensuing conversation, she had felt sufficiently black and
bitter to have satisfied any fiend who might have been
waiting about for the chance of gratifying his malignity by
the coming to grief of human affairs. But it was when she
was left alone, when her friend had gone away, and she was
in her solitary room—all the trivial occupations of the day
at an end, and only the long hours of the night, often sleepless hours to her, to be faced—that she gave way to the
intensity of the bitterness of her spirit; that she looked
into and sounded the darkness and the depth of the gulf
of sorrow which had opened before her feet.

That her husband sought and found all his happiness
in the duties of his profession; that he had no consciousness, comprehension, or care for the disappointed feelings
which occupied her wholly, had been hard enough to bear
—how hard, the lonely woman who had borne the burden

G

knew; but such a state of things, the state from which only
a few hours divided her, was happy in comparison with
that which now opened suddenly before her. He had neglected her for the profession he preferred; he was going to
neglect his own interests, to depart from his accustomed
law of life, to throw the best friend he had in the world over
—for a woman: yes, a woman, a sick girl had done what
she had failed to do: she had never swayed his judgment,
or turned him aside from a purpose for a moment; and now
he was changed by the touch of a more potent hand than
hers, and there was an end of the old settled melancholy
peacefulness of her life; active wretchedness had come in,
and the repose, dear-bought in its deadness of disappointment and blight, was all gone.

Mabel Wilmot sat opposite the long glass in her room
that night, and turned the branch-candles so as to throw a
full light upon her face, at which she gazed steadily and
long, frowning as she did so. It was a fair face, and the
fresh bloom of youth was still upon it. It was a face in
which a skilful observer might have read strange matters;
but there were none curious to read the story in the face
of the pretty wife of the prosperous rising man. Her eyes
were soft and dark, well shaded by long lashes, and marked
by finely-arched eyebrows; and there were none to see
that there was frequent gloom and brooding in their darkness—a shadow from the gloominess of the soul within.
She was fair rather than pale, and had abundant dark hair;
and as she sat and gazed in the glass, she let its dusky masses
loose, and caught them in her hands. The fair face was
not pleasant to look upon; and so she seemed to think, for
she muttered:

" She is very pretty, I suppose, and a great deal younger
than I am; never looks sullen, and has no cause. And
yet he's not a man I should have thought to have been beguiled by any woman. *I* never beguiled him, and I was

pretty in my time; ay, and *new* too! And I have lived in
his sight all these years, and he has never sacrificed an hour
of time or thought to me. And now he leaves me without
hesitation, though I am ill. I have not talked about it, to
be sure; but what is his skill worth if he did not see it in my
face and hear it in my voice without being told! I was not a
case—I was only his wife; and he never thought of looking,
never thought of caring whether I was ill or well. I appear at breakfast, and I go out every day; that's quite
enough for him. I wonder if he knew what I suspect,
what I should once have said *I hope*, is the cause; but that
is a long time ago. Would it have made any difference?
I don't mean now; of course it would not *now;* nothing
makes any difference to a man when once his heart is turned
aside, and quite filled by another. I don't think I ever
touched his heart; I know only too well I never filled
it."

Mabel Wilmot was right. She had never filled her
husband's heart. She had touched it though, for a time
and after a light holiday kind of fashion, which had subsided when life began in earnest for them, and which he
had laid aside and forgotten, as a boy might have abandoned
and lost sight of the toys with which he had amused himself during a school vacation. And the girl had been
deceived; had built silently in the inveterately undemon-
strative recesses of her heart and fancy a fairy palace,
destined to stand for ever empty. It had been swept and
garnished; but the prince had never come to dwell there:
he with busy feet had passed by on the other side, and she
had nothing to do but to sit and mourn in the empty
chambers. She had borne her grief valiantly until now;
she had only known the passive side of it. But that was
all over for ever; and the day that dawned after Wilmot's
wife had received his letter found her a different woman
from what she had been.

"Are you sure you are not ill, Mabel?" asked Mrs Prendergast the day after their colloquy over the letter. "You are so black under the eyes, and your face is so pinched, I fancy you must be ill."

"Not more so than usual," said Mrs Wilmot shortly.

"Than usual, my dear! What *do* you mean? Have you been feeling ill lately?"

"Yes, Henrietta, very ill."

"And have you been doing nothing for yourself? Have you not had advice?"

"You know I have not. You have seen me very nearly every day, and you know I have done nothing without your knowledge."

"But Wilmot?" said Mrs Prendergast.

"Oh, Wilmot! Much he knows and much he cares about me! Don't talk nonsense, Henrietta. If I were dying, he would not see it while I could keep on my feet, which I certainly should do as long as I could."

"My dear Mabel," remonstrated Henrietta, "do you mean to tell me that, feeling very ill, you have actually suffered your husband to leave you? Is that right, Mabel? Is it right to yourself or fair to him?"

"Fair to *him!*" returned Mrs Wilmot with a scornful emphasis. "The idea of anything I do being fair or unfair to *him*. I am so important to him, am I not? His life is so largely influenced by me? Really, Henrietta, I don't understand you."

"O yes, you do," said her friend; and she seated herself beside her, and took her feverish hands firmly in hers; "you understand me perfectly. What is the illness, Mabel? How do you suffer, and why are you concealing it?"

"I suffer always, and in all ways," said Mabel, twitching her hands impatiently from her friend's grasp, and averting her face, down which tears began slowly to trickle. "I have not been well for a long time; and would not one think that *he* might have seen it? He can be full of skill and perception in every one's case but mine."

Henrietta Prendergast was troubled. She was a woman with an odd kind of conscience. So long as a fact did not come too forcibly before her, so long as a duty did not imperatively confront her, she would ignore it; but she would not do the absolutely, the undeniably wrong, nor leave the obviously and pressingly right undone. Here was a dilemma. She believed that Wilmot's ignorance of his wife's state of health was solely the result of her own studious avoidance of complaint, or of letting him see, during the short periods of every day that they were together, that she was suffering in any way. Any man whose perceptions were not quickened by the inspiration of love would be naturally deceived by the calm tranquillity of Mrs Wilmot's manner, which, if occasionally sullen, was apparently influenced in that direction by trivial causes,—household annoyances, and so forth. And though Henrietta Prendergast had a grudge against Chudleigh Wilmot, which was all the stronger and the more lasting that it was utterly unreasonable, she could not turn a deaf ear to the promptings of her conscience, which told her she must speak the truth on his behalf now.

"I must say, Mabel," she began, "that I think it is your fault that Wilmot has not perceived your state of health. You have carefully concealed it from him, and now you are angry at your own success. You must not continue to act thus, Mabel; you will destroy his happiness and your own."

"*His* happiness!" repeated Mrs Wilmot with indescribable bitterness; "*his* happiness *and* mine I know nothing about his happiness, or what he has found it in hitherto, and may find it in for the future. I only know that it has nothing to do with mine; and that I have no happiness, and never can have any now."

The sullen conviction in Mabel Wilmot's voice impressed

her friend painfully, and kept her silent for a while. Then she said :

"You are unjust, Mabel. You have concealed your suffering and illness from me as effectually as from him."

"Do you attempt to compare the cases?" said Mrs Wilmot with a degree of passion extremely unusual to her. "I deny that they admit of comparison. However, there is an end of the subject; let us talk of something else. If I am not better in a day or so, I can do as Mr Foljambe has had to do: I can call in Whittaker, or somebody else. It does not matter. Let us turn to some more agreeable topic."

And the friends talked of something else. They lunched together, and they went out driving; they did some very consolatory shopping, and paid a number of afternoon calls. But Henrietta Prendergast watched her friend closely and unremittingly; and came to the conclusion that she was really ill, and also that it was imperatively right her husband should be informed of the fact. Henrietta dined at Charles-street; and when the two women were alone in the evening, and the confidence-producing tea-tray had been removed, she tried to introduce the interdicted subject. Ordinarily she was anything but a timid woman, anything but likely to be turned from her purpose; but there was something new in Mabel's manner, a sad intensity and abstraction, which puzzled and distressed her, and she had never in her life felt it so hard to say the things she had determined to say.

Argument and persuasion Mrs Wilmot took very ill; and at length her friend told her, in an accent of resolution, that she had made up her mind as to her own course of action.

"It is wrong to leave Wilmot in ignorance, Mabel," she said; "wrong to him and wrong to you. If only a little of all you have acknowledged to me were the matter with you, it would still be wrong to conceal it from him. If you *will* not tell him, I *will*. If you will not promise me to write to him to-night, I will write to him to-morrow. Mind, Mabel, I mean what I say ; and I will keep my word."

Mrs Wilmot had been leaning, almost lying, back in a deep easy-chair, when her friend spoke. She raised herself slowly while she was speaking, her dark eyes fixed upon her, and when she had finished, caught her by the wrist.

"If you do this thing, Henrietta, I most solemnly declare to you that I will never speak to you or see you again. In this, in all that concerns my husband and myself, I claim, I insist upon, perfect freedom of action. No human being —on my side at least—shall come between him and me. I am thoroughly in earnest in this, Henrietta. Now choose between him and me."

"Choose between him and *you* ! What *can* you mean, Mabel ?"

"I know what I mean, Henrietta, and I am determined in this. When you know all, you will see that only I can speak to him ; and that I must speak, not write."

"Then you *will* speak ? "

"Yes, I will speak. I suppose he will return in a few days ; and then I will speak."

Then Mabel Wilmot told her friend intelligence which surprised her very much, and they stayed together until late ; and when they parted Mrs Prendergast looked very thoughtful and serious.

"This will make things either better or worse," she said to herself that night. " If he returns soon, and receives the news well, all may go on well afterwards ; but if he stays away for this girl's sake much longer, I don't think even the child will do any good."

Many times within the next few days, in thinking of her friend, Mrs Prendergast said, "There's a desperation about her that I never saw before, and that I don't like."

The days passed over, and Wilmot's patients were obliged either to content themselves with the attendance of the insinuating Whittaker, or to exercise their own judgment and call in some other physician of their own choice. There was no doubt that the delay was injuring Wilmot. He might have had his week's holiday, and passed it with Sir Saville Rowe, and welcome; but he was not at Sir Saville's, and the week had long been over. As for Mr Foljambe, his indignation was extreme.

"Hang it!" he observed, "if Chudleigh can't come back when he might, why does he pretend to keep up a London practice? And to send me Whittaker too; a fellow I hate like—like colchicum. I suppose I can choose my doctor for myself, can't I?"

Thus the worthy and irascible old gentleman, who was more attached to Chudleigh Wilmot than to any other living being, would discourse to droppers-in concerning his absent favourite; and as the droppers-in to the invalid room of the rich banker were numerous, and of the class to whom Wilmot was especially well known, the old gentleman's talk led to somewhat wide and varied speculation on the causes and inducements of his absence. Mr Foljambe had ascertained all the particulars which Wilmot had given his wife; and Kilsyth of Kilsyth was soon a familiar phrase in connection with the rising man. Everybody knew where he was, and "all about it;" and when the unctuous and deprecating Whittaker talked of the "specially interesting case" which was detaining Wilmot, glances of unequivocal intelligence, but of somewhat equivocal meaning, were interchanged among his hearers; and guesses were made that Miss Kilsyth was a "doosed nice" girl, or her step-mother Lady Muriel,—"young enough to be Kilsyth's daughter, you know, and never lets him forget it, by Jove"—was a "doosed fine" woman. "The Kilsyths" began to be famous among Wilmot's *clientèle* and the old banker's familiars; the *Peerage*, lying on his book-shelves, and hither-to serenely undisturbed, with its covering of dust, was fre-quently in demand; and young Lothbury, of Lombard, Lothbury, & Co., made quite a sensation when he informed a select circle of Mr Foljambe's visitors that he knew Ronald Kilsyth very well—was in his club in fact.

"Old Kilsyth's son," he explained; "a very good fellow in his way, and quite the gentleman, as he ought to be of course, but a queer-tempered one, and a bit of a prig."

"Have you written to your husband, Mabel?" said Mrs Prendergast with solemn anxiety, when the third week of Wilmot's absence was drawing to a close, and his wife's ill-ness had increased day by day, so that now it was a com-mon topic of conversation among their acquaintance.

"No," returned Mabel, "I have not. I have told you I will not write, but speak to him; and I am resolved."

"But Whittaker? Surely he does not know your hus-band is ignorant of your state?"

"O, dear no," returned Mrs Wilmot, with a smile by no means pleasant to see. "He is the jolliest and simplest of men in all matters of this kind. Mrs Whittaker wouldn't, in fact couldn't, have a finger ache unknown to him; and he never suspects that things are different with me."

"Mabel," said her friend, "you do very, very wrong; but I will not interfere or argue with you. Only, remember, I believe much will depend on your reception of him."

"Don't be alarmed, Henrietta," said Mabel Wilmot. "I promise you, unhesitatingly, that Wilmot will not be dissatisfied with the reception he shall have from me."

CHAPTER VIII.

KITH AND KIN.

IT was a good thing for Kilsyth that he had a soft, sweet, affectionate being like Madeleine on whom he could vent the fund of affection stored in his warm heart, and who could appreciate and return it. In the autumn of life, when the sad strange feeling first comes upon us, that we have seen the best of our allotted time, and that the remainder of our pilgrimage must be existence rather than life; when the ears which tingled at the faintest whisper of love know that they will never again hear the soft liquid language once so marvellously sweet to them; when the heart which bounded at the merest promptings of ambition beats with unmoved placidity even as we recognize the victories of our juniors in the race; when we see the hopes and cares and wishes which we have so long cherished one by one losing their sap and strength and verdure, one by one losing their hold on our being, and borne whirling away, lifeless and shrivelled, on the sighing wind of time,—we need be grateful indeed if we have anything so cheering and promiseful as a daughter's affection. It is the old excitement that has given a zest to life for so many years; administered in a very mild form indeed, but still there. The boys are well enough, fine gentlemanly fellows, making their way in the world, well spoken of, well esteemed, doing credit to the parent stock, and taking—ay, there's the deuce of it!—taking the place which we have vacated, and making us feel that we have vacated it. Their mere presence in the world brings to us the consciousness which arose dimly years ago, but which is very bright and impossible to blink now—that we no longer belong to the present, to the generation by which the levers of the world are grasped and moved; that we are tolerated

gently and genially indeed, with outward respect and with
a certain amount of real affection; but that we are in
effect *rococo* and bygone, and that our old-world notions are
to be kindly listened to, not warmly adopted. Ulysses is
all very well; in fact, was a noted chieftain in his day,
went through his wanderings with great pluck and spirit,
had his adventures, dear old boy. You recollect that story
about the Gräfinn von Calypso, and that scandalous story
which was published in the Ogygian *Satirist?* But it is
Telemachus who is the cynosure of Ithaca nowadays, whom
we watch, and on whom we wait. But with a girl it is a
very different matter. To her her father—until he is supplanted by her husband—still stands on the old heroic pedestal where, through her mother's interpretation, she saw
him long since in the early days of her childhood; in her
eyes "age has not withered him, nor custom staled his infinite variety;" all his fine qualities which she was taught to
love,—and how easily she learned the lesson!—have but
mellowed and improved with years. Her brothers, much
as she may love them, are but faint copies of that great
original; their virtues and good qualities are but reflected
lights of his—his the be-all and end-all of her existence;
and the love between him and her is of the purest and most
touching kind. No tinge of jealousy at being supplanted
by her sullies that great love with which he regards her,
and which is free from every taint of earthiness; towards
her arises a chastened remembrance of the old love felt towards her mother, with the thousand softened influences
which the old memories invest it with, combined with that
other utterly indescribable affection of parent to child, which
is one of the happiest and holiest mysteries of life.

So the love between Kilsyth and his girl was the happiness of his existence, the one gentle bond of union between
him and the outer world. For so large-hearted a man, he
had few intimate relations with life; looking on at it bene-

volently, rather than taking part even in what it had to
offer of gentleness and affection. This was perhaps because
he was so thoroughly what is called "old-fashioned." Lady
Muriel he honoured, respected, and gloried in. On the few
occasions when he was compelled to show himself in London society, he went through his duty as though enjoying
it as much as the most foppish Osric at the court; supported chiefly by the universal admiration which his wife
excited, and not a little by the remembrance that another
month would see him freed from all this confounded nonsense, and up to his waist in a salmon stream. There could
be no terms of praise too warm for "my lady," who was in
his eyes equally a miracle of talent and loveliness, to whom
he always deferred in the largest as in the smallest matters
of life; but it was Madeleine

> "who had power
> To soothe the sportsman in his softer hour."

It was Madeleine who had his deepest, fondest love—a
love without alloy; pure, selfless, and eternal.

These feelings understood, it may be imagined Kilsyth
had the warmest feelings of gratitude and regard towards
Dr Wilmot for having, as every one in the house believed,
and as was really the fact, saved the girl's life, partly by
his skill, principally by his untiring watchfulness and devotion to her at the most critical period of her illness. In
such a man as Kilsyth these feelings could not remain long
unexpressed; so that within a couple of days of the interview between Lady Muriel and Dr Wilmot, Kilsyth took
an opportunity of meeting the doctor as he was taking his
usual stretch on the terrace, and accosting him.

"Good-morning, Dr Wilmot; still keeping to the terrace as strictly as though you were on parole?"

"Good-morning to you. I'm a sanitarian, and get as
much fresh air as I can with as little labour. This terrace

seems to me the only level walking ground within eyeshot;
and there's no more preposterous mistake than overdoing
exercise. Too much muscularity and gymnastics are amongst
the besetting evils of the present day, depend upon it.

"Very likely; but I'm not of the present day, and
therefore not likely to overdo it myself, or to tempt you
into overdoing it. But still I want you to extend your
constitutional this morning round to the left; there's a
path that skirts the craig—a made path in the rock itself,
merely broad enough for two of us to walk, and which has
the double advantage that it gives us peeps of some of the
best scenery hereabouts; and it is so little frequented, that
it will give us every chance of uninterrupted conversation.
And I want to talk to you about Madeleine."

Whatever might have been Chudleigh Wilmot's previous
notions as to the pleasure derivable from an extended
walk with the old gentleman, the last word decided him;
and they started off at once.

"I won't pretend to conceal from you, Dr Wilmot," said
Kilsyth, after they had proceeded some quarter of a mile,
talking on indifferent subjects, and stopping now and then
to admire some point in the scenery,—"I won't pretend to
conceal from you, that ever since your arrival here I have had
misgivings as to the manner in which you were first summoned. I—"

"Pray don't think of that, sir."

"I don't—any more than, I am sure, you do. My
Madeleine, who is dearer to me than life, was, I knew, in
danger. I heard of your being in what one might almost
call the vicinity from Duncan Forbes; and without thought
or hesitation I at once telegraphed to you to come on
here."

"Thereby giving me the pleasantest holiday I ever enjoyed in my life, and enabling me to start away, as I was on
the point of doing, with the agreeable reflection that I have

been of some comfort to some most kind and charming people."

"I am delighted to hear you say those friendly words, Dr Wilmot; but I am not convinced even now. So far as —as the honorarium is concerned, I hope you will allow me to make that up to you; so that you shall have no reminder in your banker's book that you have not been in full London practice; and as to the feeling beyond the honorarium, I can only say that you have earned my life-long gratitude, and that I should be only too glad for any manner of showing it."

Wilmot waited a minute before he said, "My dear sir, if there is anything I hate, it is conventionality; and I am horribly afraid of being betrayed into a set speech just now. With regard to the latter part of your remarks, your gratitude for any service I may have been to you cannot be surpassed by mine for my introduction to my charming patient and your delightful family circle. With regard to what you were pleased to say about the honorarium, you must be good enough to do as I shall do—forget you ever touched upon the subject. You don't know our professional etiquette, my dear sir—that when a man is on a holiday he does no work. Nothing on earth would induce me to take a fee from you. You must look upon anything I have done as a labour of love on my part; and I should lose all the pleasure of my visit if I thought that that visit had not been paid as a friend rather than as a professional man."

Kilsyth must have changed a great deal from his former self if these words had not touched his warm generous heart. Tears stood in his bright blue eyes as he wrung Chudleigh Wilmot's hand, and said, "You're a fine fellow, Doctor; a great fellow altogether. I'm an old man now, and may say this to you without offence. Be it as you will. God knows, no man ever left this house carrying with him so deep a debt of its owner's gratitude as will hang round you. Now as to Madeleine. You're off, you say, and I can't gainsay your departure; for I know you've been detained here far too long for the pursuance of your own proper practice, which is awaiting you in London; and I feel certain you would not go if you felt that by your going you would' expose her to any danger of a relapse. But I confess I should like to hear from your own lips just your own candid opinion about her."

Now or never, Chudleigh Wilmot! No excuse of miscomprehension! You have examined yourself, probed the inmost depths of your conscience in how many midnight vigils, in how many solitary walks! You know exactly the state of your feelings towards this young girl; and it is for you to determine whether you will renounce her for ever, or continue to tread that pleasant path of companionship—so bright and alluring in its present, so dark and hopeless in its future—along which you have recently been straying. Professional and humanitarian considerations? Are you influenced by them alone, when you reply—

"My dear sir, you ask me rather a difficult question. Were I speaking of your daughter's recovery from the disease under which she has been labouring, I should say with the utmost candour that she has so far recovered as to be comparatively well. But I should not be discharging my professional duty—above all, I should not be worthy of that trust which you have reposed in my professional skill, and of the friendship with which you have been so good as to honour me—if I disguised from you that during my constant attendance on Miss Kilsyth, and during the examinations which I have from time to time made of her system, I have discovered that—that she has another point of weakness totally disconnected from that for which I have been treating her."

He was looking straight into the old man's eyes as he said this—eyes which dropped at the utterance of the words, then raised themselves again, dull, heavy-lidded, with all the normal light and life extinguished in them.

"I heard something of this from Muriel, from Lady Muriel, from my wife," muttered Kilsyth; "but I should like to know from you the exact meaning of your words. Don't be afraid of distressing me, Doctor," he added, after a short pause; "I have had in my time to listen to a sentence as hard—almost as hard "—his voice faltered here—" as any you could pronounce; and I have borne up against it with tolerable courage. So speak."

"I have no hard, at least no absolute, sentence to pronounce, my dear sir; nothing that does not admit of much mitigation, properly taken and properly treated. Miss Kilsyth is not a hoyden, you know; not one of those buxom young women who, according to French notions, are to be found in every English family—"

"No, no!" interrupted the old gentleman a little querulously.

"On the contrary, Miss Kilsyth's frame is delicate, and her constitution not particularly strong. Indeed, in the course of my investigation during her recent illness, I discovered that her left lung was not quite so healthy as it might be."

"Her lungs! Ah, good heavens! I always feared that would be the weak spot."

"Are any of her family so predisposed?"

"One brother died of rapid consumption."

"Ay, indeed! Well, well, there's nothing of that kind to be apprehended here,—at least there are no urgent symptoms. But it is only due to you and to myself to tell you that the lungs are Miss Kilsyth's weak point, and that every care should be exercised to ward off the disease which at present, I am happy to say, is only looming in the distance."

"And what should be the first step, Dr Wilmot?"

"Removal to a softer climate. You have a London house, I know; when do you generally make a move south?"

"Lady Muriel and the children usually go south in October,—about five weeks from hence,—and I go down to an old friend in Yorkshire for a month's cover-shooting. But this is an exceptional year, and anything you advise shall be done."

"My advice is very simple; it is, that you so far make an alteration in your usual programme as to put Miss Kilsyth into a more congenial climate at once. This air is beginning now to be moist and raw in the mornings and evenings, and at its best is now unfit for any one with delicate lungs."

"Would London do?"

"London would be a great improvement on Kilsyth—though of course it's treason to say so."

"Then to London she shall go at once; and I hope you will allow me the pleasure of anticipating that my daughter, when there, will have the advantage of your constant supervision."

"Anything I can do for Miss Kilsyth shall be done, you may depend on it, my dear sir. And now I want to say good-bye to you, and to you alone. I have a perfect horror of adieux, and dare not face them with women. So you will make my farewell to Lady Muriel, thanking her for all the kindness and hospitality; and—and you will tell Miss Kilsyth—that I shall hope to see her soon in London; and—so God bless you, my dear sir, *au revoir* on the flags of Pall-Mall."

Half an hour afterwards he was gone. He had made all his arrangements, ordered his horses, and slipped away while all the party was engaged, and almost before his absence from the luncheon-table was remarked. He knew that the road by which he would be driven was not overlooked by the dining-room where the *convives* would be assembled; but he knew well enough that it was commanded by one particular window, and to that window he looked up with flashing eyes and beating heart. He caught a momentary glimpse of a pale face surrounded by a nimbus of golden hair; a pale

H

face on which was an expression of sorrowful surprise, and which, as he raised his hat, shrunk back out of sight, without having given him the smallest sign of recognition. That look haunted Chudleigh Wilmot for days and days; and while at first it distressed him, on reflection brought him no little comfort, thinking, as he did, that had Madeleine had no interest in him, her expression of face would have been simply conventional, and she would have nodded and bowed as to any ordinary acquaintance. So he fed his mind on that look, and on certain kindly little speeches which she had made to him from time to time during her illness; and when he wanted a more tangible reminiscence of her, he took from his pocket-book a blue ribbon with which she had knotted her hair during the earlier days of her convalescence, and which, when she fell asleep, he had picked from the ground and carefully preserved.

Bad symptoms these, Chudleigh Wilmot; very bad symptoms indeed! Bad and easily read; for there shall be no gawky lad of seventeen years of age, fresh from the country, to join your class at St Vitus's, who, hearing them described, shall not be able to name the virulent disease from which you are suffering.

When Lady Muriel heard the result of her husband's colloquy with the Doctor, she was variously affected. She had anticipated that Chudleigh Wilmot would take the first opportunity of making his escape from Kilsyth, where his presence was no longer professionally needed, while his patients in London were urgent for his return. Nor was she surprised when her husband told her that Dr Wilmot had, when interrogated, declared that the air of Kilsyth was far too sharp for Madeleine in her then condition, and that it was peremptorily necessary that she should be moved south, say to London, at once. Only one remark did she make on this point: "Did Madeleine's removal to London—I mean

did the selection of London spring from you, Alick, or Dr
Wilmot?"

"From me, dear—at least I asked whether London
would do; and he said, at all events London would be infinitely preferable to Kilsyth; and so knowing that we should
have the advantage of his taking charge of Madeleine, I
thought it would be best for us to get away to Rutland-gate
as soon as possible."

To which Lady Muriel replied, "You were quite right;
but it will take at least a week before all our preparations
will be complete for leaving this place and starting south."

Lady Muriel Kilsyth did not join any of the expeditions
which were made up after luncheon that day; the rest of
the company went away to roaring linns or to heather-covered
mountains; walked, rode, drove; made the purple hills re-
sound with laughter excited by London stories, and flirted
with additional vigour, though perhaps without the subtlety
imparted by the experience of the season. But Lady Muriel
went away to her own room, and gave herself up to thought.
She had great belief in the efficacy of "thinking out" anything that might be on her mind, and she resorted to the
practice on this occasion. Her course was by no means
clear or straightforward, but a little thorough application to
the subject would soon show her the way. Let her look at
it in all its bearings, and slur over no salient point. This
man, this Dr Wilmot—well, he was wondrously fascinating,
that she must allow! His eyes, his earnestness of manner,
his gravity, and the way in which he slid from grave to gay
topics, as his face lit up, and his voice—ah, that voice, so
mellow, so rich, so clear, and yet so soft, and capable of such
exquisite modulation! The remembrance of that face, only
so recently known, has stopped the current of Lady Muriel's
thoughts: she sits there in the low-backed chair, her chin
resting on her breast, her hands clasped idly before her, her
eyes vaguely looking on the fitfully flaming logs upon the

hearth. Wondrously fascinating; in his mere earnestness
so different from the men, young and old, amongst whom
her life was passed; by whom, if thought were possible to
them, it was held as something to be ashamed of, while
frivolity resulting in vice ruled their lives, and frivolity garnished with slang governed their conversation. Wondrously
fascinating; in the modesty with which he exercised the great
talent he possessed, and the possession of which alone would
have turned the head of a weaker man; in his brilliant
energy and calm strength; in his unwitting superiority to
all around him, and the manner in which, apparently unconsciously and without the smallest display, he took his place
in the front rank, and, no matter who might be present,
drew rapt attention and listening ears to himself. So much
for him. Now for herself. And Lady Muriel rose from the
soft snuggery of her cushioned chair, and folded her arms
across her breast, and began pacing the room with hurried
steps. This man had established an influence over her?
Agreed. What was worse, established his influence without
intending it, without absolutely wishing it? Agreed again.
Lady Muriel was far too clever a woman to shirk any item
or gloss over any replies to her cross-examination of herself.
And was she, who had hitherto steered her way through life,
avoiding all the rocks and shoals and quicksands on which
she had seen so much happiness wrecked, so much hope in-
gulfed—was she now to drift on for the same perilous voy-
age, without rudder or compass, without even a knowledge
whether the haven would be open to her? Not she. For
her husband's, for her own sake, for her own and her children's credit, she would hold the course she had held, and
play the part she had played. A shudder ran through her
as she pictured to herself the delight with which the thousand-and-one tongues of London scandal would whisper and
chuckle over the merest hint that their prophecy of years
since was beginning to be fulfilled—how the faintest breath

of suspicion with which a name could be coupled would fly over the five miles of territory where Fashion reigns. She stopped before the glass, put her hand to her heart, and saw herself pale and trembling at the mere idea.

And yet to be loved! Only for once in her life to know that she loved and was loved again, not by a man whom she could tolerate, but by one whom she could look up to and worship. Not reverence—that was not the word; she reverenced Kilsyth—but whose intellect she could respect, whose self she could worship. Oh, only for once in her life to experience that feeling which she had read so much about and heard so much of; to feel that she was loved heart and soul and body; loved with wild passion and calm devotion —for such a man as this was capable of both feelings simultaneously—loved for herself alone, independently of all advantages of state and position; loved by the most lovable man in the world. Loved! the word itself was tabooed amongst the women with whom she lived, as being too strong and expressive. They 'liked' certain men in a calm, easy, *laissez-aller* kind of way at the height of their passion; then married them, with proper amount of bishop, bridesmaid, and wedding present, all duly celebrated in the fashionable journal; and then "gave up to parties what was meant for mankind." Ah, the difference between such an existence and that passed as this man's wife! cheering him in his work, taking part in his worries, lightening his difficulties, always ready with a smiling face and bright eyes to welcome him home, and—Jealous? Not she! there would be no such feeling with her in such a case. Jealous! And as the thought rose in her mind, simultaneously appeared the blue eyes and the golden hair of her step-daughter.

That must be nipped in the bud at once! There was nothing on Dr Wilmot's part—probably there might be nothing on either side; but sentimental friendship of that kind generally had atrociously bad results; and Madeleine was a very impressionable girl, and now, as Kilsyth had determined, was to be constantly thrown with Wilmot, to be under his charge during her stay in London, and therefore likely to have all her thoughts and actions influenced by him. Such a combination of circumstances would be necessarily hazardous, and might be fatal, if prompt measures were not taken for disposing of Madeleine previously. This could only be done by making Ramsay Caird declare himself. Why that young man had never prospered in his suit was inexplicable to Lady Muriel; he was not so good-looking as poor Stewart certainly—not one-tenth part so intense—having an excellent constitution, and looking at life through glasses of the most roseate hue; but Madeleine was young and inexperienced and docile—at least comparatively docile even to Lady Muriel, who, as she knew perfectly well, possessed very little of the girl's love; and it was through her affection that she must be touched. Who could touch her? Not her father: he was too much devoted to her to enter into the matter; at least in the proper spirit. Who else then? Ah, Lady Muriel smiled as a happy thought passed through her mind. Ronald, Madeleine's brother,—he was the person to exercise influence in a right and proper way over his sister; and to him she would write at once.

That night the butler took two letters from the post-box in Lady Muriel's handwriting; one of them was addressed to Ramsay Caird, in George-street, Edinburgh, and ran thus:

" Kilsyth.

"MY DEAR RAMSAY,—For reasons which I have already sufficiently explained to you, you will, I think, be disposed to admit that my interest in you and your career is unquestionable, and you will be ready to take any step which I may strongly urge upon you. In this conviction, I feel sure that you will unhesitatingly adopt the suggestion which I now make, and start for London at the very earliest opportunity.

You will be surprised at this recommendation, and at the manner in which I press it; but, believe me, I do not act without much reflection, and without thorough conviction of the step I am taking, and which I am desirous you should take. I have so often talked the matter over with you, that there is no necessity for me to enter upon it now, even if there were no danger in my so doing. It will be sufficient to say that we all go to London in a week's time, and that it is specially desirable that you should be there at the same time; otherwise you may find the ground mined beneath your feet. When you arrive in town, I wish you to call upon Captain Kilsyth at Knightsbridge Barracks. You will find him particularly clear-headed, and thoroughly conversant with the ways of the world; and I should advise you to be guided by him in everything, but specially in *the* matter in question. Let me have a line to say you are on the point of starting; and believe me

"Your sincere friend,
"Muriel Kilsyth."

The other letter was addressed to "Captain Kilsyth, First Life-guards, Knightsbridge Barracks, London."

"(*Confidential.*) Kilsyth.

"My dear Ronald,—You have heard from your father of Madeleine's illness and convalescence. She is rapidly recovering her strength, and will be her old self *physically* very shortly.

"You smile as you see that the word 'physically' is underlined; but this is not, believe me, one of those 'unmeaning women's dashes' which I have so often heard you unequivocally condemn. I underlined the word specially, because I think that Madeleine's recovery will be, so far as she is concerned, physical, and physical only.

"Not that I mean in the least that her reason has been

affected, otherwise than it always is most transiently in the access of fever; but that I think that the occasion which you and I have so often talked of has come, and come in a most undeniable manner. In a word, Madeleine has lost her heart, if I am not much mistaken, and lost it in a quarter where she herself, poor child, can hope for no return of her affection, and where, even if such return were possible, it would only bring misery on her, *and him,* and degradation to us all.

"We are coming to London at once, and therein lies simultaneously the danger to Madeleine and my hope of rescuing her from it, principally through your aid. You will see that is impossible to enter upon this subject at length in a letter; but I could not let you be in ignorance of what I know will possess an acute and painful interest for you. Of course I have not hinted a word of this to your father, so that you will be equally reticent in any of your communications with him. You shall hear the day we expect to arrive in town, and I hope to see you in Brook-street on the next morning.

"You will recollect all I said to you about Ramsay Caird. He will probably call on you very shortly after you receive this letter. Bear in mind the cue I gave you, when we last parted, about this young man, and act up to it: he is a little weak, a little hesitating; but I am more convinced than ever of the advisability of pursuing the course I then indicated. God bless you!

"Your affectionate

"M. K."

CHAPTER IX.

RONALD.

WHEN Ronald Kilsyth was little more than four years old his nurses said he was " so odd ; " a phrase which stuck by him through life. As a child his oddity consisted in his curious gravity, and preoccupation, his insensibility to amusement, his dislike of companionship, his love of solitude, his old-fashioned thoughts and manner and habits. He had a dogged honesty which prevented him from using the smallest deception in any way, which prevented him from ever prevaricating or telling those small fibs which are made so much of in the child, but to which he looks back as trivial sins indeed when compared with the duplicity of his after-life,— which rendered him obnoxious even to the children whom he met as playfellows in the square-garden, and who found it impossible to get on with young Kilsyth on account of the rigidity of his morals, displeasing to them even at their tender years. When a delicious *guet-apens*, made of string stretched from tree to tree, had been, with great consumption of time and trouble, prepared for the downfall of the old gardener ; and when the youthful conspirators were all laid up in ambush behind the Portugal laurels, waiting to see the old man, plodding round with rake and leaf-basket in the early dusk of the autumnal evening, fall headlong over the snare,—it was provoking to see little Ronald Kilsyth, in his gray kilt, step out and go up to the old man and show him the pitfall, and assist him in removing it. The conspirators were highly incensed at this treachery, as they called it, and would have sent Ronald then and there to Coventry,—not that that would have distressed him much,—had it not been for his magnanimity in refusing, even when under pressure, to give up the names of those in the plot. But as in this, so in everything else ; and the little frequenters of the square soon found Ronald Kilsyth " too good " for them, and were by no means anxious to secure his companionship in their sports.

At Eton, whither he was sent so soon as he arrived at the proper age, he very shortly obtained the same character. Pursuing the strict path of duty,—industrious, punctual, and regular, with very fair abilities, and scrupulously making the most of them,—he never lost an opportunity and never made a friend. All that was good of him his masters always said; but they stopped there ; they never said anything that was kind. In school they could not help respecting him ; out of school they would as soon have thought of making Ronald Kilsyth their companion as of taking *Hind's Algebra* for pleasant reading. And it was the same with his schoolfellows. They talked of his steadiness and of his hard-working with pride, as reflecting on themselves and the whole school. They speculated as to what he would do in the future, and how he would show that the stories that had been told about Eton were all lies, don't you know ? and how Kilsyth would go up to Cambridge, and show them what the best public school—the only school for English gentlemen, you know— could do ; and *Floreat. Etona*, and all that kind of thing, old fellow. But Ronald Kilsyth, during the whole of his Eton pupilage, never had a chum—never knew what it was to share a confidence, add to a pleasure, or lighten a grief. Did he feel this ? Perhaps more acutely 'than could have been imagined ; but being, as he was, proud, shy, sensitive, and above all queer, he took care that no one knew what his feelings were, or whether he had any at all on the subject.

Queer ! that was the word by which they called him at Eton, and which, after all, expressed his disposition better than any other. Strong-minded, clear-headed, generous, and brave, with an outer coating of pride, shyness, reserve, and a mixture of all which passed current for *hauteur*. With a

strong contempt for nearly everything in which his con-
temporaries found pleasure,—save in the excess of exercise,
as that he thoroughly understood and appreciated,—and
with a wearying desire to find pleasure for himself; with an
impulse to exertion and work, accountable to himself only on
the score of duty, but having no definite end or aim; with a
restless longing to make his escape from the thraldom of
conventionality, and rush off and do something somewhere
far away from the haunts of men. With all the morbidness
of the hero of *Locksley Hall*, without the excuse of having
been jilted, and without any of the experience of that sweetly
modulated cynic, Ronald Kilsyth, obeying his father's wish,
and thereby again following the path of duty, was gazetted
to the Life-Guards—the exact position for a young gentleman
in his condition.

The donning of a scarlet tunic instead of a round jacket,
and the substitution of a helmet for a pot-hat, made very
little difference in Ronald. Several of his brother officers
had known him personally at Eton, so that the character he
had obtained there preceded him, inspiring a wholesome awe
of him before he appeared on the scene; and he had not
been two days in barracks before he was voted a prig and
a bore. There was no sympathy between the dry, pedantic,
rough young Scotsman and those jolly genial youths. His
hard, dry, handsome, clean-cut face, with its cold gray eyes,
thin aquiline nose, and tight lips, cast a gloom over the
cheery mess-table around which they sat; their jovial beam-
ing smiles, and curling moustaches, and glittering shirt-studs
reflected in the silver *épergne*, with its outposts of mounted
sentries and its pleasant mingling of feasting and frays at the
Temple of Mars and the London Tavern. His grim presence
robbed many a pleasant story of its point, which indeed, in
deference to him, had to be softened down or given with
bated breath. The young fellows—no younger than him in
years, but with, oh, such an enormous gulf between them as

regards their elasticity and charm of youth—were afraid of him, and from fear sprung dislike.   They had not much fear of their elders, these youths of ingenuous countenance and ingenuous modesty.   They had a wholesome awe, tempering their hearty love, of Colonel Jefferson ; but less on account of the strictness of his discipline and of a certain *noli-me-tangere* expression towards those whom he did not specially favour, than on account of his age ; and as for the jolly old Major, who had been in the regiment for ever so many years,—for him they had neither fear nor respect ; and when he was in command—which befell him during the cheerful interval between July and December—the lads did as they liked.

But they could not get on with Ronald Kilsyth ; and though they tolerated him quietly for the sake of his people, they never could be induced to regard him with anything like the fraternal good fellowship which they entertained towards each other.   As it had been at Eton, so it was at Knightsbridge, at Windsor, in Albany-street, in all those charming quarters where the Household Cavalry spend their time for their own and their country's advantage.   Ronald Kilsyth was respected by all, loved by none.   Charley Jefferson himself, fascinated as he was by Ronald's devotion to the mysteries of drill and by all the young man's unswerving attention to his regimental duties—qualities which weighed immensely with the martinet Colonel—had been heard to confess, with a prolonged twirl at his grizzled moustache, that "Kilsyth was a d—d hard nut to crack,"—an enigmatic remark which, from so plain a speaker as the Colonel, meant volumes.   The Major, whom Ronald, under strong provocation, had once designated a "tipsy old atheist," had, in the absence of his enemy and under the influence of two-thirds of a bottle of brandy, retorted in terms which were held to justify both Ronald's epithets ; and the men nad a very low opinion of him, who at the time of writing was senior lieutenant of the regiment. He had no sympathy with the men, no care for them; he would have liked to have made them more domestic, less inclined for the public-house and the music-hall; he would have subscribed to reading-rooms, to institutes, to anything for their mental improvement; but he never thought of giving them a kind word or an encouraging speech; and they much preferred Cornet Bosky—who cursed them roundly for their talking, for their silence, for their going too fast, for their going too slow, for their anything in fact, on those horrible mornings when he happened to be in charge of them exercising their horses, but who off duty always had a kindly word, an open purse at their service—to the senior lieutenant, who never used a bad expression, and who, as they confessed, was, after the Colonel, the best soldier in the regiment.

It was like going into a different world to leave the smoky atmosphere, the wild disorder, and reckless confusion of most of the other rooms in barracks, and go into Donald Kilsyth's trim orderly apartment. Instead of tables ringed with stains of long-since-emptied tumblers, and littered with yellow-paper-covered French novels, torn playbills, old gloves, letters, unpaid bills, opera-glasses, pipes, shreds of tobacco, heaps of cigar-ash, rolls of comic songs, trophies from knock'em-downs at race-courses, empty soda-water bottles, scattered packs of cards, and such-like examples of free living —to find perfect order and decorum; the walls covered with movable bookcases filled with valuable books, Raphael Morghen prints, proofs before letters after the best modern artists, and charming bits of water-colour sketches, instead of coloured daubs of French *écuyères* and *lionnes* of the Quartier Breda, photographs of Roman temple or Pompeian excavation, and Venetian glass and delicate eggshell china, and Chinese carving, and Indian beadwork. They used to look round at these things in wonder, the other young fellows of the regiment, when they penetrated into Ronald's room,

and point to the pictures and ask who " that queer old party
was," and depreciate the furniture by inquiring " what was
that old rubbish ? " They could not understand his friends
either ; men asked to the mess by them or seen in their
rooms were generally well known in the Household Brigade,
other officers in the Blues or the Foot Regiments, or idlers
and dawdlers with nothing to do, men in the Treasury or
Foreign Office, people whom they were safe to meet in society
at least every other night in the season. But Ronald Kilsyth's
guests were of a different stamp. Sometimes he brought
Wrencher the novelist or Scumble the Royal Academician to
dinner ; and the fellows who knew the works of both made
much of the guests and did them due honour ; but when
occasionally they had to receive Jack Flokes the journalist,
who looked on washing as an original sin, or Dick Tinto the
painter, who regarded a dirty brown velvet shooting-coat as
the proper costume for the evening, or Klavierspieler the
pianist, a fat dirty German in spectacles, who made a perfect
Indian juggler of himself in trying to swallow his knife
during dinner—they were scarcely so much gratified. Innate
gentlemanliness and entire good-breeding made them receive
the gentlemen with every outward sign of hospitality ; but
afterwards, round the solemn council fire in the little mess-
room and midst deep clouds of tobacco-smoke, they delivered
a verdict anything but complimentary either to guest or
host.

What possessed him ? That was what they could not
understand. Nicest people in the world, sir ! father, dear
delightful jolly old fellow, give you his heart's blood if you
wanted it—but you don't want it, so gives the best glass of
claret in London ; and at home—at Kilsyth—'gad, you can't
conceive it ; no country-house to be named in the same
breath with it. Perfect shooting and all that kind of thing,
and thoroughly your own master, by Jove ! do just as you
like, I mean to say, and have everything you want, don't you

know! Lady Muriel quite charming; holding her own, don't you know, with all the younger women in point of attractiveness and that sort of thing, and yet respected and looked up to, and the best mistress of a house possible. And Miss Kilsyth, Madeleine, deuced nice little girl; very pretty, and no nonsense about her; meant for some big fish! Well, yes, suppose so; but meantime extremely pleasant and chatty, and sings nice little songs and *valses* splendidly, and all that kind of thing. That was what they said of the Kilsyth *ménage* in the Household Brigade, in which pleasant joyous assemblage of gallant freethinkers it would have been difficult to point out one who would not have been delighted at an autumn visit to Kilsyth. Ah! what we believe and that we know! The humorous articles of the comic writers, the humorous sketches of the comic artists, lead us to think that the gentlemen officers of the regiments specially accredited for London service are, in the main, good-looking, handsome dolts, who pull their moustaches, eliminate the " r's " from their speech, and are but the nearest removes from the inmates of Hanwell Asylum. But a very small experience will serve to remove this impression, and will lead one to know that the reading and appreciation of character is nowhere more aptly read and more shrewdly hit upon than in the barrack-rooms of Knightsbridge or the Regent's Park.

People who knew, or thought they knew, Ronald Kilsyth, declared that he was solitary and oyster-like, self-contained, and caring for no one but himself. They were wrong. Ronald had strong home affections. He loved and reverenced his father more than any one in the world. He saw plainly enough the few shortcomings—the want of modern education, the excessive love of sport, the natural indolence of his disposition, and the intense desire to shirk all the responsibilities of his position, and to shift the discharge of them on to some one else. But equally he saw his father's warm-heartedness, honour, and chivalry; his unselfishness, his disposition to look upon the bright side of all that happened, his cheery *bonhomie*, and his unfailing good temper. Lady Muriel he regarded with feelings of the highest respect—respect which he had often tried to turn into affection, but had tried in vain. With a woman's quickness, Lady Muriel had seen at a glance, on her first entering the Kilsyth family, that her hardest task would be to win over her stepson, and she had laid herself out for that victory with really far more care and pains than she had taken to captivate his father. With great natural shrewdness, quickened by worldly experience, Lady Muriel very shortly made herself mistress of Ronald Kilsyth's character, and laid her plans accordingly. Never was shaft more truly shot, never was mine more ingeniously laid. Ronald Kilsyth, boy as he was at the time of his father's second marriage, had scarcely had three interviews with his stepmother before she found a corroboration of the fact which had so often whispered itself in his own bosom, that he, and he alone, was the guiding spirit of the family; that he had knowledge and experience beyond his years : and that if she, Lady Muriel, only got him, Ronald, to coöperate with her, everything would be smooth, and between them the felicity and well-being of all would be assured. It was a deft compliment, and it succeeded. From that time forth Ronald Kilsyth was Lady Muriel's most pliant instrument and doughtiest champion. In the circles in which during the earlier phases of his succeeding life he found himself, there were plenty to carp at his stepmother's conduct, to impugn her motives,—worst of all, to drop side hints of her integrity; but to all of these Ronald Kilsyth gave instant and immediate battle, never allowing the smallest insinuation which reflected upon her to pass unrebuked. He thought he knew his stepmother thoroughly : whether he did or not time must show; but at all events he thought highly enough of her to permit himself to be guided by her in some of the most important steps in his career.

And what were his feelings with regard to Madeleine? If you wanted to find the key to Ronald Kilsyth's character, it was there that you should have looked for it. Ronald loved Madeleine with all the love which such a heart as his was capable of feeling; but he watched over her with a strictness such as no duenna ever yet dreamed of. Years ago, when they were very little children, there occurred an episode which Miss O'Grady—who was then Kilsyth's governess, and now happily married to Herr Ohm, a wine-merchant at Heidelberg—to this day narrates with the greatest delight. It was in Hamilton Gardens, where the Kilsyth children and a number of others were playing at *Les Graces*—a pleasing diversion then popular with youth—and little Lord Claud Barrington, in picking up and restoring her hoop to Madeleine, had taken advantage of the opportunity to kiss her hand. Ronald noticed the gallantry, and at once resented it, asking the youthful libertine how he dared to take such a liberty. " Well, but she liketh it!" said Lord Claud, ingenuously pointing to Madeleine, who was sucking and biting the end of her hoop-stick, by no means ill-pleased. "Very likely," said Ronald; "but these girls know nothing of such matters. *I* am my sister's guardian, and call upon you to apologize." Lord Claud, humiliated, said he was " wewy thorry; " and the three,—he, Ronald, and Madeleine,—had some bath-pipe and some cough-lozenges as a banquet in honour of the reconciliation.

This odd watchfulness, never slumbering, always vigilant, perpetually unjust, and generally *exigeant*, characterized Ronald's relations with his sister up to the time of our story. When she first came out, his mental torture was extraordinary; he, so long banished from ball-rooms, accepted every invitation, and though he never danced, would invariably remain in the dancing-room, ensconced behind a pillar, lounging in a doorway, always in some position whence he could command his sister's movements, and throughout the evening never taking his eyes from her. His friends, or rather his acquaintances, who at first watched his rapt attention without having the smallest idea of its object, used to chaff him upon his devotion, and interrogate him as to whether it was the tall person with the teeth, the stout virgin with the shells in her hair, or the interesting party with the shoulders, who had won his young affection. Ronald stood this chaff well, confident in the fact that hitherto his sister had performed her part in that grand and ludicrous mystery termed "Society," and had escaped heart-whole. He began to realize the truth of the axiom about the constant dropping of water. So long as Madeleine had had sense to comprehend, he had instilled into her the absolute necessity of consulting him before she even permitted herself to have the smallest liking for any man. During the first two months of her first season she had confessed to him twice : once in the case of a middle-aged, well-preserved peer; and again when a thin, black-bearded *attaché* of the Brazilian embassy was in question. Ronald's immediate and unmistakable veto had been sufficient in both cases; and he was flattering himself that the rest of the season had passed without any further call on his self-assumed judicial functions.

Imagine, then, his state of mind at the receipt of Lady Muriel's letter! The assault had been made, the mine had been sprung, the enemy was in the citadel, and, worst of all, the enemy was masked and disguised, and the guardian of the fortress did not know who was his assailant, or what measures he should take to repel him.

CHAPTER X.

CROSS-EXAMINATION.

THE hall-porter at Barnes's Club in St James's-street, whose views of life during the last two months had been remarkably gloomy and desponding, began to revive and to feel himself again as the end of October drew on apace. He had had a dull time of it, that hall-porter, during August and September, sitting in his glazed box, cutting the newspapers which no one came to read, and staring at the hat-pegs which no one used. He had his manuscript book before him, but he did not inscribe ten names in it during the day, for nearly everybody was out of town ; and the few members who perforce remained—gentlemen in the Whitehall offices, or officers in the Household Brigade—found scaffolding and ladders in the hall of Barnes's, and the morning-room in the hands of the whitewashers, and the coffee-room closed, and the smokers relegated to the card-room, and such a general state of discomfort, that they shunned Barnes's, and went off to the other clubs to which they belonged. But with the end of October came a change. The men who had been shooting in the North, the men who had been travelling on the Continent, the men who had been yachting, and the men who had been lounging on the sea-coast, all came through town on their way to their other engagements ; those who had no other engagements, and who had spent all their available money, settled down into their old way of life; all paid at least a flying visit to the club to see who was in town, and to learn any news that might be afloat.

It is a sharp bright afternoon, and the morning-room at Barnes's is so full that you might actually fancy it the season. Sir Coke Only's gray cab horse is, as usual, champing his bit just outside the door, and Lord Sumph's brougham is there, and Tommy Toshington's chestnut cob with the white face is being led up and down by the red-jacketed lad, who has probably been out of town too, as he has not been seen since Parliament broke up, and yet is there and to the fore directly he is wanted. Tommy Toshington himself, an apple-faced little man, who might be any age between sixteen and sixty, but who is considerably nearer the latter than the former, gathers his letters from the porter as he passes, looks through them quickly, shaking his head the while at two or three written on very blue paper, and addressed in very formal writing, and proceeds to the morning-room. Everybody there, everybody knowing Tommy, universal chorus of welcome from all save three old gentlemen reading evening papers, two of whom don't know Tommy, and all of whom hate him.

"And where have you come from, Tommy?" says Lord Sumph, who is a charming nobleman, labouring under the slight eccentricity of occasionally imagining that he is a steam-engine, when he whistles, and shrieks, and puffs, and has to be secluded from observation until the fit is over.

"Last from East Standling, my lord," says Tommy; "and very pleasant it was."

"Must have been doosid pleasant, by all I hear," says Sir Thomas Buffem, K.C.B., and late of the Madras army. "Dook had the gout, hadn't he? and we all know how pleasant he is then!"

"That feller was there of course—what's his name?— Bawlindor the barrister," says Sir Coke Only. "Can't bear that feller, dev'lish low-bred feller; was a dancin'-master or something of that sort—can't bear low-bred fellers;" and Sir Coke, whose paternal grandfather had been a pedlar, and who himself combined the intellect of an Esquimaux with the manners of a Whitechapel butcher on a Saturday night, cleared his throat, and thumped his stick, and looked ferocious.

"Yes, Mr Bawlindor was there," says Tommy Toshington, looking round with a queer twinkle in his little gray eyes; "and he was very pleasant, very pleasant indeed. I hardly know how the duchess would have got on without him. He said some doosid smart things, did Mr Bawlindor."

"I hate a feller who says smart things," said Sir Coke Only; "making a buffoon of himself."

"Ha, ha!" said Duncan Forbes, joining the group—

"the carrier is jealous of the tumbler; it's a mere question of pigeons."

"What do you mean, Sir Duncan? I don't understand you," said Sir Coke angrily.

"Don't suppose you do—never gave you credit for anything of the sort.—How are you, all you fellows? What were the smart things that Bawlindor said, Tommy?"

"Well, I don't know; perhaps you wouldn't think 'em smart, Duncan, because you're a devilish clever chap yourself, and—"

"Yes, yes, we know all about that; but tell us some smart things that Bawlindor said—tell us one."

"Well, you know Tottenham? you know he gives awful heavy dinners? He was bragging about them one day at luncheon at East Standling, and Bawlindor said, 'There's one thing, my lord, I always envy when I'm dining with you.' 'What's that?' says Tottenham. 'I envy your gas,' says Bawlindor, 'and *it escapes.*'"

"Ye-es! that was not bad for Bawlindor. I hate the brute though; I dare say he stole it from somebody else. Well, how are you all, and what's the news?"

"You ought to be able to tell us that," said Lord Sumph. "We're only just back in town, and you've been here all the time, haven't you, in the Tower or somewhere?"

"Not I; I'm only just back too."

"And where have you come from?"

"Last from Kilsyth."

"Devil you have!" growled Sir Thomas Buffem, edging away. "They've had jungle-fever—not jungle, scarlet-fever there, haven't they?"

"Oh, ah, Duncan," said Clement Walkinshaw of the Foreign Office, "tell us all about that! It was awful, wasn't it? Towcester cut and run, didn't he? Mrs Severn said he turned pea-green, and sent such a stunning caricature of him to her sister, who was staying at Claverton! We stuck it up in the smoking-room, and had no end fun about it."

"I'm glad you were so much amused. It wasn't no end fun for Miss Kilsyth, however, as she was nearly losing her life."

"Was she, by Jove!" said Walkinshaw, who was a "beauty boy," examining himself in the glass, and smoothing his little moustaches,—"was she, by Jove! What! our dear little Maddy?"

"Our dear little Maddy," said Duncan Forbes calmly, "if you are on sufficient terms of intimacy with the young lady to speak of her in that manner in a public room. I call her Miss Kilsyth; but then we were only brought up together as children, whereas you had the advantage of having been introduced to her last season, I think, Walkinshaw."

"That was a hot 'un for that d—d little despatch-box!" said Sir Thomas Buffem, as Walkinshaw walked off discomfited. "Serve him quite right—conceited little brute!"

"Well, but what was it, Duncan?" asked Lord Sumph. "It wasn't only the gal, heaps of people were down with it, eh?—regular hospital, and that kind of thing? I saw the Northallertons on their way south, and the duchess said it was awfully bad up there."

"The duchess is a—very nice person," said Forbes, checking himself, "and, like Sir Thomas here, an old soldier."

"But it was a great go, though, Duncan,—infection and all that, eh?" asked Captain Hetherington, who had joined the talkers. "There's no such thing as getting Poole's people to make you a coat; the whole resources of the establishment are concentrated on building a new rig-out for Towcester, who had sacrificed his entire get-up, and had his hair cut close, and taken no end of Turkish baths, for fear of being refused admittance at places where he was going to stay."

"All I can say is, then, that it's a capital thing for Towcester's man, or whoever gets his wardrobe," said Forbes. "Charley Jefferson might have made a good thing by buying his tunics, only there's a slight difference in their size—*he* wouldn't have feared the infection."

"No, not in that way perhaps," said Hetherington. "Charley's like the Yankee in Dickens's book, 'fever-proof and likewise ague;' but he *can* be got at, we all know. How about the widow? She bolted too, didn't she?"

"She did—more shame for her. No! the fact was, that at Kilsyth—"

"*Cave canem!*" said Tommy Toshington, holding up a monitory finger—"*Cave canem*, as we used to say at school. Here's Ronald Kilsyth just come into the room and making towards us!"

You can get a good view of Ronald Kilsyth now as he advances up the room. Rather under than over the middle height, with very broad shoulders, betokening great muscular strength, and square limbs. His head is large, and his thick brown hair is brushed off his broad forehead, and hangs almost to his coat-collar. He has a well-moulded but rather a stern face, with bushy eyebrows, piercing gray eyes, and close thin lips. He is dressed plainly but in good taste, and his whole appearance is perfectly gentlemanlike. It would have been as hard to have mistaken Ronald for a snob as to have passed him by without notice; and there was something about him that infallibly attracted attention, and made those who saw him for the first time wonder who he was. It would have been quite impossible to divine his profession from his appearance; neither in look nor bearing was there the smallest trace of the plunger. He might have been taken for a deep-thinking Chancery barrister, had it not been for his moustache; or, more likely still, a shrewd, long-headed engineer, a man of facts and figures and calculation; but never a dragoon. He had been the innocent cause of extreme disappointment to many young ladies in various parts of the country where he had stayed—quiet unsophisticated girls, whose visits to London had been very rare, and who knew nothing of its society, and who hearing that a Life-Guards' officer was coming to dinner, expected to see a gigantic creature, all cuirass and jack-boots, an enlarged and ornamental edition of the sentries in front of the Horse-Guards. Ronald Kilsyth in his plain evening dress was a great blow to them; in bygone days his moustache would have been some consolation; but now the young farmers in the neighbourhood, the sporting surgeon, and all the volunteers wore moustaches; and though in subsequent conversation they found Ronald very pleasant, he neither drawled, nor lisped, nor made love to them; all of which proceedings they had believed to be necessary attributes of his branch of the military profession.

And many persons who were not young ladies in the country were disappointed in Ronald Kilsyth, more especially old friends of his father, who expected to find his son resembling him. Ronald inherited his father's love of honour, truth, and candour, his keen sense of right and wrong, his manliness and his courage; but there the likeness between the men ceased. Kilsyth's warmth of heart, warmth of temper, and largeness of soul were not reflected by Ronald, who never lost his self-control, who never gave anybody credit for more than they deserved, and who—save perhaps for his sister Madeleine, and his love for her was of a very stern and Spartan character—had never entertained any particularly warm feelings for any human being.

Ronald Kilsyth is not popular at Barnes's, being decidedly an unclubbable man. The members, if ever they speak of him at all, want to know what he joined for. He belonged to the Rag, didn't he, and some other club, where he could sit mumchance over his mutton, or stare at the lads from Aldershott drinking five-guinea Heidzeck champague. What did he want among this sociable set? He always looked straight down his nose when Guffoon came up with a sad story, and he never cared about any scandal that was foreign. But he was not disliked, at least openly. It was considered that he was a doosid clever fellow, with a doosid sharp tongue of his own; and at Barnes's, as at other clubs, they are generally polite to fellows with doosid sharp tongues. And his father was a very good fellow, and gave very good dinners during the season; and Kilsyth was a very pleasant house to stop at in the autumn; so that, for these various reasons, Ronald Kilsyth, albeit in himself unpopular at Barnes's, was never suffered to hear of his unpopularity.

Not that, if he had, it would have troubled him one jot. No man in the world was more careless of what people thought of him, so long as he had the approval of his own conscience; and by dint of long course of self-schooling and the presence of a certain amount of self-satisfaction, he could generally count upon that. He could not tell himself why he had joined Barnes's Club, unless it was that Duncan Forbes was a member, and had asked him to join; and he liked Duncan Forbes in his way, and wanted some place where he could be pretty certain of finding him when in town. There were few points of resemblance between Ronald Kilsyth and Duncan Forbes; but perhaps their very dissimilarity was the bond of the union, such as it was, that existed between them. Ronald knew Duncan to be weak, but believed him, and rightly, to be thorough. Duncan Forbes would assume a languid haw-hawism, an almost idiotic rapidity, a freezing *hauteur* to any one he did not know and did not care for, for the merest caprice; but he would stand or fall by a friend, and not Charley Jefferson himself would be firmer and truer under trial. Ronald knew this; and knowing it, was not disposed to be hard on his friend's less stable qualities—was rather amused indeed

"by Duncan's nonsense," as he phrased it, and showed
more inclination for his society than that of any other of
his acquaintance.

The group of talkers in the window opened as Ronald
approached, and he shook hands with its various members ;
Tommy Toshington, who always had something pleasant to
say to anybody out of whom there was any possibility of
his ever getting anything, complimenting him on his appearance.

" Look as fresh as paint, Ronald, my boy—fresh as paint,
by Jove ! Where have you been to pick up such a colour
and to get yourself into such focus, eh ? "

" The marine breezes of Knightsbridge have contributed
to my complexion, Toshington, and the vigorous exercise of
walking four miles a day on the London flags has brought
me into my present splendid condition."

" What ! not been away from town at all ? " asked Sir Coke
Only, who would almost as soon have acknowledged his poor
relations as confessed to having been in London in September.

" Not at all. In the first place, I was on duty, and
could not get away ; not that I think I should have moved
under any circumstances. London is always good enough
for me."

" But not when it's quite empty," said Lord Sumph.

" It can't be quite empty with two millions and a half of
people in it, Sumph," said Ronald.

" Oh, ah, cads and tradesmen, and all that sort of thing,—
devilish worthy people in their way, of course ; but I mean
people that one knows."

" *I* know several of those ' devilish worthy people,'
Sumph," said Ronald, with a smile ; " and besides, country-
house life is not much in my way."

" Don't meet those d—d radical fellows that he thinks so
much of, there," growled Sir Thomas Buffem to Sir Coke
Only.

"No, nor those painters and people that my boy says this chap's always bringing to mess," replied Sir Coke.

"There, he's gone away with Duncan now," said Toshington, "and they'll be happy. They're too clever, those two are, for us old fellows! Not that you're an old fellow, Sumph, my boy."

"You're old enough for several, ain't you, Tommy?" said Lord Sumph; "and I'm old enough to play you a game of billiards before dinner, and give you fifteen; so come along."

Meanwhile Ronald Kilsyth and Duncan Forbes had walked away to the far end of the room, which happened to be deserted at the time; and seating themselves on an ottoman, were soon engaged in earnest conversation.

"What on earth made you remain in town, Ronald?" asked Duncan. "I heard what you said to those fellows; but I know well enough that you could have got leave if you had wished. Why did you not come up to Kilsyth?"

"Principally because there was no particular inducement for me to do so, Duncan?"

"You always were polite, Ronald—"

"Ah, you were there! No, no; you know perfectly well what I mean, Duncan. With you and the governor and Madeleine I'm always perfectly happy; and her ladyship is very friendly, and we get on very well together. But then I like you all quietly and by yourselves; I'm selfish enough to want the entire enjoyment of your society. And the life at Kilsyth would not have suited me at all."

"Well, I don't know; it was very jolly—"

"Yes, of course it was, and—By the way, Duncan, tell me all about it; who were there, and what you did?"

"Oh, heaps of people there—the Northallertons, and the Thurlows, and—"

"Yes, yes; but what men—younger men, I mean?"

"Let me see; there was Towcester—"

" No, not he ; her ladyship would not have thought him objectionable, whatever I might."

" What ? what the deuce are you muttering, Ronald ? "

" I beg your pardon, Duncan—thinking aloud only; it's a horrible habit I've fallen into. Well, who besides Towcester ? "

" Oh, Severn, and Roderick Douglas, and Charley Jefferson—"

" Ah, Charley Jefferson; he's just the same, of course ? "

" Oh yes, he's as jolly as ever."

" Yes; but I mean, is he as devoted as he was to Lady Fairfax ? "

" Oh, worse; most desperate case of—no, by the way, though, I forgot ; I think he has cooled off—"

" Cooled off ! since when ? "

" Since your sister's illness."

" Since my sister's illness ! What, what could that have to do with them ? "

" Well, you see, some of the people in the house got frightened at the notion of infection and that kind of thing, and bolted off. Lady Fairfax was one of the first to rush away ; and Charley, who is loyalty itself in everything, as you know, was deucedly annoyed about it. My lady had been leading him a pretty dance for a few days previously, playing off little Towcester against him, and—"

" Ah, yes. No doubt Charley was right, quite right. And that was all about him, eh ? And so the people were frightened at poor Madeleine's illness, were they ? "

" Gad, they were, and not without reason too. The poor child was awfully bad; and indeed, if it had not been for Wilmot, I much doubt whether she would have pulled through."

" Hadn't been for Wilmot ? Wilmot ! Oh, yes, the London doctor who was staying somewhere near, and who was telegraphed for. Tell me about Dr Wilmot—a clever man, is'nt he ? "

" Clever ! He's wonderful ! Keen, clear-headed fellow ;

sees his way through a brick wall in a minute. Not that at Kilsyth he did not do as much by his devotion to his patient as by his skill."

"Devotion? Oh, he was devoted to his patient, eh?" said Ronald, biting his nails.

"Never saw such a thing in all your life. Went in a regular perisher," said Duncan Forbes, dropping his hands to emphasize his words. "Put himself in regular quarantine; cut himself off from all communication with anybody else, and shut himself up in the room with his patient for days together. It's the sort of thing you read of in poems, and that kind of thing, don't you know, but very seldom meet with in real life. If Wilmot had been a young man, and your sister had had any chance of making him like her, I should have said it was a case of smite. But Wilmot is an old married man; and these doctors don't indulge much in being captivated, especially by patients in fevers, I should think!"

"No; of course not, of course not. Now, this Wilmot —what's he like?"

"Well, he's rather a striking-looking man; looks very earnest, and speaks with a very effectively modulated voice."

"Ah! And he's gentlemanly, eh?"

"Oh, perfectly gentlemanly. No mistake in that."

"And he was wonderfully devoted to Madeleine, eh? Very kind of him, I'm sure. Shut himself up in her room, and—What did Lady Muriel think of him, by the way?"

"I scarcely know. I never heard her say; and yet I gathered somehow that Lady Muriel was not so much impressed in the doctor's favour as the rest of us."

"That's curious, for there are few keener readers of character than Lady Muriel. And the doctor was not a favourite of hers?"

"Well, no; I should say not. But the rest of the party were so strongly in his favour that we looked with some suspicion on all who did not shout as loudly as ourselves."

"And Madeleine, was she equally enthusiastic?"

"Poor Miss Kilsyth, she was not well enough to have much enthusiasm on any subject, even on her doctor. Gratitude is, I imagine, the strongest sentiment one is capable of after a long and severe illness."

"Exactly—yes—I should suppose so. And what aged man is Dr Wilmot?"

"Oh, what we should have called some years ago very old, but what we now look upon as the commencement of middle age—just approaching forty, I should think."

"He is married, you say?"

"Yes; so we all understood. Oh yes, I heard him once mention his wife to Lady Muriel.—I say, Ronald, what an unconscionable lot of questions you are asking about Wilmot; one would think that—"

"Gentleman waiting to speak to you, sir," said a servant, handing a card to Ronald; "says he won't detain you a moment, sir."

Ronald took the card, and read on it "DR WILMOT."

"I will come to the gentleman at once," said he; and the servant went away.

"Who is it? Any one I know?" asked Duncan Forbes.

"He is a stranger to me," said Ronald, blinking the question.

He found Dr Wilmot in that wretched little waiting-room about the size of a warm bath, and having for its furniture a chair, a table, and a map of England, which is dedicated at Barnes's to the reception of "strangers." The gas was low, and the Doctor was heavily wrapped up, and had a shawl round the lower part of his face; but Ronald made him out to be a gentlemanly-looking man, and specially noticed his keen flashing eyes. The Doctor was sorry to disturb Captain Kilsyth, but his father had sent up to him just before he started a parcel which he wished delivered personally to the Captain; so he had brought it on his way from the Great

Northern, by which he had just arrived. It was some law-deed, about the safety of which Kilsyth was a little particular. It would have been delivered two days since, but, passing through Edinburgh, the Doctor had found his old friend Sir Saville Rowe staying at the same hotel, and had suffered himself to be persuaded to accompany him to see the new experiments in anæsthetics which Simpson had just made, and which— Ah! but the Captain did not care for medical details. The Captain was very sorry that he had not a better room to ask the Doctor into; but the regulations at Barnes's about strangers were antediluvian and absurd. He should take an early opportunity of thanking Dr Wilmot for his exceeding kindness in going to Kilsyth, and for the skill and attention which he had bestowed on Miss Kilsyth. The Doctor apparently to Ronald, even in the dull gas-light, with a heightened colour disclaimed everything, asserting that he had merely done his duty. Exchange of bows and of very cold hand-shakes, the Doctor jumping into the cab at the door, Ronald turning back into the hall, muttering, "That's the man! Taking what Duncan Forbes said, and that fellow's look when I named Madeleine—taking them together, that's the man that Lady Muriel meant. That's the man, for a thousand pounds!"

In the cab Dr Wilmot is thinking about Ronald. A blunt rough customer rather, but with a wonderful look of his sister about him; not traceable to any feature in particular, but in the general expression. His sister! now a memory and a dream—with the bit of blue ribbon as the sole tangible reminiscence of her. She is among her friends now; and probably at this moment some one is sitting close by her, close as he used to sit, and he is forgotten already, or but thought of as—Not a pleasant manner, Captain Kilsyth's. Studiously polite, no doubt, but with an under-current of badly-veiled suspicion and reserve. What could that mean? Dr Wilmot knew that his conduct towards the Kilsyth family, so far at least as its outward expression was concerned, had merited nothing but gratitude from every member of it. Why, then, was the young man embarrassed and suspicious? Could he—pshaw! how could he by any possible means have become aware of the Doctor's secret feelings towards Miss Kilsyth—feelings so secret that they had never been breathed in words to mortal? Perfectly absurd! It is conscience that makes cowards of us all; and the Doctor decides that it is conscience which has made him pervert Captain Kilsyth's naturally cold manner so ridiculously.

Well, it is all over now! He is just back again at his old life, and he must give up the day-dreams of the past month and fall back into his professional habits. Looking out of the cab window at the long monotonous row of dirty-brown houses, at the sloppy street, at the pushing crowds on the foot-pavement, listening to the never-ceasing roar of wheels, he can hardly believe that he has only just returned from mountain, and heather, and distance, and fresh air, and comparative solitude! Back again! The reception at home from "ten till one," the old ladies' pulses and the old gentlemen's tongues, the wearied listening to the symptoms, the stethoscopical examination, and the prescription-writing; then the afternoon visits, with the repetition of all the morning's details; the hospital lecture; the dull, cold, formal dinner with Mabel; and the evening's reading and writing, —without one bright spot in the entire daily round, without one cheering hope, one—

A smell of tan!—the street in front of his door strewed with tan! Some one ill close by. What is this strange sickness that comes over him—this sinking at his heart—this clamminess of his brow and hands? The cab has scarcely stopped before he has jumped out, and has knocked at the door. Not his usual sharp decisive knock, but feebly and hesitatingly. He notices this himself, and is wondering about it, when the door opens, and his servant, always solemn, but now preternaturally grave, appears.

Glad to see you at last, sir," says the man, "though you're too late!"

"Too late!" echoes Wilmot vacantly; "too late!—what for?"

"For God's sake, sir," says the man, startled out of his ordinary quietude; "you got the telegram?"

"Telegram! no—what telegram?" What did it say? What has happened?"

"Mrs Wilmot, sir!—she's gone, sir!—died yesterday morning at eight o'clock!"

CHAPTER XI.

IRREPARABLE.

CHUDLEIGH WILMOT was a strong man, and he possessed much of the pride and reticence which ordinarily accompany strength of character. Hitherto he can hardly be said to have suffered much in his life. Affliction had come to him, as it comes to every man born of woman; but it had come in the ordinary course of human life, unattended by exceptional circumstances, above all not intensified, not warped from its wholesome purposes by self-reproach. His life had been commonplace in its joys and in its griefs alike, and he had never suffered from any cause which was not as palpable, as apparent, to all who knew him as to himself. His had been the sorrows, chiefly his parents' death, which are rather gravely acknowledged and respected, than whispered about in corners with dubious head-shaking and suggestive shoulder-shrugging. So far the experience of the rising man had in it nothing distinctive, nothing peculiarly painful.

But there was an end of this now. A new phase of life had begun for Chudleigh Wilmot, when he recoiled, like one who has received a deadly thrust, and whose life-blood rushes

K

forth in answer to it, from the announcement made to him
by his servant.   He realized the truth of the man's statement as the words passed his lips ; he was not a man whose
brain was ever slow to take any impression, and he knew in
an instant and thoroughly understood that his wife was dead.
A very few minutes more sufficed to show him all that was
implied by that tremendous truth.   His wife was dead ; not
of a sudden illness assailing the fortress of life and carrying
it by one blow, but of an illness that had had time in which
to do its deadly work.   His wife was dead ; had died alone,
in the care of hirelings, while he had been away in attendance upon a stranger, one out of his own sphere, not even a
regular patient, one for whom he had already neglected
pressing duties—not so sacred indeed as that which he could
now never fulfil or recall, but binding enough to have brought
severe reflections upon him for their neglect.   The thought
of all this surged up within him, and overwhelmed him in a
sea of trouble, while yet his face had not subsided from the
look of horror with which he had heard his servant's awful
announcement.

He turned abruptly into his consulting-room and shut
the door between him and the man, who had attempted to
follow him, but who now turned his attention to dismissing
the cab and getting in his master's luggage, during which
process he informed cabby of the state of affairs.

"I thought there were something up," remarked that
individual, "when I see the two-pair front with the windows
open and the blinds down, and all the house shut up ; but
he didn't notice it."   An observation which the servant
commented upon later, and drew certain conclusions from,
considerably nearer the truth than Wilmot would have liked,
had he had heart or leisure for any minor considerations.
Presently Wilmot called the man ; who entered the consulting-room, and found his master almost as pale as the corpse
upstairs in "the two-pair front," where the windows were

open and the blinds were down, but perfectly calm and quiet.

"Is there a nurse in the house?"

"Yes, sir; a nurse has been here since this day week, sir."

"Send her here—stay—has Dr Whittaker been here to-day?"

"No, sir; he were here last night, a half an hour after my missus departed, sir; but he ain't been here since. He said he would come at one, sir, to see your answer to the telegraft, sir."

"Very well; send the nurse to me;" and Wilmot strode towards the darkened window, and leaned against the wire-blind which covered the lower compartment. He had not to wait long. Presently the man returned.

"If you please, sir, the nurse has gone home to fetch some clothes, and Susan is a-watchin' the body."

Chudleigh Wilmot started, and ground his teeth. It was perfectly true; the proper phrase had been used by this poor churl, who had no notion of fine susceptibilities and no intention of wounding them, who would not have remained away from his own wife if she had been ill, not to say dying, for the highest wages and the best perquisites to be had in any house in London, but to whom a corpse was a corpse, and that was all about it. The phrase did not make the dreadful truth a bit more dreadful or more true, but it made Wilmot wince and quiver.

"Is there no one else—upstairs?" he asked.

"No, sir. Mrs Prendergast were here all night, sir, and she is coming again to meet Dr Whittaker; but there's no one but Susan a-watchin' now, sir. We was waiting for orders from you."

Wilmot turned away from the man, and spoke without permitting him to see his face.

"Tell Susan to leave the room, if you please; I am going upstairs."

The man went away, and returned in a few minutes with a key, which he laid upon the table, and then silently withdrew. His master was still standing by the window, his face turned away. A considerable interval elapsed before the silent group of listeners, comprising all the servants of the establishment, upon the kitchen-stairs, heard the widower's slow and heavy step ascending the front staircase.

The sight which Chudleigh Wilmot had to see, the strife of feeling which he had to encounter, were none the less terrible to him that death was familiar to him in every shape, in every preliminary of anguish and fear, in all that distorts its repose and renders its features terrible. It is an error surely to suppose that the familiarity of the physician with suffering and death, with all the ills that render the pilgrimage of life burdensome and the earthy vesture repulsive, makes the experience of these things when brought home to him easier to bear. The sickness that defies his skill, the life that eludes his grasp, is as dark an enigma, as terrible a defeat to him as to the man who knows nothing about the dissolving frame but that it holds the being he loves and is doomed to lose.

If Chudleigh Wilmot had had a deadly, vindictive, and relentless enemy,—one of those creatures of romance, but incredible in real life, who gloat over the misery of a hated object, and would increase it by every fiendish device within their ingenuity and power,—that fabulous being might have been satisfied with the mental torture which he endured when he found himself within the room, so formally arranged, so faultlessly orderly, so terribly suggestive of the cessation of life, in which his dead wife lay. As he turned the key in the lock, for the first time a sense of unreality, of impossibility came over him, with a swift bewildering remembrance —rather a vision than a recollection—of the last time he had seen her. He saw her standing in the hall, in the low light of the autumn evening, her pretty fresh dinner-dress lifted daintily out of the way of the servant carrying his portmanteau to the cab; her head, with its coronet of dark hair, held up to receive her husband's careless kiss, as he followed the man to the door. He remembered how carelessly he had kissed her, and how—he had never thought of it before—she had not returned the caress. When had she kissed him last? This was a trifling thing, that he had never thought about till now—a question he could not answer, and had never asked till now; and in another moment he would be looking at her dead face!

The window-blinds fluttered in the faint autumn wind as Wilmot opened the door, then quickly closed and locked it; and the rustling sound added to the impressiveness of the great human silence. The hands of the stern woman who loved her had ordered all the surroundings of the dead tenderly and gracefully; and the tranquil form lay in its deep rest very fair and solemn, and not terrible to look upon, if that can ever be said of death, in its garments of linen and lace. The head was a little bent, the face turned gently to one side, and the long dark eyelashes lay on the cheek, which was hardly at all sunken, as if they might be lifted up again and the light of life seen under them. Death was indeed there, but the sign and the seal were not impressed upon the face yet for a little while. Wilmot looked upon the dead tearless and still for some minutes, and then a quick short shudder ran through him, and he replaced the covering which had concealed the features, and sat down by the bed-side, hiding his face with his hands.

Who could put on paper the thoughts that swept over him then, and swept his mind away in their turmoil, and tossed him to and fro in a tempest of anguish which even the majestic tranquillity of death in presence was powerless to quell? Who could measure the punishment, the tremendous retribution of those hours, in which, if the world could have known anything about them, the world would have seen the

natural, the praiseworthy grief of bereavement ? Who shall
say through what purifying fires of self-knowledge and self-
abasement the nature of the erring man passed in that dreadful vigil ? And yet he did not know the truth. His conscience had been rudely awakened, but his comprehension
had not yet been enlightened. He did not yet know the
terrible depths of meaning which he had still to explore in
the words which were the only articulate sounds that had
formed themselves amid the chaos of his grief—"Too late ;
too late ! " The failure in duty, the poverty, the niggardli-
ness in love, the negligence, the dallying with right, in so far
as his wife had been concerned, were all there, keeping him
ghastly company, as he sat by the side of the dead ; but the
grimmest and the ghastliest phantoms which were to swarm
around him were not yet evoked.

To do Chudleigh Wilmot justice, he had no notion that
his wife had been unhappy. That he had never rightly understood her character or read her heart, was the soundest
proof that he had not loved her; but he had never taken
himself to task on that point, and had been quite satisfied to
impute such symptoms of discontent as he could not fail to
notice to her sullenness of temper, of which he considered
himself wonderfully tolerant. So little did this wise, rising
man understand women, that he actually believed that indifference to his wife's moods was a good-humoured sort of
kindness she could not fail to appreciate. She had appreciated it only too truly. The source of much of the remorse and self-condemnation which tortured him now was
to be traced to his own newly-awakened feelings, to the
fresh and novel susceptibility which the experience of the
past few weeks had aroused, and in which lay the germs of
some terrible lessons for the man whose studies in all but
the lore of the human heart had been so deep, whose knowledge of that had been so strangely shallow. And now no
knowledge could avail. The harm, the wrong, the cruel ill

that had been done, was gone before him to the judgment; and he must live to learn its extent, to feel its bitterness with every day of life, which could never avail to lessen or repair it.

When Dr Whittaker arrived, he found Wilmot in his consulting-room, quite calm and steady, and prepared to receive his professional account of the "melancholy occurrence," on which he condoled with the bereaved husband after the most approved models. He did not attempt to disguise from Wilmot that he had been disagreeably surprised by his non-return under the circumstances. "Also," he added, "by your not sending me any instructions; though indeed at that stage nothing could have availed, I am convinced."

Wilmot received these observations with such unmistakable surprise that an explanation ensued, which elicited the fact that he had never received any letter from Dr Whittaker, and indeed had had no intimation of his wife's illness, beyond that conveyed in a letter from herself a fortnight previous to her death, and in which she treated it as quite a trifling matter.

"Very extraordinary indeed," said Dr Whittaker in a dry and unsatisfactory tone. "I can only repeat that I sent you the fullest possible report, and entreated you to return at once. I was particularly anxious, as Mrs Wilmot confessed to me that you were unaware of her situation."

"I never had the letter," said Wilmot; "I never heard of or from you, beyond the memoranda enclosed in my wife's letters."

"Very extraordinary," repeated Dr Whittaker still more drily than before. "She took the letter at her own particular request, saying she would direct it, that the sight of her handwriting on the envelope, she being unable to write more, might reassure you."

Wilmot coloured deeply and angrily under his brother

physician's searching gaze. He had not looked for his wife's
infrequent letters with any anxiety ; he had had no quick,
love-inspired apprehension to be assuaged by her womanly
considerateness.   He felt an uneasy sort of gladness that
she had thought he had had such apprehension—better so,
even now, when all mistakes were doomed to be everlasting,
—or when they were quite cleared up.   Which was it?
He did not know ; he did not like to think.   All was over ;
all was too late.

"I never received any such letter," he said again ; "and
I am astonished you did not write again when you got no
answer."

"I did not write again, because Mrs Wilmot gave me so
very decidedly to understand that you had told her you
could not, under any circumstances, leave Kilsyth ; and
danger was not imminent until Monday, when I telegraphed,
just too late to catch you."

No more was said upon the point ; but on Wilmot's
mind was left a painful and disagreeable impression that Dr
Whittaker had received his explanation with distrust.   The
colloquy between the two physicians lasted long ; and Wilmot was further engaged for a long time in giving the
necessary attention to the distressing details which claim
a hearing just at the time when they most disturb and jar
with the tone of feeling.   A sense of shock and hurry—a
difficulty of realizing the event which had occurred, quite
other than the stunned feeling of conviction which had
come with the first reception of the intelligence—beset
him, while the nameless evidences of death were constantly
pressed upon his attention.   He sat in his consulting-room,
receiving messages and communications of every kind,
hearing the subdued voices of the servants as they replied
to inquiries, feeling as though he were living through a
terrible feverish dream, conscious of all around him, and
yet strangely, awfully conscious too of the dead white face

upstairs growing, as he knew, more stiff and stark and awful as the hours, so crowded yet so lonely, so busy yet so dreary, flew, no, dragged—which was it?—along.

Many times that day, as Chudleigh Wilmot sat cold and grave, and, although deeply sad, more composed, more like himself than most men would have been in similar circum stances—a vision rose before his mind. It was a vision such as has come to many a mourner—a vision of *what might have been*. For it was not only his wife's death that the new-made widower had learned that day; he had learned that which had made her death doubly sad, far more untimely. The vision that Chudleigh saw in his day-dream was of a fair young mother and her child, a happy wife in the summer-time of her beauty and her pride of motherhood—this was what might have been. What was, was a dead white face upstairs upon the bed, waiting for the coffin and the grave, and a blighted hope, a promise never to be fulfilled, which had never even been whispered between the living and the dead.

Mrs Prendergast had been in the darkened house for many hours of that long day. Wilmot knew she was there; but she had sent him no message, and he had made no attempt to see her. He shrank from seeing her; and yet he wished to know all that she, and she alone, could tell him. If he had ever loved his wife sufficiently to be jealous of any other sharing or even usurping her confidence, to have resented that any other should have a more intimate knowledge of Mabel's sentiments and tastes, should have occupied her time and her attention more fully than he, Henrietta Prendergast's intimacy with her might have eli-cited such feeling. But Chudleigh Wilmot had not loved his wife enough for jealousy of the nobler, and was too much of a gentleman for jealousy of the baser kind. No such insidious element of ill ever had a place in his nature; and, except that he did not like Mrs Prendergast, whom he considered a clever woman of a type more objectionable than common—and Wilmot was not an admirer of clever women generally—he never resented, or indeed noticed, the exceptional place she occupied among the number of his wife's friends. But there was something lurking in his thoughts to-day; there was some unfaced, some unquestioned misery at work within him, something beyond the tremendous shock he had received, the deep natural grief and calamity which enshrouded him, that made him shrink from seeing Henrietta until he should have had more time to get accustomed to the truth.

When the night had fallen, he heard the light tread of women's feet in the hall and a gentle whispering. Then the street-door was softly shut, and carriage-wheels rolled away. The gas had been lighted in Wilmot's room, but he had turned it almost out, and was sitting in the dim light, when a knock at the door aroused his attention. The intruder was the "Susan" already mentioned. Mrs Wilmot had not boasted an "own maid;" but this girl, one of the housemaids, had been in fact her personal attendant. She came timidly towards her master, her eyes red and her face pale with grief and watching.

"Well, what is it now?" said Wilmot impatiently. He was weary of disturbance; he wanted to be securely alone, and to think it out.

"Mrs Prendergast desired me to give you this, sir," the girl replied, handing him a small packet, "and to say she wants to see you, sir, to-morrow—respecting some messages from missus."

He took the parcel from her, and Susan left the room. Before she reached the stairs, her master called her back.

"Susan," he said, "where's the seal-ring your mistress always wore? This parcel contains her keys and her wedding-ring; where is the seal-ring? Has it been left on her hand?"

"No, sir," said Susan; "and I can't think where it can have got to. Missus hasn't wore it, sir, not this fortnight; and I have looked everywhere for it. You'll find all her things quite right, sir, except that ring; and Mrs Prendergast, she knows nothing about it neither; for I called her my own self to take off missus's wedding-ring, as it was missus's own wish as she should do it, and she missed the seal-ring there and then, sir, and couldn't account for it no more than me."

"Very well, Susan, it can't be helped," replied Wilmot; and Susan again left him.

He sat long, looking at the golden circlet as it lay in the broad palm of his hand. It had never meant so much to him before; and even yet he was far from knowing all it had meant to her from whose dead hand it had been taken. At last, and with some difficulty, he placed the ring upon the little finger of his left hand, saying as he did so, " I must find the other, and always wear them both."

CHAPTER XII.

THE LEADEN SEAL.

WHEN Chudleigh Wilmot arose on the following morning, with the semi-stupefied feeling of a man on whom a great calamity had just fallen, not the least painful portion of the task, not the least difficult part of the endurance that lay before him, was the inevitable interview with his dead wife's friend. Mrs Prendergast had requested that he would receive her early. This he learned from the servant who answered his bell; and he had directed that she should be admitted as soon as she arrived. He loitered about his room; he dallied with the time; he dared not face the cold

silent house, the servants, who looked at him with natural
curiosity, and, as he thought, avoidance. If the case had
not been his own, Wilmot would have remembered that the
spectacle of a new-made widow or widower always has attractions for the curiosity of the vulgar : strong, if the grief
in the case be very violent, and stronger, if it be mild or non-
existent. Wilmot was awfully shocked by his wife's death,
terribly remorseful for his own absence, and perhaps for another reason—at which, however, he had not yet had the
hardihood to look—almost stunned by the terrible sense, the
conviction of the irrevocable ill of the past, the utterly irreparable nature of the wrong that had been done. But all
these warring feelings did not constitute grief. Its supreme
agony, its utter sadness, its unspeakable weariness were
wanting in the strife which shook and rent him. The
thought of the dead face had terror and regret for him ; but
not the dreadful yearning of separation, not the mysterious
wrenching asunder of body and spirit, almost as powerful as
that of death itself, which comes with the sentence of parting, which makes the possibility of living on so incomprehensible and so cruel to the true mourner. Not the fact
itself, so much as the attendant circumstances, caused Wilmot to suffer, as he undoubtedly did suffer. He knew in
his heart that had there been no self-reproach involved in
this calamity, he would not have felt it as he felt it now
and in the knowledge there was denial of the reality of grief.

No such thought as " How am I to live without her ? "
the natural utterance of bereavement, arose in Wilmot's
heart ; though neither did he profane his wife's memory or
do dishonour to his own higher nature by even the most
passing reference to the object which had so fatally engrossed
him. The strong hand of death had curbed that passion for
the present, and his thoughts turned to Kilsyth only with
remorse and regret. But the wife who had had no absorbing
share in his life could not by her death make a blank in it
of wide extent or long duration.

He was still lingering in his room, when he was told that Mrs Prendergast had arrived and was in the drawing-room. The closely-drawn blinds rendered the room so dark that he could not distinguish Henrietta's features, still further obscured by a heavy black veil. She did not rise, and she made no attempt to take his hand, which he extended to her in silence, the result of agitation. She bowed to him formally, and was the first to speak. Her voice was low and her words were hurried, though she tried hard to be calm.

"I was with your wife during her illness and at her death, Dr Wilmot," she said; "and I am here now not to offer you ill-timed condolences, but to fulfil a trust."

Her tone surprised Wilmot, and affected him disagreeably. There had never been any disagreement between himself and Mrs Prendergast; he was not a man likely to interfere or quarrel with his wife's friends; and as he was wholly unconscious of the projects she had entertained towards him, he had not any suspicion of hidden malice on her part. Emotion he was prepared for—would indeed have welcomed; he was ready also for blame and reproaches, in which he would have joined heartily, against himself; but the calm, cold, rooted anger in this woman's voice he was not prepared for. If such a thing had been possible—the thought flashed lightning-like across his mind before she had concluded her sentence—he might have had in her an enemy, biding her time, and now at length finding it.

He did not speak, and she continued:

"I presume you have heard from Dr Whittaker the particulars of Mabel's illness, its cause, and the means used to avert—what has not been averted?--"

"I have," briefly replied the listener.

"Then I need not enter into that—beyond this: a portion of my trust is to tell you that Dr Whittaker is not to blame."

"I have not blamed him, Mrs Prendergast."

"that is well. When Mabel knew. or thought, I fear

hoped, that her life was in danger, her strongest desire was that you should be kept in ignorance of the fact."

"Good God! why?" exclaimed Wilmot.

"I think you must know why better than I can tell you," replied Henrietta pitilessly. "But, at all events, such was the case. Dr Whittaker wrote to you, but she suppressed the letter. She gave it to me on the night she died. Here it is."

Chudleigh Wilmot took the letter from her hand silently. Astonishment and distress overwhelmed him.

"She bade me tell you that she laid her life down gladly; that she had nothing to leave, nothing to regret; that she was glad she had succeeded in keeping you in ignorance of her danger—for she knew, for the sake of your reputation, you would have left even Miss Kilsyth to be here at her death. But she preferred your absence; she distinctly bade me tell you so. She left no dying charge to you but this, that you should allow me to see her coffin closed on the second day after her death, and that you should wear her wedding-ring. I sent it to you last night, Dr Wilmot. I hope you got it safely."

"I did; it is here on my finger," answered Wilmot; "but, for God's sake, Mrs Prendergast, tell me what all this means. Why did my wife charge you with such a message for me; how have I deserved it? Why did she, how should she, so young, and to all appearance not unhappy, wish to die, and to die in my absence? Did she persevere in that wish, or was it only a whim of her illness, which, had there been any one to remonstrate with her, would have yielded later?"

"It was no whim, Dr Wilmot. A wretched truth, I grant you, but a truth, and persisted in. So long as consciousness remained, she never changed in that."

A dark and angry look came into Wilmot's face, and he raised his voice as he asked the next question:

"Do you mean to explain this extraordinary circumstance, Mrs Prendergast? Are you going to give me the clue to this mystery? My wife and I always lived on good terms; we parted on the same. No man or woman living can say with truth that I ever was unkind to her, or that she had cause given her *by me* to wish her life at an end, to welcome death. I believe the communication you have just made to me is utterly without example. I never heard, I don't believe any one ever heard of such a thing. I ask you to explain it, if you can."

"You speak as though you asked, or desired me to *account* for it too," said Henrietta in a cold and cutting tone, which rebuked the vehemence of his manner, and revealed the intense, unsleeping egotism of her disposition. "I could do so, I daresay; but I cannot see the profitableness of such a discussion between you and me. It is too late now; nothing can undo the wrong, no matter what it was, or how far it extended. It is all over, and I have nothing more to do than to carry out the last wishes of my dear friend. Have I your permission to do so?" she asked, in the most formal possible tone, as she rose and stood opposite him.

Wilmot put his hands up to his face, and walked hurriedly about the room. Then he came suddenly towards Henrietta, and said with intense feeling:

"I beg your pardon; I did not mean to speak roughly: but I am bewildered by all this. I am sure you must feel for me; you must understand how utterly I am unable to comprehend what has occurred. To come home and receive such a shock as the news of my wife's death, was surely enough in itself to try me severely. And now to hear what you tell me, and tell me too so calmly, as if you did not understand what it means, and what it must be to me to hear it! You were with her, her chosen friend. I think you knew her better than any one in the world."

"And if I did," said Henrietta,—all her assumed calm
gone, and her manner now as vehement as his own,—"if I
did, is not that an answer to all you ask me? If I am to
explain her motives, to lay bare her thoughts, to tell her
sorrows, *to you*, her husband, is *that* not your answer?
Surely you have it in that fact! They are not true husband
and true wife who have closer friends. You never loved
her, and you never knew or cared what her life was; and
so, when she was leaving it, she kept you aloof from her."

Wilmot made no sound in reply. He stood quite still,
and looked at her. His eyes had grown accustomed to the
gloom, and she had raised her veil. He could see her face
now. Her pale cheeks, paler than usual in her grief and
passion, her deep angry sorrowful eyes, and her trembling
lips, made her look almost terrible, as she stood there and
told him out the truth.

"No," she went on, "you did not know her, and you
were satisfied not to know her; you went complacently on
your way, and never thought whether hers was lonely and
wearisome. You never were unkind to her, you say; no, I
daresay you never were. She had all the advantages to
which your wife was entitled, and she did you and them due
honour. Why, even I, who did, as you say, know her best,
had suspected only recently, and learned fully only since her
illness began, all she suffered; no, not all—*that* one heart
can never pour into another—but I have only read the story
of her life lately, and you have never read it at all. You
were a physician, and you did not see that your own wife, a
dweller under your own roof, whose life was lived in your
sight, had a mortal disease."

"What do you mean?" he said; "she had no such
thing."

"*She had!*" Henrietta repeated impetuously; "she had
a broken heart. You never ill-treated her—true; you never
neglected her—true,—until she was dying, that is to say;—

but did you ever love her, Dr Wilmot? Did you ever consider her as other or more than an appendage of your position, an ornament in your house, a condition of your social success and respectability? What were her thoughts, her hopes, her disappointments to you? Did you ever make her your real companion, the true sharer of your life? Did you ever return the love, the worship which she gave you? Did you ever pity her jealous nature; did you ever interpret it by any love or sensitiveness of your own, and abstain from wounding it? Did you know, did you care, whether she suffered when you shut yourself up in your devotion to a pursuit in which she had no share? All women have to bear that, no doubt, and are fools if they quarrel with the bread-winner's devotion to his work. Yes; but all women have not her silent, brooding, jealous, sullen nature; all women are not so little frivolous as she was; all women, Dr Wilmot, do not love their husbands as Mabel loved you."

She paused in the torrent of her words, and then he spoke.

"All this is new and terrible to me; as new as it is terrible. Mrs Prendergast, do me the justice to believe that."

"It is not for me to do you justice or injustice," she made answer; "your punishment must come from your own heart, or you must go unpunished."

"But"—he almost pleaded with her—"Mabel never blamed me, never tried to keep me more with her; rarely indeed expressed a wish of any kind. I declare, before God, I never dreamed, it never occurred to me to suspect that she was unhappy."

"No," she said; "and Mabel knew that. She interested you so little, you cared so little for her, that you never looked below the surface of her life; and her pride kept that surface fair and smooth. She would have died before she would have complained,—she has died, in fact, and made no sign."

"Yes," said Wilmot suddenly and bitterly; "but she

L

has left me this legacy, brought me by your hands, of miserable regret and vain repentance. She has insured the destruction of my peace of mind; she has taken care that mine shall be no ordinary grief, sent by God and to be dispelled by time; she has added bitterness to the bitter, and put me utterly in the wrong by her unwarrantable concealment and reticence."

"How truly manlike your feelings are, Dr Wilmot! She has hurt your pride, and you can't forgive her even in death! She has put *you* in the wrong,—and all her own wrongs, so silently borne, sink into nothing in comparison!"

"I deny it!" Wilmot said vehemently; "she *had* no wrongs,—no woman of her acquaintance had a better husband. What did I ever deny her?"

"Only your love, only a wife's true place in your life, only all she longed for, only all she died for lack of."

"All this is absurd," he said. "If she really had these romantic notions, why did she conceal them? Have *I* nothing to complain of in this? Was she just to me, or candid with me?"

"What encouragement did you give her? Do you think a proud, shy, silent woman like Mabel was likely to lay her heart open to so cold and careless a glance as yours? No; she loved you as few women can love; but if she had much love, so she had much pride and jealousy; and all three had power with her."

"Jealousy!" said Wilmot in an angry tone; "in God's name, of whom did she contrive to be jealous."

"Her jealousy was not of a mean kind," said Henrietta. "Ever since your marriage it had nourished itself, so far as I understood the matter, upon your devotion to your profession, upon the complacent ease with which you set *her* claims aside for those which so thoroughly engrossed you, that you had no heart, no eyes, no attention for her. Of late—" she paused.

" Well ? " said Wilmot ;—" of late ? "

" Of late," repeated Henrietta, speaking now with some more reserve of manner, " she believed you devoted—to a degree which conquered your devotion to your profession and to the interests of your own advancement—to the patient who detained you at Kilsyth."

" What madness! what utter folly !" said Wilmot; but his face turned deeply red, and he felt in his heart that the arrow had struck home.

" Perhaps so," said Henrietta, and her voice resumed the cutting tone from which all through this painful interview Wilmot had shrunk. " But Mabel was not more reasonable or less so than other jealous women. You had never neg- lected your business for *her*, remember, or been turned aside by any sentimental attraction from your course of professional duty. Friendship, gratitude, and interest alike required you to attend to Mr Foljambe's summons. You did not come, and people talked. Mr Foljambe himself spoke of the at- tractions of Kilsyth, and joked, after his inconsiderate manner."

" In *her* presence ? " said Wilmot incautiously.

" Yes, in *her* presence," said Henrietta, who perfectly appreciated the slip he had made. " She knew some people who knew the Kilsyths, and she heard the remarks that were made. I daresay she imagined more than she heard. No matter. Nothing matters any more. She was not sorry to die when her time came ; she would not have you troubled, —that is all. And now I will leave you. I am going to her."

The last sentence had a dreadful effect on Wilmot. In the agitation, the surprise, the pain of this interview, he had almost forgotten time ; the present reality had nearly escaped him. He had been rapt away into a world of feel- ing, of passion ; he had been absorbed in the sense of a discovery, and of something which seemed like an impossible injustice. With Henrietta's words it all vanished, and he

L 2

remembered, with a start, that his wife lay dead upstairs. They were not talking of a life long extinguished, which in former years might have been made happier by him, but of one which had ended only a few hours ago; a life whose forsaken tenement was still untouched by " decay's effacing fingers." With all this new knowledge fresh upon him, with all this bewildering conviction of irreparable wrong, he might look upon the calm young face again. Not as he had looked upon it yesterday; not with the deep sorrow and the irresistible though unjustified compassion with which death in youth is always regarded, but with an exceeding and heart-rending bitterness, in comparison with which even that repentant grief was mild and merciful. The fixedness, the blank, the silence, would be far more dreadful, far more reproachful now, when he knew that he had never understood, never appreciated her—had unwittingly tortured her; now when he knew that, in all her youth and beauty, she had been glad to die. Glad to die! The words had a tremendous, an unbearable meaning for him. If even the last month could have been unlived! If only he had not had *that* to reproach himself with, to justify *her!* In vain, in vain. In that one moment of unspeakable suffering Wilmot felt that his punishment, however grave his offence, was greater than he could bear.

He turned away from Henrietta with the air of a man to whom another word would be intolerable, and sat down wearily. She stood still looking at him, as if awaiting an answer or a dismissal.

At length she said, "Have you forgotten, Dr Wilmot, that I asked your permission to carry out Mabel's wish?"

"No," he said drearily, "I remember. Of course do as you like; I should say, as she directed. I suppose the object of her request was, that I should see her no more, in death either. Well, well—it is fortunate that did not succeed too." He spoke in a patient, broken tone, which touched Henrietta's heart. But her perverted notion of truth and loyalty to the dead held her back from showing any sign of softening. Just as she was leaving the room he said:

"Such a course is very unusual, is it not?"

"I believe so," she replied; "but the servants know it was her desire."

Then Henrietta Prendergast went away; and presently he heard a slight sound in that awful room overhead, and he knew she had taken her place beside the dead. He felt, as he sat for hours of that day quite alone, like a banished man. His wife was doubly dead to him now. All his married life had grown on a sudden unreal; and when he thought of the still white face which he was to see once, and only once more, for ever, it was with a strange sense of dread and avoidance, and not with the tender sorrow which, even amid the shock and self-reproach of yesterday, had come to his relief.

Somehow, he could not have told how, with the inevitable interruptions, the wretched necessary business of such a time, the hours of that day passed over Chudleigh Wilmot's head, and the night came. He had looked his last upon his wife, had taken his solemn leave of the death-chamber. She lay now in her coffin, sealed, hidden from sight for evermore, and there was nothing now but the long dreary waiting. In its turn that too passed, and in due time the funeral day; and Chudleigh Wilmot was quite alone in his silent house, and had only to look back into the past. Forward into the future he did not dare, he had not heart to look. A kind of blank, the reaction from intense excitement, had set in with him, and for the first time in his life his physical strength flagged. The claims of his business began to press upon him; people sent for him, respectfully and hesitatingly, but with some confidence that he would come, nevertheless. And Wilmot went;

and was received with condoling looks, which he affected
not to see, and compassionating tones, of which he took no
notice.

He had no more to do with the past—he had buried it;
his sole desire was that others should aid him in this apparent oblivion; how far from real it was, he alone could
have told. He had written to Kilsyth a few indispensable
lines, and had had a formal report of Madeleine's health,
which he had conscientiously tried to range with other professional documents, and lay by with them.   It was certainly a dark and dreary time, endless in length, and so
hopeless, so final, that it seemed to have no outlet; a time
than which Chudleigh Wilmot believed life could never
bring him a darker. But trouble was new to him.   He
learned more about it later on in his day.

When a fortnight had elapsed after Wilmot's return to
London, and the tumult of his mind had subsided, though
the bitterness of his feelings was not yet allayed, he chanced
one morning to require a paper, which he knew was to be
found in a certain cabinet which filled a niche in the wall
of his consulting-room. The cabinet in question was one
he rarely opened; and the moment he attempted to turn
the key, he felt confident that the lock had been tampered
with.   The conviction was singularly unpleasant; for the
cabinet was a repository of private papers, deeds, letters,
and professional notes. It also contained several poisons,
which Wilmot kept there in what he supposed to be inviolable security. Closer inspection confirmed his suspicions. The lock had been opened by the simple process
of breaking it; and the doors, merely laid together, had
caught on a jagged piece of metal, and thus presented the
slight obstacle they had offered. With a mere shake they
unclosed.

This circumstance puzzled Wilmot exceedingly.   He
made a careful examination of the contents of the cabinet.

All was precisely as he had left it; not a paper missing or disturbed.

"Who can have been at the cabinet?" he thought, "and with what motive? Nothing has been taken; nothing, so far as I can discover, has been touched. Mere curiosity would hardly tempt any one to run such a risk; and no one knew that there was anything of value here. Stay," he reflected; "one person knew it. *She* knew it; she knew that I kept private papers here. No doubt it was she who opened the cabinet. But with what motive? What can she possibly have wanted which she could have hoped to find here?"

No answer to this query presented itself to Wilmot's mind. He thought and thought over it, painfully recurring to all Mrs Prendergast had told him, and trying to help himself to a solution of this mystery by the aid of those which had preceded it. For some time he thought in vain; at length the idea struck him that the jealous woman, restless and miserable in her unhappy curiosity—he could understand *now* what she had felt, he could pity her *now*—had opened the cabinet to seek for letters from some fancied rival in his affections. Nothing but his belief in the perversion of mind which comes of the indulgence of such a passion as jealousy could have led Wilmot to suspect his wife of such an act for a moment. But he was a wise man, now that it was too late, in that lore which he had never studied while he might have read the book, and he recognized the transforming power of jealousy. Yes, that was it doubtless; she had sought here for the material wherewith to feed the flame that had tortured her.

Chudleigh Wilmot took the paper he wanted from the place where it had lain, and was about to close the doors of the cabinet once more—restoring them, until he could have the lock repaired, to their deceptive appearance of security—when his attention was caught by a dark-coloured

spot, about the size of a shilling, upon the topmost sheet of
a packet of papers which lay beside a small mahogany case
containing the before-mentioned poisons. He took the
packet out and examined it. The spot was there, and extended to every paper in the packet. A sudden flush and
expression of vague alarm crossed Wilmot's face. He took
up the case and examined the exterior. A dark mark, the
stain of some glutinous fluid, ran down the side of the box
next which the papers had lain. For a moment he held
the case in his hands, and literally dared not open it. Then
in sickening fear he did so, and found its contents apparently
undisturbed. The box was divided into ten little compart-
ments, in each of which stood a tiny bottle, glass-stoppered
and covered with a leaden capsule. To the neck of each
was appended a little leaden seal, the mark of the French
chemist from whom Wilmot had purchased the deadly
drugs. He took the bottles out one by one, examined
their seals, and held them up to the light. All safe for
nine out of the number; but as he touched the tenth, the
capsule with the leaden seal attached to it fell off, and
Wilmot discovered, with ineffable horror, that the bottle,
which had contained one of the deadliest poisons known to
science, was half empty.

He set down the case, and reeled against the corner of
the mantelshelf near him, like a drunken man. He could
not face the idea that had taken possession of him; he
could not collect his thoughts. He gasped as though water
were surging round him. Once more he took up the bottle
and looked at it. It was only too true; one half the contents was missing. He closed the case, and pushed it back
into its place. It struck against something on the shelf of
the cabinet. He felt for the object, and drew out *his wife's
seal-ring !*

And now Chudleigh Wilmot knew what was the terror
that had seized him. It was no longer vague; it stood

before him clear, defined, unconquerable; and he groaned:
"My God! she destroyed herself!"

CHAPTER XIII.

A TURN OF THE SCREW.

CHUDLEIGH WILMOT had not seen Mrs Prendergast
since the day on which his wife's funeral had taken place;
and it was with equal surprise and satisfaction that she received a brief but kindly-worded note from him, requesting
her to permit him to call upon her.

"I wonder what it's all about," she thought, as she
wrote with deliberation and care a gracious answer in the
affirmative. Mrs Prendergast had been thinking too since
her friend's death, and her cogitations had had some practical
results. It was true that Mabel Darlington had not been
happy with Wilmot; but Mrs Prendergast, thinking it all
over, was not indisposed to the opinion that it was a good
deal her own fault, and to entertain the very natural
feminine conviction that things would have been quite otherwise had she been in Mabel's place. Why should she not—
of course in due time, and with a proper observance of all
the social decencies—hope to fill that place now?" She
was a practical, not a sentimental woman; but when the
idea occurred to her very strongly, she certainly did find
pleasure in remembering that Mabel Wilmot had been very
much attached to her, and would perhaps have liked the
notion of her being her successor as well as any woman ever
really likes any suggestion of the kind, that is to say, re-
signedly, and with an " it-might-be-worse " reservation.

Henrietta Prendergast had cherished a very sound dislike to Chudleigh Wilmot for some time; but it was, though

quite real—while the fact that he had chosen another than herself, though she had been so ready and willing to be chosen, was constantly impressed upon her remembrance—not of a lasting nature. Besides, she had had the satisfaction of making him understand very distinctly that the choice he had made had not been a wise one; and ever since her feelings towards him had been undergoing a considerable modification.

How much ground had Mabel had for her jealousy of Miss Kilsyth? What truth was there in the suspicions they had both entertained respecting the influence which his young patient had exercised over Wilmot? She had no means of determining these questions. It would have been impossible for her, had she been a woman capable of such a meanness, to have watched Wilmot during the interval which had elapsed since his wife's death. His numerous professional duties, the constant demands upon his time, all rendered her attaining any distinct knowledge of his proceedings impossible; and beyond the announcement in the *Morning Post* that Kilsyth of Kilsyth and his family had arrived in town, she knew nothing whatever concerning them. Henrietta Prendergast had, on the whole, been considerably occupied with the idea of Chudleigh Wilmot when his note reached her, and she prepared to receive him with feelings which resembled those of long-past days rather than those which had actuated her of late.

It was late in the afternoon when the expected visitor made his appearance, and Henrietta had already begun to feel piqued and angry at the delay. His note indicated a pressing wish to see her—she had answered it promptly. What had made him so dilatory about availing himself of her permission?

The first look she caught of Wilmot's face convinced her that the motive of his visit was a grave one. He was pale and sedate, even to a fixed seriousness far beyond that which had fallen upon him after the shock of Mabel's death, and a painful devouring anxiety might be read in the troubled haggard expression of his deep-set dark eyes. He entered at once upon the matter which had induced him to ask Mrs Prendergast for an interview; and though her manner was emphatically gracious, and designed to show him that she desired to maintain their former relations intact, he took no notice of her courtesy This was a mistake. All women are quick to take cognizance of a slight, and Henrietta was no slower than the rest of her sex. He showed her much too plainly that he had an object in seeking her presence entirely unconnected with herself. It was not wise; but the shock of the discovery which he had made had shaken Wilmot's nerves and overthrown his judgment for the time. He briefly informed Mrs Prendergast that he came for the purpose of asking her to recapitulate all the circumstances of his wife's illness and death; to entreat her to tax her memory to the utmost, to recall everything, however trivial, bearing upon the progress of the malady, and in particular every detail bearing upon her state of mind.

Henrietta listened to him with profound astonishment. Previously he had shunned all such details. When she had met him, prepared to supply them, he had asked her no questions; he had been apparently satisfied with the medical report made to him by Dr Whittaker; he had been almost indifferent to such minor facts as she had stated; and the painful revelation which she had made to him had not been followed up by any close questioning on his part. And now, when all was at an end, when the grave had closed over the sad domestic story, as over all the tragedies of human life, hidden or displayed, the grave must close,—now he came to her with this preoccupied brooding face and manner to ask her these vain and painful questions. Thus she was newly associated with dark and dismal images in his mind, and this was precisely what Henrietta had no desire to be. She answered him, therefore, in her coldest tone (and no woman knew how to ice her answers better than she did), that the subject was extremely painful to her for many reasons. Was it absolutely necessary to revive it ? Wilmot said it was, and expressed no consideration for her feelings nor regret for the necessity of wounding them.

" Well, then, Dr Wilmot," said Henrietta, " as I presume you wish to question me in some particular direction, though I am quite at a loss to understand why, you are at liberty to do so."

Wilmot then commenced an interrogatory, which, as it proceeded, filled Henrietta with amazement. Had he any theory of his wife's illness and death incompatible with the facts as she had seen and understood them ? Did he suspect Dr Whittaker of ignorance and mismanagement in the case ? Even supposing he did, what would it avail him now to convince himself that such suspicion was well founded ? All was inevitable, all was irreparable now. While these thoughts were busy in her brain, she was answering question after question put to her by Wilmot in a cold voice, and with her steady neutral-tinted eyes fixed in pitiless scrutiny upon him. He asked her in particular about the period at which Mabel had suppressed Dr Whittaker's letter to him. Had she been particularly unhappy just then ; had the " unfortunate notion she had conceived about—about Miss Kilsyth, been in her mind before, or just at that time ? "

This question Mrs Prendergast could not, or would not, answer very distinctly. She did not remember exactly when Mabel had heard so much about Miss Kilsyth ; she did not know what day it was on which Dr Whittaker had written. Wilmot produced the letter, and pointed out the date. Still Mrs Prendergast's memory refused to aid her reliably. She really did not know ; she could not answer this. Could she remember whether Mabel had ever left her room after that letter had been written ? or whether she had been confined to her room when she had received his (Wilmot's) letter from Kilsyth; the letter which Mrs Prendergast had said had distressed her so much, had brought about the confidence between Mabel and herself relative to the feelings of the former, and had led Mabel to say that she had no desire to live? Wilmot awaited the reply to these questions in a state of suspense not far removed from agony. He could not indeed permit himself to cherish a hope that the dreadful idea he entertained was unfounded; but in the answer awful confirmation or the germ of hope must lie.

Henrietta replied, after a few moments' thoughtful silence. She could remember the circumstances, though not the precise date. Mabel had left her room on the day on which she had received Wilmot's letter; she had been in the drawing-rooms, and even in the consulting-room on that day. It was on the night that she had told Mrs Prendergast all, and had expressed her desire to die, her conviction that she could not recover. Henrietta was not certain whether that day was the same as that on which Dr Whittaker's letter was written, but she was perfectly clear on the point on which Wilmot appeared to lay so much stress; she knew it was the day after his last letter from Kilsyth had reached her.

The intense suffering displayed in every line of Wilmot's face as she made this statement touched Henrietta as much as it puzzled her. Had she mistaken this man? Had he really deep feelings, strong susceptibilities? Had the shock of his wife's death been far otherwise felt than she had believed, and was he now groping after every detail, in order to feed the vain flame of love and memory? Such a supposition accorded very ill with all she knew and all she imagined of Chudleigh Wilmot; but she could find no other within her not infertile brain.

"What became of my letter to her?" Wilmot asked her abruptly.

"It is in her coffin, together with every other you ever

wrote her. I placed them there at her own request. She had them tied up in a packet,—the others I mean; but she gave me that one separately."

"Why?" asked Wilmot in a hoarse whisper.

"Why!" repeated Henrietta. "I don't know. It was only a few hours before she died. She hardly spoke at all after, but she told me quite distinctly that I was to give you her wedding-ring, and to place those letters in her coffin. 'I could not destroy those,' she said, touching the packet in my hand; 'and this,' she drew it from under her pillow as she spoke, 'I want to be placed with me too. It is my justification.'"

"My justification!" repeated Wilmot. "What did she mean? What did you understand that she meant by that?"

"I did not think much about it. The poor thing was near her end then, and I thought little of it; though of course I did what she desired."

"Yes, yes, I understand," said Wilmot. "But her justification—justification in what—for what?"

"In her gloomy and miserable ideas, of course, and, above all, in her desire to die. She believed that your letter contained the proof of all she feared and suffered from, and so justified her longing to escape from further neglect and sorrow."

"You did not suspect that it had any further meaning?"

Henrietta stared at him in silence.

"I beg your pardon," he said; "my mind is confused by anxiety. I am afraid, Mrs Prendergast, there may have been features in this case not rightly understood. Could it be that Whittaker was deceived?"

"I think not—I cannot believe that there was any error. Dr Whittaker never expressed any anxiety on *that* point, any uncertainty, any wish to divide the responsibility, except with yourself. I understood him to say that he had gone into the case very fully with you, and that you were satisfied everything had been done within the resources of medicine."

" Yes, he did. I don't blame him ; I don't blame any one but myself. But, Mrs Prendergast, that is not the point. What I want to get at is this : did she—my wife I mean— did she hide anything from Whittaker's knowledge ? "

" Anything ? In her physical state do you mean ? Of her mental sufferings no one but myself ever had the smallest indication. Will you wrong her dead as well as living ? " said Henrietta angrily.

" No," he answered, " I will not,—I trust I will not, and do not. I meant did she tell Whittaker all about her illness ? Did she conceal any symptoms from him ? Did she suffer more or otherwise than he knew of ? "

" Frankly, I think she did, Dr Wilmot. She was extremely, almost painfully patient ; I would much rather have seen her less so. She answered his questions and mine, but she said nothing except in answer to questioning. She suffered, I am convinced, infinitely more than she allowed to appear ; and especially on the night of her death, just before the stupor set in, she was in great agony."

" Yes," said Wilmot hurriedly. " Was Whittaker there ? Did he know it ? "

" He was not there ; he had been sent for a little while before, when she was tranquil ; and she was quite insensible when he returned in about three hours. He told you, of course, that we had had good hope of her during the day,— in fact, up to the evening ? "

" Yes, he said there had been a rally, but it had not lasted. Did she know that there was hope ? "

" She did," said Henrietta slowly and reluctantly. " You ask me very painful questions, Dr Wilmot,—painful to me in the extreme ; and I am sure my answers must be acutely distressing to you. I cannot understand your motive."

" No," he said, " I am sure you cannot ; neither can I explain it. But indeed I am compelled to put these questions; I cannot spare either you or myself. You say she knew there was hope of her recovery on the day before her death; and yet while the rally lasted,—before the suffering of which you speak set in,—she gave you those solemn charges which you fulfilled?"

"Yes," said Henrietta—and her voice was soft now and her eyes were full of tears—"she did. She did not trust the rally. She told me, with such a dreadful smile, that it would not avail to keep her from her rest. She was right. From the moment she grew worse the progress of death was awfully rapid."

"What medicine did you give her during the brief improvement?"

"Only some restorative drops. Dr Whittaker gave them to her himself several times, and when he left I gave them to her."

"Did she ever take this medicine of her own accord? Was she strong enough in the interval of improvement to take medicine, or to move without assistance?"

Again Henrietta looked at him for a little while before she replied:

"If you are afraid, Dr Wilmot, that any mistake was made about the medicine, dismiss such a fear. There was no other medicine in the room but the bottle containing the drops; and now your strange question reminds me that she did take them once unassisted."

Wilmot rose and came towards her.

"How? when?" he said eagerly. "How could she do so in her weak state?"

"The bottle was on the table, close by her bed. Only one dose was left. She had asked me to raise the window-blind; and I was doing so, when she stretched out her arm and took the bottle off the table. When I turned round she was drinking the last drops, and the next moment she dropped the bottle on the floor, and it was broken."

" Was she fainting, then ? "

" O no," said Henrietta, "she was quite sensible, until the pain came on. Indeed I remember that she told me to keep away from the bed until the broken glass had been swept up."

" Was that done ? "

" Yes, I did it myself at once."

" One more question, Mrs Prendergast," said Wilmot, who had put a strong constraint upon himself, and spoke calmly now. " When did she charge you to have her coffin closed within two days of her death ? Was it within the interval during which her recovery seemed possible ? "

" It was," answered Henrietta,—" it was when she told me that the rally was deceitful, and was not to keep her from her rest. Then I undertook to carry out her wish."

" Did she give any reason for having formed it ? "

" She did—the reason you surmised when I first told you of it. I need not repeat it."

" I would wish you to do so—pray let me hear the exact words she said."

" Well, then, they were these. 'You will promise me to see it done, Henrietta. He cannot get home, even supposing he could leave at once, when he hears that I am dead, until late on the second day.' I told her it was an awful thing that she should wish you not to see her again, and she said, ' No, no, it is not. If he thinks of my face at all, I want him to see it in his memory as it was when I thought he liked to look at it. I could not bear him to remember it black and disfigured.' These were her exact words, Dr Wilmot ; and like all the rest she said, they proved to me how much she loved you."

Wilmot made no answer, and neither spoke for some minutes. Then Wilmot extended his hand, which Henrietta took with some cordiality, and said, " I thank you very much, Mrs Prendergast, for the patience with which you have

M

heard me and answered me. I have no explanation to give
you. I shall never forget your kindness to my wife, and I
hope we shall always be good friends."

He pressed her hand warmly as he spoke; and before
Henrietta could reply, he left her to cogitations as vain and
unsatisfactory as they were absorbing and unceasing.

Chudleigh Wilmot went direct to his own house after
his interview with Henrietta, and gave himself up to the
emotions which possessed him. Not a shadow of doubt
did he now entertain that his wife had destroyed herself.
In the skill and ingenuity with which he invested the act,
in his active fancy, which had read the story from the
unconscious narrative of Henrietta, he recognized a touch
of insanity, which his experience taught him was not very
rare in cases similar to that of his wife. To a certain
extent he was relieved by the conviction that when she had
done the irrevocable deed she was not in her right mind.
But what had led to it? what had been the predis-
posing causes? His conscience, awakened too late, his
heart, softened too late, gave him a stern and searching
answer. Her life had been unhappy, and she had made her
escape from it. He was as much to blame as if he had
voluntarily and actively made her wretched. He saw this
now by the light of that keener susceptibility, that higher
understanding, which had been kindled within him. It
had been kindled by the magic touch of love. Another
woman had made him see into his wife's heart, and understand her life. What was he to do now? how was it to
be with him in the future? He hardly dared to think.
Sometimes his mind dwelt on the possibility that it might
not be as he believed it was, and the only means of
resolving his doubts suggested itself. He might have
Mabel's body exhumed, and then the truth would be
known. But he shrank with horror from the thought, as
from a dishonour to her memory. If he took such a step,
it must be accounted for; and could he, would he dare to

cast such a slur upon the woman who, if she had done this deed, had. resorted to it because, as his wife, she was miserable? Had he any right, supposing it was all a dreadful delusion, that she had meddled with his poisons for some trivial motive, however inexplicable,—had he any right to solve his own doubts at such a price as their exposure to cold official eyes? No—a resolute negative was the reply of his heart to these questions; and he made up his mind that his punishment must be lifelong irremediable doubt, to be borne with such courage as he could summon, but never to be escaped from or left behind.

Utter sickness of heart fell upon him and a great weariness. From the past he turned away with vain terrible regret; to the future he dared not look. The present he loathed. He must leave that house, he thought impatiently—he could not bear the sight of it. It had none of the dear and sorrowful sacredness which makes one cling to the home of the loved and lost; it was hateful to him; for there the life his indifference, his want of comprehension, had blighted, had been terminated—he shuddered as he thought by what means. And then he thought he would leave England; he could not see Madeleine Kilsyth again; or if he had to do so, he could not see her often. To think of her, in her innocent youth and beauty, as one to be loved or wooed, or won—if even in his most distant dreams such a possibility were approached by a man whose life had such a story in it, such a dreadful truth, setting him apart from other men—was almost sacrilegious. No, he would go away. Fate had dealt him a tremendous blow; he could not stand against it; he must yield to it for the present, at all events. Under the influence of the terrible truth which he was forced to confront, all his ambition, all his energy, seemed suddenly to have deserted the rising man.

*　　*　　*　　*　　*　　*

"But, my dear fellow, I can't bring myself to believe
that you are serious; I can't indeed, just as the ball is at
your foot too.   I protest I expected you to distance them
all in another year.   Everybody talks of you; and what is
infinitely better, every one is ready to call you in if they
require your services or fancy they require them.   Why,
there's Kilsyth of Kilsyth—ah, Wilmot, you threw me over
in that direction, but I don't bear malice—he swears by
you.   The fine old fellow came to the bank yesterday; I
met him in the hall, and he got into my brougham, and
came home with me, for no other reason on earth than to
talk about you.   Wilmot's skill and Wilmot's coolness,
Wilmot's kindness and Wilmot's care—nothing but Wilmot.   I should have been bored to death by so much talking all about one man, if it had been any man but yourself.
And now to tell me that you are going away, going to make
a gap in your life, going to give up the running, and for-
feit such prospects as yours—because you must remember,
my dear fellow, you must not calculate on resuming
exactly where you have left off, in any sort of game of life;
to do such a thing as this because you have met with a loss
which thousands of men have to bear, and work on just as
usual notwithstanding!   Impossible, my dear Wilmot;
you are not in earnest—you have not considered the
thing!"

Thus emphatically spoke Mr Foljambe to Chudleigh
Wilmot, all the more emphatically because his friend's
resolution had astonished as much as it had displeased and
disquieted him.   Mr Foljambe had never looked upon
Wilmot at all in the light of a particularly devoted husband; and when he alluded to the loss of a wife being one
which he had to bear in common with many other sufferers,
he had done so with a shrewd conviction that Wilmot must
be trusted to find all the fortitude necessary for the
occasion.

Mr Foljambe, of Portland-place, was a very rich and influential banker; gouty enough to bear out the tradition of his wealth, and courteous and wise enough to do credit to his calling. He was not describable as a City man, however, but was, on the contrary, a pleasure and fashion-loving old gentleman, who was perfectly versed in the ways of society, *au courant* of all the gossip of "town," very popular in the gayest and in the most select circles, an authority upon horses, though he never rode, learned in wines, though he consumed them in great moderation, believed not to possess a relative in the world, and more attached to Chudleigh Wilmot than to any human being alive, at his present and advanced period of existence. The old gentleman and Chudleigh Wilmot's father had been chums in boyhood and friends in manhood; and the friendship he felt for the younger man was somewhat hereditary, though Wilmot's qualities were precisely of a nature to have won Mr Foljambe's regard on their own merits. He had watched Wilmot's course with the utmost interest, pride, and pleasure. His unflagging industry, his determined energy, commanded his sympathy; and he anticipated a triumphant career of professional success and renown for his favourite. The intelligence that he had determined, if not to relinquish, at least to suspend his professional labours, gave the kind old gentleman sincere concern. He did not understand it, he repeated over and over again; he could not make it out; it was not like Wilmot. Of course he could not say distinctly to him that he had never supposed his wife to be so dear to him that her death must needs revolutionize his life. But if he did not say this, Wilmot discerned it in his manner; but still he offered no explanation. He could not remain in England; he must go. His health, his mind would give way, if he did not get away into another scene, into new associations. All remonstrance, all argument, proved unavailing; and when Wilmot bade his old friend farewell, he left him half angry and half mistrustful, as well as altogether depressed and sorrowful.

CHAPTER XIV

HIS GRATEFUL PATIENT.

SHE has destroyed herself! That was the keynote to all his thoughts. Destroyed herself, made away with herself! Destroyed herself! He was not much of a reading man—had not time for it in all his occupations; but what were those two lines which would keep surging up into his beating brain, and from time to time finding expression on his trembling tongue—

> " Rashly importunate,
> Gone to her death ! "

Gone to her death! He repeated the words a thousand times. Dead now; gone to her last account, as Shakespeare says, "with all her imperfections on her head." Gone, without chance or power of recall; gone without a word of explanation between them, without a word of sympathy, without a word of forgiveness on either side. He had often pictured their parting, he dying, she dying, and had imagined the scene; how, whichever of them found life ebbing away, would say that they had misunderstood the other perhaps, and that perhaps life might have been made more to each, had they been more suitable; but that they had been faithful, and so on; and perhaps hereafter they might, &c. He had thought of this often; but the end had come now; and his ideas had not been realized. There had been no parting, no mutual forgiveness, no last words of tenderness and hope. He had not been there to soothe her dying hour; to tell her how he acknowledged all her goodness, and how, though perhaps he had not made much outward manifestation, he had always thoroughly appreciated the discharge of her wifely duties to him. He had not been present to have one whispered explanation of how each had misunderstood the other, and how both had been in the wrong; to share in one common prayer for forgiveness, and one common hope of future meeting. There had been no explanation, no forgiveness; he had parted from her almost as he might from any everyday acquaintance; he had written to her such a letter as he might have written to Whittaker, who had taken his practice temporarily; and now he returned to find her dead! Worse than dead! Dead probably by her own act, by her own hand!

Stay! He was losing his head now; his pulse was at fever-heat, his skin dry and hot. Why had this terrible supposition taken such fast hold upon him? There was the evidence of the ring and of the leaden seal. Certainly practical evidence; but the motive—where was the motive? Suppose now—and a horrible shudder ran through him as the supposition crossed his mind—suppose now that this had become a matter for legal inquiry? suppose—Heaven knows how—suppose that the servants had suspected, and had talked, and—and the law had interfered—what motive would have been put forward for Mabel's self-destruction? He and she had never had a word of contention since their marriage; no one could prove that there had ever been the smallest disagreement between them; her home had been such as befitted her station; no word could be breathed against her husband's character; and yet—

> "Anywhere, anywhere,
> Out of the world!"

that was another couplet from the same poem that was
fixed in his brain, and that he found himself constantly
quoting, when he was trying to assign reasons for his
wife's suicide. Was Henrietta Prendergast right, after
all? Had his whole married life been a mistake, a Dead-
Sea apple without even the gorgeous external, a hollow
sham, a delusion, and a mockery culminating in the semblance of a crime? "Anywhere out of the world," eh?
And "out of the world" had meant at first, in the early
days, when the first faint dawnings of discontent rose in
her mind,—then "anywhere out of the world" was a poor
dejected cry of repining at her want of power to influence
her husband, to make herself the successful rival of his
profession, to wean him from the constant pursuit of
science to the exclusion of all domestic bliss, and to render
him her companion and her lover. But if Henrietta Prendergast were right, that must have been a mere fancy,
which, compared to the wild despair that prompted the
heart-broken shriek of "anywhere out of the world" at the
last, and which, according to that authority, meant—anywhere for rest and peace and quiet, anywhere where I may
stifle the love which I bear him, may be no longer a fetter
and a clog to him, and might have to suffer the knowledge
that though bound to me, he loves Madeleine Kilsyth.

He loves Madeleine Kilsyth! As the thought rose in his
mind, he found himself audibly repeating the sentence. His
dead wife thought that; and in that thought found life
insupportable to her, and destroyed herself! His dead
wife! Straightway his thoughts flew back through a
series of years, and he saw himself first married,—young,
earnest, and striving. Not in love with his wife—that he
never had been, he reflected with something like self-excuse
—not in love with Mabel, but actually proud of her.
When he first commenced his connection, and earned the
gratitude of the great railway contractor's wife at Clapham,

and that great dame, who was the ruling star in her own circle, intimated her intention of calling on Mrs Wilmot, Wilmot remembered how he had thanked his stars that while some of his fellow-students had married barmaids of London taverns, or awkward hoydens from their provincial pasture, he had had the good luck to espouse a girl than whom the great Mrs Sleepers herself was not more thoroughly presentable, more perfectly well-mannered. He recollected the first interview at his little, modest, badly-furnished house, with the dingy maid-servant decorated with one of Mabel's cast-off gowns (not cast off until every scrap of bloom had been ruthlessly worn off it), and the arrival of the great lady in her banging, swinging barouche, with her tawdry ill-got-up footman, and her evident astonishment at the way in which everything was made the most of, and at the taste which characterized the rooms, and her open-mouthed wonder at Mabel herself, in her turned black-silk dress and her neat linen cuffs and collar, and her impossibility to patronize, and her declaration delivered to him the next day, that his wife was "the nicest little woman in the world, and a real lady!"

Out of the gloom of long-since vanished days came a thousand little reminiscences, each "garlanded with its peculiar flower," each touchingly remindful of something pleasant connected with the dead woman whom he had lost. Long dreary nights which he had passed in reading and working, and which she had spent in vaguely wondering what was to be the purport and result of all his labour. No sympathy! that had been his cry! Good God!—as though he had not been demented in fancying that a young woman could have had sympathy with his dry studies, his physiological experiments. No sympathy! what sympathy had he shown to her? The mere physical struggle in the race, the hope of winning, the dawning of success, had irradiated his life, had softened the stony path, and pushed aside the briers, and

tempered the difficulties in his career; but how had she
benefited? In sharing them? But had he permitted her
to share them? had he ever made her a portion of himself?
had he not laughed aside the notion of her entering into the
vital affairs of his career, and told her that any assistance
from her was an impossibility? That she was self-contained
and unsympathetic, he had said to himself a thousand times.
Now, for the first time, he had asked himself who had made
her so;—and the answer was anything but consoling to him
in his then desolate frame of mind.

These thoughts were constantly present to him; he found
it impossible to shake them off; in the few minutes' interval
between the exit of one patient and the entrance of another,
in his driving from house to house, his mind instantly gave
up the case with which it had recently been occupied, and
turned back to the dead woman. He would sit apparently
looking vacantly before him, but· in reality trying to recall
the looks, words, ways of his dead wife. He tried—oh, how
hard!—to recall one look of content, of happiness, of thorough
trust and love; but he tried in vain. A general expression
of quiet suffering, which had become calm through continuance, varied by an occasional glance of querulous impatience
when he might have been betrayed into dilating on the importance of some case in which he happened to be engaged
and the interest with which it filled him,—these were his
only recollections of Mabel's looks. Nor did his remembrance of her words and ways afford him any more comfort.
True she had never said, certainly had never said to him, that
her life was anything but a happy one; but she had looked
it often. Even he felt that now, reading her looks by the
light of memory, and wondered that the truth had never
struck him at the time. He remembered how he would
look up off his work and see her, her hands lying listlessly
in her lap, her eyes staring vacantly before, so entranced, so
rapt in her own thoughts, that she would start violently

when he spoke to her. She always had the same answer for his questions at those times. What was the matter with her? Nothing! What should be the matter with her?— What was she thinking of? Nothing, at least nothing that could possibly interest him. Did her presence there annoy him, because she would go away willingly if it did? And the voice in which this was said—the cold, hard, dry, unsympathizing voice! Good God! if he had not been sufficiently mindful of her, if he had not bestowed such attention and affection as is due from a husband to his wife, surely there was some small excuse for him in the manner in which his clumsy approaches had been received!

At times he felt a wild inexplicable desire to have her back again with him, and fell into a long train of thought as to what he should do supposing all the events of the past three months were to turn out to have been a dream—as indeed he often fancied they would; and on his return he were to go up into the drawing-room, whither he had never penetrated since his return, and were to find Mabel sitting there, prim and orderly, among the prim and orderly furniture. Should he alter his mode of life, and endeavour to make it more acceptable to her? How was it to be done? It would be impossible for him now to give up his confirmed ways; impossible for him to give up his reading and his work, and fritter away his evenings in taking his wife to the gaieties to which they were invited. Perkins might do that—did it, and found it answer; but the profession knew that Perkins was a charlatan, and he— What wild nonsense was he thinking of! It was done—it was over; he should never find his wife waiting for him again when he returned: she was dead; she had destroyed herself!

As this horrible thought burst upon him again with tenfold its original horror, he buried his face in his hands, and bowed his head upon the writing-table in front of him in an agony of despair. He could bear it no longer; it was

driving him mad. If he only knew—and yet he dared not
inquire more closely; the presumptive evidence was horribly strong, was thoroughly sufficient to rob him of his
peace of mind, of his clearness of intellect. Then the
terrible consequences of the discovery, the awful duty which
it imposed upon him, flashed upon his labouring consciousness. He dared not inquire more closely? No, not he.
As a physician he knew perfectly well what the result of
any such inquiry would be. He knew perfectly well that
in any other case, where he was merely professionally and
not personally interested, his first idea for the solution of
such doubts as then oppressed him, had they existed in any
one else, would have been to suggest the exhumation of the
body, and its rigid examination. He knew perfectly well
that, harbouring such doubts as were then racking and torturing his distracted mind, it was clearly his duty to insist
on such steps being taken. He was no squeamish woman,
no nervous man, to be alarmed at the sight of death's dread
handiwork; that was familiar to him from constant experience, from old hospital custom, from his education and his
studies. Should this dread idea of Mabel's self-destruction,
now ever haunting him, ever present to his mind—should it
cross the thoughts of any one else, would not the necessity
for exhumation be the first notion that would present itself?
Suppose he were to suggest it? Suppose he were to pro-
fess himself dissatisfied with the accounts of Mabel's illness
given him by Whittaker, and were to insist upon positive
proof, professionally satisfactory to him, of his wife's disease?
Of course he would make a deadly enemy of Whittaker;
but that he thought but little of: his name stood high
enough to bear any slur that might be thrown upon it from
that quarter, and his reputation would stand higher than
ever from the mere fact of his boldly determining to face a
disagreeable inquiry, rather than allow such a case to be
slurred over. And the inquiry made, and Whittaker's state-

ment proved to be generally correct, at best it would be thought that Dr Wilmot was somewhat morbidly anxious as to the cause of his wife's death; an anxiety which would be anything but prejudicial to him in the minds of many of his friends, while the relief to his own overcharged mind would be immediate and complete. Relief! Ah, once more to feel relief would be worth all the responsibility. He would see about it at once; he would give the necessary information, and—But suppose the result did not turn out as he could hope to see it? suppose all the information given, the coroner's warrant obtained, the exhumation made, the examination complete, and the result—that Mabel had destroyed herself? The first step taken in such a matter would be an immediate challenge to public attention; the press would bear the whole matter broadcast on its wings; Dr Wilmot and his domestic affairs would become a subject for gossip throughout the land; and if it proved that Mabel had destroyed herself, her memory would, at his instance, remain ever crime-tainted. Even if the best happened; if Whittaker's judgment were indorsed, would not people ask whether it was not odd that a suspicion of foul play should have crossed the husband's mind, whether Mrs. Wilmot in her lifetime may not have used such a threat; and if so, might not the circumstances which led to the supposed use of the threat be inquired into, the motives questioned, the home-life discussed? Hour after hour he revolved this in his mind, purposeless, wavering. Finally he decided that he would leave matters as they were, saying to himself that such a course was merely justice to his dead wife, on whose memory, were she guilty of self-slaughter, he should be the last to bring obloquy, or even suspicion. He felt more comfortable after having come to this decision—more comfortable in persuading himself that he was guided by a tender feeling towards the dead woman. He said " Poor Mabel!" to himself several times in thinking over it, and shook his head dolefully; and actually felt that if she had been prompted by his neglect to take this step, his omitting to call public attention to it was in itself some *amende* for his neglect. But even to himself he would not allow this soul-guiding influence in the matter. He blinked it, and shut his eyes to it; refused to listen to it, and—was led by it all the same. Chudleigh Wilmot tried to persuade himself, did persuade himself, that he was acting solely in deference to his dead wife's memory; but what really influenced his conduct was the knowledge that the arousal of the smallest suspicion as to the cause of his wife's death, the smallest scandal about himself, would inevitably separate him hope-lessly, and for ever, from Madeleine Kilsyth. The great question as to whether Mabel had destroyed herself still re-mained unanswered. He was powerless to shake off the impression, and under the impression he was useless; he could do justice neither to himself nor his patients. He must get away; give up practice at least for a time, and go abroad; go somewhere where he knew no one, and where he himself was quite unknown—somewhere where he could have rest and quiet and surcease of brain-work; where he could face this dreadful incubus, and either get rid of it, or school himself to bear it without its present dire effect on his life.

He would do that, and do it at once. The death of his wife would afford him sufficient excuse to the world, which knew him as a highly nervous and easily impressible man, and which would readily understand that he had been shat-tered by the suddenness of the blow. As to his practice, he was well content to give that up for a short time: he knew his own value without being in the least conceited—knew that he could pick it up again just where he left it, and that his patients would be only too glad to see him. He had felt that when he was at Kilsyth.

At Kilsyth! The word jarred upon him at once. To give up his practice even for a time meant a temporary estrangement from Madeleine; meant a shutting out, so far as he was concerned, of sun and warmth and light and life, at the very time when his way was darkest and his path most beset. His mind had been so fully occupied since his return, that he had only been able to give a few fleeting thoughts to Madeleine. He felt a kind of horror at permitting her even in his thoughts to be connected with the dreadful subject which filled them. But now when the question of departure was being considered by him, he naturally turned to Madeleine.

To leave London now would be to throw away for ever his chance with Madeleine Kilsyth. His chance with her? Yes, his chance of winning her! He was a free man now— free to take his place among her suitors, and try his chance of winning her for himself. How wonderful that seemed to him, to be unfettered, to be free to woo where he liked! Last time he had drifted into marriage carelessly and without purpose—it should be very different the next time. But to leave London now would be throwing away for ever his chance with Madeleine. He knew that; he knew that he had established a claim of gratitude on the family, which Kilsyth himself, at all events, would gladly allow, and which Lady Muriel would probably not be prepared to deny. As for Madeleine herself, he knew that she was deeply grateful to him, and thoroughly disposed to confide in him. This was all he had dared to hope hitherto; but now he was in a position to try and awaken a warmer feeling. Gratitude was not a bad basis to begin on, and he hoped, he did not know it was so long since the days of Maria Strutt—and thinking it over, he looked blankly in the glass at the crows'-feet round his eyes and the streaks of silver in his dark hair; but he thought then that he had the art of pleasing women, unfortunate as was the result of that particular case. But if he were to go away, the advantageous position he had so luckily gained would be lost, the ground would be cut away from under his feet, and on his return he would have great difficulty in being received on a footing of intimacy by the family; while it would probably be impossible for him to regain the confidence and esteem he then enjoyed from all of them.

Was, then, Madeleine Kilsyth a necessary ingredient in his future happiness? That was a new subject for consideration. Hitherto, while that—that barrier existed, he had looked upon the whole affair merely as a strange sort of romance, in which ideas and feelings of which he had never had much experience, and that experience long ago, had suddenly revived within him. Pleasantly enough; for it was pleasant to know that his heart had not yet been enough trodden down and hardened by the years which had gone over it to prevent it receiving seed and bearing fruit;— pleasantly enough; for an exchange of the stern reality of his work, a dry world with the bevy of cares which are ready waiting for you as you emerge from your morning's tub, and which only disappear—to change into nightmares—as you extinguish your bed-room gas—an exchange of this for a little of that glamour of love which he thought never to meet with again, could not fail to be pleasant. But the affair was altered now; the occurrence which had made him free had at the same time rendered it necessary that he should use his freedom to a certain end. Under former circumstances he could have been frequently in Madeleine's company,— happy as he never had been save when with her,—and the world would have asked no question, have lifted no eyebrow, have shrugged no shoulder. Dr Wilmot was a married man, and his professional position warranted his visiting Miss Kilsyth, who was his patient, as often as he thought necessary. But now it was a very different matter. Here was a man, still young, at least quite young enough to marry again; and if it were said, as it would be, that he was "constantly at the house," people—those confounded anonymous persons, the *on* who do such an enormous amount of mischief in the world—would begin to talk and whisper and hint; and the girl's name might be compromised through him, and that would never do.

Did he love her? did he want to marry her? As he asked himself the question, his thoughts wandered back to Kilsyth. He saw her lying flushed and fevered, her long golden hair tossing over her pillow, a bright light in her blue eyes, her hot hands clasped behind her burning head—or, better still, in her convalescence, when she lay still and tranquil, and looked up at him timidly and softly, and thanked him in the fullest and most liquid tones for all his kindness to her. And he remembered how, gazing at her, listening to her, the remembrance of what Love really was had come to him out of the far-away regions of the Past, and had moved his heart within him in the same manner, but much more potently than it had been moved in the days of his youth. Yes; the question that he had put to himself admitted but of one answer. He did love Madeleine Kilsyth; he did want to marry her! To that end he would employ all his energies; to secure that he would defer everything. What nonsense had he been talking about giving up his practice and going away? He would remain where he was, and marry Madeleine!

And Henrietta Prendergast? The thought of that woman struck him like a whip. If he were to marry Madeleine Kilsyth, would not that woman, Henrietta Prendergast, Mabel's intimate and only friend—would not she proclaim to the world all that she knew of the jealousy in which the dead woman held the young girl? Would not his marriage be a confirmation of her story? Might it not be possible that the existence of such a talk might create other talk; that the manner of her death might be discussed; that it might be suspected that, driven to it by jealousy—that is how they would put it—Mrs Wilmot had destroyed herself?

And if "they" put it so, it would be in vain to deny it. The mere fact of his having been successful in his profession had created hosts of enemies, who would take advantage of the first adverse wind, and do their best to blast his renown and bring him down from the pedestal to which he had been elevated. Then bit by bit the scandal would grow—would permeate his practice—would become general town-talk. He would see the whispers and the shoulder-shrugs and the up-lifted eyebrows, and perhaps the cool manner or the possible cut. Could he stand that? Could a man of his sensibility endure such talk? could he bear to feel that his domesticity was being laid bare before the world for the comment of each idler who might choose to wile away his time in dis-cussing the story? Impossible! No; sooner keep in his present dreary, hopeless, isolated position, sooner give up all chances of winning Madeleine, sooner even retrograde. He had no children to provide for, and could always have enough to support him in a sufficient manner. He would give it all up; he would go away; he would banish for ever that day-dream which he had permitted himself to enjoy, and he would—

A letter was brought in by his servant—an oblong note, sealed with black wax, in an unfamiliar handwriting. He turned it over two or three times, then opened it, and read as follows:

"Brook-street, Thursday.

"DEAR DR WILMOT,—We have heard with very great regret of your sad loss, and we all, Lady Muriel, papa, and myself, beg you to receive our sincere condolence. I know how difficult it is at such a time to attempt to offer consola-tion without an appearance of intrusion; but I think I may say that we are especially concerned for you, as it was your attendance on me which kept you from returning home at the time you had originally intended. I can assure you. I have thought of this very often, and it has given me a great deal of uneasiness. Pray understand that we can none of us ever thank you sufficiently for your kindness to us at Kilsyth. With united kind regards, dear Dr Wilmot, your grateful patient,

"MADELEINE KILSYTH.

"P.S. I have a rather troublesome cough, which worries me at night. You recollect telling me that you knew about this?"

So the Kilsyths were in town. His grateful patient! He could fancy the half-smile on her lips as she traced the words. No; he would give up his notion of going away—at least for the present!

CHAPTER XV.

FAMILY RELATIONS.

WHEN the Kilsyths were in London, which, according to their general practice, was only from February until June, they lived in a big square house in Brook-street,—an old-fashioned house, with a multiplicity of rooms, necessary for their establishment, which demanded besides the ordinary number of what were known in the house-agent's catalogue as "reception rooms," a sitting-room for Kilsyth, where he could be quiet and uninterrupted by visitors, and read the *Times*, and Scrope's *Salmon Fishing*, and Colonel Hawker on *Shooting*, and *Cyril Thornton*, and Gleig's *Subaltern*, and Napier's *History of the Peninsular War*, and one or two other books which formed his library; where he could smoke his cigar, and pass in review his guns and his gaiters and his waterproofs, and hold colloquy with his man, Sandy

N 2

MacCollop, as to what sport they had had the past year, and what they expected to have the next—without fear of interruption. This sanctuary of Kilsyth's lay far at the back of the house, at the end of a passage never penetrated by ordinary visitors, who indeed never inquired for the master of the house. Special guests were admitted there occasionally; and perhaps two or three times in the season there was a council-fire, to which some of the keenest sportsmen, who knew Kilsyth, and were about to visit it in the autumn, were admitted,—round which the smoke hung thick, and the conversation generally ran in monosyllables.

Lady Muriel's boudoir—another of the extraneous rooms which the house-agent's catalogue wotteth not of—led off the principal staircase through a narrow passage; and, so far as extravagance and good taste could combine in luxury, was the room of the house. When you are not an appraiser's apprentice, it is difficult to describe a room of this kind; it is best perhaps to follow little Lord Towcester's description, who, when the subject was being discussed at mess, offered to back Lady Muriel's room for good taste against any in London; and when asked to describe it, said,

"Lots of flowers; lots of cushions; lots of soft things to sit down upon, and nice things to smell; and jolly books—to look at, don't you know: needn't say I haven't read any of 'em; and forty hundred clocks, with charming chimin' bells; and china monkeys, you know; and fellows with women's heads and no bodies, and that kind of thing; and those round tables, that are always sticking out their confounded third leg and tripping a fellow up. Most charmin' place, give you my word."

Lord Towcester's description was not a bad one, though to the initiated in his peculiar phraseology it scarcely did justice to the room, which was in rose-coloured silk and walnut-wood; which had *étagères*, and what-nots, and all the frivolousness of upholstery, covered with all the most expensive and useless china; which opened into a little conservatory, always full of sweet-smelling plants, and where a little fountain played, and little gold-fish swam, and the gas-jets were cunningly hidden behind swinging baskets on pendent branches. There was a lovely little desk in one corner of the room, with a paper-stand on it always full of note-paper and envelopes radiant with Lady Muriel's cipher and monogram worked in all kinds of expensive ways, and with a series of drawers, which were full of letters and sketches and albums, and were always innocently open to everybody; and one drawer, which was not open to everybody,—which was closed indeed by a patent Bramah lock, and which, had it been inspected, would have been found to contain a lock of Stewart Caird's hair (cut from his head after death), a packet of letters from him of the most trivial character, and a copy of Owen Meredith's *Wanderer*, which Lady Muriel had been reading at the time of her first and only passion, and in which all the passages that she considered were applicable to or bearing on her own situation were thickly pencil-scored. But it never was inspected, that drawer, and was understood by any who had ever had the hardihood to inquire about it, to contain household accounts. Lady Muriel Kilsyth in connection with a lock of a dead man's hair, a bundle of a dead man's letters, a pencil-marked copy of a sentimental poet! The idea was too absurd. Ah, how extraordinarily wise the world is, and in what a wonderful manner our power of reading character has developed!

Madeleine's rooms—by her stepmother's grace she had two, a sitting-room and a bed-room—are upstairs. Small rooms, but very pretty, and arranged with all the simple taste of a well-bred, right-thinking girl. Her hanging book-shelves are well filled with their row of poets, their row of " useful " works, their *Thomas à Kempis*, their Longfellow's *Hyperion*, their *Pilgrim's Progress*, their *Scenes of Clerical Life*—with all the Amos Barton bits dreadfully underscored

—their *Christmas Carol*, and their *Esmond*. The neat little writing table, with its gilt mortar inkstand, and its pretty costly nicknacks—birthday presents from her fond father—stood in the window: and above it hung the cage of her pet canary. There were but few pictures on the walls: a water-colour drawing of Kilsyth, bad enough, with impossible perspective and a very coppery sunset over very spotty blue hills, but dear to the girl as the work of the mother whom she had scarcely known; a portrait of her father in his youth, showing how gently time had dealt with the brave old boy; a print from Grant's portrait of Lady Muriel; and a photograph of Ronald in his uniform, looking very grim and stern and Puritan-like. There is a small cottage-piano too, and a well-filled music-stand,—well-filled, that is to say, according to its owner's ideas, but calculated to fill the souls of musical enthusiasts with horror or pity; for there is very little of the severe and the classical about Madeleine even in her musical tastes: Glück's *Orfeo*, some of Mendelssohn's *ieder ohne Wörte*, and a few selections from Mozart, quite satisfied her; and the rest of the music-stand was filled with Bellini, Donizetti, Rossini, and Verdi, English ballads, and even dance music. Upon all the room was the impress and evidence of womanly taste and neatness; nothing was prim, but everything was properly arranged; above all, neither in books, pictures, music, nor on the dressing-table or in the wardrobe in the bed-room, was there the smallest sign of fastness or slanginess, that almost omnipresent drawback to the charms of the young ladies of the present day.

Nigh to Madeleine's rooms was a big airy chamber with a shower-bath, an iron bedstead, a painted chest of drawers, and a couple of common chairs, for its sole furniture. This was the room devoted to Captain Kilsyth whenever he stayed with his relatives, and had been furnished according to his exact injunctions. It was like Roland himself, grim and stern, and was regarded as a kind of Blue Chamber of Horrors by Lady Muriel's little children, who used to hurry

past its door, and accredited it as a perfect stronghold of
bogies. This feeling was but a reflection of that with which
the little girls Ethel and Maud regarded their elder brother.
His visits to their school-room, periodically made, were always
looked forward to with intense fright both by them and by
their governess, Miss Blathers—a worthy woman, untouchable in Mangnall, devoted to the backboard, with a fair pro-
ficiency in music and French, but with an unconquerable
tendency towards sentimentality of the most snivelling kind.
Miss Blathers' sentiment was of the G. P. R. James's school;
she was always on the look-out for that knight who was to
come and deliver her from the bonds of governesshood, who
was to fling his arm over her, as Count Gismond flung his
round Mr Browning's anonymous heroine, and lead her off to
some land where Ollendorf was unknown, and Levizac had
never been heard of. A thoroughly worthy creature, Miss
Blathers, but horribly frightened of Ronald, who would come
into the school-room, make his bow, pull his moustache, and
go off at once into the questions, pulling his moustache a
great deal more, and shrugging his shoulders at the answers
he received.

It was not often, however, that Ronald came to Brook-
street, at all events for any length of time. When he was
on duty, he was of course with his regiment in barracks;
and when he had opportunities of devoting himself to his own
peculiar studies and subjects, he generally took advantage of
those opportunities with his own particular cronies. He
would ride with Madeleine sometimes, in a morning, occasionally in the Row, but oftener for a long stretch round the
pretty suburbs; and he would dine with his father now and
then; and perhaps twice in a season would put in an appearance in Lady Muriel's opera-box, and once at a reception
given by her. But, except perhaps by Madeleine, who
always loved to see him, he was not much missed in Brook-
street, where, indeed, plenty of people came.

Plenty of people and of all kinds. Constituents up from

Scotland on business, or friends of constituents with letters
of introduction from their friends to Kilsyth ; to whom also
came old boys from the clubs, who had nothing else to do,
and liked to smoke a morning cigar or drink a before-lun-
cheon glass of sherry with the hospitable laird ; old boys who
never penetrated beyond the ground-floor, save perhaps on
one night in the season, which Lady Muriel set apart for the
reception of "the House" and "the House" wives and
daughters, when they would make their way upstairs and
cling round the lintels of the drawing-room, and obstruct all
circulation, and eat a very good supper, and for three or four
days afterwards wag their heads at each other in the bow-
windows of Brookes's or Barnes's, and inform each other
with great solemnity that Lady Muriel was a "dayvilish
fine woman," and that "the thing had been doosid well done
at Kilsyth's the other night, eh ? " Other visitors, nominally
to Kilsyth, but in reality after their reception by him relegated to Lady Muriel, keen-looking, clear-eyed, high-cheek-
boned men, wonderfully "canny"-looking, thoroughly Scotch,
only wanting the pinch of snuff between their fingers, and
the kilt round their legs, to have fitted them for taking their
station at the tobacconists' doors,—factors from different
portions of the estate, whom Lady Muriel took in hand, and
with them went carefully through every item of their accounts, leaving them marvellously impressed with her qualities as a woman of business.

No very special visitors to Lady Muriel. Plenty of
carriages with women, young and old, elegant and dowdy,
aristocratic and plebeian, on the front seat, and the *Court
Guide* in all its majesty on the back. Plenty of raps, preposterous in their potency, delivered with unerring aim by
ambrosial mercuries, who disengaged quite a cloud of powder
in the operation ; packs of cards, delivered like conjuring
tricks into the hands of the hall-porter, over whose sleek
head appeared a charming perspective of other serving-men

kind regards, tender inquiries, congratulations, condolence,
P.P.C.'s, all the whole formula duly gone through between
the ambrosial creatures who have descended from the
monkey-board and the plethoric giant who has extricated
himself from the leathern bee-hive—one of the principals in
the mummery stolidly looking on from the carriage, the
other sitting calmly upstairs, neither taking the smallest part,
or caring the least about it.   The lady visitors did not come
in, as a rule, but the men did, almost without exception.
The men arrived from half-past four till half-past six, and,
during the season, came in great numbers.   Why?   Well,
Lady Muriel was very pleasant, and Miss Kilsyth was
" charmin', quite charmin' " They said this parrot-wise;
there are no such parrots as your modern young men; they
repeat whatever they have learnt constantly, but between their
got-by-rote sentences they are fatally and mysteriously dumb.

" Were you at the Duchess's last night, Lady Muriel?"

" Yes!   You were not there, I think?"

" No; couldn't go—was on duty."

*Pause.   Dead silence.   Five clocks ticking loudly and
running races with each other.*

" Yes, by the way, knew you were there."

" Did you—who told you?"

" Saw it in the paper, 'mongst the comp'ny, don't you
know, and that kind of thing."

*Awful pause.   Clocks take up the running.   Lady Muriel
looks on the carpet.   Visitor calmly scrutinizes furniture
round the room, at length he receives inspiration from lengthened contemplation of his hat-lining.*

" Seen Clement Penruddock lately?"

" Yes, he was here on—when was it?—quite lately—Oh,
the day before yesterday."

" Poor old Clem!   Going to marry Lady Violet Dumanoir,
they say.   Pity Lady Vi don't leave off putting that stuff on
her face and shoulders, isn't it?"

" How ridiculous you are ! "

" No, but really ! she does ! "

" How can you be so silly ! "

Grand and final pause of ten minutes, broken by the visitor's saying quietly, " Well, good-bye," *and lounging off to repeat the invigorating conversation elsewhere.*

Who ? Youth of all kinds. The junior portion of the Household Brigade, horse and foot, solemn plungers and dapper little guardsmen ; youth from the Whitehall offices, specially diplomatic and erudite, and disposed to chaff the military as ignorant of most things, and specially of spelling ; idlers *purs et simples*, who had been last year in Norway, and would be the next in Canada, and who suffered socially from their perpetual motion, never being able to retain the good graces which they had gained or to recover those they had lost ; foreign *attachés ;* junior representatives of the plutocracy, who went into society into which their fathers might never have dreamed of penetrating, but who found the " almighty dollar," or its equivalent, when judiciously used, have all the open-sesame power ; an occasional Scotch connection on a passing visit to London, and—Mrs M'Diarmid.

Who was Mrs M'Diarmid ? That was the first question every one asked on their introduction to her ; the second, on their revisiting the house where the introduction had taken place, being, " Where is Mrs M'Diarmid ? " Mrs M'Diarmid was originally Miss Whiffin, daughter of Mrs Whiffin of Salisbury-street in the Strand, who let lodgings, and in whose parlours George M'Diarmid, second cousin to the present Kilsyth, lived when he first came to London, and enrolled himself as a student in the Inner Temple. A pleasant fellow George M'Diarmid, with a taste for pleasure, and very little money, and an impossibility to keep out of debt. A good-looking fellow, with a bright blue eye, and big red whiskers (beards were not in fashion then, or George would have grown a very Birnam-Wood of hair), and broad shoulders, and a genial jovial manner with " the sex." Deep into Mrs Whiffin's books went George, and simultaneously deep into her daughter's heart; and finally, when Kilsyth had done his best for his scapegrace kinsman, and could do no more, and nobody else would do anything, George wiped off his score by marrying Miss Whiffin, and, as she expressed it to her select circle of friends, "making a lady of her." It was out of his power to do that. Nothing on earth would have made Hannah Whiffin a lady, any more than anything on earth could have destroyed her kindness of heart, her devotion to her husband, her hard-working, honest striving to do her duty as his wife. Kilsyth would not have been the large-souled glorious fellow that he was if he had failed to see this, or seeing, had failed to appreciate and recognize it. George M'Diarmid hemmed and hawed when told to bring his wife to Brook-street, and blushed and stuttered when he brought her; but Kilsyth and Lady Muriel set the poor shy little woman at her ease in an instant, and seeing all her good qualities, remained her kind and true friends. After two years or so George M'Diarmid died in his wife's arms, blessing and thanking her; and after his death, to the astonishment of all who knew anything about it, his widow was as constant a visitor to Brook-street as ever. Why? No one could exactly tell, save that she was a shrewd, clever woman, with an extraordinary amount of real affection for every member of the family. There was no mistake about that. She had been tried in times of sickness and of trouble, and had always come out splendidly. A vulgar old lady, with curious blunt manners and odd phrases of speech, which had at first been dreadfully trying; but by degrees the regular visitors to the house began to comprehend her, to make allowance for her *gaucheries* and her quaint sayings—in fact, to take the greatest delight in them. So Mrs M'Diarmid was constantly in Brook-street, and the frequenters of the five-o'clock tea-table professed to be personally hurt if she absented herself.

A shrewd little woman too, with a special care for Madeleine; with a queer old-world notion that she, being herself childless, should look after the motherless girl. For Lady Muriel Mrs M'Diarmid had the highest respect; but Lady Muriel had children of her own, and, naturally enough, was concerned about, or as Mrs M'Diarmid expressed it, "wropped up" in them, and Madeleine had no one to protect and guide her—poor soul! So this worthy little old woman devoted herself to the motherless girl, and watched over her with duenna-like care and almost maternal fidelity.

Five o'clock in the evening, two days after Wilmot had received Madeleine's little note; the shutters were shut in Lady Muriel's boudoir, the curtains were drawn, a bright fire burned on the hearth, and the tea-equipage was ready set on the little round table close by the hostess. Not many people there. Not Kilsyth, of course, who was reading the evening papers and chatting at Brookes's,—not Ronald, who scarcely ever showed at that time. Madeleine, looking very lovely in a tight-fitting high violet-velvet dress, a thought pale still, but with her blue eyes bright, and her golden hair taken off her face, and gathered into a great knot at the back of her pretty little head. Near her, on an ottoman, Clement Penruddock, half-entranced at the appearance of his own red stockings, half in wondering why he does not go off to see Lady Violet Dumanoir, his *fiancée*. Clem is always wondering about this, and never seems to arrive at a satisfactory result. Next to him, and vainly endeavouring to think of something to say, the Hon. Robert Brettles, familiarly known as "Bristles," from the eccentric state of his hair, who is supposed to be madly in love with Madeleine Kilsyth, and who has never yet made greater approaches in conversation with her than meteorological observations in regard to the weather, and blushing demands for her hand in the dance. By Lady Muriel, Lord Roderick Douglas, who still finds his nose too large for the rest of his face, and strokes it thoughtfully in the palm of his hand, as though he could thereby quietly reduce its dimensions. Frank Only, Sir Coke's eldest son, but recently gazetted to the Body Guards, an ingenuous youth, dressed more like a tailor's dummy than anything else, especially about his feet, which are very small and very shiny; and Tommy Toshington, who has dropped in on the chance of hearing something which, cleverly manipulated and well told at the club, may gain him a dinner. In the immediate background sits Mrs M'Diarmid, knitting.

Lady Muriel has poured out the tea; the gentlemen have handed the ladies their cups, and are taking their own; and the usual blank dulness has fallen on the company. Nobody says a word for full three minutes, when the silence is broken by Tommy Toshington, who begins to find his visit unremunerative, as hitherto he has not gleaned one atom of gossip. So he asks Lady Muriel whether she has seen anything of Colonel Jefferson.

"No, indeed," Lady Muriel replies; Colonel Jefferson has not been to see us since our return."

"Didn't know you were in town, perhaps," suggests the peace-loving Tommy.

"Must know that, Toshington," says Lord Roderick Douglas, who has no great love for Charley Jefferson, associating that stern commander with various causes of heavy field-days and refusals of leave.

"I don't see that," says Tommy, who has never been Lord Roderick's guest at mess or anywhere else, and who does not see a chance of hospitality in that quarter; consequently is by no means reticent,—"I don't see that; how was he to know it?"

"Same way that everybody else did—through the *Post*."

"Tommy can't read it," said Clement Penruddock; "they didn't teach spellin' ever so long ago, when Tommy was a boy."

"They taught manners," growled Tommy, "at all events, but they seem to have given that up."

"Charley Jefferson isn't in town," said "Bristles," cutting in quickly to stop the discussion; "he's down at Torquay. Had a letter from him yesterday, my lady; last man in the world, Charley, to be rude—specially to you or Miss Kilsyth."

"I am sure of that, Mr Brettles," said Lady Muriel; "I fancied Colonel Jefferson must be away, or we should have seen him."

"People go away most strangelike," observed Mrs M'Diarmid from the far distance. "The facilities of the road, the river, and the rail, as I've seen it somewhere expressed, is such, that one's here to-day, Lord bless you, and next week in the Sydney Isles or thereabouts."

By "the Sydney Isles or thereabouts," Mrs M'Diarmid's friends had by long experience ascertained that she meant Australia.

"Scarcely so far as that in so short a time, Aunt Hannah," said Madeleine with a smile.

"Well, my dear, far enough to fare worse, as the expression is. I don't hold with such wanderings, thinking home to be home, be it ever so homely."

"You would not like to go far away yourself, would you, Mrs M'Diarmid?" asked Lord Roderick.

"Not I, my lord; Regent-street for me is quite very, and beyond that I have no inspiration."

"You've never been able to get Mrs M'Diarmid even so far as Kilsyth, have you, Lady Muriel?" said Clement.

"No; she has always refused to come to us. I think she imagines we're utter barbarians at Kilsyth."

"Not at all, my dear, not at all," said the old lady; "but everybody has their fancies, and knows what they can do, and where they're useful; and fancy me at my time of life tossing my cabers, or doing my Tullochgorums or whatever they're called, between two crossed swords on the top of a mountain! Scarcely respectable, I think."

" You're quite right, Mrs Mac, and I honour your sentiments," said Clem with a half-grin.

" Not but that I would have gone through all that and a
good deal more, my darling," said the old lady, putting down
her work, crossing the room, and taking Madeleine's pale face
between her own fat little hands, " to have been with you in
your illness, and to have nursed you. Duchesses indeed ! "
cried Mrs Mac, with a sniff of defiance at the remembrance
of the Northallerton defection—" I'd have duchessed 'em, if
I'd had my way ! "

" You would have been the dearest and best nurse in the
world, I know, Aunt Hannah," said Madeleine ; then added,
with a half-sigh, "though I could not have been better
attended to than I was, I think."

Lady Muriel marked the half-sigh instantly, and looked
across at her step-daughter. Reassured at the perfect calm
of Madeleine's face, on which there was no blush, no tremor,
she said, " You wrote that note, Madeleine, according to
your father's wish ? "

" Two days ago, mamma."

" Two days ago ! I should have thought that—"

" Perhaps he is very much engaged, mamma, and knew
that there was no pressing need of his services. Dr Wilmot
told me that—" and the girl hesitated, and stopped.

" Is that Dr Wilmot of Charles-street, close by the
Junior ? Are you talking of him ? " said Penruddock.
" Doosid clever feller they say he is. He's been attending
my cousin Cranbrook—you know him, Lady Muriel ; been
awfully bad, poor Cranbrook has ; head shaved, and holloing
out, and all that kind of thing—frightful ; and this doctor
has pulled him through like a bird—splendidly, by Jove ! "

" He drives an awful pair of screws," said " Bristles,"
who was horsey in his tastes ; " saw 'em standing at Cranbrook's door. To look at 'em, you wouldn't think they
could drag that thundering big heavy brougham—C springs,

don't you know, Clem?—and yet when they start they nip along stunningly."

"Ah, those poor doctors!" said Mrs M'Diarmid; "I often wonder how they live, for they take no exercise now all the streets are M'Adam and wood and all sorts of nonsense! When there was good sound stone pavement, one was bumped about in your carriage like riding a trotting-horse, and that was all the exercise the poor doctors got. Now they don't get that."

"And Dr Wilmot attended Lord Cranbrook, did he, Clem?" asked Madeleine softly; "and brought him safely through his illness. I'm glad of that; I'm glad—"

"Dr Wilmot, my lady!" said the groom of the chambers.

"What a bore that doctor coming," said Clement Penruddock, looking round, "just as I was going to have a pleasant talk with Maddy!"

"You leave Maddy alone," said Mrs M'Diarmid with a grunt, "and go off to your financier!"

"My financier, Aunt Hannah?" said Clem in astonishment; "I haven't one; I wish to Heaven I had."

"Haven't one?" retorted the old lady. "Pray, what do you call Lady Vi?"

And 'then Clement Penruddock understood that Mrs M'Diarmid meant his *fiancée*.

Dr Wilmot and Madeleine went, at Lady Muriel's request, into the drawing-room.

He was with her once again; looked in her eyes, heard her voice murmuring thanks to him for all his past kindness, touched her hand—no longer hot with fever, but tremblingly dropping into his—saw the sweet smile which had come upon her with the earliest dawn of convalescence. At the same time Wilmot remarked a faint flush on her cheek and a baleful light in her eyes, which recalled to him the discovery which he had made at Kilsyth, and which he had mentioned to her father. His diagnosis had been short

then and hurried, but it had been true: the seeds of the
disease were in her, and, unchecked, were likely to bear
fatal fruit. Could he leave her thus? could he absent himself, bearing about with him the knowledge that she whom
he loved better than anything on earth might derive benefit
from his assistance—might indeed owe her life and her
earthly salvation to his ministering care? He knew well
enough that though her father had given him his thorough
trust and confidence, his friendship and his warm gratitude,
yet there were others about her who had no share in these
feelings, by whom he was looked upon with doubt and suspicion, and who would be only too glad to relegate him to
his position of the professional man who had fulfilled what
was required of him, and had been discharged—not to be
taken up again, until another case of necessity arose. There
was no doubt that his diagnosis had been correct, and that
her life required constant watching, perpetual care. Well,
should she not have it? Was not he then close at hand?
Had his talent ever been engaged in a case in which he took
so deep, so vital an interest? Had he not often given up
his every thought, his day's study, his night's repose, for
the mere professional excitement of battling the insidious
advances of Disease—of checking him here, and counter-
checking him there, and finally cutting off his supplies, and
routing him utterly? and would he not do this in the
present instance, where such an interest as he had never
yet felt, such an inducement as had never yet been held
out to him, urged him on to victory?

Ah, yes; "his grateful patient" should have greater
claims on his gratitude than she herself imagined. He had
seen her safely through a comparatively trifling illness; he
would be by her side in the struggle that threatened her
life. Come what might, win or lose, he should be there,
able, as he thought, to help her in danger, whatever might
be the result to himself of his efforts.

o

He has her hand in his now, and is looking into her eyes —momentarily only; for the soft blue orbs droop beneath his glance, and the bright red flush leaps into the pale cheek. Still he retains her hand, and asks her, in a voice which vainly strives to keep its professional tone, such professional questions as admit of the least professional putting. She replies in a low voice, when suddenly a shadow falls upon them standing together; and looking up, they see Ronald Kilsyth. Dr Wilmot utters the intruder's name; Madeleine is silent.

"Yes, Madeleine," says Ronald, addressing her as though she had spoken; "I have come to fetch you to Lady Muriel.—I was not aware, sir," he added, turning to Wilmot, "that you were any longer in attendance on this young lady. I thought that her illness was over, and that your services had been dispensed with."

Constitutionally pale, Ronald now, under the influence of strong excitement, was almost livid; but he had not one whit more colour than Chudleigh Wilmot, as he replied: "You were right, Captain Kilsyth: my professional visits are at an end; it is as a friend that I am now visiting your sister."

Ronald drew himself up as he said, "I have yet to learn, Dr Wilmot, that you are on such terms with the family as to justify you in paying these friendly visits.—Madeleine, come with me."

The girl hesitated for an instant; but Ronald placed her arm in his, and walked off with her to the door, leaving Chudleigh Wilmot immovable with astonishment and rage.

CHAPTER XVI.

GIVING UP.

RAGE was quite a novel passion for Chudleigh Wilmot, and one which, like most new passions, obtained for the time complete mastery over him. In his previous career he had been so steeped in study, so overwhelmed by practice—had had every hour of his time so completely and unceasingly occupied, that he had had no leisure to get into a rage, even if he had had the slightest occasion. But the truth is, the occasion had been wanting also. During the time he had been at the hospital he had had various tricks played upon him,—such tricks as the idle always will play upon the industrious,—but he had not paid the least attention to them; and when the perpetrators of the practical jokes found they were disregarded, they turned the tide of their humour upon some one else less pachydermatous. Ever since then his life had flowed in an even stream, which never turned aside into a whirlpool of passion or a cataract of rage, but continued its calm course without the smallest check or shoal. In the old days, when driven nearly to madness by the calm way in which her husband took every event in life, undisturbed by public news or private worry, finding the be-all and the end-all of life in the prosecution of his studies, the correctness of his diagnoses, and the number of profitable visits daily entered up in his diary, Mabel Wilmot would have given anything if he had now and then broken out into a fit of rage, no matter for what cause, and thus cleared the dull heavy atmosphere of tranquil domesticity for ever impending over them. But he never did break out; and the atmosphere, as we have seen, was never cleared.

But Chudleigh Wilmot was in a rage at last. By

nature he was anything but a coward, was endowed with a
keen sensitiveness, and scrupulously honourable.   His
abstraction, his studiousness, his simple unworldly ways—
for there were few more unworldly men than the rising
fashionable physician—all prevented his easily recognizing
that he was a butt for intentional ribaldry or insult; but
when, as in this case, he did see it, it touched him to the
quick.   As a boy he could laugh at the practical jokes of
his fellow-students; as a man he writhed under and rebelled
against the first slight that since his manhood he had received.   What was to be done?   This young man, this
Captain Kilsyth, her brother, had studiously and purposely
insulted him, and insulted him before her.   As this thought
rushed through Wilmot's mind, as he stood as though
rooted to the spot where they had left him in the drawing-
room in Brook-street, his first feeling was to rush after
Ronald and strike him to the ground as the penalty of his
presumption.   His fingers itched to do it, clenched themselves involuntarily, as his teeth set and his nostrils dilated
involuntarily.   What good would that do?   None.   Come
of it what might, Madeleine's name would be mixed up
with it, and—Ah, good God! he saw it all; saw the newspaper paragraph with the sensation-heading, "Fracas in
private life between a gallant Officer and a distinguished
Physician;" he saw the blanks and asterisks under which
Madeleine's name would be concealed; he guessed the club
scandal which—No, that would never do.   He must give
up all thoughts of avenging himself in that manner, for her
sake.   Better bear what he had borne, better bear slight
and insult worse a thousandfold, than have her mixed up
in a newspaper paragraph, or given over to the genial talk
of society.

He must bear it, put up with the insult, swallow his
disgust, forego his revenge.   There was not enough of the
Christian element in Chudleigh Wilmot's composition to

render this line of conduct at all palatable to him; but it was necessary, and should be pursued. He had gone through all this in his thought and arrived at this determination before he moved from the drawing-room. Then he walked quietly down to Lady Muriel's boudoir, entered, chatted with her ladyship for five minutes on indifferent topics, and took his leave, perfectly cool without, raging hot within.

As he had correctly thought, his long absence from London had by no means injured his practice; if anything, had improved it. In every class of life there is such a thing as making yourself too cheap, and the healthy and wealthy hypochrondriacs, who form six-sevenths of a fashionable physician's *clientèle*, are rather incited and stimulated when they find the doctor unable or unwilling to attend their every summons. So Wilmot's practice was immense. He had a very large number of visits to pay that day, and he paid them all with thorough scrupulousness. Never had his manner been more *suave* and bland; never had he listened more attentively to his patients' narratives of their complaints; never had his eyebrow-upliftings been more telling, the noddings of his head thrown in more *apropos*. The old ladies, who worshipped him, thought him more delightful than ever; the men were more and more convinced of his talent; but the truth is, that having no really serious case on hand, Dr Wilmot permitted himself the luxuries of thought; and while he was clasping Lady Cawdor's pulse, or peering down General Donaldbain's throat, he was all the time wondering what line of conduct he could best pursue towards Ronald and Madeleine Kilsyth. In the course of his afternoon drive he passed the carriages of scores of his brother practitioners, with whom he exchanged hurried bows and nods, all of whom returned to the perusal of the *Lancet* or of their diaries, as the case might be, with envy at their hearts, and jealousy of the successful man who succeeded in everything, and who, if they had only known it, was quivering under the slight and insult which he had just received.

His visits over, he went home and dined quietly. The romantic feelings connected with an "empty chair" troubled Chudleigh Wilmot very little. He had never paid very much attention to the person by whom the chair had been filled; indeed very frequently during Mabel's lifetime he had done what he always had done since her death, taken a book, and read during his dinner. But he could not read on this occasion. He tried, and failed dismally; the print swam before his eyes; he could not keep his attention for a moment on the book; he pushed it away, and gave up his mind to the subject with which it was preoccupied.

Fair, impartial, and judicial self-examination—that was what he wanted, what he must have. Captain Kilsyth had insulted him, purposely no doubt; why? Not for an instant did Wilmot attempt to disguise from himself that it was on Madeleine's account; but how could Captain Kilsyth know anything of his (Wilmot's) feelings in regard to Madeleine; and if he did know of them, why should he now object? Captain Kilsyth might be standing out on the question of family; but that would never lead him to behave in so *brusque* and ungentlemanly a manner; he might object to the alliance—to the alliance!—good God! here was he giving another man credit for speculating on matters which had only dimly arisen even in his own brain!

Still there remained the fact of Captain Kilsyth's conduct having been as it had been, and still remained the question—why? To no creature on earth had he, Chudleigh Wilmot, confided his love for this girl; and so far as he knew—and he searched his memory carefully—he had never in his manner betrayed his secret in the remotest degree. Had his wife been alive, Ronald Kilsyth might have objected to finding him in close converse with his sister; yet in the fact of his having a wife lay—

It flashed across him in an instant, and sent the blood rushing to his heart. The manner of his wife's death— was that known? The causes which, as Henrietta Prendergast had hinted to him, had led Mabel to the vial with the leaden seal—had they leaked out? had they reached the ears of this young man? Did he suspect that jealousy —no matter whether with or without foundation—of his sister had led Mrs Wilmot to lay violent hands upon herself? And if he suspected it, why not a hundred others? The story would fly from mouth to mouth. This Captain Kilsyth—no; he would not lend his aid to its promulgation; he could not for his sister's sake; but—And yet, with or against Captain Kilsyth's wish, it must come out. When his visits ceased in Brook-street, as they must cease —he had determined on that; when he no longer saw Madeleine, who, as he perfectly well knew, had been brought to London with the view of being under his care, would not old Kilsyth make inquiries as to the change in the intended programme, and would not his son have to tell him all he had heard? It was too horrible to think of. With such a rumour in existence—granting that it was a rumour merely, and all unproved—it would be impossible for Kilsyth, however eagerly he might wish it, to befriend him—at least in the manner in which he could best befriend him, by encouraging his addresses to Madeleine. Lady Muriel would not listen to it; Ronald would not listen to it, even if those two were in some way—he could not think how, but there might be a way of getting round those two and winning them to his side—even if that were done, while that horrible story or suspicion was current— and it was impossible to set it at rest without the chance of establishing it firmly for ever—Kilsyth would never consent to his marriage with Madeleine.

He must at once free himself from the chance of any story of this kind being promulgated. The more he thought the matter over, the more he saw the impossibility of again going to Brook-street, after what had occurred; the impossibility of his absence passing without remark and inquiry by Kilsyth; the impossibility of Ronald's withholding his statement of his own conduct in the matter, and his reasons for that conduct. For an instant a ray of hope shot through Chudleigh Wilmot's soul, as he thought that perhaps the reasons might be infinitely less serious and less damaging than he had depicted them to himself; but it died out again at once, and he acknowledged to himself the hopelessness of his situation. He had been indulging in a day-dream from which he had been rudely and ruthlessly waked, and his action must now be prompt and decisive. There was an end to it all; it was Kismet, and he must accept his fate. No combined future for Madeleine and him; their paths lay separate, and must be trodden separately at once; her brother was right, his own dead wife was right—it is not to be!

There must be no blinking or shuffling with the question now, he thought. To remain in London without visiting in Brook-street would evoke immediate and peculiar attention; and it was plain that Ronald Kilsyth had determined that Dr Wilmot's visits to Brook-street were not to be renewed. He must leave London, must leave England at once. He must go abroad for six months, for a year; must give up his practice and seek change and repose in fresh scenes. He would spoil his future by so doing, blow up and shatter the fabric which he had reared with such industry and patience and self-denial; but what of that? He should ascribe his forced expatriation and retreat to loss of health, and he should at least reap pity and condolence; whereas now every moment that he remained upon the scene he ran the chance of being overwhelmed

with obloquy and scorn. He could imagine, vividly
enough, how the patients whom he had refused to flatter,
whose self-imagined maladies he had laughed at and ridi-
culed, would turn upon him; how his brother practitioners,
who had always hated him for his success, would point to
the fulfilment of their never-delivered prophecies, and make
much of their own idleness and incompetency; how the
medical journals which he had riddled and scathed would
issue fierce diatribes over his fall, or, worse than all, sympathize with the profession on—he could almost see the
words in print before him—"the breach of that confidence
which is the necessary and sacred bond between the physician and the patient."

Anything better than that; and he must take the decisive step at once! He must give up his practice. Whittaker should have it, so far at least as his recommendation
could serve him. He should have that, and must rely upon
himself for the rest. Many of his patients knew Whittaker
now, had become accustomed to him during the time of
Wilmot's absence at Kilsyth, and Whittaker had not behaved badly during that—that horrible affair of Mabel's
last illness. Moreover, if Whittaker suspected the cause
of Mabel's death—and Wilmot shuddered as the mere
thought crossed his mind--the practice would be a sop to
him to induce him to hold his tongue in the matter. And
he, Wilmot, would go away—and be forgotten. Better that,
bitter as the thought might be—and how bitter it was none
but those who have been compelled, for conscience' sake,
for honour's sake, for expediency's sake even, to give up in
the moment of success, to haul down the flag and sheath
the sword when they knew victory was in their grasp,
could ever tell;—better that than to remain, with the
chance of exposure to himself, of compromise to *her*. The
mental overthrow, the physical suffering consequent upon
the sudden death of his wife, would be sufficient excuse for

this step to the world; and there were none to know the
real cause of its being taken.   He had saved sufficient
money to enable him to live as comfortably as he should
care to live, even if he never returned to work again; and
once free from the torturing doubt which oppressed him, or
rather from the possibility of all which that torturing
doubt meant to his fevered mind, he should be himself
again.

Beyond his position, so hardly struggled for, so recently
attained, he had nothing to leave behind him which he
should particularly regret.   He had been so self-contained,
from the very means necessary for attaining that position,
had been so circumscribed in the pleasures of his life, that
his opportunities for the cultivation even of friendship had
been very rare.   He should miss the quaint caustic conversation, the earnest hearty liking so undeniably existing,
even under its slight veneer of eccentricity, of old Foljambe; he should miss what he used laughingly to call his
" dissipation " of attending a few professional and scientific
gatherings held in the winter, where the talk was all " shop,"
dry and uninteresting to the uninitiated, but full of delight
to the listeners, and specially to the talkers; he should
miss the excitement of the lecture-theatre, where perhaps
more than anywhere else he thoroughly enjoyed himself,
and where he shone at his very brightest, and—that was
all.   No! Madeleine! this last and keenest source of enjoyment in his life, this pure spring of freshness and vigour,
this revivification of early hopes and boyish dreams, this
young girl, the merest acquaintance with whom had softened and purified his heart, had given aim and end to his
career, had shown him how dull and heartless, how un-
loved, unloving, and unlovely had been his bygone time,
and had aroused in him such dreams of uncensurable ambition for the future,—she must be given up, must become
a " portion and parcel of the dreadful past," and be dead to

nim for ever! She must be given up! He repeated the words mechanically, and they rang in his ears like a knell. She must be given up! She was given up, even then, if he carried out his intention. He should never see her again, should never see the loving light in those blue eyes—ah, how well he minded him of the time when he first saw it in the earliest days of her convalescence at Kilsyth, and of all the undefined associations which it awakened in him!— should never hear the grateful accents of her soft sweet voice, should never touch her pretty hand again. For all the years of his life, as it appeared to him, he had held his eyes fixed upon the ground, and had raised them at the rustle of an angel's wings, only to see her float far beyond his reach. For all the years of his life he had toiled wearily on through the parching desert; and at length, on meeting the green oasis, where the fresh well sparkled so cheerily, had had the cup shattered from his trembling hand.

She must be given up! She should be; that was the very keystone of the arrangement. He had looked the whole question fairly in the face; and what he had proposed to himself, and had determined on abiding by, he would not shrink from now. But it was hard, very hard. And then he lay back in his chair, and in his mind retraced all the circumstances of his acquaintance with her; last of all, coming upon their final interview of that morning in the drawing-room at Brook-street. He was sufficiently calm now to eliminate Ronald and his truculence from the scene, and to think only of Madeleine; and that brought to his remembrance the reason of their having gone into the drawing-room together, to consult on her illness, the weakness of the lungs which he had detected at Kilsyth.

That was a new phase of the subject, which had not occurred to him before. Not merely must he give her up and absent himself from her, but he must leave her at a time when his care and attention might be of vital importance to

her.   Like most leading men in his profession, Chudleigh
Wilmot, with a full reliance on himself, combined a wholesome distrust of and disbelief in most of his brother practitioners.   There were few—half a dozen at the most, perhaps
—in whose hands Madeleine might be safely left, if they had
some special interest, such as he had, in her case.   Such as
he had! Wilmot could not avoid a grim smile as he thought
of old Dr Blenkiron, with his snuff-dusted shirt-frill, or little
Dr Prater, with his gold-rimmed spectacles, feeling similar
interest to his in this sweet girl.   But unless they had special
interest—unless they could have given up a certain amount
of their time regularly to attending to her—it would have
been of little use, as her symptoms were for ever varying, and
wanted constant watching.   And as for the general run of
the profession, even men so well thought of as Whittaker or
Perkins, he—stay, a good thought—old Sir Saville Rowe
would probably be coming to town for the winter ; and the
old gentleman, though he had retired from active practice,
would, Wilmot made sure, look after Madeleine for him as a
special case.   Sir Saville's brain was as clear as ever ; and
though his strength was insufficient to enable him to continue
his practice, this one case would be an amusement rather than
a trouble to him.   Yes, that was the best way of meeting this
part of the difficulty.   Wilmot could go away at least without the additional anxiety of his darling's being without com-
petent advice.   So much of his burden could be lightened by
Sir Saville ; and he would sit down at once and write to the
old gentleman, asking him to undertake the charge.

He moved to his writing-table and sat down at it.   He
had arranged the paper before him and taken up his pen, when
he suddenly stopped, threw aside the pen, and flung himself
back in his chair.   What excuse was he about to make to his
old master for his leaving London at so critical a period in
his career ?   He had not sufficiently considered that.   He
had intended saying that Mrs Wilmot's sudden death had

had such an effect upon him physically and mentally, that he felt compelled to relinquish practice, at least for the present, and to seek abroad for that rest and change of scene which was absolutely necessary for him. He had turned the phrases very neatly in his mind, but he had forgotten one thing. He had forgotton his conversation with the old gentleman on the garden walk overhanging the brawling Tay on the morning when he received the telegram from Kilsyth. He had forgotten how he had laughed in derision when Sir Saville had asked him whether he was in love with his wife; how he had curtly hinted that Mabel was all very well in her way, but holding a decidedly inferior position in his estimation to his practice and his work. He remembered all this now, and he saw how utterly futile it would be to attempt to put off his old friend with such a story. What, then, should be the excuse? That his own health had given way under pressure of work? Sir Saville knew well how highly Wilmot appreciated his professional opinion; and had he believed the story—which was very unlikely—would have been hurt at his old pupil's rushing away without consulting him. In any case he must not see Sir Saville, who would undoubtedly cross-question him in detail about Mrs Wilmot's illness. He must write to the old gentleman, giving a very general statement and avoiding all particulars, and requesting him to take Madeleine under his charge.

He did so. He wrote fully and affectionately to his old friend. He touched very slightly on the death of his wife, beyond hinting that that occurrence had necessitated his departing at once for the Continent on some law-business concerning property, by which he might probably be detained for some time. He went on to say that he had made arrangements for the transfer of his practice to Whittaker, who had had it, as Sir Saville would remember, during Chudleigh's absence in Scotland; but there was one special case, which he could only leave in the hands of Sir Saville himself: this was Miss Kilsyth. Sir Saville would remember his (Wilmot's) disinclination to accede to the request contained in the telegram on that eventful morning; and indeed it seemed curious to himself now, when he thought of the interest which he took in all that household. Kilsyth himself was the most charming, &c., and the best specimen of an, &c.; Lady Muriel was also, and her little girls were angels. Miss Kilsyth was mentioned last of all the family in Wilmot's letter, and was merely described as " an interesting, amiable girl." This portion of the letter was principally occupied with details of her threatened disease; and on reperusing it before sending it away, Wilmot was greatly struck by, as it seemed to him, the capital manner in which he had made his interest throughout assume a purely professional form. But whether professionally or not, the interest was very earnestly put; and the desire that the old gentleman should break through his retirement and attend to this particular case was very strongly expressed. In conclusion, Wilmot said that he should send his address to his old friend, and that he hoped to be kept acquainted with Miss Kilsyth's state.

Dr Wilmot did not send his letter to the post that night. He read it over the next morning after seeing his home patients, and when the carriage was at the door to take him off on his rounds. He was quite satisfied with the tone of the letter, which he placed in an envelope and was just about to seal, when his servant entered and announced " Captain Kilsyth."

CHAPTER XVII.

FACE TO FACE.

" CAPTAIN KILSYTH ! " No time for Chudleigh Wilmot to deny himself, if even he had so wished ; no time to recover himself from the excitement which the announcement had aroused. He saw the broad dark outline of his visitor behind the servant.

" Show Captain Kilsyth in."

Captain Kilsyth came in. Wilmot noticed that he was very pale and stern-looking, but that there was no trace of yesterday's excitement about him. It had become second nature to Wilmot to notice these things ; and he found himself critically examining Ronald's external appearance, as he would that of a patient who had sought his advice.

The men bowed to each other, and Ronald spoke first. " You will be surprised to see me here, Dr Wilmot," he said ; " but be assured that it is business of importance that brings me."

Wilmot bowed again. He was fast recovering from his agitation, but scarcely dared trust himself to speak just yet.

" I see your carriage is at the door, and I will detain you but a very few moments. You can give me, say, ten minutes ? "

Wilmot muttered that his time was at Captain Kilsyth's disposal ; an avowal which apparently annoyed his visitor, for he said testily, " You and I should be above exchanging the polite trash of society, Dr Wilmot. I am come here to speak on a matter which concerns me deeply, and those very near and dear to me even more deeply still. Are you prepared to hear me ? "

Those very near and dear to him ! Oh yes ; Wilmot was prepared to hear him fully, and said as much. Would Captain Kilsyth be seated ?

"I have come to talk to you, Dr Wilmot, as a friend," commenced Ronald, dropping into a chair. "I daresay you are scarcely prepared for that avowal, considering my conduct at our interview yesterday in Brook-street. Then I was hasty and inconsiderate; and for my conduct then I beg to tender my apologies frankly and freely. I trust they will be received?" There was an odd square blunt honesty even in the manner in which he said this that prepossessed Wilmot.

"As frankly and freely as they are offered," he replied.

"So far agreed," said Ronald. "Now, look here. I am a very bad hand at beating about the bush; and I have come here to say things the mere fact of saying which is, where men of honour are not concerned, compromising to one of the persons spoken of. I have every belief that you are a man of honour, and therefore I speak."

Dr Wilmot bowed again, and said that Captain Kilsyth complimented him.

"No. I think too highly of you to do that. I simply speak what I believe to be true, from all I have heard of your doings at Kilsyth."

Of his doings at Kilsyth? A man of honour, from his doings at Kilsyth? Though perfectly conscious that Ronald was watching him narrowly, Chudleigh Wilmot's cheeks coloured deeply at this point, and he was silent.

"Now, Dr Wilmot, I must begin by talking to you a little about myself—an unprofitable subject, but one necessary to be touched upon in this discourse between us. The men who are supposed to know me intimately—my own brother officers, I mean—will tell you that I am an oddity, an extraordinary fellow, and that they know nothing about me. Nothing is known of my likes or dislikes. I am believed not to have any of either. Now this is an exaggerated view of the question. I don't know that I dislike any one in particular; but I have my affections. I am very fond of my father; I adore my sister Madeleine."

He spoke with such earnestness and warmth, that Wilmot looked up at him, half in pleasure, half in wonder. Ronald noticed the glance, and said, " If you have heard me mentioned at all, Dr Wilmot, you have probably heard it said that I am a man with a stone instead of a heart, with the *Cavalry Officer's Instructions* instead of a Bible; and therefore I cannot wonder at your look of astonishment. But what I have stated to you is pure and simple fact. I love these two infinitely better than my life."

Wilmot bowed again. He felt ashamed of his reiterated acquiescence, but had nothing more satisfactory to proffer.

"Now, I don't see much of my family," pursued Ronald. "Their ways of life are different from mine ; and except when they happen to be in London we are seldom thrown together. This may be to be regretted, or it may not; at all events the fact is so. But whether I see them or not, my interest in them never slackens. There are people, I know—most people, I believe—to whom propinquity is a necessary ingredient for affection. They must be near those they love—must be brought into constant communication, personal communication with them, or their love dies out. That is affection of a type which I cannot understand ; it is a great deal too spaniel-or ivy-like for my comprehension. I could go on for years without seeing those I love, and love them all the same. Consequently, although when the eight or nine weeks' whirl which my family calls the London season is at an end, and I scarcely see them until it begins again, I do not take less interest in their proceedings, nor is my keen affection for those I love one whit diminished. You follow me ? "

" So far, perfectly."

" I was detained here on duty in London during last August and September; and even if I had been free, I doubt whether I should have been with my people at Kilsyth. As I have just said, their ways of life, their amusements and pursuits, are different from mine, and I should probably have

P

been following my own fancies somewhere else.   But I always
hear from some of them with the greatest regularity; and I
heard, of course, of my sister's illness, and of your being called
in to attend upon her.   Your name was thoroughly familiar
to me.   What my friends call my 'odd ways' have made me
personally acquainted with several of the leading members of
your profession; and directly I heard that you had arrived at
Kilsyth, I knew that Madeleine could not possibly be in
better hands."

To any one else Wilmot would have said that she could
not have been under the charge of any one who would have
taken greater interest in her case; but he had not forgotten
the interview of yesterday, and he forbore.

"I was delighted to hear of your arrival at Kilsyth," continued Ronald, "and I was deeply grateful to you for the
unceasing care and anxiety which, as reported to me, you bestowed upon my sister.   The accounts which I received vied
with each other in doing justice to your skill and your constant attention; and I believe, as I know all at Kilsyth believed, that, under Providence, we owe Madeleine's life to
you."

"You will pardon my interrupting you, Captain Kilsyth,"
said Wilmot, speaking almost for the first time; "but you
give me more credit than I deserve.   Miss Kilsyth was very
ill; but what she required most was constant attention and
watching.   The excellent doctor of the district—I forget his
name, I'm ashamed to say—Joyce, Dr Joyce, would have
been thoroughly efficient, and would have doubtless restored
Miss Kilsyth to health as speedily as I did; only unfortunately others had a claim upon him, and he could not devote
his time to her."

"Exactly what I was saying.   I presume it will not
be doubted that Dr Wilmot, of Charles-street, St James's—
in his own line the principal physician of London—had as
many calls upon his time even as the excellent doctor of the

district, and yet he sacrificed all others to attend on Miss Kilsyth."

"Dr Wilmot was away from his patients on a holiday, and no one had a claim upon his time."

"And he made the most of his holiday by spending a great portion of it in the sick-room of a fever-stricken patient ! No, no, Dr Wilmot; you made a great sacrifice undoubtedly. Now, why did you make it ?"

He turned suddenly upon Wilmot as he spoke, and looked him straight in the face. Wilmot's colour came again; he moved restlessly in his chair, pressed his hands nervously together, but said nothing.

"I told you, Dr Wilmot, that I was about to speak of things the mere mention of which, were we not men of honour, would be compromising to some of the persons spoken. I ask you why you made that sacrifice of your professional time. I ask you not for information, because I know the reason. Before you left Kilsyth, I heard that my sister was receiving attention from a most undesirable quarter—from a quarter whence it was impossible that any good could arise. My sister is, as I have told you, dearer to me than my life, and the news distressed me beyond measure. I turned it over and over in my mind; I made every possible kind of inquiry. At length, on the evening on which you arrived in London and called on me at my club, I knew that you were the man alluded to by my informant."

No change in Chudleigh Wilmot. His cheek is still flushed, his eyes still cast down; still he moves restlessly in his chair, still his hands pluck nervously at each other.

"I knew it, and yet I hardly could believe it. I knew that men of your profession, specially men of such eminence in your profession, were in the habit of being received and treated with the utmost confidence; which confidence was never abused. I knew that bystanders and lookers-on, unaccustomed to illness, might very easily misconstrue the attention which a physician would pay to a young lady whose case had excited his strong professional interest. I —well, constrained to take the worst view of it—I knew that you were a married man, and I thought that you might have admired Miss Kilsyth, and that—that when you left her—there—there would be an end of the feeling."

No change in Chudleigh Wilmot. His cheek is still flushed, his eyes still cast down; still he moves restlessly in his chair, still his hands pluck nervously at each other. Something in his appearance seemed to touch Ronald Kilsyth as he looked at him earnestly, for he said:

"I wish to God I could think so now, Dr Wilmot! I wish to God I could think so now! But though I don't pretend to be versed in these matters, I have a certain amount of insight; and when I saw you standing by my sister's side in the drawing-room in Brook-street yesterday, I knew that the information I had received was correct." He paused for an instant, and passed his hand across his forehead, then resumed. "I am a blunt man, Dr Wilmot, but I trust neither coarse nor unsympathetic. I want to convey to you as quietly as possible that you have made a mistake; that for every one's sake—ours, Madeleine's, your own—this thing cannot, must not be."

A change in Chudleigh Wilmot now. He does not look up; he covers his brow with his left hand; but he says in a deep husky voice:

"There is—as you are aware—a change in my circumstances: I am—I am free now; and perhaps—in the future—"

"In no future, Dr Wilmot," interrupted Ronald gravely but not unkindly. "Listen to me. If, as I half suspected you would, you had flung yourself into a rage,—denied, stormed, protested,—I should simply have said my say, and left you to make the best or the worst of it. But you have not done this, and—and I pity you most sincerely.

You are, as you say, free now. You think probably there is no reason why, at some future time, you should not ask my sister to become your wife. You would probably urge your claims upon her gratitude—claims which you think she might possibly be brought to allow. It can never be, Dr Wilmot. I, who am anything but, in this sense, a worldly man, even I know that your presence at Kilsyth, your long stay there, to the detriment of your home interests, your devotion to my sister, have already given matter for talk to the gossips of society, and received the usual amount of malicious comment. And if you have real regard for Madeleine, you would give up anything to shield her from that, indorsed as would be the imputation and intensified as would be the malice, if your relations with her were to be on any other footing than—they ought to have been."

Quite silent now, Chudleigh Wilmot; his hand still covering his brow, his head sunk upon his breast.

"I said I pitied you; and I do," continued Ronald. "And here, understand me, and let me explain one point in our position, Dr Wilmot. What I have to say, though it may pain you in one way, will, I think, be satisfactory to you in another. You may think that Madeleine may be destined by her family for some—I speak without the least offence— some higher destiny; that her family would wish for her a husband higher in social rank. I give you my honour that, as far as I am concerned, I could not, from all I have heard of you, wish my sister's future confided to a more honourable man. Social rank and dignity weigh very little with me. My life is passed generally with those who have won their spurs, rather than inherited their titles; and I would infinitely sooner see my sister married to a man whose successful position in life was due to himself than to one who merely wore the reflected glory of his ancestors. So far you would have been a suitor entirely acceptable to me, had there not been the other unfortunate element in the

Ronald ceased speaking, and for some minutes there was a dead silence. Then Chudleigh Wilmot raised his head, rose from his chair, and commenced pacing the room with long strides; Ronald, perfectly understanding his emotion, remaining passively seated. At length Wilmot stopped by Ronald's chair, and said:

" When you entered this room, you told me you had come here to speak to me as a friend. I am bound to say that you have perfectly fulfilled that implicit promise. No one could have been more frank, more candid, and, I may say, more tender than you have been with me. My profession," said Wilmot with a dreary smile,—"my profession teaches us to touch wounds tenderly, and you seem to be thoroughly imbued with the precept. You will do me the justice to allow that I have listened to you patiently; that I have heard without flinching almost, certainly without complaint."

Ronald bowed his head in acquiescence.

" Now, then, I must ask you to listen to me. What I have to say to you is as sacred as what you have said to me, and will not, could not be mentioned by me to another living soul. When I received your father's telegram summoning me to your sister's bedside, there was no more heart-whole man in Britain than myself. When I use the word 'heart-whole,' I do not intend it to convey the expression of a perfect content in the affections I possessed, as you, knowing I was married and settled, might understand it. I was heart-whole in the sense that, while I was thoroughly skilled in the physical state of my heart, its mental condition never gave me a thought. I had, as long as I could recollect, been a very hard-working man. I had married, when I first established myself in practice, principally, I believe, because I thought it the most prudent thing for a young physician to do; but certainly not from any feeling that ever caused my heart one extra pulsation. You must not be shocked at this

plain speaking. Recollect that you are listening to an anatomical lecture, and go through with it. All the years of
my married life passed without any such feeling being called
into existence. My—my wife was a woman of quiet domestic
temperament, who pursued her way quietly through life;
and I, thoroughly engrossed in my professional pursuits,
never thought that life had anything better to engage in
than ambition, better to offer than success. I went to Kilsyth, and for weeks was engaged in constant, unremitting
attendance upon your sister. I saw her under circumstances
which must to a certain extent have invested the most uninteresting woman in the world with interest; I saw her
deserted and shunned by every one else, and left entirely to
my care; I saw her in her access of delirium, and afterwards,
when prostrate and weak, she was dependent on me for
everything she wanted. And while she and I were thus
together—I now combating the disease which assailed her,
now watching the sweet womanly patience, the more than
womanly courage, with which she supported its attacks—I,
witnessing how pure and good she was, how soft and gentle,
and utterly unlike anything I had ever seen, save perhaps in
years long past, began to comprehend that there was, after
all, something to live for beyond the attainment of success
and the accumulation of fees."

Wilmot stopped here, and looked at his companion; but
Ronald's head was turned away, and he made no movement;
so Wilmot proceeded.

" I—I scarcely know how to go on here; but I determined
to tell you all, and I will go through with it. You cannot
tell, you cannot have the smallest idea of what I have suffered.
You were pleased to call me a man of honour : God alone
knows how I struggled to deserve that title from you, from
every member of Miss Kilsyth's family. I succeeded so well,
that until I noticed the expression of your face yesterday,
I believed no one on earth knew of the state of my feel-

ings towards that young lady. At Kilsyth, when I first felt the fascination creeping over me; when I found that there was another, a better and a brighter be-all and end-all for human existence than I had previously imagined; when I found that the whole of my career had hitherto lacked, and under then existent circumstances was likely to lack, all that could make it worth running after, the want had been discovered; I did my best to shut my eyes to what might have been, and to content myself with what was. I knew that though my—my wife and I had never professed any extravagant affection for each other; that though we had never been lovers, in the common acceptation of the word, she had discharged her duty most faithfully to me, and that I should be a scoundrel to be untrue to her in thought—in word, of course, from other considerations, it was impossible. I did my best, and my best availed. I succeeded so far, that I left your father's house with the knowledge that my secret was locked in my own breast, and that I had never made the slightest tentative advance to your sister, to see if she were even aware of its existence. More than this. During my attendance on Miss Kilsyth, I had discovered that she was suffering from a threatening of what the world calls consumption. I felt it my duty to mention this to your father, and he requested me to attend her professionally when the family returned to London. I agreed—to him; but I had long reflection on the subject during my return journey, and had almost decided to decline, on some pretext or another.

"Hear me but a little longer. I need not dwell to you upon the event which has occurred since I left Scotland, and which has left me a free man—free to enjoy legitimately that happiness, a dream of which dawned upon me at Kilsyth, and which I shut out and put aside because it was then wrong and almost unattainable. Circumstances are now so altered, that it is certainly not the former, and it is yet to be proved whether, so far as the young lady is con-

cerncd, it is the latter. In my desire to do right, even with
the feeling of relief and release which I had, even with the
hope which I do not scruple to confess I have nourished, I
kept from Brook-street until a line from Miss Kilsyth summoned me thither. When you met me yesterday, I was
there in obedience to her summons. You know that, I suppose, Captain Kilsyth ? "

" I made inquiries yesterday, and heard so. I said at the
outset, Dr Wilmot, that you were a man of honour. Your
conduct since your return, and since the return of my family,
weighed with me in the utterance of that opinion."

" I did not go to Brook-street—not that I did not fully
comprehend the change in the nature of my position since I
had last seen Miss Kilsyth, not that I had not a certain
half-latent feeling of hope that I might, now I had the legitimate chance, be enabled to rouse an interest in her, but because I thought it was better to stay away. If I did not see
her again, I preposterously attempted to argue to myself, the
feeling that I had for her might die out. I *have* seen her
again. I have heard from you that my feelings towards
your sister are known—at least to you ; and now I ask you
whether you still think that, under existing circumstances, it
is impossible for me to ask Miss Kilsyth to be my wife at
some future date ? "

As Chudleigh Wilmot stopped speaking, he bent over
the back of the chair by which he had been standing during
the latter part of his speech, and looked long and earnestly
at Ronald. It was very seldom that Captain Kilsyth dropped
his eyes before any one's gaze ; but on this occasion he passed
his hand hastily across them, and kept them for some minutes
fixed upon the ground. A very hard struggle was going on
in Ronald Kilsyth's mind. He was firmly persuaded that
the decision he had originally taken, and which he had come
to Charles-street for the purpose of insisting on with Wilmot, was the right one. And yet Wilmot's story, in itself

so touching, had been so plainly and earnestly told, there was such evident honesty and candour in the man, that Ronald's heart ached to be compelled to destroy the hopes which he felt certain that his companion had recently cherished. Moreover, in saying that in considering Madeleine's future, his aspirations for her marriage took no heed of rank or wealth, Ronald simply spoke the truth. He had a slight tendency to hero-worship; and a man of Wilmot's talent, and, as he now found, of Wilmot's integrity and gentlemanly feeling, was just the person of whose friendship and alliance he would have been proud. Madeleine too? In his own heart Ronald felt perfectly certain that Madeleine was already gratefully fond of her preserver, and would soon become as passionately attached to him as the mildness of her nature would admit; while he knew that she would not feel that she was descending from her social position—that she was "marrying beneath her," to use the ordinarily accepted phrase, in the smallest degree. And yet—no, it was impossible! He, Ronald Kilsyth, the last man in the world to care for the talk of "on," "they," "everybody," the social scandal, and the club chatter, while it concerned himself, shrunk from it most sensitively when it threatened any one dear to him. Physicians were all very well—every one knew them of course, necessarily; but their wives— Ronald was trying to recollect how many physicians' wives he had ever met in society, when he recollected that it was Madeleine, who could of course hold her own position; and then came a thought of Lady Muriel, and the influence which she had over his father when they were both tolerably agreed upon the subject. It was impossible; and he must say so.

He looked up straightforwardly and honestly at his companion, and said, "I wish to God that I could give you a different answer, Dr Wilmot; but I cannot. I still think it is impossible."

"I think so too," said Wilmot sadly. "I have looked at

it, as you may imagine, from the most hopeful aspect; and even then I am compelled to confess that you are right. But, see here, Captain Kilsyth; whatever I make up my mind to I can go through with,—all save slow torture. My doom must be short and sharp—no lingering death. What I mean to say is," he continued, striving to repress the knot rising in his throat,—"what I mean to say is, that as I am to give up this hope of my life, I must quench it utterly and at once, not suffer it to smoulder and die out. You tell me —no!" he added, as Ronald put out his hand. "I do not mean you personally, believe me. I am told that I must abandon any idea of asking Miss Kilsyth to be my wife, and —and I agree. But—I must never see Miss Kilsyth again. I could not risk the chance of meeting her here, there, and everywhere. I would not run the chance of being thrown with her again. I should do my best to hold to the line of conduct I have marked out for myself; but I am but mortal, and, as such, liable to err."

"Then, in heaven's name, what do you intend to do with yourself?" asked Ronald, with one hand plucking at his moustache, and the other hooked round the back of the chair.

"To do with myself!" echoed Wilmot. "To fly from temptation. The thing that every sensible man does when he really means to win. It is only your braggarts who stop and vaunt the excellence of their virtue, and give in after all. Read that letter, Captain Kilsyth, and you will see that I have anticipated the object of your visit."

Ronald took the letter to Sir Saville Rowe which Wilmot handed to him, and read it through carefully. The tears stood in his eyes as he handed it back.

"You're a noble fellow, Dr Wilmot," said he; "such a gentleman as one seldom meets with. But this will never do. You must never think of giving up your practice."

"For a time at least; it is the only way. I must cure

myself of a disease that has laid firm hold upon me before I can be of any use to my patients, I fancy "

" When do you purpose going ? "

" At once, or within the week."

" And where ? "

" I don't know.   Through Germany—to Vienna, I imagine.   Vienna is a great stronghold of the *savans* of our profession; and I should give out that I was bound thither on a professional mission."

" I feel as though there is nothing I would not give to dissuade you from carrying out what only half an hour since my heart was so earnestly set upon.   But is. it absolutely necessary that you should thus exile yourself?   Could you not—"

" I can take no half measures," said Wilmot decisively. " I go, or I stay; and we have both decided what I had better do."

Five minutes more and Ronald was gone, after a short and earnest speech of gratitude and thanks to Wilmot, in which he had said that it would be impossible ever to forget his manly chivalry, and that he hoped they would soon meet under happier auspices.   He wrung Wilmot's hand at parting, and left, sensibly affected.

Wilmot's servant heard the hall-door shut behind the departing visitor, and wondered he had not been rung for. Five minutes more elapsed, ten minutes, and then the man, thinking that his master had overlooked the fact that the carriage was waiting for him, went up to the room to make the announcement.   When he entered the room, he found his master with his head upon the table in front of him clasped in his hands.   He looked up at the sound of the man's voice, and murmured something unintelligible, seized his hat and gloves from the hall-table, and jumped into his brougham.

" He was ghastly pale when he first looked up," said the man to the female circle downstairs, "and had great red lines round his eyes. Sometimes I think he's gone off his 'ead! He's never been the same man since missus's death."

CHAPTER XVIII.

NOTHING LIKE WILMOT.

Mr Foljambe did not easily throw off the painful impression which his interview with Chudleigh Wilmot had made upon him. The old gentleman had always found Wilmot, though not an expansive, a singularly frank person; he had not indeed ever spoken much to him concerning his wife or his domestic affairs generally; but men do not do so habitually; and the men to whom their wives are most dear and important rarely mention them at all. The circumstance had therefore made no impression upon Mr Foljambe, himself a confirmed old bachelor, who, though very kind and considerate to women and children, regarded them rather as ornamental trifles, with a tendency to degenerate into nuisances, than otherwise.

He began by wondering why Wilmot should have been so thoroughly upset by his wife's death, and went on to speculate how long that very unexpected and undesirable result might be likely to last. Becoming sanguine and comparatively cheerful at this point, he made up his mind that Chudleigh would get over it before long. Perhaps all had not gone very smooth with the Wilmots. Not that he had any particular reason to think so; but Wilmot was not a remarkably domestic man, and there might be perhaps a little spice of self-reproach in his sorrow. At all events, it would not last; *that* might be looked upon as certain. In

the mean time, and in order that the world might not think
Wilmot's conduct silly, sentimental, or mysterious, Mr Foljambe would be beforehand with the gossips and the curious,
and, by assigning to his absence from England a motive in
which the interests of his profession and those of his health
should be combined, prevent the risk of its being imputed to
anything so *rococo* as deep feeling.

"Gad, I'll do it," said Mr Foljambe, as he took his seat
in his faultless brougham, having carefully completed an irreproachable afternoon toilette, in which every article of
costume was integrally perfect and of the highest fashion,
but as scrupulously adapted to his time of life as the dress of
a Frenchwoman of middle or indeed of any age. "I'll go
and inquire for that Kilsyth girl, and set the right story
afloat there," he said, as he gave his coachman the necessary
orders; "it will soon find its way about town, especially if
that carrier-pigeon Caird is in the way"

And the old gentleman, chuckling over his own cleverness in hitting on so happy a device, felt almost reconciled
already to the deprivation which he was doomed to suffer in
the loss of Wilmot's society by the opportunity which it
afforded him of exercising the small social talents, of which
he really possessed a good many, and believed himself to
be endowed with a good many more.

Lady Muriel Kilsyth was at home, likewise Miss Kilsyth;
and her ladyship "received" that afternoon. So Mr Foljambe, who, though an admittedly old man, long past the
elderly stage, and no longer *à prétention* in any sense, was as
welcome a visitor in a London drawing-room as the curliest
of darlings and most irresistible of guardsmen, made his way
nimbly upstairs, and was ushered into the presence of the
two ladies, who formed an exceedingly pretty and effective
domestic group.

Madeleine Kilsyth, who had recovered her beauty, though
a little of her brilliance and her bloom was still wanting, was

drawing, while her step-mother stood a little behind her chair, her dark graceful head bent over her shoulder, and directed her pencil. Mr Foljambe's glance lighted on the two faces as he entered the room, and they inspired him with an instantaneous compliment, which he turned with grace, a little old-fashioned, but the more attractive. They answered him pleasantly ; Lady Muriel gave him her hand ; Madeleine suffered him to take both hers, and repaid the long look of interest with which he regarded her with her sweetest smile ; then resumed her occupation, and listened, as she drew, to the conversation between Lady Muriel and Mr Foljambe.

At first their talk was only of generalities : what the ladies had been doing since they came to London, the extent of Madeleine's drives, how many of their acquaintance had also arrived, the prospects of society for the winter, and cognate topics. They had seen a good deal of Ronald, Lady Muriel told Mr Foljambe ; and her brother's presence had been a great pleasure to Madeleine. A close observer might have thought that Madeleine's expression of countenance did not altogether confirm this statement ; but her old friend was not a close observer of young ladies, and Lady Muriel did not look at her step-daughter as she spoke. After a while Mr Foljambe turned the conversation upon Madeleine's illness, and so, in the easiest and most natural way, introduced Wilmot's name. Lady Muriel's manner of meeting this topic was admirable. She never failed in the *aplomb* which is part of the armour of a woman of the world ; and though she never again could hear Wilmot's name mentioned with real composure, she had the mock article always at hand ; so skilful an imitation as successfully to defy detection.

" A fine fellow, is he not, Lady Muriel ? " said Mr Foljambe, in the tone of a father desirous of hearing the praises of his favourite son.

" Indeed he is," responded Lady Muriel heartily. " He

has laid us under an obligation which we can never discharge or forget. I am sure Kilsyth and I reckon him among the most valued of our friends."

" He took the deepest interest in Miss Kilsyth's case, I know," said Mr Foljambe; "and of course there was everything to excite such a feeling;" and the gallant old gentleman bowed in the direction of Madeleine, who acknowledged the compliment with a most becoming blush.

" It was a very anxious, a very trying time," said Lady Muriel, in the precise tone which suited the sentiment. " I don't know how Kilsyth would have borne it, had it not been for Dr Wilmot. We were much distressed to hear that such bad news awaited him on his return. He found his wife dying, did he not ? "

" He found her dead, Lady Muriel."

There was a pause, during which Madeleine laid aside her pencil, and shaded her face with her hand. The tears were standing in her blue eyes; and while Mr Foljambe proceeded, they streamed unchecked down her face.

" Yes, he found her dead. It was a sudden termination to an illness which had nothing serious in it, to all appearance. But, as many another illness has done, it set all human calculations at naught; and when the bad symptoms set in, it was too late for him to reach her in time. I suppose he has not told you anything about it ? "

" No," said Lady Muriel; "beyond a few words of condolence, to which he made a very brief reply, nothing has been said. I fancy Dr Wilmot is a man but little given to talking of his own affairs or his own feelings."

" Not given to talking of them at all, Lady Muriel. I never met a more reticent man, even with myself; and I flatter myself he has no closer friend, none with whom he is on more confidential terms; he is very reserved in some things. I did not know much of his wife."

" Did you not ? " said Lady Muriel; "how was that ?"

" When I say I did not know much of her," Mr Foljambe explained, " I do not mean that it was from any fault of mine. I called once or twice, but there was something sullen and impenetrable and uninteresting about her, and I never felt any real intimacy with her."

" Indeed ! " said Lady Muriel, " it is impossible to know Dr Wilmot without feeling interested in all that concerns him ; and I have often wished to know what sort of woman his wife was."

" Well, that is precisely what very few persons in the world could have told you ; and I, for one, acknowledge myself astonished at the effect her death has had on Wilmot."

" He is dreadfully cut up by it certainly," said Lady Muriel ; " but I hope, and suppose, he will recover it, as other people have to recover troubles of that and every other kind."

" He is taking the best means of getting over it," said Mr Foljambe ; " and I heartily enter into the notion, and have encouraged him in it. He thinks of going abroad for some time. I know he has been very anxious to study the foreign treatment of diseases in general, and of fever in particular ; and he came to me yesterday and told me he meant to leave London for six months at least. He assigned sound reasons for such a determination, and I think it is the wisest at which he could possibly have arrived."

Lady Muriel rose and rang the bell. The fire required mending, and the brief afternoon twilight rendered the lamps a necessity earlier than usual. When these things had been attended to, she took up the dialogue where it had been broken off with all her accustomed grace and skill.

" I did not know we were about to lose Dr Wilmot for a time," she said. " If all his friends and patients miss him as much as Madeleine Kilsyth and myself are likely to do his absence is likely to create a sensation indeed. And so poor Mrs Wilmot was not a very amiable woman ? "

Mr Foljambe had not said anything about Mrs Wilmot's amiability, or the opposite, but he let the observation pass in sheer bewilderment; and that Lady Muriel Kilsyth understood as well as he did. She went on. " A man like Dr Wilmot must miss companionship at home very much. Of course he can always command the resources of society, but they would not be welcome to him yet awhile. How long does he speak of remaining away, Mr Foljambe ? "

" He did not mention any particular time in talking the matter over with me. His destination is Berlin, I believe. He is anxious to investigate some medical system carried on there, which I need not say neither you nor I know anything about. He was very eloquent upon it, I assure you; and I am glad to perceive that all his trouble has not decreased his interest in the one great object of his life."

" His professional advancement, I suppose ? " said Lady Muriel.

" Well, not exactly that. I think he must retard that by any, and especially by an indefinite, absence. It is rather to his profession itself, to science in the abstract, I allude. He always had a perfect thirst for knowledge, and the greatest powers of application I have ever known any man possessed of. A ' case ' was in his eyes the most important of human affairs. He would throw himself into the interest of his attendance upon a patient with preternatural energy. I am sure you discovered that while he was at Kilsyth."

" Yes indeed; his care of Madeleine was beyond all praise, or indeed description. No doubt, had any other opportunity offered, we should have found, as you say, that such devotion was not a solitary instance."

" Oh no, Wilmot is always the same. You know, I presume, that I required his services very urgently indeed just then; but he would not leave Miss Kilsyth's case for ever so old and near a friend as I am."

Madeleine's colour deepened, and she listened to th.

conversation, in which she had taken no share, with increased
eagerness.

"I know that some one telegraphed to him, but that he
kindly said Madeleine's case being the more urgent of the
two, he would remain with her. And you were none the
worse, it seems, Mr Foljambe?"

"No indeed, Lady Muriel," replied the old gentleman
with a good-humoured smile. "Wilmot's deputy did quite
as well for me as the mighty potentate of medicine himself.
But I acknowledge I was a little annoyed; and if any one
but my old friend Kilsyth's daughter had been the detaining
cause, I should have been tempted to play Wilmot a trick,
by pretending that some extraordinary and entirely novel
symptoms had appeared. He would have come fast enough
then, I warrant you, for the chance of finding out something
new about gout."

Lady Muriel laughed, but Madeleine apparently did not
perceive the joke. Soon some other callers dropped in, and
Mr Foljambe took his leave. But the subject of Wilmot
and his contemplated abandonment of London was not
abandoned on his departure. He was well known to the
" set " in which the Kilsyths moved, though their own acquaintance with him was so recent, and every one had something to say about the rising man. The sentimental view of
the subject was very general. It was so very charming to
think of any man, especially one so talented, so popular, so
altogether delightful as Wilmot, being " broken-hearted " by
the death of his wife. Lady Muriel gently insinuated, once
or twice, a doubt whether there was any ground for this
very congenial but rather romantic supposition : her doubts,
however, were by no means well received, and she found
herself overwhelmed with evidence of the irremediably desolate condition of Wilmot's heart.

When the afternoon calls had come to an end, and Lady
Muriel and her step-daughter were in their respective rooms

and about to dress for dinner, the mind of each was in accord
with that of the other, inasmuch as the same subject of contemplation engrossed both. But the harmony went no
farther. Nothing could be more opposite than the effect
produced upon Madeleine and Lady Muriel by Mr Foljambe's news, and by all the desultory discussion and speculation which had followed its announcement.

To Madeleine the knowledge that she should see Wilmot no more for an indefinite period was like a sentence of
death. The young girl was profoundly unconscious of the
meaning of her own feelings. That the sentiment which she
entertained towards Wilmot was love, she never for a
moment dreamed. In him the ideal of an elevated and
refined fancy had found its realization; he was altogether
different from the men she had hitherto met since her
emancipation from the schoolroom; different from the hunting, shooting devotees of field-sports, or the heavy country
gentlemen given to farming and local politics, who frequented Kilsyth; different from the associates of her brother,
who, whether they were merely fashionable and empty, or
formal and priggish like Ronald himself, were essentially
distasteful to her. She was of a dreamy and romantic
temperament, to which the delicacy of health and the not
quite congenial conditions of her life at home contributed
not a little; and she had seen in Wilmot the man of talent,
action, and resolve, the realization of the nineteenth-century
heroic ideal. To admire and reverence him; to find the
best and most valuable of resources in his friendship, the
wisest and truest guidance in his intellect, the most exquisite
of pleasures in his society; to triumph in his fame, and try
to merit his approval,—such was the girl's scheme for the
future. But it never occurred to her that there was one
comprehensive and forbidden word in which the whole of
this state of feeling might be accurately defined. She had
grieved for Wilmot's grief when she heard of the death of

his wife, but at the same time a subtle instinct, which she
never questioned and could not have defined, told her that
his marriage had not been a happy one, according to her
enthusiastic girlish notion of a happy marriage. She did
not know anything about it; she had no idea what sort of
woman Chudleigh Wilmot's wife was, but she had felt, by
the nameless sense which, had she been an elder woman
with ever so little experience, would have enlightened her
as to the nature of her own feelings, that he was not really
attached to her to the extent which alone seemed to her to
imply happiness in the conjugal relation. So, when Madeleine heard that Wilmot was going abroad, and heard her
step-mother's visitors talk about his being "broken-hearted,"
she felt equally wretched and incredulous. Sentimental
reason for this resolution she did not, she could not accept;
the other was exquisitely painful to her. Had he, indeed,
so absorbing a love for his professional studies? Was he
really occupied by them to the exclusion of all else; had
her "case," and not herself, been his attraction at Kilsyth?
If Mr Foljambe had really resorted to the device he had
spoken of, would Wilmot have left her? To none of these
questions could Madeleine find an answer inside her own
breast, or without it; so they tortured her. Her vision of
seeing him frequently, of making him her friend—the vision
which had so strangely beautified the prospect of her stay
in London,—faded suddenly; and unconscious of all the
idea meant and implied, the girl said to herself, "If he had
cared for me—not as I care for him, of course that could
not be—but ever so little, he would not go away."

Very different were Lady Muriel's meditations. To her
this resolve on the part of Wilmot was peculiarly welcome.
In the first place, she was a thorough woman of the world,
and free from the impetuosity of youth. She was quite
willing to be deprived of Wilmot's society for the present,
if, as she calculated would be the case, he should return

under circumstances which would enable her to reckon with increased security upon gaining the influence over him to which she ardently aspired, to which she aspired more and more ardently as each day proved to her how strong an impulse her life had taken from this new source. She cared little from what motive Wilmot's resolve had sprung. If indeed he had deeply loved, and if indeed he did desperately mourn his wife, the very power and violence of the feeling would react upon itself, and force him to accept consolation all the sooner that he had proved the greatness of his need of it. He would be absent during the dark time when grief forms an eclipse, and he would emerge from its shadow into the brightness which she would cause to shine upon his life. She did not anticipate that his absence would be greatly prolonged, but she did not shrink, even supposing it should be, from the interval. She had enough to do within its duration. Lady Muriel was as thoroughly acquainted with Madeleine's love for Wilmot as the girl was ignorant that she loved him. There was not a corner of her innocent heart which the keen experienced eye of her step-mother had not scanned and examined narrowly.

In Madeleine's perfect ignorance of the real nature of her own feelings Lady Muriel's best security for the success of her wishes and designs lay. As she had no notion that her love was aught but liking, she would be the more easily persuaded that her liking was love. She had a liking for Ramsay Caird. The gay, careless, superficial good-nature of the young man, his easy gentlemanly manners, and the familiarity with which his intercourse with the Kilsyth family was invested in consequence of his relationship to Lady Muriel, were all pleasing to the young girl; and probably, "next to Ronald," she preferred Ramsay Caird to any man of her acquaintance. Of late, too, an unexplained something had come between Madeleine and her brother—a certain restraint, a subtle sense of estrangement—which

Lady Muriel thoroughly understood, but for which Madeleine could not have accounted, and shrunk from acknowledging to herself. This unexplained something, which made her look forward to Ronald's visits with greatly decreased pleasure, and made her involuntarily silent and depressed in his presence, told considerably in Ramsay Caird's favour; for it led to Madeleine's according him an increased share of her attention. The young man was a constant visitor at the Kilsyths'; and there was so much decision in Madeleine's liking for him, that she missed him if by any chance he was absent of an evening, and occasionally was heard to wonder what could have kept Mr Caird away.

Madeleine's delicate health furnished Lady Muriel with a sufficient and reasonable pretext for keeping her at home in the evenings; and she contrived to make it evident that Ramsay Caird's presence constituted a material difference in the dulness or the pleasantness of the little party which assembled with tolerable regularity in the drawing-room. Ronald would come in for an hour or so, and then Madeleine would be particularly *prévenante* towards Ramsay Caird; an innocent and unconscious hypocrisy, poor child, which her step-mother perfectly understood, and which she saw with deep though concealed satisfaction.

On the evening of the day when Mr Foljambe had discussed Wilmot's departure with Lady Muriel and Madeleine, the elder lady was a little embarrassed by the manifest effect on the looks and the spirits of the younger which the intelligence had produced. At dinner Kilsyth perversely chose to descant on the two themes with all a single-minded man's amiable pertinacity, and, of course, without the smallest conception that any connection existed between them. He was quite aggrieved at Wilmot's departure, and called on every one to take notice of Madeleine's looks in confirmation of the loss he and his in particular must sustain by his absence. Ronald was of the party; and he preserved so marked and ungracious a silence, that at length even Kilsyth could not avoid noticing it, and said:

"I suppose you are the only man who knows him, Ronald, who underrates Wilmot; and I really believe you think we make quite an unnecessary fuss about him."

"I by no means underrate the abilities of your medical attendant, sir," Ronald answered in his coldest and driest tone, and, as Madeleine felt in all her shrinking nerves, though she dared not look up to meet it, with a moody searching glance at her; "but, admirable as he may be in his proper capacity and his proper place, I cannot quite appreciate his social importance."

"Just listen to him, Muriel," said Kilsyth in a provoked but yet good-humoured tone. "What wonderful fellows these young men are! He actually talks of a man like Wilmot as if he were a general practitioner or an apothecary's apprentice!"

Lady Muriel interposed, and turned off this somewhat perilous and peace-breaking remark with one of the graceful, skilful generalities of which she always had a supply ready for emergencies. Ronald contented himself with a half-smile of contempt at his father's enthusiastic misrepresentation. Madeleine talked energetically to Ramsay Caird; and the matter dropped.

To be resumed in the drawing-room, however. Madeleine's looks were not improved when her father and the two young men joined her and Lady Muriel. She was dreaming over a book which she was pretending to read, when Kilsyth came up to her, took her chin in his hand, and turned up her face to his and to the light.

Tears were trembling in her blue eyes.

"Hallo, Maddy," said her father, "what's this? You're nervous, my darling! I knew you were not well. Has anything fretted you?—Has anything vexed her, Muriel?"

"No, papa, nothing; nothing at all," said Madeleine, making a strong effort to recover herself. "I have got hold of a sorrowful book, that's all."

"Have you, my dear? then put it away. Let's look at it. Why, it's *Pickwick*, I declare! Maddy, what can ail you? How could you possibly cry over anything in *Pickwick*?"

"I don't know that, sir," said Ramsay, jantily and jovially coming to Madeleine's assistance, without the faintest notion of anything beyond her being "badgered by the governor." "There's the dying clown, you know, and the queer client. I've cried over them myself; or at least I've been very near it." And he sat down beside Madeleine, and applied himself with success to rousing and amusing her. Ronald said nothing, and very soon went away.

"I'm determined on one thing, Muriel," said Kilsyth to his wife when they were alone; "I'll have a long talk with Wilmot before he goes, and get the fullest instructions from him about Madeleine. I have no confidence in any one else in her case, and I'll write to Wilmot about it, and ask him to come here professionally, as soon as he can, the first thing to-morrow morning."

CHAPTER XIX.

ANOTHER TURN OF THE SCREW.

If the interview which had taken place between Chudleigh Wilmot and Henrietta Prendergast had had unfortunate results for the one, it had been proportionably, if not equally, unpleasant to the other. It was impossible that Henrietta could have sustained a more complete discouragement, a more telling and unmistakable defeat, than she felt had befallen her when, after Wilmot had left her, she went over every point of their conversation, and considered the interview in every possible aspect. She had at once, or at least at a very early stage, discerned that some fresh disturbing cause existed in Wilmot's mind. She had seen him, on the memorable occasion of their first interview after his wife's death, horrified, confounded, and unfeignedly distressed. However little he had loved his wife, however passing and shallow the impression made upon him by the sudden and untimely event might prove—and Mrs Prendergast was prepared to find it prove shallow and passing—it had been real, single, intelligible. He had received the painful communication which she had been charged to make to him with surprise, with sorrow—no doubt, in his secret soul, with bitter, regretful, vain remorse. She could only surmise this part of his feelings. He had not departed from the manly reticence which she had expected from him, and for which she admired him; but she never doubted that he had experienced such remorse,—vain, bitter, and regretful.

All the information which had drifted to her knowledge since—and though she was not a distinctly curious or mean-natured woman, Mrs Prendergast was not above cultivating and maintaining friendly relations with Dr Wilmot's household, to all of whom she was as well known, and had been nearly as important, as their late mistress—had confirmed her in the belief that the conduct of the suddenly-bereaved husband had been all that propriety, good feeling, good taste, and good sense could possibly require. She had not precisely defined in her imagination what it was that she looked for and expected in the interview which Wilmot had requested, with a little too much formality, certainly, to be reassuring with regard to any notions she might possibly have entertained with respect to the freedom and intimacy of their future relations. But she did not suffer herself to dwell on that matter of the formality. It was not unnatural;

there are persons, she knew, to whom that sort of thing seems proper when a death—what may be called an intimate death, that is to say—has taken place, who change all their ways and manners for a time, just as they put on mourning and use lugubrious stationery. It was not very like what she would have expected of Wilmot, to enrol himself in the number of these formalists; but she did not allow the circumstance to impress her disagreeably. She possessed patience in as marked a degree as she possessed intelligence—patience, a much rarer and nearly as valuable a quality—and she was satisfied to wait until time should enable her to arrive at the free and frequent association with Wilmot, which was the first step to the end she had in view, and meant to keep in view. She was perfectly clear upon that point; none the less clear that she did not discuss it in her own thoughts, or ponder over it; but she laid it quietly aside, to be produced and acted on when it should be required.

Therefore Henrietta Prendergast was disquieted and disconcerted by the tone and manner which Wilmot had assumed during their interview. Disquieted, because there was something in and under them which she could not fathom; disconcerted, because everything in the interview betrayed and disappointed the expectations she had formed, and because her intention of conveying to Wilmot, by a frank and friendly manner, that it was within his power to continue in his own person the intimacy which had subsisted between herself and his wife, had been utterly routed and nullified.

"There was something in his mind with regard to Mabel," she said to herself, as she sat at her tea in her snug drawing-room on the same afternoon; "there certainly was something in his mind about her which was not in it when I saw him last. I wonder what it is. I wonder whether he has found anything? I am sure she never kept a journal;

I shouldn't think so; I fancy no one ever does in real life, except they are so important as to be wanted for public purposes, or so vain as to think such demand likely. Besides, Mabel's trouble was not tragical; it was only monotonous and uneventful. No; I am sure she did not keep a journal. So he has not found one; and he has not found any letters either. Mabel had very few to keep, and she burnt the scanty collection just as her illness began. I remember coming suddenly into the room, and fluttering the ashes all over her bed and toilet-table by opening the door. Yes, to be sure, the window was open; and she had had a fire kindled on purpose."

Mrs Prendergast leaned her face upon her hand, struck her teaspoon thoughtfully against the edge of the tea-tray, and pondered deeply. She was trying to recall every little incident connected with the dead woman, in the endeavour to discover the secret of Wilmot's demeanour that day.

"Yes, she was sitting by the fire; a sandalwood box was on the floor, and a heap of ashes in the grate. I remember looking rather surprised, and she said, 'You know, Hettie, one never can tell what may happen. You nor I either cannot tell whether I shall ever recover; and it is well to have all things in readiness.' I thought the observation rather absurd particularly, however true it might be generally, and told her so, for she was by no means seriously ill then. She still persisted, however. What a remarkable feature of poor Mabel's illness, by the bye, was her persistent and unalterable belief that she should die! To wish to die, no doubt, assisted it much at the end; but the conviction laid hold on her from the first."

Then Mrs Prendergast remembered how Mrs Wilmot had left everything in readiness; every article of household property, all her own private possessions, everything which had claimed her care, provided for; and though she knew that instances of such a morbid state of mind were not altogether wanting in the case of women in Mrs Wilmot's state of health, she did not feel that such an hypothesis accounted for this particular case satisfactorily. In all other respects there had been such equality of disposition, common sense, and absence of fancifulness about her friend, that she could not accept the explanation which suggested itself. This was not the first time that she had thought over this circumstance. It had been brought before her very forcibly when a packet was sent to her, with a kind but formal note from Wilmot, a day or two after his wife's funeral; which packet contained a few articles of jewelry and general ornament, and a strip of paper, bearing merely the words: "I wish these to be given to Mrs Prendergast.—M. W "

But now it assumed a more puzzling importance and deeper interest. Had Wilmot found anything among all her orderly possessions which had thrown any new light upon her life? Had he had a misunderstanding with Dr Whittaker? Did he think his wife's life had been sacrificed by want of care, or want of attention or of skill? Had remorse seized him on this account, when he had succeeded in defeating its attacks, in consequence of the revelation which she had made to him?. Had he regained incredulity or indifference as regarded the years which had passed in miscomprehension, to be roused into inquietude and stern self-reproach by an appeal to his master-passion, his professional knowledge and attainments? If this were so, there would at least be some measure of punishment allotted to Chudleigh Wilmot; for he was a proud man, and sensitive on that point, if not on any other.

Henrietta Prendergast was well disposed towards Wilmot now, in the new aspect of affairs, and contemplating as she did certain dim future possibilities very grateful to her pertinacious disposition. But she was not sorry to think that he had something to suffer; and that something of a nature to oppress his spirits considerably, and render him indifferent to the attractions of society. Before this desirable effect should have worn off, she would have contrived to make herself necessary to him. She had but little doubt of her power to accomplish this, if only the opportunity were afforded her. She knew she had plenty of ability, not of a kind which Wilmot would dislike, and certainly of a quality for which he did not give her credit. She had less attraction than Mabel, so far as good looks would go, but that would not be very far, she thought, with Dr Wilmot. He might never care for her even so much as he had cared for Mabel; but his feelings towards her, if evoked at all, would be different, much more satisfactory, and to her mind, which was properly organized, quite sufficient.

If Henrietta's day-dreams were of a more sober colour, they were no less unreal than the rosiest and most extravagant vision ever woven by youthful fancy. She had not seen Madeleine Kilsyth. She had indeed understood and witnessed Mabel's jealousy, aroused by the devotion of her husband to the young Scotch girl. But she thought little of danger from this quarter. She had always understood —having a larger intellect and a wider perception, and above all, being an unconcerned spectator, uninjured by it in her affections or her rights—Wilmot's absorption in his profession much better than his wife had understood it. Something in her own nature, dim and undeveloped, answered to this absorption.

" If I had had any pursuit in life, I should have followed it just as eagerly; if I had had a career, I should have devoted myself to it just as entirely," had been her frequent mental comment upon Wilmot's conduct. She quite understood the effect it produced on a woman of Mabel's temperament, was perfectly convinced that it could not produce a similar effect on a woman of her own; but also believed that no such conduct would ever have been pursued towards her. The very something which enabled her to sympathize with him would have secured her from exclusion from the reality and the meaning of his life. "At least I should interest him," she had often said to herself, when she had seen how entirely Mabel failed to inspire him with interest; and in her lengthened cogitations on the evening of the day which had been marked by Wilmot's visit, she repeated the assurance with renewed conviction.

It was not that the remembrance of Miss Kilsyth did not occur to her very strongly; on the contrary, it occupied its full share of her mind and attention. But she disposed of the subject very comfortably and finally by dwelling on the following points:

First, the distinction of rank and the difference in age between Miss Kilsyth and Dr Wilmot were both considerable, important, and likely to form very efficient barriers against any extravagant notions on his part. Supposing— an unlikely supposition in the case of a man who added remarkable good sense to exceptional talent—he were to overlook this distinction of rank and difference of age, it was not probable that the young lady's relatives would accommodate themselves to any such blindness; while it was extremely probable they would regard any project on his part with respect to her as unmitigated presumption.

So far she had pursued her cogitations without regard to the young girl herself—to this brilliant young beauty, upon whom, endowed with youth, beauty, rank, the prestige of one of the most fashionable and popular women in London (for Henrietta Prendergast had her relations with the great world, though she was not of it), life was just opening in the fulness of joy and splendour. But when she turned her attention in that direction, she found nothing to discourage her, nothing to fear. What could be more wildly improbable than that Chudleigh Wilmot should have made any impression on Miss Kilsyth of a nature to lead to the realization of any hope which might suggest itself to the new-made widower? Henrietta Prendergast was not a woman of much delicacy of mind or refinement of sentiment—if she had been, such self-communing as that of this evening would have been impossible within three weeks of her friend's death—but she was not so coarse, or indeed so ignorant of the nature and training of women like Madeleine Kilsyth, as to conceive the possibility of the girl's having fallen in love with a married man, even had that married man been of a far more captivating type than that presented by Chudleigh Wilmot. Madeleine's stepmother had not been restrained from such a suspicion by any superfluous delicacy; but Lady Muriel had an incentive to clear-sightedness which was wanting in Henrietta's case; and it must be said in justification of the acute woman of the world, that she was satisfied of the girl's perfect unconsciousness of the real nature of the sentiment which her jealous quick-sightedness had detected almost in the first hours of its existence.

The disqualification of his marriage removed, Henrietta still thought there could be nothing to dread. The reminiscences attached to the doctor who had attended her through a long illness, was said to have saved her life and had made himself very agreeable to his patient, were no doubt frankly kind and grateful; but they were very unlikely to be sentimental, and the opportunities which might come in his way for rendering the tie already established stronger would be probably limited. "If anything were to be feared in that quarter," thought Henrietta, "and one could only manage to get a hint conveyed to Lady Muriel, the thing would be done at once."

Henrietta pronounced this opinion in her own mind with perfect confidence. And she was right. If Lady

Muriel Kilsyth had had no more interest in Wilmot than that which during his sojourn at Kilsyth he might have inspired in the least important inmate of the house, she would have acted precisely as she had done. This was her strong tower of defence, her excuse, her justification. If Wilmot's admiration of her step-daughter had not had in it the least element of offence to herself, she would at once have opposed it, have endeavoured to prevent its growth and manifestation, just as assiduously as she had done. Herein was her safety. So, though Henrietta Prendergast was entirely unaware of anything that had taken place; though she had never spoken to Lady Muriel in her life, she had, as it happened, speculated upon her quite correctly. So her self-conference came to a close, without any misgiving, discouragement, or hesitation.

"Mabel knew some people who knew the Kilsyths," Henrietta Prendergast had said to Wilmot in their first interview; but she had not mentioned that the people who knew the Kilsyths were acquaintances of hers, and that she had been present on the occasion when Mabel had acquired all the information which she had taken to heart so keenly. Such was, however, the case; and Henrietta made up her mind, when she had reasoned herself out of the first feeling of discouragement which her interview with Wilmot had caused, though not out of the conviction that there was something in his mind which she had not been able to come at, that she would call on Mrs and Miss Charlwood without delay. She might not learn anything about Wilmot by so doing, but she could easily introduce the Kilsyths into the conversation; and it could not fail to be useful to her to gain a clear insight into what sort of people they were, and especially to know whether Miss Kilsyth had any declared or supposed admirers as yet. So she went to bed that night with her mind tolerably easy on the whole, though her last waking thought was of the strange something in Chudleigh

Wilmot's manner which she had not been able to penetrate.

It chanced, however, that Mrs Prendergast did not fulfil her intention so soon as she had purposed. On waking the following morning, she found that she had taken cold, a rather severe cold. She was habitually careful of her health, and as the business on which she had intended to go out was not pressing, she thought it wiser to remain at home. The next day she was no better; the day after a little worse. On the fourth day she thought she should be justified in asking Wilmot to give her a call. On the very rare occasions when she had required medical attendance she had had recourse to her friend's husband; and it occurred to her that the present opportunity was favourable for impressing him with a sense that she desired to maintain the former relation unbroken. To increase and intensify it would be her business later.

So Mrs Prendergast sent for Dr Wilmot; but in answer to the summons Dr Whittaker presented himself.

They had not met since they had stood together by Mabel's death-bed, and the recollection softened Henrietta, though she felt at once surprised and angry at the substitution.

"I am doing Wilmot's work, except in the very particular cases," Dr Whittaker explained.

"Indeed! Then Dr Wilmot knew, in some strange way, that mine was not a particular case!" Henrietta answered, with an exhibition of pique as unusual in her as it was unflattering to Dr Whittaker.

"My dear Mrs Prendergast," expostulated the doctor mildly, "your note—I saw it in the regular way of business—said 'merely a cold;' and Wilmot and I both know you always say what you mean—no more and no less."

Henrietta smiled rather grimly as she replied, "I must say, you are adroit in turning a slight into a compliment. And now we will talk about my cold."

They did talk about her cold, and Dr Whittaker duly prescribed for it, emphatically forbidding exposure to the weather. Just as he rose to take leave, Henrietta asked him what sort of spirits Wilmot appeared to be in.

" Very low indeed," said Dr Whittaker; " but I think the change of air will do him good."

The change was likely to be sufficiently profitable to Dr Whittaker to make it only natural that he should regard it with warm approbation, without reflecting very severely upon his sincerity either; he was but human, and not particularly prosperous.

" What change ?" asked Henrietta in a tone which had not all the indifference which she had desired to lend it. (Dr Whittaker had seen and guessed enough to make it just that he should not look for much warmth from Mabel's friend in speaking of Mabel's husband; and Mrs Prendergast never overlooked the relative positions in any situation.)

" What! don't you know, then ? He is going abroad— going to Paris, and then to Berlin, partly to recruit, and partly to inquire into some new theory about fever they've got there. I don't generally think much of their theories myself, especially in Berlin."

But Dr Whittaker's opinions had no interest for Henrietta. His news occupied her. She did not altogether like this move. She did not believe in either of the reasons assigned; she felt certain there was something behind them both, and that that something had been in Wilmot's mind when she last saw him. What was it ? Was he flying from a memory or a presence ? If the former, then something more than she was in possession of had come to his knowledge concerning Mabel; for much as he had been shocked, and intensely as he had felt all she had told him, Henrietta knew Wilmot too well to believe for a moment that the present resolution was to be traced to that source. If the latter, the presence must be that of Miss Kilsyth ; and there

must be dangers in her way, complications in this matter
she did not understand, some grave error in her calculation.
True, he might be flying away in despair; but that could
hardly be. In so short an interval of time it was impossible
he could have dared or even tried his fate. It was the un-
expectedness of this occurrence that gave it so much power
to trouble Henrietta. She had made a careful calculation;
but this was outside it, and it puzzled her. She took leave
of Dr Whittaker, while these and many more equally distracting thoughts passed through her mind, in a sufficiently
absent manner, and listened to his expression of a sanguine
hope of finding her much better on the morrow through a
sedulous observance of his advice, with as much indifference
as though he had been talking about somebody else's cold.
When he had left her, she sat still for a while; then put on
her warmest attire, sent for a cab, and, utterly regardless of
Dr Whittaker's prohibition, drove straight to Mrs Charlton's
house in South-street, Park-lane.

Mrs Prendergast's cab drew up behind a carriage which
had just stopped before Mrs Charlton's door, at that moment
opened in reply to the defiant summons of the footman, who
was none other than one of the ambrosial Mercuries in attendance on Lady Muriel Kilsyth. An elderly lady, rather
oddly dressed, descended from the equipage, bestowed a
familiar nod upon its remaining occupant from the steps,
and walked into the house. Mrs Prendergast was then admitted; and as the carriage which made way for her was
displaced, she recognized in the face of the lady who sat in it
Lady Muriel Kilsyth.

"That is very odd," she thought; "I wonder who she
has set down here, and why she has not come in herself."

Immediately afterwards she was exchanging the customary *fadeurs* with Mrs Charlton, and had been presented by
that lady to Mrs M'Diarmid.

Wonderfully voluble was Mrs M'Diarmid, to be sure, and

communicative to a degree which, if her audience did not
happen to be vehemently interested in the matter of her discourse, must have been occasionally a little overpowering
and wearisome. Mrs M'Diarmid, being at present staying
with the Kilsyths, could not talk of anything but the Kilsyths ; a state of things rather distressing to Mrs Charlton,
who was an eminently well-bred person, and perfectly aware
that Mrs Prendergast was not acquainted with the people
under discussion. But to arrest Mrs M'Diarmid in the full
tide of her discourse was a feat which a few adventurous
spirits had indeed attempted, but in which no one had ever
succeeded. Mrs Charlton's was not an adventurous spirit ;
she merely suffered, and was not strong, but derived sensible
consolation after a while from observing that Mrs Prendergast either had the tact and the manners to assume an aspect
of perfect contentment, or really did feel an interest in the
affairs of strangers, which to her, Mrs Charlton, was inexplicable. She had much regard for Henrietta, and considerable
respect for her intellect ; so she preferred the former hypothesis, and adopted it.

"And she told me to tell you how sorry she was she
could not possibly come in to-day; but she had to fetch
Kilsyth at his club, and then go home and dress for a ride
with him, and send the carriage for me. I must run away
the moment it comes, and get back to Maddy." This, after
Mrs M'Diarmid had run on uninterruptedly for about a
quarter of an hour, with details of every kind concerning the
house and the servants, the health, spirits, employments,
and engagements of the family.

"Miss Kilsyth is still delicate, I think you said ?" Mrs
Charlton at length contrived to say.

"Yes, indeed, very delicate. My dear, the child mopes
—she really mopes; and I can't bear to see young people
moping, though it seems the fashion nowadays for all the
young people to think themselves not only wiser but sadder

than their elders. Just to see Ronald beside his father, **my
dear!** The difference! And to think he'll be Kilsyth of
Kilsyth some day; and what will the poor people do then?
He'll make them go to school, and have 'em drilled, I'm sure
he will; not that he is not a fine young man, my dear, and
a good one—we must all admit that; but he is not like his
father, and never will be—never. And, for my part, I don't
wonder Maddy's afraid of him, for I'm sure I am."

"But I thought Miss Kilsyth and her brother were so
particularly attached to each other," said Mrs Charlton,
yielding at length to the temptation to gossip.

"So they are, so they are.—I'm sure, Mrs Prendergast,"
said Mrs M'Diarmid, turning to Henrietta, "a better brother
than Ronald Kilsyth never lived; but then he *is* dictatorial,
I *must* say that; and he never will believe or remember that
Madeleine is not a child now, and that it is absurd and useless to treat a woman just as one would treat a child. He
makes such a fuss about every one Maddy sees, and everywhere she goes to, and is positively disagreeable about any
one she seems to fancy."

"Well," said Mrs Charlton, "but I'm not sure that he
is wrong to be particular about his sister's fancies. The
fancies of a young lady of Miss Kilsyth's beauty and pretensions are not trifling matters. Has she any *very* strongly
pronounced?"

"Bless your heart, no!" exclaimed Mrs M'Diarmid, her
vulgarity evoked by her earnestness. "The girl is fonder of
himself and her father than of any one in the world, and I
really don't think she ever had a thought hid from them.
But Ronald *will* interfere so; he bothered about the silliness
of young ladies' correspondence until he worried her into
giving up writing to Bessy Ravenshaw; and he lectured for
ten minutes because she wrote to poor Dr Wilmot on her
own account."

"How very absurd!" said Mrs Charlton; "he had better take care he does not worry her by excess of brotherly love and authority into finding her home so unbearable, that she may make a wretched hurried marriage in order to get away from it. Such things *have* been;" and Mrs Charlton sighed, as if she spoke from some close experience of "such things."

"Very true, very true—I am sure I often wish the poor dear child was well married. I must say for Lady Muriel, I think she is an admirable step-mother. It is such a difficult position, Mrs Prendergast, so invidious; still, you know, it never can be exactly the same thing; and then, you know, there are the little girls to grow up, and there will be the natural jealousy—about Maddy's fortune, you know; and altogether *I do* think it would be very nice."

"I should think a good many others think it would be very nice also," said Mrs Charlton.

"Well, I don't know—it is hard to say—young men are so different now-a-days from what they were in my time; they seem to be afraid of marrying. I really don't think Maddy has ever had an offer."

"Depend on it that story will soon be changed. She is, to my knowledge, immensely admired. Her illness made quite a sensation, and the romantic story of the famous Dr Wilmot's devotion to the patient."

"I think you should say to the *case*," struck in Henrietta. "I know Dr Wilmot very well, and I can fancy any amount of devotion to the fever and its cure; but Wilmot devoted to a patient I cannot understand."

Something in her voice and manner conveyed an unpleasant impression to both her hearers. Mrs Charlton looked calmly surprised; Mrs M'Diarmid looked distressed and rather angry. She wished she had been more cautious in telling of the Kilsyths before this lady, who did not know them, but who did know Dr Wilmot. She felt that Mrs Prendergast had put a meaning into what Mrs Charlton had said, in which there was something at least indirectly slighting and derogatory to Madeleine; and the feeling made her hot and angry. Mrs Charlton's suavity extricated them from the difficulty, which all felt, and one intended.

"I didn't quite understand the distinction," she said; "of course I understand it as you put it, but mine was merely a *façon de parler*. Dr Wilmot's devotion to his profession has long been known, and he has succeeded as such devotion deserves."

"Yes, indeed, Mrs Charlton," said Henrietta heartily, and slipping with infinite ease into the peculiar manner which implies such intimacy with the person complimented as to make the praise almost a personal favour. "He has paid dearly indeed for his devotion, in the very instance you mention, Mrs M'Diarmid."

"How so?" said Mrs M'Diarmid, off her guard, and rather huffily.

"Ah, poor fellow! I can hardly bear to talk of it; but as I was his poor wife's closest friend, and with her when she died, I think it is only fair and just to him to tell the truth. Of course he had no notion of his wife's danger—no one could have had; but he never can or will forgive himself for his absence from her. You will not wonder that he should feel it dreadfully, and that his self-reproach is intolerable. 'I suppose,' he said, in one of his worst fits of grief, 'people will think I stayed at Kilsyth because Kilsyth is a great man; but you, Henrietta, you know me better. If she had been his dairymaid, instead of his daughter, it would have been all one to me.' And that was perfectly true; he knows no distinction in the pursuit of his duties. It was a terrible coincidence; but nothing can persuade him to regard it merely as a coincidence. It is fortunate your young friend is restored to health, Mrs M'Diarmid."

"Yes," said that lady, now pale, and looking the image of disconcerted distress.

"Fortunate for her, of course; but also fortunate for him. You will excuse my telling you, of course; nothing in the whole matter reflects in the least on the Kilsyth family —and I cannot forbear from saying what must exalt him still more in your esteem, but you cannot conceive how painful to him any reference to that fatal time is. He has wonderful self-control and firmness; but they were severely taxed, I assure you, when he had to make a call on Lady Muriel and Miss Kilsyth. I daresay he didn't show it."

"Not in the least," said Mrs M'Diarmid.

Oh no; he is essentially a strong man. But he suffered. You would know how much, if you had seen him when he had finally made up his mind to go abroad, and get out of the remembrance of it all, so far as he could. Poor Miss Kilsyth! one pities a young girl to have been even the perfectly innocent cause of such a calamity to any man, and especially to one who rendered her such a service. However, people who talk about it now will have forgotten it all long before he comes back."

At this juncture Miss Charlton entered the room and warmly greeted Henrietta. Mrs Prendergast was an authority in the art of illuminating, to which Miss Charlton devoted her harmless life.

Presently Lady Muriel's carriage came for Mrs M'Diarmid, and that good woman went away, and might have been heard to say many times during the silent drive:

" My poor Maddy! my poor dear child! "

Chudleigh Wilmot had entertained, it has been seen, vague fears that Mrs Prendergast might talk about him; but of all possible shapes they had never taken this one.

CHAPTER XX.

A COUP MANQUÉ.

IT has been said that Mrs M'Diarmid took an earnest motherly interest in Madeleine Kilsyth; but the bare statement is by no means sufficient to explain the real feelings entertained towards the somewhat forlorn motherless girl by the brisk, energetic, vulgar little woman of the world, who was her connection by marriage. Such affections spring up in many female breasts which, to all outward appearance, are most unpromising soil; they need no cultivation, no looking after, no watering with the tears of sympathy or gratitude, no raking or hoeing or binding up. They are ruthlessly lopped off in their tenderest shoots; but they grow again, and twine away round the "object" as parasitically as ever. Mrs M'Diarmid's regard for Madeleine was quite of the parasitical type in its best sense, be it always understood. She loved the young girl with all her heart and soul, and would as soon have dreamed of inspiring as of "carneying" her, as she expressed it. Her love for Madeleine was pure and simple and unaffected, deep-seated and capable of producing great results; but it was of the "poor-dear" school after all.

Nothing, for instance, could persuade Mrs M'Diarmid that Madeleine was not very much to be pitied in every act and circumstance of her life. The fact of having a step-mother was in itself a burden sufficient to break the spirit of any ordinarily-constituted young woman, according to Mrs Mac's idea. Not but that Mrs Mac and Lady Muriel "got on very well together," according to the former lady's phraseology; not but that Lady M. (whom she was usually accustomed to speak of when extra emphasis was required, as Lady Hem) did her duty by Madeleine perfectly and thoroughly; but still, as Mrs Mac would confess, "she was not one of them; she was of a different family; and what could you expect out of your own blood and bone?" "One of them" meant of the Kilsyth family, of which Mrs M'Diarmid, to a certain portion of her acquaintance, described herself as a component part. In the late summer and the early autumn, when the Kilsyths and all their friends had left town, dear old Mrs M'Diarmid would revel in the light with which, though her suns of fashion had set, her horizon was still illumined. When the grandees of Belgravia and Tyburnia have sped northward in the long pre-engaged seat of the limited mail; when they are coasting round the ever-verdant Island, or lounging in all the glory of pseudo-naval get-up on the pier at Ryde, there is yet corn in Egypt, balm in Gilead, and fine weather in the suburbs of London. Many of Mrs M'Diarmid's acquaintance, formed in the earlier and ante-married portion of her life, were found in London during those months. Some had been away to Ramsgate and Margate with their children in June; others, unable to "get away from business," had compromised the matter with their wives by taking a cottage at Richmond or Staines, and running backwards and forwards from town for a month, and staying at home on the Saturday. To these worthy people Mrs M'Diarmid was the connecting link between them and that fashionable world, of whose doings they read so religiously every Saturday in the fashionable journal. For her news, her talk, her appearance, they loved this old lady, and paid her the greatest court. From some of them she received brevet rank, and was spoken of as the Honourable Mrs M'Diarmid; from all she received kindness and—what she never gave herself—toadyism. Pleasant dinners at the furnished cottages at Richmond and Staines, Star-and-Garter refections, picnics on the river; what was even more delicious, a croquet-party on the lawn, tea, and an early supper, with some singing

afterwards—all these delights were provided by her acquaintances for Mrs M'Diarmid, who had nothing to do
but to sit still, and be taken about; to recall a few of the
scenes of her past season's gaiety; to drop occasionally the
names of a few of her grand acquaintance, and to have it
thoroughly understood that she was "one of them."

Use is second nature; and by dint of perpetually repeating that she was "one of them," Mrs M'Diarmid had
almost begun to forget the lodging-house and its associations, and to believe that she was a blood-relation of the
old house of Kilsyth. It did the old lady no harm, this innocent self-deception, it did not render her insolent, arro-
gant, or stuck-up; it did not for an instant tend to render
her forgetful of her position in the household, and it did
perhaps increase the fond maternal affection which she entertained for Madeleine. How could Lady Muriel feel for
that girl like one of her own blood? Besides, had she not
now children of her own, about whose future she was
naturally anxious, and whose future might clash with that
of her step-daughter? Whose future? Ay, it was about
Madeleine's future that she was so anxious; and just about
this stage in our history Mrs M'Diarmid, revolving all
these things in her mind, set herself seriously to consider
what Madeleine's future should be.

To a woman of Mrs M'Diarmid's stamp the future of a
young girl, it is almost needless to say, meant her marriage.
Notwithstanding all the shams which, to use Mr Carlyle's
phrases, have been exploded, all the Babeldoms which have
been talked out, all the mockeries, delusions, and snares
which have been exposed, it yet remains that marriage
is the be-all and end-all of the British maiden's existence.
That accomplished, life shuts up, or is of no account, with
the orange-flowers and the tinkling bells, the ring, the oath,
and the blessing; all that childhood has played at, and
maidenhood has dreamed of, is at an end. The husband is

secured; and so long as he is in the requisite position and possesses the requisite means—*vogue la galère*, in its most respectable translation, be it understood—all that is requisite on friends' part has been done. We laugh when we hear that a charwoman offers to produce her "marriage-lines" in proof of her respectability; but we slur over the fact that in our own social status we are content to aim at the dignity achieved by the charwoman's certificate, and not to look beyond into the future thereby opened

Madeleine's marriage? Yes; Mrs M'Diarmid had turned that subject over in her mind a hundred thousand times; had chewed the cud of it until all taste therein had been exhausted; had had all sorts of preposterous visions connected therewith, none of which had the smallest waking foundation. Madeleine's marriage? It was by her own marriage that Mrs M'Diarmid had made her one grand *coup* in life, and consequently she attached the greatest value to it. She was always picturing to herself Madeleine married to each or one of the different visitors in Brook-street; seeing her walking up the aisle with one, standing at the altar-rails with another, muttering "I will" to a third, and shyly looking up after signing the register with a fourth. The old lady had the good sense to keep these mental pictures in her own mental portfolio, but still she was perpetually drawing them forth for her own mental delectation. None of the young men who were in the habit of dropping in in Brook-street for a cup of afternoon tea and a social chat had any notion of the wondrous scenes passing through the brain of the quiet elderly lady, whom they all liked and all laughed at. None of them knew that in Mrs Mac's mind's eye, as they sat there placidly sipping their tea and talking their nonsense, they were transfigured; that their ordinary raiment was changed into the blue coat and yellow waistcoat dear to this valentine artist; that from their coat-collar grew the attenuated spire of a village

church, and that sounds of chiming bells drowned their
voices.   Madeleine as a countess presented at a drawing-
room "on her marriage;" Madeleine receiving a brilliant
circle as the wife of a brilliant member of the House of
Commons; Madeleine doing the honours of the British
embassy at the best and most distinguished legation which
happened at the time to be vacant.   All these pictures had
presented themselves to Mrs M'Diarmid, and been filled
up by her mentally in outline and detail.   Other supple-
mentary pictures were there in the same gallery. Madeleine
presenting new colours to the gallant 140th as the wife of
their colonel; Madeleine landing from the Amphitrite,
amidst the cheers of her crew, as the wife of their admiral;
Madeleine graciously receiving the million pounds' worth
of pearls and diamonds which the native Indian princes offered to the wife of their governor-general.   All these different shiftings of the glasses of the magic lantern appeared
to Mrs M'Diarmid as she noticed the attention paid to
Madeleine by the different visitors in Brook-street.

But these, after all, were mere day-dreams, and it was
time Mrs M'Diarmid thought that some real and satisfactory
match should be arranged for her dear child.   Since the
return of the family from Scotland, after Madeleine's illness,
Mrs M'Diarmid either had noticed, or fancied she had
noticed, that Lady Muriel was less interested in her step-
daughter than ever, more inclined to let her have her own
way, less particular as to who sought her society.   Under
these circumstances, not merely did Mrs M'Diarmid's dragon
watchfulness increase tenfold, but the necessity of speedily
taking her darling into a different atmosphere, and surrounding her with other cares and hopes in life, made itself doubly
apparent.   For hours and hours the old lady sat in her own
little room, cosy little room,—neat, tidy, clean, and whole-
some-looking as the old lady herself,—revolving different
matrimonial schemes in her mind, guessing at incomes,

weighing dispositions, thinking over the traits and character-
istics, the health and position of every marriageable man of
her acquaintance. And all to no purpose; for the old lady,
though a tolerably shrewd and worldly-wise old lady, was a
good woman: in the early days of the lodging-house she had
had a spirit of religion properly instilled into her; and this,
aided by her genuine and unselfish love for Madeleine, would
have prevented her from wishing to see the girl married to
any one, no matter what were his wealth, position, and
general eligibility, unless there was the prospect of her darling's life being a happy one with him. "I don't see my way
clear, my dear," she would say to Mrs Tonkley, the most
intimate of her early life acquaintances, and the only one
whom the old lady admitted into her confidence (Mrs Tonkley had been Sarah Simmons, daughter of Simmons's private
hotel, and had married Tonkley, London representative of
Blades and Buckhorn of Sheffield),—"I don't see my way
clear in this business, my dear, and that's the truth. Powers
forbid my Madeleine should marry an old man, though
among our people it's considered to be about the best thing
that could happen to a girl, provided he's old enough, and
rich into the bargain. Why, there are old fellows, tottering
old wretches, that crawl about with mineral teeth in their
mouths and other people's hair on their heads, and they'd
only have to say, 'Will you?' to some of the prettiest and
the best-born girls in England, and they'd get the answer
'Yes' directly minute! No, no; I've seen too much of
that. Not to name names, there's one old fellow, a lord and
a general, all stars and garters and crosses and ribbons, and
two seasons ago he carried off a lovely girl. I won't put a
name to her, my dear, but you've seen her photographic
likeness in the portrait-shops; and what is it now? Divorced?
Lord, no, my dear; that sort of thing's never done amongst
us, nor even separation, so far as the world knows. Oh no;
they live very happily together, to all outward show, and she

has her opera-box, and jewels as much as she can wear; but, Lor' bless you, I hear what the young fellows say who come to our house about the way she goes on, and the men who are always about her, and who was meant by the stars and blanks in last week's *Dustman*. No, no; no old wretch for Madeleine; nor any of your fast boys either, with their drags and their yachts, and their hunters and their Market Harboroughs, and their Queen's Benches, I tell 'em; for that's what it'll come to. You can't build a house of paper, specially of stamped paper, to last very long; and though you touch it up every three months or so, at about the end of a year down it goes with a run, and you and your wife and the lot of you go with it! That would be a pleasant ending for my child, to have to live at Bolong on what her husband got by winning at cards from the foreigners; and that's not likely to be much, I should think. No; that would never do. I declare to you, my dear Sarah, when I think about that dear girl's future, I am that driven as to be at my wits' end."

There was another reason for the old lady's feeling "driven" when thinking over her dear girl's future which she never imparted to her dear Sarah, nor indeed to any one else, but which she crooned over constantly, and relished less and less after each spell of consideration, and that was the evident intention of Lady Muriel with regard to Ramsay Caird. Mrs M'Diarmid, though a woman of strong feelings, rarely, if ever, took antipathies; but certainly her strong aversion to Ramsay Caird could be called by no other name. She hated him cordially, and took very little pains to conceal her dislike, though, if she had been called upon, she would have found it difficult to define the reasons for her prejudice. It was probably the obvious purpose for which he had been introduced into the family, which the old lady immediately divined and as immediately execrated, that made her his enemy; but she could not put forward this reason, and she had no other to offer. She used to say to herself that he was a "down-looking fellow," which was metaphorical, inasmuch as Ramsay Caird had rather a frank and free expression, though, to one more versed in physiognomy than Mrs M'Diarmid, there certainly was a shifty expression in his eyes. She hated to see him paying attention to Madeleine, bending over her, hovering near her—in her self-communion the old lady declared that it gave her "the creeps"—and it was with great difficulty that she refrained when present from actually shuddering. It was lucky that she did so refrain; for Lady Muriel, who brooked no interference with her plans, would have ruthlessly given Mrs Mac her *congé*, and closed the doors of Brook-street against her for ever.

To find some one so eligible that Kilsyth would take a fancy to him—a fancy which Lady Muriel could not, in common honesty, combat—and thus to get rid of Ramsay Caird and his pretensions to Madeleine's hand,—this was Mrs M'Diarmid's great object in life. But she had pottered hopelessly about it; and it is probable that she would never have succeeded in getting the smallest clue to what, if properly carried through, might really have led to the accomplishment of her hopes, had it not been for her own kindness of heart, which led her to spend many of her leisure half-hours in the nursery with Lady Muriel's little girls. Sitting one day with these little ladies, but in truth not attending much to their prattle, being occupied in her favourite daydream, Mrs M'Diarmid was startled by hearing an observation which at once interested her, and caused her to attend to the little ladies' conversation.

"When you grow up, Maud, will you be like Maddy?" asked little Ethel.

"I don't know," replied her sister. "I think I shall be quite as pretty as Maddy; and I'm sure I sha'n't be half so dull."

"You don't know that! People are only dull because

they can't help it. They're not dull on purpose; only because they can't help it."

"Well, then, I shall help it," said Maud in an imperious way. "Besides, it's not always that Maddy's dull; she's only dull since we've been back in London; she wasn't dull at Kilsyth."

"Ah, no one was dull at Kilsyth," said little Ethel with a sigh.

"Oh, we all know what you mean by that, Ethel," said Maud. "You silly sentimental child, you were happy at Kilsyth because you had *some one* with you."

"Well, it's no use talking to you, Maud; because you're a dreadful flirt, and care for no one in particular, and like to have a heap of men always round you. But wasn't Madeleine happy at Kilsyth because she had *some one* with her?"

"Why, you don't mean that Lord Roderick?"

"Lord Roderick, indeed! I should think not," said little Ethel, flushing scarlet. "Madeleine's 'some one' was much older and graver and wiser and sterner, and nothing like so good-looking."

"Ethel dear, you talk like a child!" said Maud, who, by virtue of her twelvemonth's seniority, gave herself quite maternal airs towards her sister. "Of course I see you're alluding to Dr Wilmot; but you can't imagine that Maddy cared for him in any way but that of a—a friend who was grateful to him—for—"

"Oh yes! 'Your grateful patient,' we know! Maddy did not know how to end her note to him the other morning, and I kept suggesting all kinds of things: 'yours lovingly,' and 'yours eternally,' and 'your own devoted;' and made Madge blush awfully; and at last she put that. 'Grateful patient'! grateful rubbish! You hadn't half such opportunities as I had of seeing them together at Kilsyth, Maud."

"I'm not half so romantic and sentimental, Ethel; and I can see a doctor talking to a girl about her illness without fancying he's madly in love with her. And now I am going to my music." And Maud pranced out of the room.

And then Mrs M'Diarmid, who had greedily swallowed every word of this conversation between the children, laid down the book over which she had been nodding; and going up to little Ethel, gave herself over to the task of learning from the child her impressions of the state of Madeleine's feelings towards Dr Wilmot, and of gleaning as much as she could of all that passed between them at Kilsyth; the result being that little Ethel, who was, as her sister had said, sentiment-ally and romantically inclined, led her old friend to believe, first, that Madeleine was deeply attached to the doctor, and, secondly, that the doctor was inclined to respond promptly to the young lady's sentiments.

That night Mrs M'Diarmid remained at home, for the purpose of " putting on her considering cap," as she phrased it, and steadily looking at the question of Madeleine's future in the new light now surrounding it. Like all other old ladies, she had a *tendresse* for the medical profession; and though she had never met Dr Wilmot, she had often heard of him, and had taken great interest in his rise and progress. And this was the man who was to fulfil her expectations, and to prevent Madeleine's being sacrificed to a sordid or disagree-able match ? It really seemed like it. Dr Wilmot was in the prime of life, was highly thought of and esteemed by all who knew him, was essentially a man of mark in the world, and must be in the enjoyment of a very lucrative practice. Practice ? ay, that was rather awkward ! Kilsyth would not care much about having a son-in-law who was in practice, and at the beck and call of every hypochondriacal old woman ; and Lady Muriel would, Mrs Mac was certain, refuse to enter-tain such a notion. And yet Dr Wilmot was in every other respect so eligible ; it was a thousand pities ! Dr Wilmot ! Yes, there it was ; that " Doctor " would stick to him through life ; and he, from all she had heard of him, was just the man

to be proud of the title, and refuse to be addressed by any
other.   Unless, indeed, they could get him knighted ; that
would be something indeed.   Sir—Sir—whatever his name
was—Wilmot would sound very well ; and nobody need ever
know that he had felt pulses and written prescriptions.
That is, of course, if he retired from his profession, as he
would do on his marriage into " our " family ; because if the
unpleasantness with Lady Muriel and—but then how were
they to live ?   Dr Wilmot could not possibly have saved
enough money to retire upon ; and though Madeleine had her
own little fortune, neither Kilsyth nor Lady Muriel would
feel inclined to accept for a son-in-law a penniless man, unless
he had some old alliance with the family.   The old lady was
very much puzzled by all these thoughts.   She sat for hour
after hour revolving plans and projects in her head, without
arriving at any definite result.   The want of adequate fortune
without continuing in practice—that was what worried Mrs
M'Diarmid.   She had already perfectly settled in her own
mind that Madeleine and Wilmot adored each other.   She
had pictured them both at the altar, and settled upon the
new dress to which she should treat herself on the occasion
of their marriage—a nice brown *moire ;* none of your cheap
rubbish—a splendid silk, stiff as a board, that would stand up-
right by itself, as one might say ; and she knew just the pew
which she would be shown into.   All the arrangements were
completed in Mrs Mac's mind—all, with the exception of
the income for the happy pair.

How could that be managed ?   What could be done ?
Were there not appointments, government things, where people were very well paid, and which were always to be had, if
asked for by people of influence ?   Straightway the inde-
fatigable old lady began questioning everybody able to give
her information about consulships, secretaryships, and com-
missionerships ; and received an amount of news that quite
bewildered her.   Two or three men in the Whitehall offices,

who were in the habit of coming to Brook-street, from whom she had endeavoured to glean information, amused themselves by telling her the wildest nonsense of the necessary qualifications for such appointments; so that the old lady was in despair, and almost at her wits' end, when she suddenly bethought her of Mr Foljambe. The very man! Wealthy and childless, with the highest opinion of Wilmot, and with a great regard for Madeleine. Mrs Mac remembered hearing it said in Brook-street, long before Madeleine's illness, that Mr Foljambe would in all probability leave his fortune to Dr Wilmot. And his fortune was a very large one—quite enough to keep up the dignity of a knight upon; though indeed, as there would be no lack of money, Mrs Mac did not see why a baronetcy should not be substituted. Lady Wilmot, and green-and-gold liveries, and hair-powder, of course; that would be the very thing, if that dear old man would only settle it, and not care to live too long after he had settled it— his attacks of gout were dreadful now, she had heard Lady Muriel say—all would be well. Would it be possible to ascertain whether there was any real foundation for the gossip whether Mr Foljambe had really made Wilmot his heir? Would it not be possible to give him such hints respecting his power of benefiting the future of two persons in whom he had the greatest interest as to settle him finally in his amiable determination? Mrs M'Diarmid was a woman of impulse, and believed much in the expediency of "clinching the nail," and "striking the iron while it was hot," as she expressed it. "In such matters as these," she was accustomed to say, "nothing is ever done by third parties, or by writing; if you want a thing done, go and see about it at once, and go and see about it yourself, Lord love you!" Acting on which wise maxims, Mrs M'Diarmid determined to call in person upon Mr Foljambe, and then and there "have it out with him."

At ten o'clock on the following morning, Mr Foljambe,

seated at breakfast, was disturbed by a sharp rap at his
street-door. Mrs M'Diarmid was right in saying that the
old gentleman's gout had been extra troublesome lately, and
his temper had deteriorated in proportion to the sharpness
and the frequency of the attacks. He had had some very
sharp twinges the previous evening, and was in anything but
a good temper ; and as the clanging knock resounded through
the hall, and penetrated to the snug little room where the old
gentleman, in a long shawl dressing-gown, such as were
fashionable five-and-twenty years ago, but are now seldom
seen out of farces, was dallying with his toast and glancing
at the *Times*, he broke out into a very naughty exclamation.
A thorough type of the old English gentleman of his class,
Mr Foljambe, as witness his well-bred hands and feet,—the
former surrounded by long and beautifully white wristbands,
one of the latter incased in the nattiest of morocco-leather
slippers, though the other was in a large list shoe,—his high
cross-barred muslin cravat, his carefully trimmed gray
whiskers, and his polished head.

"Visitors' bell!" muttered the old gentleman to himself,
after giving vent to the naughty exclamation. "What the
deuce brings people calling here at this hour ? Just ten!"
with a glance at the clock. "'Pon my word, it's too bad ;
as though one were a doctor, or a dentist, and on view from
now till five. Who can it be ? Collector of some local
charity, probably, or some one to ask if somebody else doesn't
live here, and to be quite astonished and rather indignant
when he find he's come to the wrong house."

"Well, Sargeant," to the servant who had just entered,
"what is it ?"

"Lady, sir, to speak with you," said Sargeant, grim and
inflexible. He objected to women anywhere in general, but
at that house in particular. Like his master, he passed for
a misogynist ; but unlike his master, he was one.

"A lady ! God bless my soul, what an extraordinary

thing for a lady to come here to see me, and at this hour, Sargeant!"

The tone of Mr Foljambe's voice invited response; but from Sargeant no response came. His master had uttered his sentiments, and there was nothing more to say.

"Why don't you answer, man?" said the old gentleman peevishly. "What sort of a lady is she? Young or old, tall or short? What do you think she has come about, Sargeant?"

"About middle 'ithe; but 'ave her veil down. Wouldn't give a message; but wanted to speak to you partickler, sir."

"Confounded fellow! no getting anything out of him!" muttered the old gentleman beneath his breath. Then aloud, "Where is she?"

"I put the lady in the droring-room, sir; but no fire, as the chimlies was swept this morning."

"I know that; I heard 'em, the scoundrels! No fire! the woman will be perished! Here, bring me down a coat, and take this dressing-gown, and just put these things aside, and poke the fire, and brighten up the place, will you?"

As soon as the old gentleman had put on his coat, and cast a hasty glance at himself in the glass, he hobbled to the drawing-room, and there found a lady seated, who, when she raised her veil, partly to his relief, partly to his disappointment, revealed the well-known features of Mrs M'Diarmid.

"God bless my soul, my dear Mrs Mac, who ever would have thought of seeing you here! I mean to say this is what one might call an unexpected pleasure. Come out of this confoundedly cold room, my dear madam. Now I know who is my visitor, I will, with your permission, waive all formality and receive you in my sanctum. This way, my dear madam. You must excuse my hobbling slowly; but my old enemy the gout has been trying me rather severely during the last few days."

Chattering on in this fashion, the old gentleman gallantly offered Mrs M'Diarmid his arm, and led her from the cold and formally-arranged drawing-room, where everything was set and stiff, to his own cheerful little room, the perfection of bachelor comfort and elegance.

"Wheel a chair round for the lady, Sargeant, there, with its back to the light, and push that footstool nearer.—There, my dear madam, that's more comfortable. You have break-fasted? Sorry for it. I've some orange pekoe that is unrivalled in London, and there's a little ham that is per-fectly de-licious. You won't? Then all I can say is, that yours is the loss. And now, my dear madam, you have not told me what has procured me the honour of this visit."

Had the old lady been viciously disposed, she might easily have pleaded that her host had not given her the chance; but as it was her policy to be most amiable, she merely smiled sweetly upon him, and said that her visit was actuated by important business.

Outside the bank-parlour, Mr Foljambe detested business visits of all kinds; and even there he only tolerated them. Female visitors were his special aversion; and the leaden-buttoned porter in Lombard-street had special directions as to their admission. The junior partner, a buck of forty-five, who dressed according to the fashion of ten years since, and who was supposed still to cause a flutter in the virgin breasts of Balham, where his residence, "The Pineries," was situate, was generally told off to reply to the questions of such ladies as required consultation with Burkinyoung, Foljambe, and Co.

So that when Mrs M'Diarmid mentioned business as the cause of her visit, the old gentleman was scarcely reassured, and begged for a further explanation.

"Well, when I say business, Mr Foljambe," said the old lady, again resuming her smile, "I scarcely know whether I'm doing justice to what lies in my own—my own bosom.

Business, Mr Foljambe, is a hard word, as I know well enough, connected with my early life—of which you know, no doubt, from our friends in Brook-street—connected with boot-cleaning, and errand-sending, and generally poor George's carryings-on in—no matter. And indeed there is but little business connected with what rules the court, the camp, the grove, and is like the red red rose, which is newly sprung in June, sir. You will perceive, Mr Foljambe, that I am alluding to Love."

"To Love, madam!" exclaimed the old gentleman with a jerk, thinking at the same time, "Good God! can it be possible that I have ever said anything to this old vulgarian that can have induced her to imagine that I'm in love with her?"

"To Love, Mr Foljambe; though to you and me, at our time of life, such ideas are generally *non compos.* Yet there are hearts that feel for another; and yours is one, I am certain sure."

"You must be a little clearer, madam, if you want me to follow you," said the old gentleman gruffly.

"Well, then, to have no perspicuity or odontification, and to do our duty in that state into which heaven has called us," pursued Mrs Mac, with a lingering recollection of the Church Catechism, "am I not right in thinking that you take an interest in our Maddy?"

"In Miss Kilsyth?" said Foljambe. "The very greatest interest that a man at—at my time of life could possibly take in a girl of her age. But surely you don't think, Mrs M'Diarmid, that—that I'm in love with her?"

"Powers above!" exclaimed Mrs Mac, "do you think that I've lost my reason; or that if you were, it would be any good? Do you think that I for one would stand by and see my child sacrificed? No, of course I don't mean that! But what I do mean is, that you're fond of our Maddy, ain't you?"

"Yes," said the old gentleman with a burst; "yes, I am; there, will that content you? I think Madeleine Kilsyth a very charming girl!"

"And worthy of a very charming husband, Mr Foljambe?"

"And worthy of a very charming husband. But where is he? I have been tolerably intimate with the family for years—not, of course, as intimate as you, my dear Mrs M'Diarmid, but still I may say an intimate and trusted friend—and I have never seen any one whom I could think in the least likely to be a *prétendu*—not in the least."

"N-no; not before they left for Scotland, certainly."

"No; and then in Scotland, you know, of course there would have been a chance—country house full of company, thrown together and all that kind of thing—best adjuncts for love-making, importunity and opportunity, as I daresay you know well enough, my dear madam; but then Maddy was taken ill, and that spoilt the whole chance."

"Spoilt the whole chance! Maddy's illness spoilt the whole chance, did it? Are you quite sure of that, Mr Foljambe? Are you quite sure that that illness did not decide Maddy's future?"

"That illness!"

"That illness. 'Importunity and opportunity,' to quote your own words, Mr Foljambe, the last if not the worst—have it how you will."

"My dear Mrs M'Diarmid, you are speaking in riddles; you are a perfect Sphinx, and I am, alas, no Œdipus. Will you tell me shortly what you mean?"

"Yes, Mr Foljambe, I will tell you; I came to tell you, and to ask you, as an old friend of the family, what you thought. More than that, I came to ask you, as an old friend of one whom I think most interested, what you thought. You know well and intimately Dr Wilmot?"

"Know Wilmot? Thoroughly and most intimately,

and—why, good God, my dear madam, you don't think that Wilmot is in love with Miss Kilsyth?"

" I confess that I have thought—"

" Rubbish, my dear madam! Simple nonsense! You have been confounding the attention which a man wrapped up in his own profession, in the study of science, pays to a case with attentions paid to an individual. Why, my dear madam, if—not to be offensive—if *you* had had Miss Kilsyth's illness, and Wilmot had attended you, he would have bestowed on you exactly the same interest."

" Perhaps while the case lasted, Mr Foljambe, while his professional duty obliged him to do so ; but not afterwards."

" Not afterwards? Does Dr Wilmot still pay attention to Miss Kilsyth?"

" The last time I was in Brook-street I saw him there," said the old lady, bridling, "paying Miss Kilsyth great 'attention.'"

" Then it was a farewell visit, Mrs M'Diarmid," replied Mr Foljambe. "Dr Wilmot quits town—and England—at once, for a lengthened sojourn on the Continent."

" Leaves town—and England?" said Mrs Mac blankly.

" For several months. Devoted to his profession, as he always has been, without the smallest variation in his devotion, he goes to Berlin to study in the hospitals there. Does that look like the act of an ardent *soupirant*, Mrs M'Diarmid?"

" Not unless he has reasons for feeling that it is better that he should so absent himself," said the old lady.

" Of that you will probably be the best judge," said Mr Foljambe. " My knowledge of Chudleigh Wilmot is not such as to lead me to believe that he would 'set his fortunes on a die' without calculating the result."

In the "off season," when her fashionable friends were away from town, Mrs M'Diarmid was in the habit of receiving some few acquaintances who constituted a whist-club, and met from week to week at each other's houses. Amongst this worthy sisterhood Mrs Mac passed for a very shrewd and clever woman; a "deep" woman, who never "showed her hand." But on turning into Portland-place after her interview with Mr Foljambe, the old lady felt that she had forfeited that title to admiration, and that too without the slightest adequate result.

CHAPTER XXI.

MADELEINE AWAKES.

It is probable that if Chudleigh Wilmot had remained in London, fulfilling his professional duties and leading his ordinary life, the declaration of love and the offer of his hand which in due course he would have made to Miss Kilsyth would have, for the first time, caused that young lady to avow the real state of her feelings towards him to herself. These feelings, beginning in gratitude, had passed into hero-worship, which is perhaps about as dangerous a phase both for adorer and adored as any in the whole category; showing as it does that the former must be considerably "far gone" before she could consent to exalt any man into an object of idolatry, and proving very perilous to the latter from the impossibility of his separating himself from the peculiar attributes which are supposed to call forth the devotion. And Wilmot was just such an idol as a girl like Madeleine would place upon a pedestal and worship with constancy and fervour. The very fact that he possessed none of those qualifications so esteemed by and in the men by whom she was ordinarily surrounded was in her eyes a point in his favour. He did not hunt; he was an indifferent shot; he professed himself worse than

a child at billiards, and his whist-playing was something
atrocious. But then, for the best man across country, the
straightest rider to hounds whom they knew, was Captain
Severn, a slangy wretch only tolerated in society for his
wife's sake. George Pitcairn was a splendid shot; but he
had never heard of Tennyson, and would probably think
that Browning was the name of a setter. Major Delapoche
was the billiard champion at Kilsyth, where he was never
seen out of the billiard-room, except at meal-times; and as
for whist, there could not be much in that when her father
declared that there were not three men at Brookes's who
could play so good a rubber as old Dr M'Johns, the Pres-
byterian clergyman in the village. Ever since she had been
emancipated from her governess, she had longed to meet
some man of name and renown, who would take an interest
in her, and whom she could reverence, admire, and look up to.
She never pined for the heroes of the novels which she read,
probably because she saw plenty of them in her ordinary
life, and she was used to them and their ways. The big
heavy dragoons of the *Guy-Livingstone* type—by his por-
trayal of whom Mr Lawrence establishes for himself such a
reputation amongst the young ladies of the middle classes,
who pine after the *beaux sabreurs* and the "cool captains,"
principally because they have never met any one in real life
like them—are by no means such sources of raving among
the girls accustomed to country-house and London-season
society, who are familiar with something like the prototype
of each character. Ronald's brother officers, Kilsyth's
sporting friends, and Lady Muriel's connections, had made
this kind of type too common for Madeleine, even if her
temperament had not been very different, to elevate it into
a hero; but she had never met any one fulfilling her ideas
until Chudleigh Wilmot crossed her path. From the earliest period of her convalescence, from the time when
slowly-returning strength gave her an interest again in

life, until the time that Wilmot left London, she had
indulged in this happy dream. She was something in that
man's life, something to which his thoughts occasionally
turned, as she hoped, as she believed, with pleasure. As
to "being in love," as it is phrased, Madeleine believed
that such a state as little applied to Wilmot as to herself,
and of her own entire innocence in the existence of such a
feeling she was confident. But there was established a
curious relation between them which she could not explain,
but which she thoroughly understood, and which made her
very happy. Hour after hour she would sit thinking over
this acquaintance, so singularly begun, so different from
anything which she had ever previously experienced, and
wondering within herself what a bright clever man like Dr
Wilmot could see to like in a silly girl like herself. If
Wilmot had been differently constituted she could have
understood it well enough; for though very free from
vanity, Madeleine was of course conscious that she had a
pretty face, and she could perfectly understand the admiration which she received from Ramsay Caird and the men of
whom he was a type. But she imagined Wilmot to be far
too staid and serious, far too much absorbed in his studies
and his "cases," to notice anything so unimportant.

What could he see in her? She asked herself this
question a thousand times without arriving at any satisfactory result. She thought that Wilmot, whom she had
exalted into her hero, would naturally not bestow his
thoughts on any but a heroine; and she knew that there
was very little of the heroine in her. Indeed I, writing
this veracious history, am often surprised at my own daring
in having, in these highly-spiced times, ventured to submit
so very tame a specimen of womanhood to public notice.
Madeleine Kilsyth was neither tawny and leopard-like, nor
hideous and quaintly-fascinating. She was merely an ordinary English girl, with about as much cleverness as girls

have at her age, when they have had no occasion to use
their brains; and she thought and argued in a girlish manner. She could not tell that the difference in each from
their ordinary acquaintance pleased them equally. If
Madeleine had been bright, clever, witty, fast, flirting, or
blasée, she would never have seen her physician after her
recovery. Wilmot was too thoroughly acquainted with
women of all these varieties to find any pleasure in an additional specimen. It was the young girl's freshness and
innocence, her frankness and trusting confidence, her bright
looks and happy thoughts, that touched the heart of the
worn and solitary man, and made him feel that there were
in life joys which he had never experienced, and which
were yet worth living for.

To admire and reverence him; to find the best and
most valuable of resources in his friendship, the wisest and
truest guidance in his intellect, the most exquisite of
pleasures in his society; to triumph in his fame, and to
try to merit his approval—such, as we have seen, had been
Madeleine's scheme. Now this was all changed: he was
gone; the greatest enjoyment of her life, his society, was
taken from her. He was gone; he would be absent for a
long time; she should not see him, would not hear his
voice, for weeks—it might be for months: it took her a
long time to realize this fact, and with its realization
flashed across her the knowledge that she loved Chudleigh
Wilmot.

Loved him! The indefinite, inexplicable sentiments so
long brooded over were gone now, and she looked into her
own heart and acknowledged its condition. So long as he
remained in London, so long as there was a chance of
seeing him, even though she knew that his departure had
been decided on, and was almost inevitable, she yet remained unconscious of the state of her feelings. It was
only when he was actually gone, when she knew that the

long-dreaded step had been taken, that all chance of seeing him again for months was at an end, that the truth flashed upon her. She loved him!—loved him with the whole warmth, truth, and earnestness of her sweet simple nature; loved him as such a man should be loved—deeply, fervently, and confidingly. In the first recognition of the existence of this feeling, she was scarcely likely to inquire psychologically into it; but she felt that her love for Wilmot had many component parts. The admiration and reverence with which he had originally inspired her still remained; but with them was now blended a passion which had never before been evoked in her. She longed to see him again, longed to throw her arms round his neck and whisper to him how she loved him. How miserably blind she had been! What childish folly had been hers not sooner to have comprehended the meaning of her feelings towards this man! She loved him, and—a fearful thought flashed across her. Had it come too late, the discovery of this passion? Had she been dreaming when the golden chance of her life came by, and had she let it pass unheeded? And again, what were Wilmot's feelings with regard to her? Was he under such a delusion as had long oppressed her? He was a man, strong-minded, clear-brained, and of subtle intellect; he would know at once whether his liking for her arose from professional interest, from the friendly feeling which, situated as they had been together at Kilsyth, would naturally spring up between them, or whether it had a deeper foundation and was of a warmer character. His manner to her—save perhaps on that one morning in Brook-street, when Ronald interrupted them so brusquely —had never been marked by anything approaching to warmth; and yet—That morning in Brook-street! there had been a difference then; she had noticed it at the time, and, now regarded in the new light which had dawned upon her, the thought was strengthened and confirmed.

She remembered the way in which he held her hand, and looked down at her with a soft earnest gaze out of those wonderful eyes; such a look as she had never had before or since. If ever love was conveyed by looks, if ever eyes spoke, it was surely then. Ah, did he feel for her as she now knew she felt for him, or was it merely warm friendship, fraternal affection, that actuated him? He had gone away; would he have done that if he had loved her? She had asked herself this question before the state of her own real feelings had dawned upon her, only then substituting the word "like" for love, and had decided that, if he had cared for her ever so little, he would have remained. But her recent discovery led her now to think very differently, and she hoped that this ardour in the cause of science, which prompted this professional visit to Berlin, and necessitated this lengthened absence, might be assumed, and that the real motive of Wilmot's departure might be his desire to avoid her, ignorant as he was of the state of her feelings towards him. Heaven grant that it might be so! for now that she knew herself, it would be easy to recall him. Some pretext could be found for bringing him back to England, back to her; and once together again they would never separate. As this thought passed through her mind her glance fell upon her hands, which were clasped before her, and upon a ring which had been given her by Ramsay Caird. By Ramsay Caird! The curtain dropped as swiftly as it had risen, and Madeleine shivered from head to foot.

It was a pretty ring, a broad hoop of gold set with three turquoises, and the word "AEI" engraved upon it. Madeleine remembered that Ramsay Caird had presented it to her on her last birthday, and while presenting it had said a few words of compliment and kindness with an earnestness and an *empressement* such as he had never before shown. He was not a brilliant man, but he had the society

T

air and the society talk; and he imported just enough seriousness into the latter when he said something about wishing he had dared to have had the ring perfectly plain —just enough to convey his intended hint without making a fool of himself. Ramsay Caird! There, then, was her fate, her future! Knowing all that had been pre-arranged, she had been mad enough to dream for a few minutes of loving and being loved by Chudleigh Wilmot, when she knew, as well as if it had been expressly stated instead of merely implied, that Ramsay Caird was looked upon by her family and by most of their intimate friends, as her future husband.

Ramsay Caird her future husband! She herself had occasionally thought of him in that position, not with dissatisfaction. Knowing nothing better, she imagined that the liking which she undoubtedly entertained for the pleasant young man was love. She had not been brought up in a very gushing school. She had no intimate friend, no one with whom to exchange confidences; and her acquaintances seemed to make liking do very well for love, at least as far as their *fiancés* or their husbands were concerned. Madeleine, when she had thought about the matter, had quite convinced herself that she liked Ramsay very much indeed; and it was only after she discovered that she loved Wilmot that she was undeceived. She thought that she had liked him well enough to marry him, but now she hated herself for ever having entertained such an idea. She knew now that she had never felt love for Ramsay Caird; and she would not marry where she did not love.

A hundred diverse and distracting thoughts and influences were at work within the young girl's mind. Doubt as to whether she was really loved by Wilmot, doubt as to how far she was pledged to Ramsay Caird, comprehension of the urgent necessity at once to take some steps towards a solution of the difficulty, inability to decide on the fittest course to pursue, disinclination to appeal to her father through bashfulness and timidity, to Lady Muriel through distrust, to Ronald through absolute fear: all these feelings alternated in Madeleine's breast; and as she experienced each and all, there hung over her a sense of an impending dreadful something which she could not explain, could not understand, but which seemed to crush her to the earth.

The cause of the feeling which for some time past had induced her to shrink from Ronald, to be silent and depressed when he was present, and to be rather glad when he stayed away from Brook-street, was now perfectly understood by her. In her new appreciation of herself she saw plainly that the fact of her brother's having always been Ramsay Caird's friend and Chudleigh Wilmot's enemy would, insensibly to herself, have caused an estrangement between them in these later days. And why was Ronald so hostile to Wilmot, so bitter in his depreciation of him, so grudging in his praise even of Wilmot's professional qualifications? Was this hostility merely a result of Ronald's normal "oddness" and sternness, or did it spring from the fact that Ronald had observed his sister narrowly, and had discovered, before she herself knew of it, the state of her feelings towards Wilmot? Thinking over this, the remembrance of her brother's manner that morning in Brook-street, when he broke in upon her interview with Wilmot, flashed across Madeleine's mind, and she felt convinced that her dread suspicions were right, and that Ronald had guessed the truth.

The reason of his hatred to Wilmot was then at once apparent to Madeleine. Ronald had always supported Ramsay's unacknowledged position in the family very strongly, not demonstratively, but tacitly, as was his custom in most things. He was essentially "thorough;" and Madeleine imagined that nothing would probably annoy him so much

as the lack of thoroughness in those whom he loved and
trusted. She saw that, actuated by these feelings, her
brother would regard, had regarded what she had previously
imagined to be her admiration and reverence, but what she
now knew, and what Ronald had probably from the first recognized, to be her love for Chudleigh Wilmot as base
treachery; and he hated Wilmot for having, however
innocently, called these feelings into play. However innocently? There was a drop of comfort even in this bitter
cup for poor Madeleine. However innocently? Ronald
was a man of the world, eminently clear-headed and far-
seeing—might not his hatred of Wilmot arise from his
having perceived that Wilmot himself was aware of Madeleine's feelings, and reciprocated them? He had never said
so—never hinted at it; but then that soft fond look into
her eyes when they were alone together in the drawing-room
in Brook-street rose in the girl's memory, and almost bade
her hope.

These mental anxieties, these vacillations between hope
and fear, doubt and despair, which furnished Madeleine
with constant food for reflection, were not without their
due effect on her bodily health. Her fond father, watching
her ever with jealous care, noticed the hectic flush upon
her cheek more frequent, her spirits lower, her strength
daily decreasing: he became alarmed, and confessed his
alarm to Lady Muriel.

"Madeleine is far from well," he said; "very far from
well. I notice an astonishing difference in her within the
last few months. After her first recovery from the fever, I
thought she would take a new lease of life. But Wilmot
was right throughout; she is very delicate; the last few
weeks have made a perceptible difference in her; and
Wilmot is not here to come in and cheer us after seeing
her"

"I think you are over-anxious about Madeleine," said Lady Muriel. "I must confess, Alick, she is not strong; she never was before her illness; and I do not believe that she ever recovered even her previous strength; but I do not think so badly of her as you do. As you say, we have not Dr Wilmot to send for. For reasons best known to himself, but which I confess I have been unable, so far as I have troubled myself, to fathom, Dr Wilmot has chosen to absent himself, and to put himself thoroughly out of any chance of his being sent for. But so far as advice goes, I suppose Sir Saville Rowe is still unequalled; and Dr Wilmot must have full confidence in him, or he would never have begged him to break through his retirement and attend upon Madeleine."

"Yes; that is all very well. Of course Sir Saville Rowe's opinion is excellent and all that, but he comes here but seldom; and one can't talk to him as one could to Wilmot; and he does not stop and talk and all that sort of thing, don't you know? Maddy's is a case where particular interest should be taken, it strikes me; and I think Wilmot did take special interest in her."

"I don't think there can be any doubt of that," said Lady Muriel, with the slighest touch of dryness in her accent. "Dr Wilmot's devotion to his patient was undeniable; but Dr Wilmot's away, and not available, and we must do our best to help ourselves during his absence. My own feeling is that the girl wants thoroughly rousing; she gets moped sitting here day after day with you and me and Mrs M'Diarmid; and Ronald, when he comes, does not tend much to enliven her. Ramsay Caird is the only one with any life and spirits in the whole party."

"He's a good fellow, Ramsay," said Kilsyth; "a genial, pleasant, brisk fellow."

"He is; and he's a true-hearted fellow, Alick, which is better still. By the way, Alick, he spoke to me again the

other day upon that subject which I mentioned to you before—about Madeleine, you recollect?"

"I recollect perfectly, Muriel," said Kilsyth slowly.

"You said then, if you remember, that there was no
reason for pressing the matter then—no reason for hurrying
it on; that Madeleine was full young, and that it would be
better to wait and let us see more of Ramsay. You were
perfectly right in what you said. I agreed with you
thoroughly, and what you suggested has been done. We
have waited now for several months; Madeleine has gone
through a crisis in her life." (Lady Muriel looked steadily
at her husband as she said these words to see if he detected
any double meaning in them; but Kilsyth only nodded his
head gravely.) "We have seen more, a great deal more, of
Ramsay Caird; and from what you just said, I conclude you
like him?"

"I was not thinking of him in that light when I spoke,
my dear Muriel," said Kilsyth; "but indeed I see no reason
to alter my opinion. He's a pleasant, bright, good-tempered
fellow, and I think would make a good husband. He has
seen plenty of life, and will be all the better for it when he
settles down."

"Exactly. Well, then, having settled that point, I think
you will agree with me that now the matter does press, and
there is reason for hurrying it on. Not the marriage,—there
is no necessity for hastening with that; but it is both necessary and proper that it should be understood that Madeleine
and Ramsay Caird are regularly engaged. As I said before,
Madeleine wants rousing. She is *fade* and weary and a little
lackadaisical. You remember how she burst out crying
about that book the other night. She wants employment
for her thoughts and her mind; and if she is engaged, and
we then find her occupation in searching for a house, then
in furnishing it, choosing *trousseau*, brougham, jewels, the
thousand-and-one little things that we can find for her to do,

you may depend upon it you will soon see her a different being."

Kilsyth said he hoped so; but his tone had little buoyancy in it, and was almost despondent as he added:

"What about Maddy herself? Has she any notion of—of what you have just said to me, Muriel?"

"Any notion, my dear Alick? Madeleine, though backward in some things, has plenty of common sense; and she must be perfectly aware what Ramsay's intentions mean and point to. Indeed my own observation leads me to believe that she not merely understands them, but is favourably disposed towards their object."

"Yes; but what I mean to say is, Maddy has never been plainly spoken to on the subject."

"No, no; not that I know of."

"But she should be, eh?"

"Of course she should be—and at once. It is not fair to Mr Caird to keep him longer in suspense; and there are other reasons which render such a course highly desirable."

Again Lady Muriel looked steadfastly at her husband, and again he evaded her glance, and contented himself with nodding acquiescence at her suggestion.

"This should be done," continued Lady Muriel, "by some one who has influence with dear Madeleine, whom she regards with great affection, and whose opinion she is likely to respect. I have never said as much to you, my dear Alick, because I did not want to worry you, in the first place; and in the second, because the thing sits very lightly on me, and the feeling is one which is natural, and which I can perfectly understand; but the fact is that I am Madeleine's step-mother only, and she regards me exactly in that light."

"Muriel!" cried Kilsyth.

"My dear Alick, it is perfectly natural and intelligible, and I make no complaint. I should not have alluded to the subject if it were not necessary, you may depend upon it. But I thought perhaps that you might expect me to broach the matter which we have been recently discussing to Madeleine; and for the reasons I have given, I think that would be wholly unadvisable. You did think so, did you not?"

"Well," said Kilsyth, who felt himself becoming rapidly 'cornered,' "I confess I was going to ask you to do it; but of course if you—and I feel—of course—that you're right. But then the question comes—as it must be done—who is to do it? I'm sure I could not."

Lady Muriel's brow darkened for a few moments as she heard this, but it cleared again ere she spoke. "There is only one person left then," said she; "and I am not sure that, after all, he is not the most fitting in such a case as this. I mean, of course, Ronald. He is perfectly straightforward and independent; he will see the matter in its right light; and, above all, he has great influence with Madeleine."

"Ronald's a little rough, isn't he?" said Kilsyth doubtfully; "he don't mean it, I know; but still in a matter like this he might—what do you think?"

I think, as I have said, that he is the exact person. His manner may be a little cold, somewhat *brusque* to most people; but he has Madeleine's interest entirely at heart, and he has always shown her, as you know, the most unswerving affection. He has a liking for Ramsay Caird; he appreciates the young man's worth; and he will be able to place affairs in their proper position."

So Kilsyth, with an inexpressible feeling that all was not quite right, but with the impossibility of being able to better it, vividly before him, agreed to his wife's proposition; and the next day Ronald had a long interview with Lady Muriel, when they discussed the whole subject, and settled upon their plan of action. Ronald undertook the mission cheerfully; he and his step-mother fully understood each other, and appreciated the necessity of immediate steps. Neither entered into any detail, so far as Chudleigh Wilmot was concerned; but each knew that the other was aware of the existence of that stumbling-block, and was impressed with the expediency of its removal.

Two days afterwards Ronald knocked at the door of Lady Muriel's boudoir at a very much earlier hour than he was usually to be found in Brook-street. When he entered the room he looked a thought more flushed and a thought less calm and serene than was his wont. Lady Muriel also was a little agitated as she rose hastily from her chair and advanced to greet him.

"Have you seen her?" she asked; "is it over? what did she say?"

"She is the best girl in the world!" said Ronald; "she took it quite calmly, and acquiesced perfectly in the arrangement. I think we must have been wrong with regard to that other person—at least so far as Madeleine's caring for him is concerned."

Oh, of course: Madeleine cared nothing for "that other person," the loss of whose love she was at that moment bewailing, stretched across her bed, and weeping bitterly.

CHAPTER XXII.

AT OUR MINISTER'S.

MEANWHILE Chudleigh Wilmot, bearing the secret of his great sorrow about with him, bearing with him also the dread horror and gnawing remorse which the fear that his wife had committed self-destruction had engendered in his breast, had sought safety in flight from the scene of his temptation, and oblivion in absence from his daily haunts,

and to a certain extent had found both.   How many of us
are there who have experienced the benefit of that blessed
change of climate, language, habit of life ?   I declare I believe that the continental boats rarely leave the Dover or the
Folkestone pier without carrying away amongst their motley
load some one or two passengers who are going not for
pleasure or profit, not with the idea of visiting foreign cities
or observing foreign manners, not with the intention of gaining bodily health, or with the vain-glory of being able to say
on their return that they have been abroad (which actuates
not a few of them), but simply in the hope that the entire
change will bring to them surcease of brain-worry and heart-
despondency, calm instead of anxiety, peace in place of
feverish longing, rest—no matter how dull, how stupid, how
torpid—instead of brilliant, baleful, soul-harrowing excitement.   After having pursued the beauty of Brompton
through the London season ; after having spent a little fortune in anonymous bouquets for her and choice camellias for
his own adornment ; after having duly attended at every
fête offered by the Zoological and Botanical Societies, danced
himself weary at balls, maimed his feet at croquet-parties,
and ricked his neck with staring up at her box from the
opera-stalls,—Jones, finding all his *petits soins* unavailing, and
learning that the rich stock-broker from Surbiton has dis-
tanced him in the race, and is about to carry off the prize,
flings himself and his portmanteau on board the Ostend boat,
and finds relief and a renewal of his former devotion to himself among the quaint old Belgian cities.   By the time he
arrives at the Rhine-bord he is calmer ; he has lapsed into
the sentimental stage, and is enabled to appreciate and, if
anybody gives him the chance, to quote all the lachrymose
and all the morbid passages.   He relapses dreadfully when
he gets to Homburg, because he then thinks it necessary to
—as he phrases it in his diary—"seek the Lethe of the
gaming-table ; " but having lost his five pounds' worth of

florins, he is generally content; and when ho arrives in
Switzerland finds himself in a proper-tempered state of mind,
quite fitted to commune with Nature, and to convey to the
Jungfrau his very low opinion of the state of humanity in
general, and of the female being who has blighted his young
affections in particular. And by the time that his holiday is
over, and he returns to his office or his chambers, he has
forgotten all the nonsense that enthralled him, and is prepared to commence a new course of idiotcy, *da capo*, with
another enchantress.

. And' to Chudleigh Wilmot, though a sensible and
thoughtful man, the change was no less serviceable. The
set character of his daily duties, the absorbing nature of
his studies, the devotion to his profession, which had
narrowed his ideas and cramped his aspirations, once cast
off and put aside, his mind became almost childishly impressionable by the new ideas which dawned upon it, the
new scenes which opened upon his view. In his wonder
at and admiration of the various beauties of nature and art
which came before him there was something akin to the
feeling which his acquaintance with Madeleine Kilsyth had
first awakened within him. As then, he began to feel now
that for the first time he lived; that his life hitherto had
been a great prosaic mistake; that he had worshipped false
gods, and only just arrived at the truth. To be sure, he
had now the additional feeling of a lost love and an unap-
peasable remorse; but the sting even of these was tempered
and modified by his enjoyment of the loveliness of nature
by which he was surrounded.

His time was his own; and to kill it pleasantly was his
greatest object. He crossed from Dover to Ostend, and
lingered some days on the Belgian seaboard. Thence he
pursued his way by the easiest stages through the flat low-
lying country, so rich in cathedrals and pictures, in Gothic
architecture and sweet-toned *carillons*, in portly burghers

and shovel-hatted priests and plump female peasants. To Bruges, to Ghent, and Antwerp; to Brussels, and thence, through the lovely country that lies round Verviers and Liege, to Cologne and the Rhine, Chudleigh Wilmot jour-neyed, stopping sometimes for days wherever he felt inclined, and almost insensibly acquiring bodily and mental strength.

There is a favourite story of the practical hard-headed school of philosophers, showing how that one of their number, when overwhelmed with grief at the loss of his only son, managed to master his extreme agony, and to derive very great consolation from the study of mathe-matics—a branch of science with which he had not pre-viously been familiar. It probably required a peculiar temperament to accept of and benefit by so peculiar a remedy; but undoubtedly great grief, arising from what-soever source, is susceptible of being alleviated by mental employment. And, thus, though Chudleigh Wilmot bore about with him the great sorrow of his life; though the sweet sad face of Madeleine Kilsyth was constantly before him; and though the dread suspicion regarding the manner of his wife's death haunted him perpetually, as time passed over his head, and as his mind, naturally clever, opened and expanded under the new training it was unconsciously receiving, he found the bitterness of the memory of his short love-dream fading into a settled fond regret, and the horror which he had undergone at the discovery of the seal-ring becoming less and less poignant.

Not that the nature of his love for Madeleine had changed in the least. He saw her sweet face in the blue eyes and fair hair of big blonde Madonnas in altar-pieces in Flemish cathedrals; he imagined her as the never-failing heroine of such works of poetry and fiction as now, for the first time for many years, he found leisure and inclination to read. He would sit for hours, his eyes fixed on some

lovely landscape before him, but his thoughts busy with
the events of the past few months—those few months into
which all the important circumstances of his life were
gathered. One by one he would pass in review the details
of his meetings, interviews, and conversations with Madeleine, from the period of his visit to Kilsyth to his last sad
parting from her in Brook-street. And then he would go
critically into an examination of his own conduct; he was
calm enough to do that now; and he had the satisfaction
of thinking that he had pursued the only course open to
him as a gentleman and a man of honour. He had fled from
the sweetest, the purest, the most unconscious temptation;
and by his flight he hoped he was expiating the wrong
which he had ignorantly committed by his neglect of his
late wife. That must be the key-note of his future conduct—expiation. So far as the love of women or the praise
of men was concerned, his future must be a blank. He had
made his mind up to that, and would go through with it.
Of the former he had very little, but very sweet experience
—just one short glimpse of what might have been, and then
back again into the dull dreary life; and of the latter—
well, he had prized it and cherished it at one time, had
laboured to obtain and deserve it; but it was little enough
to him now.

Among the old Rhenish towns, at that time of year
almost free of English, save such as from economical motives
were there resident, Wilmot lingered lovingly, and spent
many happy weeks. To the ordinary tourist, eager for his
next meal of castles and crags, the town means simply the
hotel where he feeds and rests for the night, while its inhabitants are represented by the landlord and the waiters,
whose exactions hold no pleasant place in his memory.
But those who stay among them will find the Rhenish burghers kindly, cheery, and hospitable, with a vein of romance
and an enthusiastic love for their great river strangely

mixed up with their national stolidity and business-like
habits. Desiring to avoid even such few of his countrymen
as were dotted about the enormous *salons* of the hotels, and
yet, to a certain extent, fearing solitude, Wilmot eagerly
availed himself of all the chances offered him for mixing
with native society, and was equally at home in the mer-
chant's parlour, the artist's *atelier*, or the student's *kneipe*.
Pleasant old Vaterland! how many of us have kindly
memories of thee and of thy pleasures, perhaps more innocent, and certainly cheaper, than those of other countries,
—memories of thy beer combats, and thy romantic sons,
our *confrères*, and thy young women, with such abundance
of hair and such large feet!

At length, when more than three months had glided
away, Wilmot determined upon starting at once for Berlin.
He had lazed away his time pleasantly enough, far more
pleasantly than he had imagined would ever have been
practicable, and he had laid the ghosts of his regret and his
remorse more effectually than at one time he had hoped.
They came to him, these spectres, yet, as spectres should
come, in the dead night-season, or at that worst of all
times, when the night is dead and the day is not yet born,
when, if it be our curse to lie awake, all disagreeable
thoughts and fancies claim us for their own. The bill which
we "backed" for the friend whose solvency and whose
friendship have both become equally doubtful within the
last few weeks; the face of her we love, with its last-seen
expression of jealousy, anger, and doubt; the pile of neatly-
cut but undeniably blank half-sheets of paper which is some
day to be covered with our great work—that great work
which we have thought of so long, but which we are as far
as ever from commencing: all these charming items present
themselves to our dreary gaze at that unholy four-o'clock
waking, and chase slumber from our fevered eyelids. Chudleigh Wilmot's ghosts came too, but less, far less frequently

than at first; and he was in hopes that in process of time they would gradually forsake him altogether, and leave him to that calm unemotional existence which was henceforth to be his.

Meantime he began to hunger for news of home and home's doings. For the first few weeks of his absence he had regularly abstained even from reading the newspapers, and up to the then time he had sent no address to his servants, choosing to remain in absolute ignorance of all that was passing in London. This was in contradiction to his original intention, but, on carefully thinking it over, he decided that it would be better that he should know nothing. He apprehended no immediate danger to Madeleine, and he knew that she could not be better than under old Sir Saville Rowe's friendly care. He knew that there was no human probability of anything more decisive leaking out of the circumstances of his wife's death. For any other matter he had no concern. His position in London society, his practice, what people said about him, were now all things of the past, which troubled him not; and hitherto he had looked on his complete isolation from his former world as a great ingredient in his composure and his better being. But as his mind became less anxious and his health more vigorous, he began to hunger for news of what was going on in that world from which he had exiled himself; and he hurried off to Berlin, anxious to secure some *pied-à-terre* which he could make at least a temporary home; and he had no sooner arrived at the Hôtel de Russe than he wrote at once to Sir Saville, begging for full and particular accounts of Madeleine Kilsyth's illness, and to his own servant, desiring that all letters which had been accumulating in Charles-street should be forwarded to him directly.

Knowing that several days must elapse before his much-longed-for news could arrive, Wilmot amused himself as best he might. To the man who has been accustomed to dwell in capitals, and who has been spending some months in provincial towns, there is a something exhilarating in returning to any place where the business and pleasure of life are at their focus, even though it be in so tranquil a city as Berlin. The resident in capitals has a keen appreciation of many of those inexplicable nothingnesses which never are to be found elsewhere; the best provincial town is to him but a bad imitation, a poor parody on his own loved home; and in the same way, though the chief city of another country may be far beneath that to which he is accustomed, nay, even in grandeur and architectural magnificence may not be comparable to some of the provincial towns of his native land, he at once falls into its ways, and is infinitely more at home in it, because those ways and customs remind him of what he has left behind. Amidst the bustle and the excitement—mild though it was—of Berlin, Wilmot's desire for perpetual wandering began to ebb. A man who has nearly reached forty years of age in a fixed and settled routine of life makes a bad Bedouin; and when the sting which first started him —be it of disappointment, remorse, or *ennui*, and the last worst of all—loses its venom, he will probably be glad enough to join the first caravan of jovial travellers which he may come across, so long as they are bound for the nearest habitable and inhabitable city. Chudleigh Wilmot knew that a return to England and his former life was, under existing circumstances, impossible; he felt that he could not take up his residence in Paris, where he would be constantly meeting old English friends, to whom he could give no valid reason for his self-imposed exile; but at Berlin it would be different. Very few English people, at least English people of his acquaintance, came to the Prussian capital; and to those whose path he might happen to cross he might, for the present at all events, plead his studies in a peculiar branch of his profession in which the German doctors had long been unrivalled; while as for the future—the future might take care of itself!

Wandering Unter den Linden, pausing in mute admiration before the Brandenburger Thor, or the numerous statues with which the patriotism of the inhabitants and the sublime skill of the sculptor Rauch has decorated the city, loitering in the Kunst Kammer of the palace, spending hour after hour in the museum, reviving old recollections, tinged now with such mournfulness as accrues to anything which has been put by for ever, in visiting the great anatomical collection, dropping into the opera or the theatre, and walking out to Charlottenburg or other of the pleasant villages on the Spree, Chudleigh Wilmot found life easier to him in Berlin than it had been for many previous months. There, for the first time since he left England, he availed himself of the fame which his talent had created for him, and found himself heartily welcome among the leading scientific men of the city, to all of whom he was well known by repute. To them, inquiring the cause of his visit, he gave the prepared answer, that he had come in person to study their mode of procedure which had so impressed him in their books; and this did not tend to make his welcome less warm. So that, all things taken into consideration, Wilmot had almost made up his mind to remain in Berlin, at least for several months. He could attend the medical schools—it would afford him amusement; and if in the future he ever resumed the practice of his profession, it could do him no harm; his life, such as it was, were as well passed in Berlin as anywhere else; and meanwhile time would be fleeting on, and the gulf between him and Madeleine Kilsyth would be gradually widening. It must widen! No matter to what width it now attained, he could never hope to span it again.

One day, on his return to his hotel after a long ramble, the waiter who was specially devoted to his service received him with a pleasant grin, and told him that a "post packet" of an enormous size awaited him. The parcel which Wilmot found on his table was certainly large enough to have created astonishment in the mind of any one, more especially a

German waiter, accustomed only to the small square thin
letters of his nation. There was but one huge packet; no
letter from Sir Saville Rowe, nor from Mr Foljambe, to
whom Wilmot had also written specially. Wilmot opened
the envelope with an amount of nervousness which was altogether foreign to his nature; his hand trembled unaccountably; and he had to clear his eyes before he could set
to work to glance over the addresses of the score of
letters which it contained. He ran them over hurriedly;
nothing from Sir Saville Rowe, nothing from Mr Foljambe,
no line—but he had expected none from any of the Kilsyths.
He threw aside unopened a letter in Whittaker's bold hand,
a dozen others whose superscriptions were familiar to him,
and paused before one, the mere sight of which gave him an
inexplicable thrill. It was a long, broad, blue-papered envelope, addressed in a formal legal hand to him at his house
in Charles-street, and marked "Immediate." There are few
men but in their time have had an uneasy sensation caused
by the perusal of their own name in that never-varying
copying-clerk's caligraphy, with its thin upstrokes and thick
downstrokes, its carefully crossed t's and infallibly dotted i's.
Few but know the "further proceedings" which, unless a
settlement be made on or before Wednesday next, the
writers are "desired to inform" us they will be "compelled to take." But Chudleigh Wilmot was among these
few. During the whole of his career he had never owed a
shilling which he could not have paid on demand, and his
experience of law in any way had been *nil*. And yet the
sight of this grim document had an extraordinarily terrifying
effect upon him. He turned it backwards and forwards,
took it up and laid it down several times, before he could
persuade himself to break its seal, a great splodge of red wax
impressed with the letters "L. & L." deeply cut. At length
he broke it open. An enclosure fell from it to the ground;
but not heeding that, Wilmot held up the letter to the fast-
fading light, and read as follows:

"Lincoln's-inn.

" SIR,—In accordance with instructions received from the late Mr Foljambe of Portland-place—"

The late Mr Foljambe! He must be dreaming! He rubbed his eyes, walked a little nearer to the window, and reperused the letter. No; there the sentence stood.

" In accordance with instructions received from the late Mr Foljambe of Portland-place, we forward to you the enclosed letter. As it appeared that in consequence of your absence from England you could not be immediately communicated with, and in pursuance of the instructions more recently verbally communicated to us by our late client in the event of such a contingency arising, we have taken upon ourselves to make the necessary arrangements for the funeral, as laid down in a memorandum written by the deceased; and the interment will take place to-morrow morning at Kensal-green Cemetery. We trust you will approve of our proceedings in this matter, and that you will make it convenient to return to London as soon as possible after the receipt of this letter, as there are pressing matters awaiting your directions.

" Your obedient servants,
" LAMBERT & LEE.

" Dr Wilmot."

The late Mr Foljambe! His kind old friend, then, was dead! Again and again he read the letter before he realized to himself the information conveyed in that one sentence: the late Mr Foljambe—pressing matters awaiting his directions. Wilmot could not make out what it meant. That Mr Foljambe was dead he understood perfectly; but why the death should be thus officially communicated to him, why the old gentleman's lawyers should express a hope that he would approve of their proceedings, and a desire that he should at once return to London, was to him perfectly inexplicable, unless—but the idea which arose in his mind was too preposterous, and he dismissed it at once.

In the course of his reflections his eyes fell upon the enclosure which had fallen from the letter to the ground. He picked it up, and at a glance saw that it was a note addressed to him in his friend's well-known clear handwriting—clearer indeed and firmer than it had been of late. He opened it at once; and on opening it the first thing which struck him was, that it was dated more than twelve months previously. It ran thus:

"Portland-place.

"My dear Chudleigh,—A smart young gentleman, with mock-diamond studs in his rather dirty shirt, and a large signet-ring on his very dirty hand, has just been witnessing my signature to the last important document which I shall ever sign—my will—and has borne that document away with him in triumph, and a hansom cab, which his masters will duly charge to my account. I shall send this letter humbly by the penny post, to be put aside with that great parchment, and to be delivered to you after my death. In all human probability you will be by my bedside when that event occurs, but I may not have either the opportunity or the strength to say to you what I should wish you to know from myself; so I write it here. My dear boy, Chudleigh—boy to me, son of my old friend—when I told your father I would look after your future, I made up my mind to do exactly what I have done by my signature ten minutes ago. I knew I should never marry, and I determined that all my fortune should go to you. By the document (the young man in the jewelry would call it a document)—by the document just executed, you inherit everything I have in the world, and are only asked to pay some legacies to a few old servants. Take it, my dear Chudleigh, and enjoy it. That you will make a good use of it, I am sure. I leave you entirely free and unfettered as to its disposal, and I have only two suggestions to make—mind, they are suggestions, and not requirements. In the first place, I should be glad if you would keep on and live in my house in Portland-place —it has been a pleasant home to me for many years; and I do not think my ghost would rest easily if, on a revisit to the glimpses of the moon, he should find the old place peopled with strangers. It has never known a lady's care— at least during my tenure—but under Mrs Wilmot's doubt- less good taste, and the aptitude which all women have for making the best of things, I feel assured that the rooms will present a sufficiently brave appearance. The other request is, that you should retire from the active practice of your profession. There! I intended to arrive at this horrible an- nouncement after a long round of set phrases and subtle argument; but I have come upon it at once. I do not want you, my dear Chudleigh, entirely to renounce those studies or the exercise of that talent in which I know you take the greatest delight; on the contrary, my idea in this suggestion is, that your brains and experience should be even more valuable to your fellow-creatures than they are now. I want you to be what the young men of the present day call a 'swell' in your line. I don't want you to refuse to give the benefit of your experience in consultation; what I wish is to think that you will be free—be your own master—and no longer be at the beck and call of every one; and if any lady has the finger-ache, or M. le Nouveau Riche has over-eaten himself, and sends for you, that you will be in a position to say you are engaged, and cannot come.

"If some of our friends could see this letter, they would laugh, and say that old Foljambe was selfish and eccentric to the last; he has had the advantage of this man's abilities throughout his own illnesses, and now he leaves him his money on condition that he sha'n't cure any one else! But you know me too well, my dear Chudleigh, to impute any- thing of this kind to me. The fact is, I think you're doing

too much, working too hard, giving up too much time aud
labour and life to your profession. You cannot carry on at
the pace you've been going; and believe an old fellow who
has enjoyed every hour of·his existence, life has‾something
better than the *renom* gained from attending crabbed valetu-
dinarians. What that something is, my dear boy, is for you
now to find out. I have done my *possible* towards realizing
it for you.

"And now, God bless you, my dear Chudleigh! I have
no other request to make. To any other man I should have
said, 'Don't let the tombstone-men outside the ʼcemetery
persuade you into any elaborate inscription in commemora-
tion of my virtues. 'Here lies John Foljambe, aged 72,' is
all I require. But I know your good sense too well to
suspect you of any such iniquity. Again, God bless you!

"Your affectionate old friend,

"JOHN FOLJAMBE."

Tears stood in Wilmot's eyes as he laid aside the old
gentleman's characteristic epistle. He took it up again after
a pause and looked at the date. Twelve months ago! What
a change in his life during that twelve months! Two allusions
in the letter had made him wince deeply—the mention of
his wife, the suggestion that undoubtedly he would be at the
death-bed of his benefactor. Twelve months ago! He did
not know the Kilsyths then, was unaware of their very existence. If he had never made that acquaintance; if he had
never seen Madeleine Kilsyth, might not Mabel have been
alive now? might he not—Whittaker was a fool in such
matters—might he not have been able once more to carry
his old friend successfully through the attack to which he
now had succumbed? Were they all right—his dead wife,
Henrietta Prendergast, the still small voice that spoke to
him in the dead watches of the night? Had that memorable
visit had such a baleful effect on his career? was it from his

introduction to Madeleine Kilsyth that he was to date all
his troubles ?

His introduction to Madeleine Kilsyth! Ah, under what
a new aspect she now appeared! Chudleigh Wilmot knew
the London world sufficiently to be aware of the very different reception which he would get from it now, how inconvenient matters would be forgotten or hushed over, and how
the heir of the rich and eccentric Mr Foljambe would begin
life anew; the doctrine of metempsychosis having been
thoroughly carried out, and the body of the physician from
which the new soul had sprung having been conveyed into
the outer darkness of forgetfulness. True, some might remember how Mr Wilmot, when he was in practice—so
honourable of him to maintain himself by his talents, you
know, and really considerable talents, and all that kind of
thing—and before he succeeded to his present large fortune,
had attended Miss Kilsyth up at their place in the Highlands, and brought her through a dangerous illness, don't
you know, and that made the affair positively romantic, you
see!—Bah! To Ronald Kilsyth himself the proposition
would be sufficiently acceptable now. The Captain had
stood out, intelligibly enough, fearing the misunderstanding
of the world; but all that misunderstanding would be set
aside when the world saw that an eligible suitor had proposed
for one of its marriageable girls, more especially when the
eligible couple kept a good house and a liberal table, and
entertained as befitted their position in society.

Wilmot had pondered over this new position with a
curled lip; but his feelings softened marvellously, and his
heart bounded within him, as his thoughts turned towards
Madeleine herself. Ah, if he had only rightly interpreted
that dropped glance, that heightened colour, that confused
yet trusting manner in the interview in the drawing-room!
Ah, if he had but read aright the secret of that childish
trusting heart! Madeleine, his love, his life, his wife!

Madeleine, with all the advantages of her own birth, the wealth which had now accrued to him, and the respect which his position had gained for him!—could anything be better? He had seen how men in society were courted, and flattered, and made much of for their wealth alone,—dolts, coarse, ignorant, brainless, mannerless savages; and he—now he could rival them in wealth, and excel them—ah, how far excel them!—in all other desirable qualities!

Madeleine his own, his wife! The dark cloud which had settled down upon him for so long a time rolled away like a mist and vanished from his sight. Once more his pulse bounded freely within him; once more he looked with keen clear eyes upon life, and owned the sweet aptitude of being. He laughed aloud and scornfully as he remembered how recently he had pictured to himself as pleasant, as endurable, a future which was now naught but the merest vegetation. To live abroad! Yes, but not solitary and self-contained; not pottering on in a miserable German town, droning through existence in the company of a few old *savans!* Life abroad with Madeleine for a few months in the year perhaps—the wretched winter months, when England was detestable, and when he would take her to brighter climes— to the Mediterranean, to Cannes, Naples, Algiers it may be, where the soft climate and his ever-watchful attention and skill would enable her to shake off the spell of the disease which then oppressed her.

He would return at once—to Madeleine! Those dull lawyers in their foggy den in Lincoln's-inn little knew how soon he would obey their mandate, or what was the motive-power which induced his obedience. In his life he had never felt so happy. He laughed aloud. He clapped the astonished waiter, who had hitherto looked upon the Herr Englander as the most miserable of his melancholy nation, on the shoulder, and bade him send his passport to the Embassy to be *viséd*, and prepare for his departure. No; he would **go** himself to the Embassy. He was so full of radiant happiness that he must find some outlet for it; and he remembered that he had made the acquaintance of a young gentleman, son of one of his aristocratic London patients, who was an *attaché* to our minister. He would himself go to the Embassy, see the boy, and offer to do any mission for him in England, to convey anything to his mother. The waiter smiled, foreseeing in his guest's happiness a good *trinkgeld* for himself; gentlemen usually sent their passports by the *hausknecht*, but the Herr could go if he wished it—of course he could go!

So Wilmot started off with his passport in his pocket. The sober-going citizens stared as they met, and turned round to stare after the eager rushing Englishman. He never heeded them; he pushed on; he reached the Embassy, and asked for his young friend Mr Walsingham, and chafed and fumed and stamped about the room in which he was left while Mr Walsingham was being sought for. At length Mr Walsingham arrived. He was glad to see Dr Wilmot; thanks for his offer! He would intrude upon him so far as to ask him to convey a parcel to Lady Caroline. *Visa?* Oh, ah! that wasn't in his department; but if Dr Wilmot would give him the passport, he'd see it put all right. Would Dr Wilmot excuse him for a few moments while he did so, and would he like to look at last Monday's *Post*, which had just arrived?

Wilmot sat himself down and took up the paper. He turned it vaguely to and fro, glancing rapidly and uninterestedly at its news. At length his eye hit upon a paragraph headed "Marriage in High Life." He passed it, but finding nothing to interest him, turned back to it again, and there he read:

"On the 13th instant, at St George's, Hanover-square, by the Lord Bishop of Boscastle, Madeleine, eldest daughter of Kilsyth of Kilsyth, to Ramsay Caird, Esq., of Dunnsloggan, N.B."

When Mr Walsingham returned with the passport he found his visitor had fainted.

CHAPTER XXIII.

THE GULF FIXED.

FAINTED! a preposterous thing for a big strong man to do! Fainted, as though he had been a school-girl, or a delicate miss, or a romantic woman troubled with nerves. Mr Walsingham did not understand it at all. He rang the bell, and told the servant to get some water and some brandy, and something—the right sort of thing; and he picked up Wilmot's head, which was gravitating towards the floor, and he bade him "Hold up, my good fellow!" and then he let his friend's head fall, and gazed at him with extreme bewilderment. He was unused to this kind of performance was Mr Walsingham, and felt himself eminently helpless and ridiculous. When the water and the brandy were brought, he administered a handful of the former externally, and a wine-glassful of the latter internally; and Wilmot revived, very white and trembling and dazed and vacant-looking. So soon as he could gather where he was, and what had occurred, he made his apologies to Mr Walsingham, and begged he would add to the kindness he had already shown by sending for a cab, and by allowing him to borrow the newspaper which he had been reading at the time of the attack; it should be carefully returned that afternoon. Mr Walsingham, who was the soul of politeness, agreed to each of these requests; the cab was fetched, and Wilmot, with many thanks to his young friend, and with the packet for his young friend's mother, his own passport, and the *Morning Post* in his pocket, went away in it. Mr Walsingham, who regarded this little episode in his monotonous life as quite an adventure, waxed very eloquent upon the subject afterwards to his friends, and made it his stock story for several days. "Doosid awkward," he used to say, "to have a fellow, don't you know, who you don't know, don't you know, gone off into fits, and all that kind of thing! Here, too, of all places in the world! If he'd gone off in my rooms, you know, it wouldn't so much have mattered; but here, where old Blowhard"—for by this epithet Mr Walsingham designated Sir Hercules Shandon, K.P., Her Britannic Majesty's Minister at the Court of Prussia—"where old Blowhard might have come in at any moment, don't you know, it might have been devilish unpleasant for a fellow. What he wanted with the *Post* I can't make out. I've looked through every column of it since he sent it back, but I can't find anything likely to upset a fellow like that. I thought at first he must have been sinking his fees in some city company that had bust-up, but there's no such thing in the paper; or that he'd read of some chap being poisoned in mistake, and that had come home to him, but there's nothing about that either. I can't make it out.—I say, Tollemache, do you see that Miss Kilsyth's married? Married to Caird, that good-looking fellow that always used to be there at Brook-street—tame cat in the house—and that used to—you know—Adalbert Villa, Omicron-road, eh? Sell for you, old boy; you were very hard hit in that quarter, weren't you, Tolly?"

So Chudleigh Wilmot went back to his hotel in the cab; and the friendly waiter, who had seen him depart so full of life and joyousness, had to help him up the steps, and thought within himself that the great English doctor would have to seek the assistance of other members of his craft. But no bodily illness had struck down Chudleigh Wilmot; he had not recovered his full strength, and the shock to his nerves had been a little too strong—that was all. So soon as he found himself alone, after refusing the friendly waiter's offer of sending for a physician, of getting him restoratives of a kind which came specially within the resources of the Hôtel de Russie, such as a roast chicken and a bottle of sparkling Moselle, and after dispensing with all further assistance or companionship, Wilmot locked the door of his room, and sat down at the table with the newspaper spread open before him. He read the paragraph again and again, with an odd sort of bewildering wonderment that it remained the same, and did not change before his eyes. No doubt about what it expressed—none. Madeleine Kilsyth, who had been worshipped by him for months past, and with whom as his companion he was looking forward to pass his future, was married to another man—that last fact was expressed in so many words. It was all over now, the hope, and the fear, and the longing; there was an end to it all. If he had only known this three months ago, what an agony of heart-sickness, of dull despair, of transient hope, of wearying feverish longing he had been spared! She was gone, then, so far as he was concerned—taken from him; the one star that had glimmered on his dark lonely path was quenched, and henceforward he was to stumble through life in darkness as best he might. That was a cruel trick of Fortune's, a wretched cruel trick, to keep him back in his pursuit, to throw obstacles of every kind in his way, but all the time to let him see his love at the end of the avenue, as he thought, beckoning to him to overcome them all, to make his way to her, and carry her off in spite of all opposition; then for all the obstacles to melt away, for him to have nought to do but gain the temple unopposed; and when he succeeded in gaining it, for the doors to be open, the shrine abandoned, the divinity gone!

Hard fate indeed! hard, hard fate! But it was not to be. His dead wife had said it; Henrietta Prendergast had said it: it was not to be. For him no woman's love, no happy home, no congenial spirit to share his thoughts, his

ambition, his success. He sighed as he thought of this, with
additional sadness as he remembered that if Henrietta Prendergast's story were true, all this had been his. Such a
companion he had had, had never appreciated, and had lost.
He had entertained an angel unawares, and he was never to
have the chance again. For him a drear blank future—
blank save when remorse for the probable fate of the woman
who had died loving him, regret for the loss of the woman he
had loved, should goad him into new scenes of fresh action.
Madeleine married! Was then his fancy that she, that
Madeleine, during that interview in the drawing-room in
Brook-street, had manifested an interest in him different
from that which she had previously shown, a mere delusion?
Had he been so far led away by his vanity as to mistake for
something akin to his own feeling the mere gratitude which
the young girl felt towards her physician? Was she, indeed,
" his grateful patient," and no more? Wilmot's heart sank
within him, and his cheeks burned, as this view of the subject presented itself to his mind. Had he, professing to be
skilled in psychology, committed this egregious blunder?
Had he, who was supposed to know what people really were
when they had put off the mummeries which they played
before the world, and when they had laid by their face-
makings and their posturings and their society antics, and
revealed to their physician perforce what no one else was
allowed to see—had he been deceived in his character study
of one who to him was a mere child? The very suddenness
of the inspiration had led him to believe in its truth. Until
that moment, just before that savage brother of hers had
burst in upon them, he had acknowledged to himself the
existence of his own passion indeed, but had struggled
against it, fully believing it to be unreciprocated, fully believing in the mere gratitude and respect which—as it now
seemed—were the sole feelings by which Madeleine had been
animated. But surely that day, in her downcast eyes and in

her fleeting blush, he had recognized——A new idea, which rushed through his mind like a flash of light, illumining his soul with a ray of hope. Had this been a forced marriage? Had she been compelled by her brother, her father, Lady Muriel—God knows who—to accept this alliance? Had it been carried out against her own free will? Had his absence from England been made the pretext for urging her on to it? Had that been shown to her as a sign of the mistake she had made in supposing that he, Wilmot, cared for her at all? He had never been so near the truth as now, and yet he scouted the notion more quickly than any of the others which he discussed within himself. Such a thing was impossible. The idea of a girl being forced to marry against her will, of her judgment being warped, and the truth perverted for the sake of warping that judgment, was incomprehensible to a man like Wilmot—man of the world in so many phases of his character, but of childlike simplicity in others. He had heard of such things as the stock-in-trade of the novelist, but in real life they did not exist. Mammon-matches, forced marriages, diabolical torturings of fact —all these various combinations, neatly dovetailed together, filled the shelves of the circulating library, but were laughed to scorn by all sensible persons when they professed to be accurate representations of what takes place in the everyday life of society.

Besides, if it were so, the mischief was done, and he was all powerless to counteract it. The marriage had taken place; there was an end of it. It could be undone by no word or deed of his. The times were changed from the old days when a sharp sword and a swift steed could nullify the priest's blessing, and leave the brave gallant and the unwilling bride to be "happy ever after." He was no young Lochinvar, to swim streams and scour countries, to dance but one measure, drink one cup of wine, and bolt with the lady on his saddle-croup. He was a sober, middle-aged

man, who must get back to England by the mail-train and
the packet-boat; and when he got there—well, make his
bow to the bride and bridegroom, and congratulate them on
the happy event. It was all over. His turn in the wheel
of Fortune had arrived too late; the bequest which his good
old friend had secured to him, had it come two months
earlier, might have insured his happiness for life : as it was,
it left him where it found him, so far as his great object in
life, so far as Madeleine Kilsyth, was concerned.

Another long pause for reflection, a prolonged pacing
up and down the room, revolving all the circumstances in
his mind. Was his whole life bound up in this young girl?
did his whole future so entirely hang upon her? Here
was he in his prime, with fame such as few men ever attained to, with fortune newly accruing to him—large fortune, leaving him his own master to do as he liked, free,
unfettered, with no ties and no responsibilities ; and was
he to give up this splendid position, or, not giving it up,
to forego its advantages, to let its gold turn into withered
leaves and its fruits into Dead-Sea apples, because a girl,
of whose existence he had been ignorant twelve months
before, preferred to accept a husband of her choice, of her
rank, of her family connection, rather than await in maidenhood a declaration of his hitherto unspoken love ? He was
pining under his solitude, the want of being appreciated,
the lack of some one to confide in, to cherish, to educate, to
love. Was his choice so circumscribed by fate that there
was only one person in the world to fulfil all these requirements ? Was it preordained that he must either win
Madeleine Kilsyth or pass the remainder of his days help-
lessly, hopelessly celibate ? Was his heart so formed as to
be capable of the reception of this one individual and none
other, to be impressionable by her and her alone? His
pride revolted at the idea; and when a man's pride under-
takes the task of combating his passion, the struggle is

likely to be a severe one, and none can tell on which side the victory may lie.

He would test it, at all events, and test it at once. The kind old man now gone to his rest had hoped that the fortune which he had bequeathed might be of service to the son of his old friend "and to Mrs Wilmot;" and why should it not, although Mrs Wilmot might not be the person whom Mr Foljambe had intended, 'or, as Chudleigh had madly hoped on reading his benefactor's letter, Madeleine Kilsyth? He would go back to England at once; he would show these people that—even if they entertained the idea which had been so plainly set before him by Ronald Kilsyth—he was not the man to sink under an injury, however much he might suffer under an injustice. "Love flows like the Solway, but ebbs like its tide," so far he would say to them with Lochinvar; they should not imagine that he was going to pine away the remainder of his life miserably because Miss Kilsyth had chosen to marry some one else. He had been a fool, a weak pliable fool, to make such a statement as he had done in that interview with Ronald Kilsyth. His cheeks tingled with shame as he remembered how he had confessed the passion which he had nurtured, and which he acknowledged beset him even at the time of speaking. And that cool, calculating young man, with his cursed priggish, pedantic airs, his lack of anything approaching enthusiasm, and his would-be frank manner, was doubtless at that moment grinning to himself at the successful result of his calm diplomacy. Chudleigh Wilmot stamped his foot on the floor and ground his teeth in the impotence of his rage.

Married to Ramsay Caird, eh? Ramsay Caird! Well, they had not made such a great catch after all! To hear them talk, to see the state they kept up at Kilsyth, to listen to or look at my Lady Muriel, one would have thought that an earl, with half England in estates at his back, was the lowest they would have stooped to for their daughter's husband. And now she was married to an untitled Scotchman, without money, and—well, if he remembered club-gossip aright, rather a loose fish. Had not Captain Kilsyth been a little too hurried in the clinching of the nail, in the completion of the bargain? As Mr Foljambe's heir, he, Chudleigh Wilmot, would have been worth a dozen such men as Ramsay Caird; and as to the question of former intimacy, of acquaintance formed during his wife's lifetime, the world would have forgotten that speedily enough.

He would go back to England at once, but when there he would show them he was not the kind of man which, from Ronald Kilsyth's behaviour, that family apparently imagined him. Still the border song rang in his head—

> "There were maidens in Scotland more lovely by far
> Would gladly be bride to the young Lochinvar."

Not more lovely, and probably never to be anything like so dear to him; but there were other maidens in England besides Madeleine Kilsyth. And why should the remainder of his life be to him utterly desolate because this girl either did not love him, or, loving him, was weak enough to yield to the interference of others? Was he to pine in solitude, to renounce all the pleasures of wifely companionship, to remain, as he had hitherto been, self-contained and solitary, because he had placed his affections unworthily, and they had not been understood, or cast aside? No; he had existed, he had vegetated long enough; henceforward he would live. Wealth and fame were his; he was not yet too old to inspire affection or to requite it; by his old friend's death he had obtained an additional claim upon society, which even previously was willing enough to welcome him; he should have the *entrée* almost where he chose, and he would avail himself of the privilege. So thus it stood. Chudleigh Wilmot left London broken-hearted at having to give up his love, and full of remorse for a crime, not of his commission indeed, but which he imagined had arisen out of his own egotism and selfish pre-occupation. He was about to start on his return, with stung sensibility and wounded pride—feelings which ren-dered him hostile rather than pitying towards the woman to whom he had imagined himself sentimentally attached, and which had completely obliterated and driven into oblivion all symptoms of his remorse.

He wrote a hurried line to Messrs Lambert and Lee, informing them of his satisfaction with their proceedings hitherto, and notifying his immediate return; and he told the friendly waiter that he should start by that night's mail, and get as far as Hanover. But this the friendly waiter would not hear of. The Herr Doctor must know perfectly well—for had not he, the friendly waiter, heard the German doctors speak of the English doctor's learn-ing?—that he was in no condition to travel that night. If he, the friendly waiter, might in his turn prescribe for the English doctor, he should say, "Wait here to-night; dine, not at the *table d'hôte*, where there is hurry and confusion, but in the smaller *speise-saal*, where you usually breakfast; and the cook shall be instructed to send up to you of his very best; and the Herr Oberkellner, a great man, but to be come over by tact, and specially kind in cases of illness, shall be persuaded to go to the cellar and fetch you Johan-nisberg—not that Zeltinger or Marcobrünner, which, under the name of Johannisberg, they sell to you in England, but real Johannisberg, of Prince Metternich's own vintage—pfa!" and the friendly waiter kissed his own fingers, and then tossed them into the air as a loving tribute to the excellence of the costly drink.

So Wilmot, knowing that there was truth in all the man had said; feeling that he was not strong, and that

what little strength ho had had gone out of him under tho
ordeal of the morning at the Embassy, gave way, and consented to remain that night. But tho next morning ho
started on his journey, and on tho evening of the third day
he arrived in London. He drove straight to his house in
Charles-street, and saw at once by the expression of his
servant's face that the news of his inheritance had preceded
him. There was a struggle between solemnity and mirth
on tho man's countenance that betrayed him at once. The
man said he expected his master back, was not in the least
surprised at his coming; indeed most people seemed to
have expected him before. What did he mean? Oh, nothing
—nothing; only there had been an uncommon number of
callers within the last few days. "Not merely the reg'-
lars," the man added; "them of course; but there have
been many people as we have not seen here these two years
past a rat-tat-tin', and leavin' reg'lar packs of cards, with
their kind regards, and to know how you were, sir." The
cards were brought, and Wilmot looked through them.
The man was right; scores of his old acquaintance, whom
he had not seen or heard of for years, were there represented; people whom ho had only known professionally,
and who had never been near him since he wrote their last
prescription and took their last fee months before, had sought
him out again. To what could this be accredited? Either
to the earnest desire of all who knew him to console him in
the affliction of having lost his friend, or to the information
sown broadcast by that diligent contributor to the *Illus-
trated News*, who had given exact particulars of the will of
the late John Foljambe, Esq., banker, of Lombard-street
and Portland-place. But there was no card from any
member of the Kilsyth family in the collection. Wilmot
searched eagerly for one, but there was none there.

He had a hurried meal—hurried, not because he had
anything to do and wanted to get through with it, but be-

cause he had no appetite, and what was placed before him was tasteless and untempting—and sat himself down in his old writing-chair in his consulting-room to ponder over his past and his future. He should leave that house ; he must. Though Mr Foljambe had made no binding requirement, the expression of his wish was enough. Wilmot must leave that house, and obey his benefactor's behests by taking up his residence in Portland-place. He had never thought much of it before, but now he felt that he loved the place in which so much of his life had been passed, and felt very loth to leave it. He recollected when he had first moved into it, when his practice began to increase and his name began to be known. He remembered how his friends had said that it was necessary he should take up his position in a good West-end street, and how alarmed he was, when the lease was signed and the furniture—rather scanty and very poor, but made to look its best by Mabel's disposition and taste—had been moved in, lest he should be unable to pay the heavy rent. He recollected perfectly the first few patients who had come to see him there : some sent by old Foljambe, some droppers-in from the adjacent military club, allured by the bright door-plate ; old gentlemen wishing to be young again, and young gentlemen in constitution rather more worn and debilitated than the oldest of the veterans. He remembered his delight when the first great person ever sent for him ; how he had treasured the note requesting his visit ; how he had gone to his club and slily looked up the family in the Peerage ; and how when he first stood before Lady Hernshaw, and listened to her account of her infant's feverish symptoms, he could, if he had been required, have gone through an examination in the origin and progress of the Hawke family, with the names of all the sons and daughters extant, and come out triumphantly. His well-loved books were ranged in due order on the walls round him ; on the table before him

stood the lamp by whose light he had gathered and repro-
duced that learning which had gained him his fame and his
position. In that house all his early struggles had been
gone through; he remembered the first dinner-parties
which had been given under Mabel's superintendence, her
diffidence and fright, his nervousness and anxiety. And
now that was all of the past; Mabel had vanished for ever
and aye; and soon the old house and its belongings, its
associations and traditions, would know him no more.
What had he gained during those few years? Fame, position, men's good word, the envy of his brother-professionals,
and, recently, wealth. What had he lost? Youth, spirit,
energy, the at one time all-sufficing love of study and progress in his science, content; and, latterly, the day-spring
of a new existence, the hope of a new world which had
opened so fairly and so promisingly before him. The
balance was on the *per-contra* side, after all.

The fashionable journals found out his return (how, his
servant of all men alone knew), and proclaimed it to the
world at large. The world at large, consisting of the sub-
scribers to the said fashionable journals, acknowledged the
information, and the influx of cards was redoubled. Some
of these performers of the card-trick lingered at the door,
and entered into conversation with the presiding genius in
black to whom their credentials were delivered. Whether
the doctor were well, whether he intended continuing the
practice of his profession, whether the rumour that he intended giving up that house and removing to Portland-
place had any substantial foundation; whether it were true
that he, the presiding genius, was about to have a new
mistress, a lady from abroad—for some even went so
far as to make that inquiry—all these different points
were put, haughtily, confidentially, jocosely, to the presiding
genius of the street-door, and all were answered by him as
best he thought fit. Only one of the queries, the last, had

any influence on that great man. He fenced with it in public with all the coolness and the dexterity of an Angelo, but in private, in the sacred confidence of the pantry engendered by the supper-beer, he was heard to declare that "the guv'nor knew better than that; or that if he didn't, and thought to introduce furreners, with their scruin' ways, to sit at the 'ead of his table and give horders to them, he'd have to suit himself, and the sooner he knew that the better."

Some of the callers on seeking admittance were admitted —among them Dr Whittaker. Perhaps amongst the large circle of Wilmot's acquaintances calling themselves Wilmot's friends, that eminent practitioner was the only one who had a direct and palpable feeling of annoyance at Wilmot's return.

Dr Whittaker's originally good practice had been considerably amplified by the patients who, under Wilmot's advice, had yielded themselves up to Dr Whittaker's direction during Wilmot's absence, and the substitute naturally looked with alarm upon the reappearance of the great original. So Dr Whittaker presented himself at an early date in Charles-street, and being admitted, had a long and, on his side at least, an earnest talk with his friend. After the state and condition of various of the leading patients had been discussed between them, Whittaker began to touch upon more dangerous, and to him more interesting, ground, and said, with an attempt at jocosity,—and Whittaker was a ponderous man, in whom humour was as natural and as easy as it might have been in Sir Isaac Newton,—

"And now that I have given account of my stewardship, I suppose my business is ended, and all I have to do is to return my trust into the hands of him from whom I received it."

He said this with a smile and a smirk, but with an anxious look in his eyes notwithstanding.

"I don't clearly understand you," said Wilmot. "If you mean to ask me whether I intend to take up my practice again, my answer is clear and distinct—No. If you wish to inquire whether those patients whom you have been attending in my absence will continue to send for you, I am in no position to say. All I can say is, that if they send for me, I shall let them know that I have retired from the profession, and that you are taking my place."

Dr Whittaker was in ecstasies. "Of course that is all I could expect," he replied; "and I flatter myself that—hum! ha! well, a man does not boast of his own proceedings—ha! Well then, and so what the little birds whispered is true, eh?"

"I—I beg your pardon," said Wilmot absently—"the—the little birds—"

"Cautious!" murmured Dr Whittaker in his blandest tone—that tone which had such an influence with female patients—"we are quite right to be cautious; but between friends one may refer to the little birds which have whispered," he continued with surprising unction, "that a certain friend of ours, whom the world delights to honour, has succeeded to wealth and station, and is about to exchange that struggle in which the—the, if I may so express it—the *pulverem Olympicum* is gathered, for a soft easy seat in the balcony, whence he can look on at the contention with a smiling *conjux* by his side."

"Little birds have peculiar information, Whittaker, if they have been so communicative as all that," said Wilmot with a rather dreary smile; "they know more than I do, at all events."

"Ha, ha! my dear friend," said Whittaker, in a gushing transport of delight at the thought of his own good fortune; "we are deep, very deep; but we must allow a little insight into human affairs to others. Why did we fly from the world, dear Bessy, to thee? as the poet Moore, or Milton—

I forget which—has it. Why did we give up our practice, and hurry off so suddenly to foreign parts, hum?" Dr Whittaker gave this last "hum" in his softest and most seductive tones, such tones as had never failed with a patient. But perhaps because Wilmot was not a patient, and was indeed versed in the behind-scenes mechanism of the profession, it had no effect on him, and he merely said: "Not for the reason you name. Indeed, you never were further out in any surmise."

"Is that really so?" said Whittaker blandly. "Well, well, you surprise me! It is only a fortnight since that I was discussing the subject at a house where you seem often spoken of, and I said I fully believed the report to be true."

"And where was that, pray?" asked Wilmot, more for the sake of something to say than for any real interest he took in the matter.

"Ah, by the way, you remind me! I intended to speak to you about that case before you left. The young lady whom you attended in Scotland—where you were when poor Mrs Wilmot died, you know—"

"In Scotland—where I was when—good God! what do you mean?"

"Miss Kilsyth, you know. Well, you left her in charge of poor old Rowe as a special case, didn't you? Yes, I thought so. Well, the poor old gentleman got a frightful attack of bronchitis, and was compelled to go back to Torquay —don't think he'll last a month, poor old fellow!—and before he went, he asked me to look after Miss Kilsyth. Thought she had phthisis—all nonsense, old-fashioned nonsense; merely congestion, I'm sure. I've seen her half-a-dozen times; and about a fortnight ago—yes, just before her intended marriage was announced—she's married since, you know—we were talking about you, and I mentioned this rumour, and—and we had a good laugh over your enthusiasm."

"It is a pity, Dr Whittaker," said Wilmot quivering with suppressed rage, "it is a pity; and it is not the first time that it has been remarked, both professionally and socially, that you offer opinions and volunteer information on subjects of which you are profoundly ignorant. Good morning!"

Just before the announcement of her intended marriage! Had the vile nonsense talked by that idiot Whittaker had any influence in inducing her to take that step? He thought of that a hundred times, coming at last to the conclusion— what did it matter now? The irrevocable step was taken. Ah, for him it was not to be! His dead wife had said so— Henrietta Prendergast had said so. It was not to be!

What was to be was soon carried out according to his old friend's expressed wish. Wilmot removed from Charles-street to Portland-place, and materially changed his manner of life. All his old patients flocked round him directly his return was announced; but, as he had promised Whittaker, he let it be understood that he had entirely retired from practice. He even declined to attend consultations, alleging as an excuse that his health was delicate, and that for some time at least he required absolute repose. He had determined to take as much enjoyment out of life as he could find in it; and that, truth to tell, was little enough. The growth and development of his love for Madeleine Kilsyth had lessened his thirst for knowledge and his desire for fame; and when the fierce flames of that love had burned out, there was still enough fire in the ashes to wither up and destroy any other passion that might seek to occupy his heart. He tried to find relief for the dead weariness of spirit, the blank desolation always upon him, in society. He gathered around him brilliant men of all classes; and "Wilmot's dinners" were soon spoken of as among the pleasantest bachelor *réunions* in

London. He dined out at clubs, he joined men's dinner-
parties ; but he resolutely declined to enter into ladies'
society. The resolution which he had formed at the Berlin
hotel of proving to the Kilsyth people that there were
families equal to theirs into which he could be received, and
girls equal to Madeleine who were willing to marry him,
never was brought to the test. Many ladies no doubt asked
their husbands about Wilmot ; but from the answers they
received they regarded him as never likely to marry again ;
and save from hearsay report, they had no opportunity of
evidence.

He went about constantly, rode on horseback a great deal,
visited theatres, and sat with a melancholy face at nearly all
the public exhibitions. The few persons who had sufficient
interest in him to discuss the reason for this change attributed
it to the impossibility of his ever recovering the shock of his
wife's sudden death ; and he was quoted perpetually before
many husbands, who sincerely wished they had the opportunity of showing how they would conduct themselves under
similar circumstances. So his life passed on, monotonous,
blank, aimless, for about three weeks after his installation in
Portland-place ; when one evening returning from a long
ride round the western suburbs, as he turned his horse
through the Albert-gate, he came full upon a carriage containing Lady Muriel and Madeleine. They were so close,
that it was impossible to avoid a recognition. Wilmot raised
his hat mechanically, Lady Muriel gave him a chilling bow,
and then turned rapidly to her companion. Madeleine
turned dead white, and sank back as though she would have
fainted ; but Lady Muriel's look recalled her, and she recovered herself in time to bow. Then they were gone. Not
much hope in that, Chudleigh Wilmot ! Not much chance
of bridging that gulf which is fixed between you !

CHAPTER XXIV

HENRIETTA.

Mrs Prendergast had heard of Chudleigh Wilmot's accession to fortune before the news had reached that more than ever "rising" man. Though she was not among Mr Foljambe's intimates, and though that sprightly old gentleman found less favour in her eyes than in those of most of his acquaintance, she knew when his illness commenced, when it had assumed a dangerous form; and she was one of the earliest outsiders to learn its fatal and rapid termination. She was indebted for all this information to Dr Whittaker, whom she had assiduously cultivated, and who was very fond of talking of all and everything that nearly or remotely concerned Wilmot. The little professional jealousy which had sometimes interfered with Dr Whittaker's genuine and generally irrepressible admiration of the genius and the success of his *confrère* and superior had given way to the influence of the superior's loftiness and liberality of mind; and with Dr Whittaker also there was, as old Mr Foljambe had said, on an occasion destined to affect many destinies, "nothing like Wilmot."

Dr Whittaker was not aware that Mrs Prendergast valued his visits chiefly because they afforded her an opportunity, which otherwise she could not have enjoyed, of hearing of Wilmot. She had too much tact to permit him to make any such mortifying discovery, and he had too much vanity to permit him to suspect the fact, except under extreme provocation. So Mrs Prendergast accounted his visits as among her most agreeable glimpses of society; and he regarded her as one of the most sensible and unaffected women of his acquaintance. Thus, when Dr Whittaker's attendance on Mr Foljambe came to a close

with the sprightly and *débonnaire* old gentleman's life, he
brought the news to his friend in Cadogan-place, and they
lamented together Wilmot's untimely absence. But Dr
Whittaker had previously conveyed to Mrs Prendergast information of another sort, which had largely influenced the
feelings with which she heard of Mr Foljambe's death.

It was the same welcome messenger who had brought
her the tidings of Madeleine Kilsyth's marriage; and never
had he been more welcome. She had steadily persevered in
denying to herself that the young Scotch girl could possibly
count for anything, one way or another, in the matter in
which she was so vividly interested; but she had not succeeded in feeling such complete conviction on the point as
to render her indifferent to any occurrence which effectually
disposed of that young lady before Wilmot's return. That
he should have come back to London, to all the former
prestige of his talent and success, with the new and brilliant addition that he had acquired the whole of Mr Foljambe's large fortune, to find Madeleine Kilsyth unmarried,
and to be brought upon an equality with her by the agency
of his wealth,—this would not have appeared to Henrietta
by any means desirable. The obstacles which the social
pride of her relations might have opposed to a *penchant* for
Wilmot on the part of Miss Kilsyth—and Mrs Prendergast
had always felt instinctively that such a *penchant*, if it did
not actually exist, would arise with opportunity—would be
considerably modified, if not altogether removed, by Wilmot's becoming a rich man by other than professional
means. Altogether there were many new sources of danger to her project, which did not relax in its intensity and
fixedness by time, silence, or leisure for consideration, in
the possibility of Madeleine Kilsyth's being again brought
within Wilmot's reach, which presented themselves very
unpleasantly to the clear perception of Mrs Prendergast.

"And so you had not heard of Miss Kilsyth's intended

marriage at all, knew nothing of it until after the event?" said Dr Whittaker, after he had imparted the intelligence to Mrs Prendergast. To him it was merely an item in the gossiping news of the day; nor had he any suspicion that it was more to his hearer.

"No; I had not heard a word of it. And I wonder I had not, for I have seen Miss Charlton several times; and I know Mrs M'Diarmid has been at their house frequently. She must have known all about it, and I can't fancy her knowing anything and not talking about it."

"No," said Dr Whittaker. "Reserve is not her *forte*, good old lady. But they say—the omnipresent, omniscient, and indefinable *they*—that Miss Kilsyth expressly stipulated that the engagement was to be kept a profound secret. She is troubled, I understand, with rather more delicacy and modesty than most young ladies at present; and she disliked the pointing and talking, the giggling and specu- lation which attend the appearance of an engaged young lady in what is politely called 'high life' on such occasions."

"The engagement was not a long one, I suppose?" said Henrietta.

"Only a few weeks, I understand. They say Lady Muriel Kilsyth was rather anxious to get her step-daughter off her hands—"

"And into those of her not particularly rich cousin, I fancy," said Henrietta. Dr Whittaker laughed.

"I daresay I shall hear a great deal about it at the Charltons'," she continued; "I am going to dine there to- morrow. I know Mrs M'Diarmid will be there, and she will have plenty to tell, no doubt. I shall hear much more about the wedding than I shall care for."

Mrs Prendergast dined at Mrs Charlton's on the follow- ing day, and she did hear a great deal about the wedding, which Mrs M'Diarmid was of opinion had not been quite worthy of the occasion either in style or in publicity, and whereat she could not say Madeleine had conducted herself altogether to her satisfaction. Not that she had been too emotional, or in the least bold in her manner, but she had taken it all so very quietly.

"I assure you it was quite unnatural, in my opinion," said the old lady, with a homely heartiness of manner calculated to convert other people to her opinion too. "Madeleine was as quiet and as unconcerned as if it was somebody else's wedding, and not her own. She positively seemed to think more of little Maud's dress and appearance than of her own, and she was as friendly as possible with Mr Caird."

"Friendly with Mr Caird, Mrs M'Diarmid!" said Henrietta. "Why should you be surprised at that? Why should she not be friendly with him?"

"Well, I'm sure I don't know, my dear," answered Mrs M'Diarmid, who called every one 'my dear;' "it did seem odd to me somehow—there, I can't explain it; and I daresay I'm an old fool—very likely; but they did seem more like friends to me, that is, Madeleine did, than lovers—that's the truth."

Miss Charlton remarked to Mrs Prendergast, with a sentimental sigh, that she perfectly understood Mrs M'Diarmid,—that Miss Kilsyth's manner had had too little of the solemnity and exaltation of such a serious and important event. "At such a moment, Henrietta," said the young lady, raising her fine eyes towards the ceiling, "earth and its restraints should fade, and the spirit be devoted to the heavenly temple, which is the true scene of the marriage."

"All I can say, then," said Mrs M'Diarmid, by no means touched by the high-flown interpretation placed upon her remarks, "is, that if any one can be reminded of a heavenly temple by St George's, Hanover-square, they must have a lively imagination; for a duller and heavier earthly one I never was in in my life."

"I suppose the wedding-party was numerous?" said Mrs Charlton, who never could endure anything like a verbal passage-at-arms; and who was moreover occasionally beset by a misgiving that her daughter was rather silly.

"Not what the Kilsyths would consider large, my dear; only their immediate connections and a few very intimate friends. Miss Kilsyth would have it so; and indeed the whole thing was got up in a hurry. It was announced in the *Morning Post* on Monday, and the marriage came off on Wednesday."

"I suppose the bride had some splendid presents?" said Miss Charlton, whose curiosity was agreeably irrepressible.

"O yes, my dear, lots. Some beautiful and expensive; some ugly and more expensive; several cheap and pretty; and a great many which could not possibly be of use to any rational being. You know Mr Foljambe, don't you, Mrs Prendergast?"

"Yes," said Henrietta; "I know him slightly."

"He is an old friend of Kilsyth's; poor man, he's very ill indeed—could not come to the wedding because he was ill then, and he is much worse since; he gave Madeleine the handsomest present of the lot—a beautiful set of pearls, and he sent her such a nice, kind, old-fashioned letter with them. He is a real old dear, though I always feel a little afraid of him somehow."

"Is Mr Foljambe really very ill?" said Mrs Charlton.

"I am sorry to say he is," said Henrietta; "I saw Dr Whittaker to-day, and he gave a very bad account of him."

"Dr Whittaker?" said Mrs Charlton inquiringly. "I don't know him; I—"

"No," interrupted Henrietta with a smile; "he is not yet famous; he is only just beginning to be a rising man. He is a great friend of Dr Wilmot's, who, when he went abroad, placed several of his principal patients in his hands."

As Henrietta mentioned Wilmot's name, she glanced

keenly at Mrs M'Diarmid, and perceived at once that the mention of him produced an effect on the old lady of no pleasing kind. Her face became overcast in a moment.

"I hope Miss Kilsyth's—I beg her pardon, Mrs Caird's health is sufficiently restored to make any such provision in her case unnecessary," said Henrietta to Mrs M'Diarmid in her best manner; which was a very good manner indeed.

"Yes, yes," the old lady said absently; then recovering herself, she continued, "Madeleine has been much better latterly; but Sir Saville Rowe has been looking after her. Dr Wilmot recommended her specially to his care."

The conversation then turned on other matters, and did not again revert to the Kilsyths; but Mrs Prendergast carried away with her from the substance of what had passed two convictions.

The first, that Wilmot had entertained sufficient feeling of some kind for Madeleine Kilsyth to render him averse to bringing her into contact with the man who attended his wife's death-bed, and who might therefore have been inconveniently communicative, or even suspicious.

The second, that there was some painful impression or association in the kind, honest, and simple mind of Mrs M'Diarmid connected with Dr Wilmot and Madeleine Kilsyth.

On that evening Mrs Prendergast settled the point, in consultation with herself, that Madeleine's marriage was an important advantage gained. How important, or precisely why, she had no means of ascertaining, but she felt that it was so; and she experienced a comfortable feeling, compounded of hope and content, at the occurrence.

A week later Dr Whittaker called on Henrietta and communicated to her the intelligence of Mr Foljambe's death; and in a few days later the accession of Wilmot to his faithful old friend's large fortune was made known to her in the same way.

And now Henrietta felt the full importance of the removal of Madeleine Kilsyth from Wilmot's path. He would return to London of course—perhaps to abandon his professional pursuits, though that she thought an unlikely step on his part. His sphere of life would, however, certainly be changed; and the best chance for the success of her project would consist in her being able to induce him to form habits of intimacy and companionship with her before the increased demands of society upon him should whirl him away out of her reach. Even supposing, which she—though more capable than most women of taking a contingency which she disliked into sensible and serious consideration—did not think likely, that Dr Wilmot would contemplate a second marriage, and that marriage purely of affection, he would certainly return to London heart-whole. If Madeleine Kilsyth had indeed possessed for him attraction which he could not disavow to himself, nor avow to the world, so much the better now as things had turned out. Madeleine would have held his fancy captive until such time as fate had set between them a second inviolable barrier; and this new and keen disappointment, even supposing he had never distinctly formulated his hope, would have turned his heart, and brought him back irresistibly to the realities of life.

Thus, knowing nothing of the actual circumstances of the case; unaware of the twofold shock which Chudleigh Wilmot had received by the events which she calmly regarded as equally fortunate; unconscious of the storm of passion, rage, grief, and helplessness in which Wilmot was wrapped and tossed, even while she was quietly discussing the matter with herself, Henrietta Prendergast arranged the present before her eyes, and questioned the future in her thoughts. But had she known all of which she was ignorant—had she been able to see Chudleigh Wilmot as he really was while she was thus thinking of him, the revela-

Y

tion would hardly have changed the current of her thoughts, though it might have robbed her of much of her composure. In that case she would have reflected that she had but mistaken the quality and the depth of his feelings, that circumstances remained unchanged. Wilmot had been passionately in love with Madeleine Kilsyth; but he was now none the less certainly, irrevocably, and eternally separated from her.

Thus, the facts which she knew, the facts which she guessed, and the facts which were effectually concealed from her, all bore encouragingly upon the projects of Henrietta Prendergast. It is only just to acknowledge that the increase to his wealth did not intensify or sharpen Mrs Prendergast's wish to marry Wilmot; indeed it rather depressed her. She felt that it might create new obstacles as strong as those which fate had removed; she would have preferred his being in his former position. "If I could have won him as he was," she thought, "and then this fortune had come, that would have been better. However, ever so poor he would have been a man worth winning; it makes no difference in that respect his being ever so rich."

After all, this appreciation, calm and passionless, yet just, clear-sighted, and true, was not a gift to be despised by a sensible man, who had had the gilding pretty nearly taken off the gingerbread of his life, but it was not likely to be valued as it deserved by a man pining desperately for the impossible love of a brilliant young beauty like Madeleine Kilsyth.

One immediate purpose which Henrietta set strongly before her was to see Wilmot as soon as possible after his return, of the time of which event she would be duly informed by Dr Whittaker. She had had no communication with him since the puzzling interview which had preceded his departure; he had neither written nor gone to take leave of her; but this omission, which would have been extremely discouraging to a less keen-sighted woman, was not discouraging to Henrietta. She knew that, as far as she was concerned, it meant simply nothing. Wilmot was deeply distressed and preoccupied; that was the cause of it. She also knew that at present, in his life, *she* meant nothing, and she was satisfied, so that the future should afford her a fair opportunity of coming to mean much. But she must attain and begin to profit by that opportunity as soon as possible —she must endeavour to anticipate other impressions; and for this purpose she resolved to seek an interview with him immediately on his return.

"I will write to him at once," she said to herself. "He has no reason to wish to avoid me; and if he had, he would conquer it at an appeal made in the name of poor Mabel."

And this strange yet matter-of-fact woman paused in the busy current of her thoughts and plans to bestow affectionate remembrance and true regret on her dead friend! Henrietta Prendergast was neither inconsistent nor insincere.

*　　　*　　　*　　　*　　　*

"I hope you did not think me intrusive in asking you to call on me so soon," said Henrietta to Chudleigh Wilmot, when he had duly presented himself in answer to a note from her, which she had written on the day Dr Whittaker had told her Wilmot had returned to London.

"You have seen him, of course?" she had asked Dr Whittaker.—"Yes, I have seen him. He looks extremely ill—wretchedly ill, in fact. As unlike a man who has just come in for a tremendous stroke of luck as any man I ever saw. I fancy he was more cut up about his wife's death than either you or I gave him credit for—eh, Mrs Prendergast?"

And now, holding Wilmot's hand in hers, and looking into his sunken eyes, marking his sallow cheek, the rigidity of the expression of his face, the thinness of his hand, she thought that Dr Whittaker's first impressions were correct. He did look ill, wretchedly ill. He did indeed look little like a favourite of fortune.

He assured her, very kindly, that her note had only fore-stalled his intention of calling upon her immediately, and apologized for his former omission.

"I ought to have come to say good-bye," he said; "but I could not indeed. I made no adieux possible to be avoided."

"And have you benefited by your absence? Have you gained health and spirits to enjoy the good fortune which has befallen you?"

She asked him these questions in a tone of more than conventional kindness; but her face told him she read the answer in his.

"I am quite well," he said quickly; "but perhaps I don't enjoy my good fortune very much. I am alone in the world, Mrs Prendergast; and my fortune has been gained by the loss of the best friend I ever had in it."

"Yes," she said thoughtfully, "that is very true. Poor Mr Foljambe! He missed you very much; but," she added, for she saw the painful expression of self-reproach which she had noticed in their first interview after Mabel's death settle down upon his face, "you must not grieve about that. He expressed the utmost confidence in Dr Whittaker."

"I know—I know," said Wilmot. "Still I wish—how-ever, that is but one of many far heavier griefs. I did not come to talk about my troubles," he said with a faint smile. "You had something to say to me—what is it? Not only to congratulate me on being a rich man now that it is too late, I am sure."

"It is not altogether too late, I think," said Henrietta in a low impressive voice; "and I wanted to speak to you of something connected alike with your grief and your fortune."

"Indeed!" said Wilmot in a tone of anxious surprise.

"Yes," said Henrietta; "I did not know how long or how short a time you might be within my reach; and so I determined to lose no time in endeavouring to gain your assent to a wish of poor Mabel's."

The conscious blood rushed into Wilmot's face. This, then, was the double connection of his present visit with his grief and his fortune. And he had not been thinking of Mabel! His dead wife's friend believed him indifferent to the wealth that had come too late to be shared by her; and except for the first sudden remembrance which the sight of Henrietta had produced, he had not thought of his dead wife at all. He thought of her now with keen remorse—keener because it had not occurred to him to think of her before, in connection with his wealth. Yes, the life which had had so dark an ending might have been very bright and prosperous now, with all this useless money to gild it. He shrunk from Mrs Prendergast's steady eyes with all the shame and uneasiness of a candid nature when given credit for motives or deeds superior to the truth. No vision of the dead face he had seen, awfully white and still, in his little loved home, had arisen to blot out the prospect of a future rich in all that wealth can give, to teach him how infinitely little is that all, how poor that richness! But he carried about for ever between him and the sunshine a vision of a fair girlish face, with pleading innocent blue eyes, with golden hair and faintly flushing cheeks, with sweet sensitive lips, and over all a look which he knew well and interpreted only too accurately. And that face, it did not lie in a coffin indeed, but as far, as hopelessly away from him—it lay on another man's breast. This was his grief; the other—well, the other was his shield from suspicion, from observation, his defence. He seized upon it, feeling unutterably the degradation of the evasion, and answered:

"I will be more than grateful, Mrs Prendergast, if you can show me any way in which I can fulfil any wish of hers,

If there is anything within the power of any effort of mine, let me know it."

Then Henrietta, in her turn, putting the dead woman forward as a pretext, began to discuss with Wilmot the provisions of a certain charitable institution, to which she knew it had been Mrs Wilmot's wish to contribute, but which she had not felt entitled by her means to assist. Wilmot acceded to all her suggestions with the utmost readiness, besought her to tax her memory for any other resource for doing honour to Mabel's memory, and prolonged his visit considerably beyond Henrietta's expectation. In her softened manner there was now no reproach, and her sense and calmness refreshed his jaded spirits. It was a relief to him to be in the company of a woman who did not expect him to be anything but sorrowful, and who yet had no suspicion of the cause and origin of his sorrow. So thought Wilmot, as he left Henrietta, having asked her permission to call on her again speedily.

And at the same moment Henrietta was thinking—

"He knows something of the torture of love unrequited and in vain now. It won't last, of course ; but for the present, if she could only know it, poor Mabel is avenged !"

CHAPTER XXV

MRS RAMSAY CAIRD AT HOME.

MR and Mrs Ramsay Caird lived, it is needless to say, in a fashionable quarter of the town. They could not have lived in any other. Their lot being essentially cast among fashionable people, it was necessary for them to reside somewhere within fashionable people's ken ; and that ken is, to say the least of it, limited. It is known to vul-

garians and common persons that there are buildings beyond
Oxford-street on the north side; but it is not known to
fashionable people. They, to be sure, know that some "old
families"—and this is said with an emphasis which conveys
that the families in question are almost pre-Adamite in their
age—reside in Portman-square. The fashionable world allows this as a kind of old-world eccentricity, as it allows
male members of said families to appear in the evening in
blue tail-coats and brass buttons, and to swathe their necks
in rolls of cravat, instead of donning the ordinary small tie.
It is a respectable eccentricity; but it is an eccentricity after
all. North of Oxford-street is as much "the other side" to
the fashionable world as is Suez to the Eastern travellers by
the Peninsular and Oriental route. The fashionable world
has heard of the big terraces of splendid mansions which
Messrs Kelk and Austin have built in the Bayswater-road
facing the Park; they have seen them occasionally when
they have been driving to Kensington-gardens; they believe
them to be inhabited by a respectable moneyed class; but
the idea of looking upon them as residences for themselves
has never once struck them. These houses are such an
enormous distance from "anywhere," which to the fashionable world is bounded by Regent-circus on the east, Belgrave-
square on the south, the Marble Arch on the west, and
Oxford-street on the north.

It is possible that if the choice of district had been
left to Madeleine herself, poor child, she, never particularly
caring about such matters, and not being in a very critical
or very argumentative state of mind at the period of her
marriage, would have fixed upon some comfortable pleasant
house, cheerful, roomy, airy, but in a wrong situation. If
the choice had been left to her father, there is no doubt that
he would have made some tremendous blunder of the like
kind; for Kilsyth when in London was always opening his
arms and expanding his chest and gasping for air. Accus-

tomed to the free atmosphere of his native Highlands, the worthy gentleman suffered torture in the dull, dead, confined and vitiated air of the London street; and amidst the many sufferings which he underwent for the sake of society during the few weeks when he remained in town was the martyrdom which he was put to in the tiny ill-ventilated rooms in which he had occasionally to dine or pass a ghastly half-hour "assisting" at a reception. But Lady Muriel and Mr Ramsay Caird took this matter in hand. Of their own express wish it was to them the task of selecting the residence of the about-to-be-married couple was to be confided; and there was no doubt that they would take care that their choice should not be open to question.

On Squab-street, Grosvenor-place, that choice fell. A curious street Squab-street; a street in a progressive state; a street which was feeling the immediate vicinity of Cubitopolis, but which was yielding to the advancing conquest piecemeal and by slow degrees; a street of small houses originally occupied by small people—doctors, clerks well-up in the West-end government offices, a barrister or two with fashionable proclivities, and several lodging-houses, always filled with good visitors from the country or eligible regular tenants; a quiet street, looked upon for many years as being a long way off, but suddenly awaking to find itself in the centre of fashion. For while the doctors had been paying their ordinary seven-and-sixpenny visits within what was then almost their suburban neighbourhood; while the West-end government-office clerks had been plodding to and fro from their offices; while the barristers had been pluming themselves on the superiority of their position to that of their brethren, who, true to old tradition, had set up their Lares and Penates in the neighbourhood of Russell-square and the Foundling Hospital; while the lodging-house-keeper had vaunted as recommendations the quietude of the vicinity and the freshness of the air, the great district now known as

Belgravia was being reclaimed from its native mud, the wild meadow called the Field of Forty Footsteps was being drained and built on, the desolate tract over which our ancestors pursued their torch-lighted way to Ranelagh and Vauxhall was being spanned by arches and undermined with gas-pipes; and when all these grand improvements were complete, Squab-street, which had held a respectable but ignominious existence as Squab-street, Pimlico, blossomed out in the *Post-Office Directory* and the *Court-Guide* as Squab-street, S.W., and thenceforward emerged from its chrysalis state, and became a recognizable and appreciated butterfly.

The effect of the change on the street itself was immediate. Two or three leases fell in about that time, and the householders, in whose families the leases had been for a couple of generations, made no doubt of their renewal. Lord Battersea was the ground landlord—not a liberal man, not a generous man; in short, a screw, and the driver of a hard bargain, but still a good landlord. He would be all right, of course. Would he? When the leaseholders went to Lord Battersea's man of business, an apple-faced old gentleman with a white head and a kind of frosty wire for beard, they learned that his lordship had fully comprehended the change in the state of affairs in Squab-street, and was prepared to act accordingly. As each lease fell in, the house which was vacant was to be increased by a couple of stories, and to have its rent trebled. Squab-street was to be a fitting accessory to Grosvenor-place. In vain the dispossessed ex-tenants declared that none of his lordship's then holders could pay the new rent: the apple-faced old gentleman was sorry; but he thought his lordship could find plenty of tenants who would. The tenants grumbled; but the man of business was firm. So were the tenants; they yielded up their leases; and so the houses were improved, and the rents were raised, and other tenants came of a class hitherto unknown to Squab-street. Married officers of the Guards, who found the situation convenient for Wellington, and not inconvenient for Portman barracks; members of parliament, who found it handy for the House; railway engineers and contractors of fabulous wealth, who could skurry to and fro their offices in Great George-street; and City magnates, who walked to Westminster-bridge, and went humbly in to the Shrine of Mammon by the penny-boat. All these newcomers lived in the enlarged houses, gorgeous stucco-fronted edifices, with porticoes which looked as if they did not belong to the house, but were leaning up against it by accident, and plate-glass windows and conservatories about the size of a market-gardener's hand-lights.

But the other houses in Squab-street, the leases of which had not run out, remained in their normal condition, and were the same little brisk, cheery, cleanly, snug common brick edifices that they had been ever since they were built. The new style of buildings had grown up round about them, and was dotted here and there amongst them; so that the range of houses in Squab-street looked like a row of uneven teeth. The original settlers, who at first had been rather overawed by the immigrants, had in time come to look upon their arrival as rather a benefit than otherwise; the doctors extended the number and the importance of their patients; the government clerks bragged judiciously of the "swells" who lived in their street; and the lodging-house-keepers, secure with leases of many unexpired years, raised their prices season after season, and found plenty of fish to swallow their hooks.

The house which Lady Muriel and Ramsay Caird, after much driving about, worrying of house-agents, search of registers, obtaining of cards to view, and general soul-depression and leg-weariness,—the house which they eventually decided upon was represented in the sibylline books of the agent as an "eligible bachelor's residence, in that fashionable locality Squab-street, S.W " Such indeed it had been for several previous years; the Honourable Peregrine Fluke, known generally as Fat Fluke, from his tendency to obesity, or Fishy Fluke, from a card transaction in which he had once been mixed up, having been its respected occupant. The Honourable Peregrine Fluke was a very eligible bachelor indeed, and led the life of the gay young fellow and the sad dog until he had passed sixty years of age. Then pale Death, knocking away with impartial rat-tat at the doors of all, the huts of the poor and the castellated turrets of kings, stopped at 122 Squab-street, and called for the Honourable Peregrine Fluke. The eligible bachelor succumbing to the summons, his executors came upon the scene ; and wishing to do the best for the lieutenant in the Marines, who was understood to be the eligible bachelor's nephew, but who was clearly proved to be his illegitimate son, put up the lease of the house—the only available thing belonging to the deceased —to auction, and found a purchaser in Kilsyth. Lady Muriel's clever tact also secured the furniture at a comparatively cheap rate. It was not first-rate furniture—a little rococo and old-fashioned ; but a few things could be imported into the drawing-rooms ; and, after all, Ramsay and his wife were not rich people—young beginners, and that kind of thing, and the place would do very well to commence their married life in. Lady Muriel always spoke of "Ramsay and his wife" when any monetary question was under debate, ignoring utterly that all the money came from Madeleine's side. For not only was there Madeleine's twenty thousand pounds, but Kilsyth, when the marriage was settled, announced his intention of making the young couple such an allowance as would prevent his favourite child from missing any of the comforts, any of the luxuries, to which she had become accustomed.

The situation was undoubtedly fashionable ; but that the house itself might have been more comfortable could not be denied. What was complimentarily called the hall, but was really the passage, was so small, that the enormous footmen, awaiting the descent of their employers from the little drawing-rooms above, dared not house themselves therein. Two of them would have filled it to overflowing; so they were compelled either to remain with the carriages, or to run the chance of being out of the way when required, and solace themselves in the tap of the Battersea Arms, down the adjacent mews. The door was so small and so low, that these great creatures rubbed their cockades and ruffled their coats in passing through it. The house stood at the corner of the mews, and every vehicle that drove in or out caused an earthquake-like sensation as it passed. Doors creaked, china rocked, floors groaned, walls trembled. The little dining-room was like a red-flocked tank; the little drawing-rooms, encumbered with the newly-imported extra furniture, were so choke-full, that it was with the utmost difficulty that visitors could thread their way between table and couch and ottoman and *etagère*. It required a knowledge of the science of navigation to tack round the piano; and the visitor, when once he had reached a seat by the hostess near the fireplace, could scarcely devote himself to conversation, owing to the trouble which filled his mind as to how he would ever get away again. It was not advisable to open any of the side-windows, even in the hottest weather, or a stably odour at once pervaded the house, and the forcible language addressed by the grooms to the horses, whose toilet was performed in the open yard, was a little too audible. It was impossible for guests to go through the ceremony of "taking down" to dinner. The steep little ladder-like staircase was only passable by one person at a time; and in the narrow little tank of a dining-room the people who sat with their backs to the fire were roasted alive, and had the additional pleasure of having to eat their meat vegetable-less and sauce-less, there being no approach to them and no passing them. Still every one said that the situation was delightful, and the house was "quite charming;" and Lady Muriel and Ramsay Caird took great credit to themselves for having secured it.

Madeleine herself was but little impressed by it. It was immaterial to her where she lived, or in what style of house. She shrugged her shoulders when they told her the rooms were charming; she raised her eyebrows when her servants complained of darkness and inconvenience. "It did very well," was her highest commendation, and she never found fault. If this girl's life had not been strangely solitary and without companionship, she would have had all sorts of confidences to exchange with some half-dozen intimates as to her new life, her new home, her new career. As it was, she dropped into it quietly, with scarcely a remark to any one. After her little and short-lived daydream had dissolved, after she had awakened to the exact realities which were about her, her period of suspense was very short. What passed between her and her brother Ronald at the interview which, as settled with Lady Muriel, he sought at his sister's hands was never known. The result was satisfactory to the prime movers in the scheme; and the result was that Madeleine was to marry Ramsay Caird. There was another interview connected with the matter which neither Lady Muriel nor Ronald ever heard of. When the news was first announced to him by his wife, Kilsyth received it very quietly. The next morning, before my lady had risen, the fond father, in pursuance of an appointment made in a note secretly sent up by the maid the night before, went to his darling's room, and had a half-hour's long and earnest conversation with her. Earnest on his side at all events: he asked her whether this engagement had been brought about of her own free will; if she had thought over it sufficiently; if she would wish the time of betrothal to be lengthened beyond the usual period; if there were anything, in fact, in which she would wish to make reference to him, and in which he could aid her. To all these inquiries, urged in the warmest and most affectionate manner, he got but the same kind of reply. Madeleine kissed her father fondly. She hated the thought of leaving him, she said; but it would do very well. It would do very well! She had not even the heart to be deceitful—to feign delight when she did not feel it. It would do very well! Kilsyth's warm heart beat more slowly as he listened to this lukewarm appreciation of the expected joys of his daughter's future; he scarcely comprehended anything so *fade* and so spiritless from a young girl about to undergo such an important change in all the phases of her existence. He again pressed his question home, and received the same answer; and then he made up his mind, for the thousandth time in his life, that women were extraordinary creatures, and that there was no dealing with them. This was a very favourite axiom of his, and had been enounced with much solemnity frequently. On this occasion, however, he kept silence, shaking his head in a very thoughtful and prophetic manner as he descended the stairs to his own dressing-room. It would do very well! Madeleine thought of the reply which she had given to the most important question ever put to her, after her father had left her and when she was alone. She knew her father well enough to be certain that a word spoken at that time by her to him would have stopped the engagement, and left her free. And what would then have ensued? She would have made an enemy of Lady Muriel, with whom she had to live; she would have deeply annoyed Ronald, who had always, in 'his odd way, shown the greatest love for her and the keenest interest in her welfare; and in the great question of her life she would have advanced not one whit. Chudleigh Wilmot was gone—gone for ever. An alliance—a continuance even of the friendship, such as it had been, with him was impossible; her friends wanted her to marry Ramsay Caird. Well, then, it would do very well!

A phrase significant of a state of mind in which marriages are often undertaken, but surely an unlucky and a pitiable state of mind. Something more than a tacit acquiescence is meant by the vows of the marriage-service; and though cynics endeavour to persuade us that these vows are far more frangible and far more often broken than they used to be, it is as well to believe in the whole force of them while we stand before the altar-rails, and before the priest utters his benediction. And the worst of it all was that the phrase expressed Madeleine's feelings thoroughly —her feelings as regarded her marriage, her feelings towards her husband. It *was* Ramsay Caird—it might have been Clement Penruddock, or Frank Only, or Lord Roderick Douglas, or half-a-dozen others. She had an equal liking for all these men; no love for any one of them. In her earlier girlish days, some year or two beforehand, she had wondered which of the young men who frequented the house would propose to her, and which of them she would marry. None of them had ever proposed to her. They saw long before she did that she was marked down for Ramsay Caird. These sort of things are concealed with the utmost discretion by long-headed mothers, are never suspected by daughters, and are discussed between male friends of the family with much openness and freedom. She had been a favourite with all these pleasant youths; but they knew perfectly well why Ramsay Caird was always at the house, and why he inevitably had the best chance; and their regard for Lady Muriel was by no means diminished by the clever manner in which she aided and assisted her protégé.

After marriage, at least during the first few months after marriage, it was very much the same. Madeleine "liked" her husband; he was quite gentlemanly, genial, cheery, very hospitable, very fond of pleasure, very fond of spending money on her, on himself, on any one. He never interfered with her in the smallest degree, and never was happier than when she was under the chaperonage of her mother, and his attendance on her was not required. During the first few months of her married life she received a vast number of callers; all of whose visits she duly repaid; went out constantly to dinners, balls, receptions of all kinds, to operas and theatres, private and public fêtes,—everywhere, in short, where people can go with decency and enjoy themselves. Not that Madeleine enjoyed herself. "It would do very well" seemed to be the keynote no less in her pleasures than in the rest of her life. In company she sat with the same ever-blank look until she was roused. Then she responded with the same smile. Oh, so unlike her old smile! With an upward glance of her blue eyes, where there was no light now, and with the little society-laugh which she had recently learned, and which was so different from the hearty ringing burst which used to greet her father's ears at Kilsyth in the old days before her illness—those days which seemed to her, to them all, but to her most of all, so long ago.

Visitors she had in plenty. Scarcely a morning passed without a call from Lady Muriel, who, still priding herself upon the admirable manner in which by her tact her stepdaughter had been "settled," looked in to see how she was getting on, to learn who had been to see her during the previous day, what parties she had been to, whom she had met, what their reception of her had been, and what invitations for forthcoming gaieties she had received. A comparison of notes on these last matters, now a favourite occupation of Lady Muriel's, with whose great name the world of fashion had begun to busy itself, proclaiming her as one of its leaders, —and she, always equal to the occasion, had accepted the tribute gracefully, and, as in everything else, conscientiously

discharged the duties of her position,—then luncheon, to which
meal Lady Muriel would frequently remain, and when some
of the more intimate friends of the family, notably Mrs
M'Diarmid, would drop in ; not that Mrs M'Diarmid's accession added much to the comfort of the meal. The dear old
lady, when her favourite project of marrying Madeleine to
Wilmot had been untimely nipped in the bud, and when
she saw that Ramsay Caird, whom she cordially disliked, was
the accepted suitor, relinquished all opposition in silence, and
contented herself with sniffing loudly, as the sole demon-
stration of her displeasure. That marriage-service, which she
had pictured to herself with so many different "eligibles"
as bridegrooms, might, but for the presence of mind of his
Right Reverence of Boscastle, have been sorely interrupted
by the defiant sniffs which came from the right-hand pew
close by the altar-rails, where Mrs Mac, dressed in the brown
moire which had so often filled her dreams, had bestowed herself, to the deep indignation of the pew-opener. But she
did not allow her disapproval of the marriage to interfere
with her love for "her dear child;" she came constantly to
Squab-street ; and the pleasantest hours of Madeleine's life
were passed in the society of this good old woman, when she
knew that there was no call upon her to exert herself in any
way, or to show herself otherwise than she really was ; when
she could lie back in her chair, and indulge herself with the
sweet sad day-dream of "what might have been," which con-
trasted so harshly and unsatisfactorily with what was.

A drive in her step-mother's carriage, or a round of calls
in her own brougham, filled up the afternoon, until it was
time to return home to preside at her tea-table and receive
her friends. After her engagement had been regularly announced there had been a good deal of fuss made about that
five-o'clock tea-table ; the young men who were intimate at
Brook-street had vowed that they would make it the
pleasantest in London ; that more news should be heard there

z

than anywhere else; and that the men who write in the *Cotillon*—a charming amateur journal of political *canards* and society gossip, published during the season—should go on their knees and implore invitations. The tea-table had been established in due course, but it had not been such a success as had been anticipated. Madeleine was *triste* and quiet to a degree. The men could not understand it, she had always been. so pleasant before her marriage; unlike most women, who are always a doosid sight pleasanter after it. They had been in the habit of finding their old partners of the two or three previous seasons, now married, by no means indisposed to listen to the compliments which they had been erst in the habit of addressing to them; and the practice had derived additional piquancy from the fact of the change of condition in the person addressed. There was Lady Violet Penruddock, for instance, only married to old Clem—oh, within a few weeks of Miss Kilsyth's marriage; and how jolly she was! Looked as fresh as possible—fresh as paint, some fellow said; but that was a confounded shame, don't you know,—only a little powder and that kind of thing, what all girls use, don't you know—doosid cruel you women are to one another! There was Lady Vi, jolly as a sand-boy! Old Clem was at his club, or some place, and didn't come home till late, and there was always tearing fun at Grosvenor-gate. Charmin' woman, Lady Vi; and very wise of old Clem to like to read the evening papers, and that kind of thing. Not that there was anything to be complained of Caird in this matter; never thought much of Caird, eh, did you? he was never at home; but his wife had grown so confoundedly dull, hipped, and that kind of thing—bored, don't you know? sits still and don't say a word except yes and no; don't help a feller out a bit, you know, and looks rather dreary and dull.

Poor Madeleine! she was beginning to be found out by her friends. If you live in society you must contribute your quota, according to your means—either your rank, your

money, your talent—towards the general stock ; but unless
your birth will warrant it, you must never be dull; and in
no case must you differ from the ordinary proceedings of
your order. Madeleine was very unlike Lady Violet Penruddock, she felt—very unlike indeed. But that was her
misfortune, not her fault. She would have been very glad
to laugh and flirt with all her old friends, to talk nonsense
and innocent scandal, and all the society chit-chat, if she had
been able ; but she was not able. Under all her quiet
manner and shyness and girlishness Madeleine Caird possessed what Lady Violet Penruddock had never pretended
to—a heart. That heart had been hurt and torn and lacer-
ated ; and as in the present day it is not possible to explain
this, or rather it is considered essential to hide it, Madeleine
was obliged to put up with the imputation of dulness, when
in reality she was merely suffering from having loved some
one who, as she thought, did not care for her, and having
been compelled to marry somebody for whom she had no real
affection.

Did Ramsay Caird ever fancy that his wife did not care
for him, or at least was not as romantically fond of him as
are most wives of their husbands during the first few months
after marriage ? If he did, did the reflection ever cost him
a moment's anxiety, a moment's distrust, a thought that
perhaps his own course of living was not precisely adapted
to enthral the affections of a young girl ? Not for an
instant. Ramsay, when Lady Muriel's half-spoken hints
had first enlightened him as to the position which, for his
dead brother's sake, her ladyship proposed to him to hold,
had cogitated over the matter in an essentially business-
like spirit, and had come to the conclusion that such an
opportunity ought by all means to be made the most of.
He was a calculating, cautious young man, entirely devoid
of impulse ; and—as had been suspected by more than one
of the frequenters of the Brook-street establishment, who,

however, were much too good fellows to hint at it openly—
he was a man fond of common, not to say gross pleasures,
which his limited means prevented him from indulging in.
A marriage with Madeline Kilsyth, herself a very nice girl,
as society girls went, would give him position, ease, and
money—leave him his own master, with power and opportunity to pursue his own devices—and was therefore for
him in every respect most desirable.   With all his easy
bearing, his *laissez-aller* manners, and his apparent *non-
chalance*, Mr Ramsay Caird possessed his full share of the
national 'cuteness; and having made up his mind to win,
looked carefully round him to see where his course lay
straightest, and what shoals were to be avoided.   He determined to make a waiting race of it, convinced that any
eagerness or ill-timed enthusiasm might spoil his chance;
he saw that his game was to be quiet and wait upon his
oars until he received the signal to dash out into mid-
stream; his complete willingness to attend to all suggestions, and to take his time from the family, quite fascinated
Ronald Kilsyth, from whom at first Caird had apprehended
opposition; and, as we have seen, when the time came he
declared himself with so strong a show that no other com-
petitor dared put in an appearance.

But when the race had been run and the prize secured,
Ramsay Caird felt that the crisis was past, that the long
course of tutelage under which he had placed himself was
at an end, and that henceforward he would enjoy those bene-
fits for the acquisition of which he had regulated his
conduct for so many months.   He had not the smallest
love for his wife; he had even but small admiration for her
looks.   Madeleine's blue eyes and golden hair were too
cold and insipid for his taste.   In his freer moments he
was accustomed to talk about " soul "—an attribute which
poor Maddy was supposed not to possess—and " liquid
eyes " and " classic features " and the " sunny South "—

which, as Tommy Toshington remarked, when told of it,
accounted for his having seen Caird on the previous Sunday
afternoon ringing at the door of the villa temporarily
tenanted by Madame Favorita, the *prima donna* of the
Opera, and situated in the Alpha-road. Tommy Toshington invariably happened to be passing by when the wrong
man was ringing at the wrong house; and got an immense
number of pleasant dinners out of the coincidence. So
that Ramsay Caird saw but little of the interior of his own
house after leaving it in the mornings. He at first had
been somewhat punctilious and deferential with Lady
Muriel, taking care to be at home when she came, and to be
in attendance when he thought she would require his
presence; but after a few weeks he threw off this restraint,
and kept the hours which suited him. Kilsyth looked
blank and uncomfortable once or twice when at dinners,
specially given in honour of the new-married couple, Madeleine had appeared alone, and Lady Muriel had proffered a
story of Ramsay's toothache or business appointment; and
Ronald had looked black, and held more than one muttered
conversation with his step-mother, in the course of which
his brows contracted, and his mouth grew very rigid. But
Madeline never uttered a word of complaint, although Lady
Muriel was in daily expectation of an outburst. She sat
quietly, sadly, uninterestedly by. Better, far better, for all
concerned if she had had sufficient feeling of her own lone-
liness, of her own neglected condition, to appeal in language
however forcible and strong. To labour under the "it-will-
do-very-well" feeling is to be on the high road to destruction.

CHAPTER XXVI.

INQUISITORIAL.

LADY MURIEL KILSYTH had carried her cherished plan into execution—had seen her wishes as regarded Madeleine and her kinsman Ramsay Caird fulfilled. With wonderfully little trouble, too. When she·thought over it all, she was surprised at the apparent ease and rapidity with which the marriage, which she had regarded, after Madeleine's illness at Kilsyth, as a difficult matter to manage, had been brought about. Time had done it all for her—time, assisted by her own tact and skill, and the accomplished fashion after which she had removed all removable obstacles, and availed herself of every circumstance and indication in favour of her cherished project. Nor had the smallest injury to her own position resulted from manœuvering which Lady Muriel would have been ready to blast, if performed by any one else, with the ruinous epithet, "vulgar matchmaking." No, not the smallest. Indeed, Lady Muriel Kilsyth was one of those fortunate individuals whose position may be generally regarded as, under all circumstances, unassailable. She stood as well with Ronald as ever; and Lady Muriel, with all her imperturbable but never offensive pride, was more anxious about standing well with her step-son than the world would have consented to believe she could have been about securing the good opinion of any human being. She stood, as she always had done, first and chief in the love and esteem of her husband, who, if he did not "understand" her—and he was none the less happy with her that he assuredly did not—made up for his want of comprehension by the most uncompromising trust, devotion, and admiration,—all manifested in his own quiet peculiar way. As this "way" included allowing her the most absolute liberty of action, and an apparent impossibility of questioning her judgment on any conceivable point, it suited Lady Muriel admirably.

Kilsyth was perfectly satisfied with Madeleine's marriage. He believed in love-matches, and it never occurred to him to doubt that this was one. He had quietly taken it for granted, first, because Ramsay Caird had spoken of their "mutual attachment," when he had formally asked Kilsyth for the precious gift of his daughter. Then, Lady Muriel had spoken so warmly of Ramsay's love for Madeleine, had shown such generous and sensitive susceptibility to the possibility of Kilsyth's thinking she had been wrong and injudicious in admitting to such close household intimacy a relative of her own, who was not qualified, as far as fortune was concerned, to pretend to his daughter's hand. Thirdly, if he never doubted Ramsay's being in love with Madeleine —and he never did doubt it for an instant—what could be more natural than that all the young men who had the chance should be in love with Madeleine? Still less could it have occurred to him to doubt that Madeleine was in love with Ramsay. Ramsay had neither rank nor fortune to give her—that was very certain; and Kilsyth knew of only two motives as possible incentives to marriage—love and money. Under any circumstances, he never could have suspected his daughter of being actuated by the latter. The fine, gallant, unsophisticated, hearty old fellow, who had had a fair share of happiness all his life, and whose knowledge of human nature was as superficial as his judgment of it was genial, had no notion that pique, thwarted love, blighted hope, wounded pride, the strong and desperate necessity of hiding suffering from kindred household eyes, or an infatuated yearning for the freedom, in certain respects, whose value a man can never estimate, and which a girl gains by her marriage, were among the not unfrequent causes of the taking of that tremendous step. He had never talked to Maddy about her love for Ramsay Caird, certainly; it would never

have occurred to him to "make the girl uncomfortable," as
he would have expressed it, by any such proceeding; but he
would as soon have suspected that Madeleine had brought
an asp to her new home among her wedding-clothes as believed that the girl's heart hid, ever so far down in its
depths, another image than her husband's.

So Kilsyth was satisfied, in his genial and outspoken
way; and Ronald was satisfied, after his grim undemonstra-
tive fashion. And Lady Muriel stood well with all concerned, especially with Madeleine. All the petty restraints
of "step-mother" authority, inevitably resented even by
the most amiable natures, however mildly exercised, were
gone now. Maddy was on a social level with Lady Muriel;
there could never more be any of the little discords between
them there had been; and Madeleine, as she took her own
place in the world, and felt, with a sudden sort of shock, as
if she had grown ever so much older, woke up to a fuller
consciousness of Lady Muriel's many attractions than she
had ever previously attained. She recognized her beauty,
her grace, her dignity, her perfect breeding, her thorough
savoir faire, with real appreciation now, and true pleasure
and admiration; and one of the happiest thoughts in which
she indulged was of how she would be such "good friends"
with Lady Muriel, and how she would take her for the
model of her conduct, and in every respect her social guide.
She was perfectly aware of the dissimilarity which existed
between them; and she never would have been guilty of the
absurdity of "copying" Lady Muriel's manners, but she
might be guided by her for all that. So much the more
readily now that she was not always in dread of hearing
Wilmot mentioned, of being reminded of him, of exciting a
suspicion by some inadvertence that she had been guilty of
the folly of thinking he had cared for her just a little. No
fear of that now. She was married and *safe*—poor child!

Unsuspicious by nature, ignorant of the world, and unconsciously living a life apart, a life in her own thoughts and reveries, Madeleine was wonderfully indifferent to the conduct of her husband. Either she was really unconscious of it for some time after it had begun to excite the fears of her father, the suspicions of Lady Muriel, the anger of her brother, and the gossip of society, or she successfully contrived to appear so. The judgment of the world leaned to the latter hypothesis; but the judgment of the world is always uncharitable, and frequently wrong. In the present instance it was both. Madeleine did not know that Ramsay Caird was behaving ill. He was always kind in his manner to her; and if he was—which there was no denying—a good deal away from home, why, he did not differ in that respect from many other men whom she knew or heard of, and it never occurred to Madeleine to resent his absence. Neither did it occur to her to ask herself whether she was not in real truth rather glad he should be so much away from her, nor to reflect that the world, which knew he was, would inevitably come to one of two conclusions, either that she was a most unhappy wife, or that she had never loved her husband.

No; Madeleine Caird thought of none of these things. She went on her way caring very little for anything; not entirely unhappy, surprised indeed at the variations in her own spirits, unable to account for the overwhelming sadness which beset her at some times, and finding equally inexplicable the ease with which she flung off this sadness at others. She was looked at and wondered at and talked of daily by scores of her acquaintances, and she was entirely unconscious that she was the subject of any such scrutiny.

Lady Muriel understood Madeleine's state of mind perfectly. She had a clue to it, which she alone possessed; and while she regarded Ramsay Caird's conduct with all the by no means inconsiderable strength of indignation of which she was capable, she was quite aware that Madeleine was only in the conventional sense an object of compassion.

Was Lady Muriel quite satisfied, was she perfectly content with her success? Hardly so; in the first place, because she was forced to condemn Ramsay Caird, and she did not like to acknowledge the necessity; in the second place, because the result of this success, personal to her, that to which it was to owe its best value, its chief sweetness, was delayed. She chafed at Wilmot's absence now; she had hailed it until Madeleine's marriage had been an accomplished fact; she had tolerated it for a little time afterwards; but now—now her impatience was undisguised to herself, now she wanted this man to return—this man who lent her life such a strange charm, in whose presence the common atmosphere took a vivid colouring, and everyday things and occurrences assumed a different meaning and value.

Lady Muriel had heard of Chudleigh Wilmot's accession to fortune reasonably soon after the occurrence of the event. Kilsyth happened to be out of town for a few days on the occasion of Mr Foljambe's death, and had therefore not attended the funeral. General report, at least in Lady Muriel's particular sphere, had not yet proclaimed the succession of one unlinked by ties of blood to the rich banker to the large fortune with which rumour correctly accredited Mr Foljambe, and it remained for Lady Muriel to learn the news from the same source whence Henrietta Prendergast had derived the account of Madeleine's marriage. It was from Mrs Charlton that Lady Muriel heard the interesting tidings, and Mrs Prendergast was present on the occasion. It was the first time she had ever been in the same room with Lady Muriel Kilsyth, and she had regarded her with lively curiosity, and much genuine, honest admiration. The finished style of Lady Muriel's beauty—the sort of style which conveys the impression that the possessor of so much beauty is beautiful as much by a sovereign act of her will as by the decree and gift of nature; her grace of manner, true stamp of the *grande dame* set upon her, had irresistible attractions for Henrietta, who was one of those women, by no means so rare as the cynics would have us believe, who can heartily and enthusiastically admire the qualities, physical and mental, of individuals of their own sex.

"I am sure you will be glad to hear the news Mrs Prendergast has just told us," Mrs Charlton had said; and then Lady Muriel learned that Mr Foljambe had made Wilmot his heir. She received the intelligence with the perfection of friendly interest; she turned courteously to Mrs Prendergast, as though taking it for granted her congratulations were to be addressed to her individually, as Wilmot's relative or friend; and as she did so her heart beat rapidly, with the pulse of one who has escaped a great danger, as she thought, "Had this happened only a few weeks sooner all might have been lost!"

It was on the same day and at the same hour that Wilmot learned the same fact, from the letter of his dead friend, at Berlin.

Had Lady Muriel been a younger, a weaker, or a less experienced woman, she must inevitably have betrayed some emotion beyond that of mere gratification at a friend's good fortune to the keen eyes of Henrietta Prendergast. But her *savoir faire* was perfect, and she said and looked precisely what she ought to have said and looked. There was a strange accord in the impulsive thoughts of each ot these women, so different, so widely separated by circumstances. As Henrietta repeated the intelligence for Lady Muriel's information which she had already communicated to Mrs Charlton, she too was thinking, "Had this happened only a few weeks sooner all might have been lost!"

Madeleine's marriage was of no less importance to the designs and the hopes of Henrietta Prendergast than to those of Lady Muriel Kilsyth.

"I wonder what he will do now?" said Miss Charlton,

who had some of the advantages of silliness, among them a happy *naïveté*, which made it always safe to calculate upon her making some remark or asking some question which others might desire to proffer on their own behalf, but for the restraints of good taste. Lady Muriel could not imagine; Mrs Prendergast could not guess. Lady Muriel remarked that Dr Wilmot would probably be guided by the nature of Mr Foljambe's property, and the terms of the bequest.

"I fancy the whole property is in money, with the exception of the house in Portland-place," said Henrietta. "I have heard my poor friend Mrs Wilmot say that Mr Foljambe hated all the responsibility of landed property, and had none. So Dr Wilmot will be free—perhaps he will live altogether abroad."

"Do you think that probable?" said Lady Muriel, very courteously implying Mrs Prendergast's more intimate acquaintance with the object of the discussion. "For a man of his turn of mind, I fancy there's no place like London—certainly no country like England."

"Ah, yes, Lady Muriel, very true," said the irrepressible Miss Charlton, making her mother wince for the twentieth time since the commencement of the visit; "but then, you see, he has such painful recollections of London. His poor wife dying as she did, you know, while he was away attending to strangers."

"Very true," said Lady Muriel—with perfect self-possession, and purposely turning her head away from Mrs Charlton, who glanced angrily and despairingly at her unconscious daughter, and towards Henrietta, who shared her friend's dismay. "We all regretted that circumstance very deeply; and I do not wonder Dr Wilmot should have felt it as he did: still, he is so strong-minded a man—"

"And so perfectly convinced that it had nothing to do with his wife's death—I mean that he could not have saved her," said Henrietta quickly.

Lady Muriel looked at her inquiringly.

" Mrs Prendergast was Mrs Wilmot's intimate friend, and was with her when she died," Mrs Charlton said; and then another visitor came in, and a *tête-à-tête* established itself between Lady Muriel and Henrietta, which caused her visit to be prolonged considerably beyond any former experience of Mrs Charlton, and gave her ladyship a good deal to think of, when she had ordered her coachman to go into the Park, and gave herself up to her thoughts, mechanically returning the numerous salutes which she received, and thinking sometimes how strange it was that there was no one in all this great crowded London whom it could interest her to see.

"She must have been a strange woman," thought Lady Muriel, "and desperately uninteresting, I am sure. That Mrs Prendergast has plenty of character. He never mentioned her, that I can remember; but then he talked so little of himself, he said so little from which any notion of his daily life and its surroundings could be gathered. Yes, I am sure his wife was a tiresome, commonplace creature, with no kind of companionship in her—an insipid doll. What wonderful things one sees under the sun in the way of unsuitable marriages! To think of such a man marrying such a woman! But it is stranger still"—and here Lady Muriel's face darkened, and a hard look came into her beautiful brown eyes— "it is stranger still to think that such a man should be attracted by Madeleine—such a merely 'pretty girl.' And he was—he was; I could not be mistaken. If this fortune had come a little sooner, what would he have done? He could not of course have proposed to her—impossible in the time —but he might have told Kilsyth, and gotten his leave, when the year should be up. What a danger! I am glad I never thought of such a thing; I am glad the possibility never occurred to me. Ronald, indeed, would have been a barrier; but I need not, I must not deceive myself, Kilsyth would not have listened to Ronald where Madeleine's happiness was concerned. When will he return? He must come soon, I suppose, to arrange his affairs. I need not fear his admiration of Madeleine now—he is not a man to admire the woman who could marry Ramsay Caird. If she did betray to him that she loved him, he would have the best and plainest proof in her marriage how fickle and flimsy such a feeling is in her case."

Lady Muriel Kilsyth was in many respects a very superior, in many respects a highly-principled woman; but she had dreamed a forbidden dream, she had cherished a perverse thought, and such speculations as she would once have shrunk from with incredulous amazement had become not only possible but easy to her.

And then all her thoughts directed themselves towards the one object—Wilmot's return. When would he come back? She wrote the news of the disposition of Mr Foljambe's will to Kilsyth; and he answered in a few jovial lines, expressing his heartfelt satisfaction. She told the news to Madeleine; carelessly, skilfully, opening a large parcel of books as she spoke, and looking at the contents. Madeleine was in her ladyship's boudoir; her bonnet lay on the sofa by her side, and she was idly twisting the strings.

"You are going to fetch Ramsay from the club, are you, Maddy?"

"Yes," said Madeleine listlessly, and looking at the clock; "presently, I suppose. Have you anything new there?"

"New? yes. Good? I can't say. Nothing you would care for, I fancy. All the magazines, though. A new volume by Merivale,—not much after your fashion. A new novel by nobody knows whom—*Squire Fullerton's Will*. By-the-by, the name reminds me—I don't think you have heard about Mr Foljambe's Will?"

"No," said Madeleine rising, and tying on her bonnet at the chimney-glass.

"Your father is delighted. Only fancy, Mr Foljambe has left all his money to Dr Wilmot."

Madeleine did not answer for a minute. Then she said,

"I am very glad. Was Mr Foljambe very rich?"

"I believe so. They talk of its being a very large fortune. What a delightful change for Dr Wilmot! Of course he will give up his profession now, and take a place in society"

"Do you think he would give up his profession for anything, Lady Muriel?" asked Madeleine.

Lady Muriel was standing at a table, still sorting the books; she could not see Maddy's face.

"Give up his profession! Of course, my dear. A man of fortune is not likely to practise as a doctor, I should think; besides, the position."

"Every one—I mean Mr Foljambe always said Dr Wilmot was so devoted to his profession," said Madeleine hesitatingly.

"Of course he was; and of course his friends said so. It is the best and wisest thing a man can have said of him—the best character he can get, while he wants it, and easily laid aside when he doesn't. What's this? *Wine of Shiraz!* Oh, another book of travels with a fantastical name! Are you going, Maddy? Will you have one of these productions to try?"

"No, thank you," said Madeleine; and she took leave of Lady Muriel, and did not call for Ramsay at the club, but went home, and passed the evening with a book lying open on her knee—a book of which she never turned a page, and wondered when Chudleigh Wilmot would come home. She wondered whether his wealth would make him happy. She wondered whether, if he had been a rich man and not a hard-working doctor, he would have cared a little about her when his wife died; and whether it was really as Lady Muriel had said, or whether his devotion to his profession was genuine and true. She wondered whether he ever thought of her; she felt sure he knew of her marriage. Well, not *ever*—something forbade her using that word in her thoughts, something told her it would be unjust and unkind; but *much?* Ronald would hear about this bequest of Mr Foliambe's; would be glad—or sorry—or neither? Supposing it had come earlier, and *he*, Wilmot, had cared for her! would things have been different? would Ronald—But no, no; she must not think of that. Let her still believe he had seen in her only a patient, only a case of fever, only an occasion for the exercise of his skill. She wondered, if "things had been different"—which was the phrase by which she translated to herself "if she had married Wilmot"—whether it would have harmed any one; she did not dare to think how happy it would have made her. Ramsay? But no; not all the simplicity, not all the credulous egotism of girlhood—and Madeleine had her fair share of those natural qualities—could persuade her that Ramsay's life would have been marred if their marriage had never taken place. And so she wondered and wondered, recurring often in her thoughts solemnly to the dead woman who had been Wilmot's wife, and thinking sadly, wonderingly, over that life, all unknown to her; and yet concerning which some mysterious instinct had whispered to her vaguely and unhappily. She hoped people would not talk much to her, or before her, of this bequest of Mr Foljambe's. It embarrassed her, though she knew it ought not; who ought to be so ready as she to speak of him, to whom no one owed so much?

Henrietta Prendergast wondered too when Dr Wilmot would return to London; and questioned Dr Whittaker, who had contrived in a wonderfully brief space of time to accumulate an extraordinary quantity of information relative to the nature and extent of Wilmot's inheritance. The worthy man possessed an inherent talent for gossip, which was likely to be of great service to him in his career, being admittedly an immense recommendation for a physician, especially when his practice lies in a class of society largely productive of *malades imaginaires*. Wilmot was left at perfect liberty, except in the matter of the house in Portland-place. It was not to be sold; and Wilmot had ·instructed the solicitors to keep up the establishment, and retain the old housekeeper and butler permanently in his service. As for his old house in Charles-street, Wilmot had behaved most generously indeed—Dr Whittaker would say he had placed it entirely at his disposal nobly: for the remainder of his lease; and by the time that should expire he had expressed his conviction that Dr Whittaker would be making his fortune.

"All the more chance of it, Mrs Prendergast," said Whittaker with his smoothest smile, "that Wilmot will be out· of my way; he's a wonderfully clever fellow, wonderfully; and I can't imagine a more popular physician. I assure you he reminds me, in his way of dealing with a case, of Carlyle's description of Frederick the Great's eyes, 'rapidity resting upon depth.' Quite Wilmot—quite Wilmot, I assure you." And Dr Whittaker, considering that he had made a remarkably good hit, took himself off, leaving Henrietta with new matter for her thoughts.

The three women who thus pondered and thought and speculated about Chudleigh Wilmot had plenty˙ of time during which to indulge in these vain occupations. Time passed on, and Mr Foljambe's heir did not present himself to the tide of congratulations which awaited him. The first interest of the intelligence died out. Other rich men died, and left their wealth to other heirs expectant or non-expectant. "Foljambe's will" and "Wilmot's luck" had almost ceased to be talked about when Chudleigh Wilmot ventured into society. Henrietta Prendergast was the first of the three who saw him. As for Lady Muriel and Madeleine, they were less likely to meet him than any women in London; for the good reason that Wilmot sedulously avoided them. And for a time successfully; but that was not always to be. He believed that the page of the book of his life on which "Madeleine Kilsyth" was written was closed for ever; Fate had written upon another, "Madeleine Caird."

CHAPTER XXVII.

AGAINST THE GRAIN.

OF all those who were in the habit of seeing Madeleine under circumstances which made it possible for them to observe her closely, her brother had been the last to perceive and the most reluctant to acknowledge that the state of her health was far from satisfactory. Ronald Kilsyth was habitually unobservant in matters of the kind; and he usually saw Madeleine in the evening, when the false spirits and deceptive flush of her disease produced an appearance of health and vivacity which might have imposed upon a closer observer. He knew she had a cough indeed; but then "Maddy always had a cough—I never remember her without one," was the ready reply to any observations made on the subject in his hearing, and to any misgivings which occasionally flitted across his own mind. It did not occur to him that in this "fact" there was no reply at all, but rather an additional reason for apprehension concerning this cough. When Madeleine was a child, it was acknowledged that she was delicate. "She had it from her poor mother," Kilsyth would say—Kilsyth, who never had a day's illness in his life, and in whose family ninety years was considered a fair age. But she was to get strong, to "outgrow her delicacy " as she grew up. When Madeleine was a girl, she was still delicate; perhaps more continuously so than she had been as a child, though no longer subject to the maladies of childhood; but she was to get stronger as she grew older. Now Madeleine had grown older; the delicate girl, with her fragile figure and poetical face, was no more; in her place was a beautiful, self-possessed young woman—a wife, with a place in the world, and a career before her. Strange, but Madeleine was still delicate; the time unhesitatingly foretold, looked forward to so anxiously with a kind of weary patience by her father, had come; but it had not brought the anticipated, the desired result. Madeleine was more delicate than ever. Her friends saw it, her father saw it; her step-mother saw it more clearly than either—saw it with feelings which would have been remorseful, had she not arrested their tendency in that direction by constantly reminding herself that Madeleine had been delicate as a child and as a girl; but her brother had not permitted the fact to establish itself in his mind.

The old affection, tacitly interrupted for a time, when Madeleine had felt the unexpressed opposition of her brother to Chudleigh Wilmot, had been as tacitly restored between them since Madeleine's marriage. She had felt during that sad interval, all whose sadness was hidden and unspoken, never taking an external shape, but formless, like a sorrow in a dream, that circumstances and her surroundings were stronger than she was; she had felt somewhat like a prisoner, against and for whom conspiracies were formed, but who had no power to meddle in them, and no distinct knowledge of their methods or objects. Mrs M'Diarmid, she vaguely felt, was for her, in the secret desire of her heart; her brother against her. Ronald would have been successful in any case, she had been quite sure, even if he had not been at once justified and relieved of all apprehensions by Wilmot's departure. He did not care for her—he had gone away; they might each and all have spared the pains they had taken—their bug-bear had been only a myth. Then Madeleine, in whose mind justice had a high place, turned again to her brother as tacitly, as completely, without explanation, as she had turned from him, and loved him, admired him, thought about him, and clung to him as she had been wont to do. Which surprised Ronald Kilsyth, who had taken it for granted that Madeleine, who had married Ramsay Caird a good deal to the Captain's surprise—who had his theories concerning affinities and analogies, into which this alliance by no means fitted—but not at all to his displeasure, would discard everybody in favour of her husband, and devote herself to him after the gushing fashion of very young brides in ordinary. He had smiled grimly to himself occasionally, as he wondered whether Lady Muriel would be altogether satisfied with a match which was so largely of her own bringing about, and by which, whatever advantages she had secured to her own family, for whom she entertained a truly clannish attachment, she had undeniably provided herself with a young, beautiful, and ever-present rival in her own queendom of fashion and social sway. "Let them fight it out," Captain Kilsyth had thought; "it would have been pleasanter if Maddy had gone farther afield; but it cannot be helped. I am sure she is glad to get away from Lady Muriel; and I am sure Lady Muriel is glad to get rid of her. I don't understand her taking to Caird in this way; for I am as strongly convinced as ever it was no false alarm about Wilmot; she was in love with him; only," and his face reddened, "thank God, she did not know it. However, it is time wasted to wonder about women, even the best and the truest of them, and no very humiliating acknowledgment to say I cannot understand them."

But Captain Kilsyth was destined to find himself unable to discard reflection on his sister and her marriage after this fashion. Madeleine put all his previously conceived ideas to rout, and disconcerted all his expectations. She was by no means engrossed by her husband; she did not assume any of the happy fussiness or fussy happiness which he had observed exhibit themselves in *jeunes ménages* constructed on the old-fashioned principle of love, as opposed to the modern expedient of *convenance*. She was just as friendly, just as kindly with Ramsay Caird as she had been in the days before their brief engagement, in the days when Ronald had found it difficult to believe that Lady Muriel's wishes and plans would ever be realized. She did not talk about her house, or give herself any of the pretty "married-woman" airs which are additional charms in brides in their teens. She led, as far as Ronald knew, much the same sort of life she had led under her step-mother's chaperonage; and Kilsyth visited her every day: Ronald too, when he was in town; and he soon felt that he was all to her he had formerly been. The innocent, girlish, loving heart had room and power for grief indeed, but none for a half-understood anger, none for the prolongation of an involuntary estrangement. So the first months of Madeleine's married life were pleasant to her brother in his relations with her; and the first thing which occurred to trouble his mind in reference to her was his suspicion and dislike of certain points in Ramsay Caird's conduct. Here, again, Madeleine puzzled him. Naturally, he had no sooner conceived this suspicious displeasure against the man to whom such an immense trust as that of his sister's happiness had been commited than he sought to discover by Madeleine's looks and manner whether and how far her happiness was compromised by what he observed. But he failed to discover any of the indications which he sought. Madeleine's spirits were unequal, but her disposition had never been precisely gay; and there was no trace of pique, sullennness, or the consciousness of offence in her manner towards her husband.

It was when Ronald's indignation against Ramsay Caird was rising fast, and he began to think Madeleine either unaccountably indifferent to certain things which women of quite

as gentle a nature as hers would inevitably and reasonably
resent, or that she was concealing her sentiments, in the
interests of her dignity, with a degree of skill and cleverness
for which he was far from having given her credit, that his
sister's delicate health for the first time attracted Ronald's
attention.   And Mrs M'Diarmid was the medium of the
first communication on the subject which alarmed him.

As in all similar cases, attention once excited, anxiety
once awakened, the progress of both is rapid.   Ronald
questioned his father, questioned Lady Muriel, questioned
Ramsay Caird.   In each instance the result was the same.
Madeleine was undoubtedly very delicate, and the danger of
alarming her, which, as her organization was highly nervous
and sensitive, was considerable, presented a serious obstacle
to the taking of the active measures which had become undeniably desirable.

One day Ronald went to see his sister earlier in the day
than usual, having been told by Mrs M'Diarmid that her
looks in the evening were not by any means a reliable indication of the state of her health.   He found her lying on a
sofa in her dressing-room, wholly unoccupied, and with an
expression of listless weariness in her face and figure which
even his unskilled judgment could not avoid observing and
appreciating with alarm.

One hand was under her head, the other hung listlessly
down; and as Ronald drew near, and took it in his tenderly,
he saw how thin the fingers were, how blue the veins, how
they marked their course too strongly under the white skin,
and how the rose-tint was gone.   As he took the gentle
hand, he felt that it was cold; but it burned in his clasp
before he had held it a minute.   Like all men of his stamp,
Ronald Kilsyth, when he was touched, was deeply touched;
when his mood was tender, it was very tender.   Madeleine
looked at him; and the love and sadness in her smile pierced
at once his well-defended heart.

"What's this I hear, Maddy, about your not being

well?" he said, as he seated himself beside her sofa, and kissed her forehead—it was slightly damp, he felt, and she touched it with her handkerchief frequently while he stayed. "You were not complaining last week, when I saw you last; and now I've just come up to town, and been to Brook-street, I find my father and my lady quite full of your not being well. What is it all, Maddy? what are you suffering from, and why have you said nothing about it?"

"I am not very ill, Ronald," said Madeleine, raising herself, and propping herself up on her cushions by leaning on her elbow, one hand under her head, its fingers in her golden hair; more profuse and beautiful than ever Ronald thought the hair was. "I am really not a bit worse than I have been; only I suddenly felt a few days ago that I could not go on making efforts, and going out, and seeing people, and all that kind of thing, any longer; and then papa got uneasy about me. I assure you that is the only difference; and you know it does grow horribly tiresome, dear, don't you? At least you don't know, because you never would do it; and you were right; but I—I hadn't much else to do, and it does not do to seem peculiar; and I went on as long as I could. But this last week was really too much for me, and I had to tell Lady Muriel I must be quiet; and so I have been quiet, lying here."

She gave her brother this simple explanation, her blue eyes looking at him with a smile, and a tone in her voice as though she prayed him not to blame her.

"My poor child, my darling Maddy!" said Ronald, "to think of your trying to go on in that way, and feeling so unequal to it, and fancying all the time you must! What a wonderful life of humbug and delusion you women lead, to be sure, either with your will or against it! Now tell me, does Ramsay know how ill you are, and how you have been doing all sorts of things which are most unfit for you, until you are quite worn out?"

"Ramsay is very kind," said Madeleine; and then she

hesitated, and the colour deepened painfully in her face; "but you know, Ronald, men are not very patient with women when they are only ailing; if I were seriously ill, it would be quite a different thing. He really is not in the least to blame," she went on hurriedly; "he gets bored at home, you know; and since I have not been feeling strong, it has been quite a relief to me to be alone."

"I see—I understand," said Ronald; but his tone did not reassure Madeleine.

"You really must not blame him," she repeated. "You know *you* yourself did not perceive that I was ill before you went away; and it is only within the last week, I assure you. I suppose the cough has weakened me; for some time, in the morning, I have felt giddy going downstairs, so I thought it better not to try it until I get stronger."

"I have not heard you cough much, Madeleine, that is, not more than usual, you know. You have always had a cough, more or less."

"Yes," said Madeleine simply, "ever since I was born, I believe; but it is never really bad, except in the morning, and sometimes at night. Up to this time I have got on very well in the day and the afternoon; and I like the evening best of all, if I am not too tired. I feel quite bright in the evening, especially when I take my drops."

"What drops, Maddy?"

"The drops Sir Saville Rowe ordered for me last winter," said Madeleine. "I got on very well with them, and I don't want anything else. Papa wants me to see some of the great doctors, but there's really no occasion; and I hate strangers. Dr Whittaker comes occasionally—as Sir Saville wished—and he does well enough. The mere idea of seeing a stranger now—in that way—would make me nervous and miserable." Indeed she flushed up again, looked excited and feverish, and a violent fit of coughing came on, and interrupted any remonstrance on Ronald's part, which perhaps she dreaded.

But she need not have dreaded such remonstrance. There was a consciousness in Ronald's heart which kept him silent; and besides, with every word his sister had spoken, with every instant during which his examination of her, close though furtive, had lasted, increasing alarm had taken firmer hold of him. How had he been so blind? How had he been content to accept appearances in Madeleine's case? how had he failed to search and examine rightly into the story of this marriage, and satisfy himself that his sister's heart was in it, that she had really forgotten Wilmot? For a conviction seized upon Ronald Kilsyth, as he looked at his sister and listened to her, that had she been really happy this state of things would not have existed. In the angry and suspicious state of his feelings towards Wilmot, he had accorded little attention, and less credence, to his father's confidences respecting Wilmot's opinion and warnings about Madeleine's health. He was too honourable, too true a gentleman, even in his anger to set down Wilmot as insincere, as acting like a charlatan or an alarmist; but he had dismissed the matter from his thoughts with disregard and impatience. How awfully, how fatally wrong he had been! And a flame of anger sprung wildly up in his heart; anger which involved equally himself and Lady Muriel.

Yes, Lady Muriel! All he had thought and done, he had thought and done at her instigation; and though, when Ronald thought the matter over calmly afterwards, as was his wont, he was unable to believe that any other course than that which had ended in the complete separation of Wilmot and Madeleine would have been possible, still he was tormented with this blind burning anger.

When Lady Muriel had aroused his suspicions, had awakened his fears, Wilmot was a married man; but when

he had acted upon these fears and suspicions, Wilmot's
wife was dead. "It might have been," then he thought.
True; but would he not, being without the knowledge, the
fear which now possessed him, have at any time, and under
any circumstances, prevented it? It cost him a struggle
now, when the knowledge and the fear had come, and his
mind was full of them, to acknowledge that he would; but
Ronald was essentially an honest man—he made the
struggle and the acknowledgment. In so far he had no
right to blame Lady Muriel.

In so far—but what about Ramsay Caird? How had
that marriage been brought about? How had his sister
been induced to marry a man whom he now felt assured
she did not love?—something had revealed it to him,
nothing she had said, nothing she had looked. How had
this marriage, by which his sister had not gained in rank,
wealth, or position, been brought about? (He thought
at this stage of his meditations, with a sigh, that Wilmot
could even have given her wealth now—how *bizarre* the
arrangements of fate are!) How had that been done?
By Lady Muriel of course, and no other. Maddy might
have remained contentedly enough at home, might have
been suffered gradually to forget Wilmot, enticed into the
amusements and distractions natural to her age and position; there was no need for this extreme measure of
inducing her to fix her fate precipitately by a marriage
with Ramsay Caird. Yes, Lady Muriel had done it; done
it to secure Madeleine's fortune to a relative of her own,
and to disembarrass herself of a grown-up step-daughter.
How blind he had been, how completely he had played
into her hands! Thus thought Ronald, as he strode about
his bare room at Brook-street, his face haggard with care,
and his heart sick with the terrible fear which had smitten
it with his first look at Madeleine.

Ronald's interview with his sister had been long and

painful to him, though nothing, or very little more, had been
said on the subject of her health. He had perceived her
anxiety to abridge discussion on that point, and had fallen
in with her humour. Once or twice, as he talked with her,
he had asked her if she was quite sure he was not wearying
her, if she did not feel tired or inclined to sleep, if he should
go, and send her maid to her. But to all his questions she
replied no; she was quite comfortable, and had not felt so
happy for a long time; and she begged him to stay with
her as long as he could. The brother and sister talked of
numerous subjects—much of Kilsyth, and their childhood;
a little of their several modes of life in the present; and
sometimes the current of their talk would be broken by
Madeleine's low musical laugh, but oftener by the miserable
cough, from which Ronald shrunk appalled, wondering that
he ever could have heard it without alarm, with indifference.
But the truth was, he had never heard it at all. The cough
had changed its character; and the significance which it had
assumed, and which crept coldly with its hollow sound to
Ronald's heart, was new.

Ronald had a dinner engagement for that day, and remained with his sister until it was time to go home and dress.
He looked into Kilsyth's room on his way to the hall-door,
when he had completed that operation; but his father was
not there. "I will speak to him in the morning," thought
Ronald. "I was impatient with him for croaking, as I
thought, about Maddy. God help him, I'm much mistaken,
or it's worse than he thinks for.'

And so Captain Kilsyth went out to dinner, and was
colder in his manner and much less lucid and decisive in his
conversation than usual. He left the party early, did not
"join the ladies;" and all the other guests, notably "the
ladies" themselves, were of opinion that they had no loss.

"If Wilmot had not gone away when he did," said Kilsyth to his son, at an advanced stage of the long and sad conversation which took place between them on the following morning, "Maddy would have been quite well now. Nobody understood her as he did; you must have seen it to have believed it, Ronald. You always had some unaccountable prejudice against Wilmot—I could not get to the bottom of it —but you must have acknowledged *that*, if you had seen it."

"It is too late to talk about that now, sir," said Ronald; "and you are quite mistaken in supposing that I undervalue Dr Wilmot's ability. But something decisive must be done at once; and as Wilmot's advice is not to be had, we must procure the best within our reach. There is no use now in looking back; but I do wonder Caird has permitted her to be without good advice all this time, and has suffered us to be so misled. He must have known of the cough being so bad in the morning, and of her exhaustion at times when neither you nor Lady Muriel saw her."

Kilsyth sighed. "I spoke to him yesterday," he said, "and I found him very easy about the matter. He says Maddy wouldn't have a strange doctor."

"Maddy wouldn't have a strange doctor! My dear father, what perfect nonsense! As if Maddy were the proper person to judge on such a subject—as if she ever ought to have been asked or consulted! As if any one in what I fear is her state ever had any consciousness of danger! I recognize Caird completely in that, his invincible easiness, his selfishness, his—"

He stopped. Kilsyth was looking at him, new concern and anxiety in his face; and Ronald had no desire to cause either, beyond the absolute necessity of the case, to his father.

"However," he said, "let us at least be energetic now. Come with me to see her now, and then we will consult some one with a first-rate reputation. Maddy will not offer any resistance when she sees your anxiety, and knows your wishes."

Kilsyth and his son walked out together; and in the street he took Ronald's arm. He was changed, enfeebled, by the fear which had captured him a few days since, and held him inexorably in its grasp.

Madeleine received her father and brother cheerfully. As usual now, she was in her dressing-room, and also, as usual, she was lying down. Ramsay Caird had told her the previous evening that her father was anxious she should have immediate advice, and she was prepared to accede to the wish. Not that she shared it; not that, as Ronald supposed, she was unconscious of her danger, as consumptive persons usually are. Quite the contrary, in fact. Madeleine Caird firmly believed that she was dying; only she did not in the least wish to live; and neither did she wish that her father should learn the fact before it became inevitable, which she felt it must, so soon as an experienced medical opinion should be taken upon her case.

But a certain dulness of all her faculties had made itself felt within the last few days, and she was particularly under its influence just then. She had neither the power nor the inclination to combat any opinion, to dissent from any wish. So she said, " Certainly, papa, if it will make your mind any easier about me ; " and twined her thin arm round her father's neck and kissed him, when he said, " I may bring a doctor to see you then, my darling, and you will tell him all about yourself."

Her arm was still about his neck, and his brow was resting against her cheek, when he said:

" Ah, if Wilmot were only here! No one ever understood you like Wilmot, my darling."

Neither Ronald nor Madeleine said a word in reply ; and when Ronald took leave of his sister, he avoided meeting her glance.

CHAPTER XXVIII.

ICONOCLASTIC.

In this great London world of ours it is our boast that we live free and unfettered by the opinions of our neighbours; that we may be unacquainted with those persons who for a score of years have resided on either side of us; that our sayings and doings, our "goings on," the company we keep, the lives we lead, and the pursuits we follow, are nothing to anybody, and are consequently unnoticed. We pride ourselves on this not a little; we shrug our shoulders and elevate our eyebrows when we talk of the small scandal and the petty spite of provincial towns; we are grateful that, in whatever state the larger vices may be, the smaller ones, at all events, do not flourish among us; and, in short, we take to ourselves enormous credit for the possession of something which has not the slightest real existence, and for the absence of something else which is of daily growth. It is true that in London a man need not be particular about the shape of his hat or the cut of his coat, so far as London itself is concerned, any more than he need fear that his having taken too much wine at a public dinner, or held a lengthened flirtation with a barmaid, will appear in the public prints; but in his own circle, be it high or low, large or small, pharisaical or liberal-minded, as much attention will be paid to all he does, his speeches, actions, and mode of life will be the subject of as much spiteful comment, as if he lived at Hull or vegetated at York. The insane desire to talk about trifles, to indulge in childish chit-chat and terrible twaddle, to erect mole-hills into mountains, and to find spots in social suns, exists everywhere amongst people who have nothing to do, and who carry out the doctrine laid down by Dr Watts by

applying their "idle hands" to "some mischief still." The
Duke of Dilworth, interested in the management of his own
estates, looking after the race-horses under his trainer's
care, hunting up his political influence, and seeing that it
sustains no diminution, marking catalogues of coming pic-
ture-sales for purchases which he has long expected must
enter the market, devising alterations in his Highland
shooting-box, planning yachting expeditions, going through,
in fact, that business of pleasure which is the real business
of his life, has no time for profitless talk and ridiculous
gossip, which, as his grace says, "he leaves for women."
But the women like what is left for them. The Duchess
and the Ladies Daffy have none of these occupations to fill
the "fallow leisure of their lives"—their calls and visits,
their fête-attendances and garden-parties, their play at
poor-visitings and High-Church-service frequentings, leave
them yet an enormous margin of waste time, which is more
or less filled up by tattle of a generally derogatory nature.
It is the same in nearly every class of life: men must work,
and women must talk; and when they talk, their conversation is robbed of half its zest and point if it be not dispara-
ging and detrimental to their dearest friends.

It was not to be imagined that the Ramsay-Caird
ménage, even had it been very differently constituted, could
have escaped criticism; as it was, it courted it. The mere
fact of Ramsay Caird himself having somehow or other
slipped into the society of *nous autres* (it was solely through
the Kilsyths that he was known in the set), and having had
the audacity to carry away one of the prizes, would in itself
have attracted sufficient attention to him and his, had other
inducements been wanting.

But other inducements were not wanting. The alteration
which had taken place in Madeleine since her illness in
Scotland, more especially since the time of the announcement
of her engagement, was matter of public comment; and all

kinds of stories were set afloat by her dearest friends to account for it. That she had had some dreadful love-affair, highly injudicious, impossible of achievement, was one of the most romantic; and being one of the most mischievous, consequently became one of the most popular theories, the only difficulty being to find for this desperate affair—which, it was said, had superinduced her illness, scarlet-fever being, as is well known to the faculty, essentially a mental disease —a hero. The list of visitors to the house was discussed in half-a-dozen different places; but no one at all likely to fill the character could be found, until Colonel Jefferson was accidentally hit upon. This, coupled with the fact that Colonel Jefferson's mad pursuit of Lady Emily Fairfax, which every one knew had so long existed, had ceased about that time, was extensively promulgated, and pretty generally accepted. So extensively promulgated, that it reached the ears of Colonel Jefferson himself, and elicited from him an expression of opinion couched in language rather stronger than that gallant officer usually permitted himself the use of —to the effect that, if he found any one engaged in the fetching and carrying of such infernal lies, he, Colonel Jefferson, should make it his business to inflict personal chastisement on him, the said fetcher and carrier. A representation of this kind coming from a very big and strong man, who in such matters had the reputation of keeping his promise, had the effect of doing away with all identification of Mrs Ramsay Caird's supposed heart-broken lover, and of restoring him his anonymity, but the fact of his existence still was whispered abroad; else why had one of the brightest girls of the past season—not that there was ever anything in her very clever, or that she was ever anything but extremely "missy," but still a pleasant, cheerful kind of girl in her way —why had she become dull and *triste*, and obviously uncaring for anything? That was what society wanted to know.

As for her husband, as for Ramsay Caird, society's

tongue said very little about him; but society's shoulders, and eyebrows, and hands, and fluttering fans, hinted a great deal. Society was divided on the subject of Mr Ramsay Caird. One portion of it threw out nebulous allusions to the fascinations of Madame Favorita of the Italian Opera, suggested the usual course pursued by beggars who had been set upon horseback, wondered how Madeleine's relations could endure the state of things which existed under their very eyes, and thought that the time could not be very far distant when Captain Kilsyth—who had the name, as you very well know, my dear, for being so very particular in such matters, not to say strait-laced—would call his brother-in-law to account for his goings on. The other portion of society was more liberal, so far at least as the gentleman was concerned. What, it asked, was the position of a man who found his newly-married wife evidently preoccupied with the loss of some previous flirtation? What was to be expected from a man who had found Dead-Sea apples instead of fruit, and utter indifference instead of conjugal love and domestic happiness? The *nous-autres* feeling penetrated into the discussion. It was not likely that a young man who had been brought up in a different sphere, who had been, if what people said was correct, a clerk or something of the kind to a lawyer in Edinburgh, could comprehend the necessity for such a course of conduct under the circumstances as the belonging to their class would naturally dictate. If Mr Caird had made a mistake—well, mistakes were often made, often without getting the equivalent which he, in allying himself with an old family in the position of the Kilsyths, had secured for himself. But they were always borne *sub silentio*—at all events the sufferer, however he might seek for distraction in private, did not let the mistake which he had made, and the means he had adopted for his own compensation, become such common gossip-matter for the world at large.

Such conversation as this is not indulged in without its
reaching the ears of those most concerned. When one says
most concerned, one means those likely to take most concern
in it. It is doubtful if Madeleine's ears were ever disturbed
by any of the rumours in which she played so prominent a
part. It is certain that her husband never knew of the interest which he excited in so many of his acquaintances;
equally certain that if he had known it, the knowledge thus
gained would not have caused him an emotion. Lady Muriel, however, was fully acquainted with all that was said.
The world, which did her homage as one of its queens of
fashion, took every possible occasion to remind her that she
was mortal, and found no better opportunity than in pointing out the mistake which she had made in the marriage of
her step-daughter and the settlement in life of her *protégé*.
Odd words dropped here and there, sly hints, innuendoes,
phrases capable of double meaning, and always receiving the
utmost perversion which could be employed in their warping,
nay, in some instances, anonymous letters—the basest shifts
to which treachery can stoop,—all these ingredients were
made use of for the poisoning of Lady Muriel's cup of life,
and for the undermining of that pinnacle to which society
had raised her.

Nor was Ronald Kilsyth ignorant of the world's talk and
the world's expressions. Isolate himself as much as he
would, be as self-contained and as solitary as an oyster, fend
off confidence, shut his ears to gossip,—all he could do was
to exclude pleasant things from him; the unpleasant had
penetrating qualities, and invariably made their way. He
knew well enough what was said in every kind of society
about Mr and Mrs Ramsay Caird. When he dined away
from the mess, he had a curiously unpleasant feeling that
advantage would be taken of his absence to discuss that unfortunate *ménage*. When he dined at his club, he had a
morbid horror lest the two men seated at the next table

should begin to talk about it. The disappointment about the whole thing had been so great as to make him morbidly sensitive on the point, to ascribe to it far greater interest than it really possessed for the world in general, and to allow it to prey on his mind, and seriously to influence his health. It had been such a consummate failure! And he, as he owned to himself,—he was primarily responsible for the marriage! If Lady Muriel had not had his assistance, she would never have carried her point of getting Madeleine for Ramsay Caird; one word from him would have nipped that acquaintance in the bud, would have stopped the completion of the project, no matter how far it had advanced. And he had never said that word. Why? He comforted himself by thinking that Caird had never shown himself in his real character before his marriage; but the fact was, although Ronald would not avow it, that he had been hoodwinked by the deference so deftly paid to him both by his step-mother and her confederate, who had consulted him on all points, and cajoled him and used him as a tool in their hands. He thought over all this very bitterly now; he saw how he had been treated, and stamped and raved in impotent fury as he remembered how he had been led on step by step, and how weak and vacillating he must have appeared in a matter in which he was most deeply interested, and which, during the whole of its progress, he thought he was managing so well.

To no man in London could such a *fiasco* as his sister's marriage had turned out be more oppressively overwhelming, productive of more thorough disgust and annoyance, than to Ronald Kilsyth. The *fiasco* was so glaring, that at once two points on which the young man most prided himself stood impugned. Every one knew that dear old Kilsyth himself would not have interfered in such a matter, and that the final settlement of it, after Lady Muriel's light skirmishing had been done, must have been left to Ronald, who was the

sensible one of the family. He had then, in the eyes of the
world, either had so little care for his sister's future as to
sanction her marriage with a very ineligible man, or so little
natural perspicacity and sharpness as to be deceived by such
a shallow pretender as Caird. That any one should entertain either of these suppositions was gall and wormwood to
Ronald. He whose reputation for clear-headedness and far-
seeing had only been equalled by the esteem in which by all
men he had been held for his strict honesty and probity and
the Spartan quality of his virtue,—that he should be suspected—more than suspected, in certain quarters accused—
of folly or want of proper caution where his sister was concerned, was to him inexpressibly painful. Perhaps the
worst thing of all was to know that people knew that he
was aware of what was said, and that he suffered under the
tittle-tattle and the gossip. He tried to forget that idea, to
dispel and do away with it by changing his usual habits ; he
went about ; he was seen—for one week—oftener in society
than he had been for months previously : but the morbid
feeling came upon him there ; he fancied that people noticed
his presence, and attributed it to its right cause ; that every
whisper which was uttered in the room had Madeleine for
its burden ; that the whole company had their minds filled
with him, and were thinking of him either pityingly, sarcas-
tically, or angrily, according to their various temperaments.

He avoided Brook-street at this time as religiously as he
avoided the little residence in Squab-street. He did not
particularly care about meeting his father, though he thought
Kilsyth would probably know nothing of what so many were
talking of ; and he had resolutely shunned a meeting with
Lady Muriel, for Ronald in his inmost heart did his step-
mother a gross injustice. He fully believed that she was
perfectly cognisant of Ramsay Caird's real character ; whereas,
in truth, no one had been more astonished at what her
protégé had proved himself than Lady Muriel—and very few

more distressed. Ronald, however, thought otherwise; and being a gentleman, he carefully avoided meeting her ladyship, lest he might lose his temper and forget himself. The Kilsyth blood *was* hot, and even in the heir to the name there had been occasions when it was pretty nearly up to boiling-point.

For the same reason he avoided all chance of running across his brother-in-law. In common with most men of strong feelings always kept in a state of repression, Ronald Kilsyth was particularly sensitive; and the idea of the publicity already accruing to this wretched business being increased by any possible tattle of open rupture between members of the family horrified him dreadfully. If he did not dare trust himself with Lady Muriel, he should certainly have to exercise a much stronger command over himself in the event of his ever meeting Ramsay Caird. Every governing principle of his life rose up within him against that young man; and on the first occasion of his hearing—accidentally, as men often hear things of the greatest import to themselves—of Mr Caird's doings, Ronald Kilsyth had for the whole night paced his barrack-room, trying in every possible form to pick such a quarrel with Caird as might leave no real clue to its origin, and enable him to work out his revenge without compromising any one. But he soon saw the futility of any such proceeding, which, carried out between *sous-officiers*, might form the basis of a French drama, but which was impossible of execution between English gentlemen, and elected absence from Squab-street, and total ignorance of Mr Caird's mode of procedure, as his best aids to a tolerably quiet life for himself. Besides, absence from Squab-street meant absence from Madeleine; and absence from Madeleine meant a great deal to Ronald Kilsyth. He, in his self-examination, found Madeleine's behaviour since her marriage the one point on which he could neither satisfy himself by a feeling of pity nor bluster himself into a fit of indignation.

He knew well enough what her abstracted manner, her dulness, her sad weary preoccupied mind, her impossibility to join in the nonsensical talk floating around her,—he knew, well enough, what all those symptoms meant. If he had ever doubted that his sister had a strong affection for Wilmot—and it is due to his perspicacity to say that no such doubt ever crossed his mind—he would have been certain of it now. If he had ever hoped—and he had hoped very earnestly—that any girlish predilection which his sister might have entertained for Wilmot was merely girlish and evanescent, and would pass away with her marriage, he could not more effectually have blighted any such chance than by marrying her to the man whose suit he, her brother, had himself urged her to accept. Perhaps under happier circumstances that childish dream would have passed away, merged into a more happy realization; but as it had eventuated, Ronald knew perfectly well that Madeleine could not but contrast the blank loveless present with the bright past, could not but compare the days when she now sat solitary and uncared for with those when the man for whom she had such intense veneration—for whom, as she doubtless had afterwards discovered, she had such honest, earnest love—had given up everything else to attend to her and shield her in the hour of danger. With such feelings as these at his heart, it was but little wonder that Ronald sedulously avoided being thrown in Madeleine's way.

He had always been so " odd ; " his comings and goings in Brook-street had been so uncertain; it was so utterly impossible to tell when he might or might not be expected at his father's house, that his prolonged absence caused no astonishment to any of the members of the family, nor to any one of their regular visitors. Lady Muriel, indeed, with a kind of guilty consciousness of participation in his feelings, guessed the reason why her stepson eschewed their society ; but no one else. And Lady Muriel, who from her first suspicion of Ramsay Caird's conduct—suspicion not entertained, be it understood, until some time after the marriage—had looked forward with great fear and trembling to a grand *éclaircissement*, a searching explanation with Ronald, in which she would have to undergo an amount of cross-questioning in his hardest manner, and a judgment which would inevitably be pronounced against her, was rather glad that this whim had taken possession of Ronald, and that her *dies iræ* was consequently indefinitely deferred. But it happened one day that Ronald, walking down to Knightsbridge barracks, came upon his father waiting to cross the road at the corner of Sloane-street, and came upon him so "plump" and so suddenly, that retreat was impossible. The young man accordingly, seeing how matters stood, advanced, and took his father by the hand.

In an instant he saw that one other, at all events, had suffered from the—well, there was no other word for it—the disgrace, the discredit, to say the least of it, which had fallen on the family during the past few months. Kilsyth seemed aged by ten years. The light had died out of his bright blue eyes, and left them glassy and colourless, with red rims and heavy dark "pads" underneath each. The bright healthy colour had faded from his cheeks, and few would have recognized the lithe and active mountaineer, the never-tiring pedestrian, and the keen shot, in the bent and shrunken form which stood half-leaning on, half-idly dallying with, its stick. He pressed his son's hand warmly, however; and something like his well-known kind old smile lighted up his face as he exclaimed—

"Ronald, I'm glad to see you, my boy! very glad! You've not been near us for ages! And not merely that—I can understand that—we're not very good company for young people now in Brook-street; there's little inducement to come there now since poor Maddy has left us. But I don't think that I was ever half so long in London without dining

with you as your guest over there at the barracks. I used
to like an outing with your fellows there; it brisked me up,
and made me forget what an old fogie I am growing; but—
but you haven't given me the chance this time, sir,—you
haven't given me the chance!"

There was something in the evidently strained attempt at
cheeriness with which his father said these words which con-
trasted so strongly with the depression under which it was
impossible for him to prevent showing he was labouring, and
with the marked alteration in his personal appearance, that
touched Ronald deeply. His heart sank within him, and his
tongue grew dry; he had to clear his throat before he replied
—and even then huskily—

"It *is* a long time since we've met, sir; and I confess
the fault is mine—entirely mine. The fact is I've been very
much engaged lately—regimental duty, and—and some
business in which I've been particularly interested—business
which I fear you would hardly care about—and—"

"Likely enough, my dear boy!" said Kilsyth, coming to
his rescue, as he floundered about in a way very unusual to
him. "Likely enough! I never did care particularly for a
good many of your pursuits, you know, Ronald, though I
tried very hard at one time—when you were quite a lad, I
recollect—to understand them and share in them. But that
was not to be. I was not bright enough. I'm of the old
school, and what we old fellows cared about seems to have
died out with our youth, and never to have interested anybody ever since. I don't say this complainingly—not in the
least—but it was deuced odd. However, I'm very glad I've
met you, Ronald, for I have long wished—and lately, within
the last few days more especially—to have a talk with you, a
serious talk, my boy, which will take up some little time.
Have you half-an-hour you can give me now? I shall be
very glad if you have."

It was coming at last. He had but put off the evil **day,**

and now it was upon him. Well—better to hear himself condemned by his father than by any one else. Let it come.

"My time is yours, sir," said Ronald, almost echoing Wilmot, as he remembered, on the day of that eventful interview in Charles-street. "I shall of course be delighted to give my best attention to anything you may have to say."

"Well, then, let's take a turn in the Park opposite," said Kilsyth, hooking his arm into his son's. "Not among the people there, where we should be perpetually interrupted by having to speak to those folks who hail one so good-naturedly at every step, but away on the grass there, by ourselves."

The two men passed through the Albert Gate, and turning to the right, struck on to the piece of turf lying between the Row and the Drive. A few children were playing about, a few nursemaids were here and there gossiping together; else they had it all to themselves.

"I want to talk to you," commenced Kilsyth, "about your sister—about Maddy. I have been a good deal to Squab-street in the last few weeks, and I've thought Maddy looks anything but as I should wish her to look. Has that struck you, Ronald?"

"I—I'm sorry to say that I haven't seen Madeleine for some little time, sir. The business which, as I just explained to you, has prevented my coming to Brook-street has equally prevented me from calling on her."

"Of course, yes! I beg pardon—I forgot! Well, Maddy looks anything but well. For a long time past—indeed ever since her marriage—she has been singularly low-spirited and dull; very unlike her usual self."

"I don't know that that is much to be wondered at. Madeleine was always a peculiar girl, in the sense that she had an extraordinary attachment for her home; and the fact of being parted from you, with whom all her life has been passed, and to whom she is devotedly attached, may explain the cause of any little temporary lowness of spirits."

"Ye-es, that's true so far; but it's not that; I wish I could think it was. What you say, though, Ronald, I think gets somewhat near the real cause. Maddy has been unlike most other girls of her class; much more homely and domestic, thinking much more of those around her with whom she has been brought into daily contact than of the outside pleasures, if I may so call them. And she's had a great deal of love. She's accustomed to it, and can't get on without it. Love's just as essential to Madeleine as light to the flowers, or the keen clear air to the stags. She's had it all her life, and she would die without it. And, Ronald, I'll say to you what I'd not say to another soul upon earth, but what's lying heavy on my heart this month past—I doubt much whether she gets it, my boy; I doubt much whether she gets it."

The old man stopped suddenly in his walk, and clutched his son's arm, and looked up earnestly into his son's face. There was so much sharp agony in the glance, hurried and fleeting though it was, that Ronald scarcely knew what to say in reply to the quivering jerky speech.

His father saved him from his embarrassment by continuing: "I don't think she gets the love that she's been accustomed to, and that she had a right to expect. I tell you that Maddy is not happy, Ronald; that her little heart aches and pines for want of sympathy, for what of appreciation, for want of love. I'm an old fellow; but in this case I suppose my affection for my darling has opened my eyes, and I can see it all plainly."

"Don't you think, sir, that your undoubted devotion to Madeleine may, on the other hand, have had the effect of warping your judgment a little, and prejudicing you in the matter? Though I've not seen my sister very lately, when I did see her I confess I did not observe any marked difference in her—any difference at all from what she has been during the last few months."

"The last few months! That's just it; that's just what —however, we'll come to that presently. I *know* you're wrong, Ronald; I *know* that Madeleine is thoroughly changed and altered from the bright darling girl of the old days. And I know why, my boy! God help me, I know why!"

Again Ronald essayed to speak, and again he only muttered unintelligibly.

"Because her home is unhappy," said Kilsyth, stopping short in his walk, and dropping his voice to a whisper; "because the marriage into which she was—was persuaded —I will use no harsh words—has proved a wretched one for her; because her husband has proved himself to be— God forgive me—a scoundrel!"

"You speak strongly, sir, notwithstanding your professions," said Ronald, on whom warm words of any kind had always the effect of rendering him even more cold and stoical than was his wont.

"I speak strongly because I feel strongly, Ronald! I don't expect you to share my feelings in this matter, but I do expect you to have some of your own, although you may not show them. For God's sake cast aside for a few minutes that cloak of frost in which you always shroud yourself, and let us talk as father and son about one who is daughter to the one and sister to the other!"

Ronald looked up in surprise. He had never seen his father so much excited before.

"I have no doubt about this," continued Kilsyth. "I have hoped against hope, and I have shut my eyes against what I have seen, hoping they might be fancies; and my ears against what I have heard, hoping they might be lies. But I can befool myself in this manner no longer. Ah! to think of my darling thus—to think of my darling thus!"

Tears started to the old man's eyes, and he smote fiercely with his stick upon the ground.

"If you are really persuaded of this, sir," said Ronald, "it is our duty to take immediate measures. Mr Caird must be taught—"

"Who brought him to our house?" asked Kilsyth in a storm of passion; "or rather—not that—but when he was brought, who backed him up and encouraged him in every way? You, Ronald! you—you—you! By your advice he was permitted free access to the house, was constantly thrown in Madeleine's company, and gave the world to understand that he was going to marry her. I postponed the settling of the engagement once; but the second time, when—when I fancied that the child might have had some other views—might have formed some other fancy—you persuaded me to agree, and—"

"You should apportion the blame properly, sir," said Ronald in his coldest tones. "I did not introduce Caird to your house, nor was I the principal advocate of his cause."

"You're quite right, Ronald, quite right—and I've been hasty and passionate and inconsiderate, I know; but if you knew how utterly heartbroken I am—"

"I think, with regard to Mr Caird," interrupted Ronald, "the best plan will be—"

"No, no; not Caird now—leave him for the present; afterwards we'll do for him. Now about Maddy—nothing but about Maddy—and not about her dulness, or anything of that kind, nor—worse, much worse—you recollect—no, you didn't know; I think you weren't there—what Wilmot, Dr Wilmot, said to me at Kilsyth about her chest? He told me that one of her lungs was threatened—that the lungs were her weak point; and he asked me whether any of our family had suffered from such disease."

"Well, sir," said Ronald, anxiously now.

"This disease has been gaining ground for months past;

I'm sure of it. I have had my opinions for some time; but Maddy never complains, you know, and I didn't like to ask her about her symptoms, lest she might be frightened. But within the last few days she has been so bad that it has been evident to us all, to myself and—and Lady Muriel, that the disease was on the increase. She caught cold at the theatre the other night, and her cough is now frightful. I have seen her just now, poor darling! She was on the sofa, but very weak—all they could do to get her there—and when the paroxysms of coughing come on it's awful to see her— she hardly seems to have the strength to live through them. My poor darling Maddy!"

"What do the doctors say, sir? Who is attending her?"

"Whittaker—Dr Whittaker—a very good man in his way, I daresay, but—I don't know—somehow I don't think much of him. Now that is the very point I wanted to talk to you about. Somehow—how, I never understood—some-body—I don't know who—offended Dr Wilmot, a man to whom we were under the greatest obligation for kindness rendered; and though he has been back in England for some time, he has never called in Brook-street, nor on Madeleine even, since his return. There is no one in whom I have such faith; there is no one, I am convinced, who understands Madeleine's constitution like Wilmot; and I want to know what is the best method for us to put our pride in our pockets and implore him to come and see her."

"You were not thinking of asking Dr Wilmot to visit Madeleine?"

"I was indeed. What objection could there possibly be?"

"I suppose you know that he has retired from practice, that he even declines to attend consultations, since he inherited Mr Foljambe's money?"

"I know that; but I am perfectly certain, from what I

saw of him at Kilsyth, that if I were to go to him and tell
him the state of affairs, he would overlook anything that
may have annoyed him, and come and see Maddy at once."

"That would be a condescension!" said Ronald. "Perhaps it might be on the other side that the 'overlooking'
might be required. However, there are other reasons, sir,
why I, for one, should think it highly inadvisable that Dr
Wilmot should be requested to visit my sister."

"What are they, then, in Heaven's name, man?" said
Kilsyth petulantly. "You don't seem to see that the
matter is of the utmost urgency."

"It is because of its urgency that I speak of it at all;
it is by no means a pleasant topic for me or for any of us.
You spoke to me just now, sir, in warm words of the part I
took in pressing Ramsay Caird to visit at your house, and
supporting his claims for Madeleine. I don't know that I
was at all eager for it at first; I'm certain I never cared
particularly for Ramsay Caird; but I freely own that latterly I did my best for him, convinced that a speedy alliance
with him was the only chance of rescuing Madeleine from
another offer which I was sure was impending—which
would have been far more objectionable, and yet which she
would have accepted."

"Another offer?—from whom?"

"From the gentleman of whom you entertain so high
an opinion—from Dr Wilmot."

"From Wilmot! An offer from Wilmot to Madeleine!
You must be mad, Ronald!"

"I never was more sane in my life, sir. I repeat, I am
perfectly certain Dr Wilmot was in love with Madeleine,
that he would have made her an offer, and that she would
have accepted him."

"And why should she not have accepted him? God
knows I would have welcomed him for a son-in-law, and—"

"I scarcely think this is the time to enter into that

subject, sir; but now that I have enlightened you, I presume you see the objection to calling in Dr Wilmot to my sister."

"I see the difficulty, Ronald; but the objection and the difficulty shall be overcome. You shall yourself go and see Wilmot; and I know he'll not refuse you."

"Don't you think, sir, before I take upon myself to do that, it would be, to say the least of it, desirable that we should consult Madeleine's husband?"

"Indeed I do not, Ronald," said Kilsyth; "indeed I do not. In giving up my daughter to Mr Caird I yielded privileges which I alone had enjoyed from her birth, and which I would gladly have retained until her death or mine. But I did not give up the privilege of watching over her health, more especially when it has been so shamefully neglected; and I shall claim the power to use it now."

"And you think, after all I have told you, that there is no objection to asking Dr Wilmot to visit Madeleine?"

"See here, Ronald!—I will be very frank with you in this matter—I think that if I had known all you have told me now seven or eight months ago, we should never have had this conversation. For I firmly believe that—granting your ideas were correct—if my darling had married Wilmot, he would have taken care both of her health and her happiness, both of which have been so grossly neglected."

The father and son took their way in silence back across the grass, each filled with his own reflections. They had only reached the Albert Gate, and were about to pass through it into the street, when a brougham passed them, and a gentleman sitting in it gravely saluted them.

"Good heavens!" exclaimed Kilsyth; "there's Wilmot!"

"Yes," said Ronald. He was surprised, and secretly agitated by the sight of the man towards whom his feelings had insensibly changed, and was hardly master of his emotion.

The carriage had passed on, but Kilsyth was standing still at the crossing.

"What an extraordinary chance—what a wonderful Providence, I should say!" said Kilsyth; "the only man I have confidence in—fancy his passing by just at this time! Thank God! No chance of his calling at Brook-street before he goes home, as he used to do; we must go on to his house at once and leave a message for him." Here the impetuous old gentleman hailed a hansom, which drew up abruptly in dangerous proximity to his toes.

"Stop a moment," said Ronald. "You had better get home, in case I can persuade Dr Wilmot to call, and tell Lady Muriel; it will save time. I will go on to his house."

"All right," said Kilsyth in a voice of positive cheerfulness. The mere sight of Wilmot had acted like a strong cordial upon him—had restored his strength and his confidence.

"Don't I recollect how he saved her before, when she was much worse, when she was actually in the clutch of a mortal disease? And he will save her again! he will save her again!" said the old man to himself as he drove homewards. He went directly to Lady Muriel's boudoir, and communicated to her the glad tidings of Ronald's mission, which had filled him with hope and joy.

The rich red colour flew to Lady Muriel's cheek, and the light shone in her dark eyes. To her too the news was precious, delicious; but not so the intelligence which formed its corollary. What! Ronald Kilsyth gone to solicit Dr Wilmot's attendance on his sister! Ronald Kilsyth bringing about the renewal of this danger which she, apparently ably assisted by fate, had put far from her! What availed Wilmot's return, if he might see Madeleine again—might be with her? What availed it that Madeleine was no longer in the house with him, that she was free to see him, to enjoy his society undisputed? As Kilsyth saw how her face lighted up, how her colour rose, he rejoiced in her sympathy with his feelings, with his hope and relief, he blessed her in his heart for her love for his Madeloine. And she listened to him, dominated in turn by irresistible joy and by burning anger.

CHAPTER XXIX.

TOO LATE.

THAT there can be such a thing as a broken heart; that love, misguided, misdirected, fixed upon the wrong object, and never finding " its earthly close," having to pine in secret, and to take out its revenge in saying deteriorating and spiteful things of its successful rival, ever kills, is now-a-days generally accepted as nonsense. In the daily round of the work-a-day life there are too many things hourly cropping up to allow a man of any spirit to permit himself to hug to his bosom the corpse of a dead joy, or to bemoan over the reminiscence of vanished happiness. He must be up and doing; he must go in to his business, read his newspaper, give his orders to his clerks, write his letters—or at least sign them ; go to his club, eat his dinner, and go through his ordinary routine, each item of which fills up his time, and prevents him from dwelling on the atrocious perfidy of the being who has deceived him. The evening has generally been considered a favourable time for indulging in those reflections which, by their bitterness, bring about the anatomical consequences so much to be deplored; but your modern Strephon either forgets his own woes in reading of the fictitious woes of others, duly supplied by Mr Mudie, or in witnessing them depicted on the stage, or in listening to the cynical wisdom of the smoking-room, which, if he duly

imbibe it, leads him rather to think he has had a wonderful
escape; or in the friendly game of whist, when deference to
his partner's interest, to say the least of it, requires that he
should keep his thoughts from wandering into that subject
so redolent of bitter-sweet. The heart-breaking business is
out of date, it is *rococo*, it is bygone; and one might as well
look to see the brazen greaves of bold Sir Lancelot flashing
in our English imitation of the sunshine, and to hear the
knight singing "Lirra-lirra!" as he rode up the banks of
the Serpentine, as to believe in its existence now-a-days.

So that those who may have imagined that Chudleigh
Wilmot had given up all relish of and interest in life must
have been grievously disappointed. When he first went
abroad grief and rage were in his heart, and he cared but
little what became of him. When he first received the news
of Mr Foljambe's bequest there sprung up in him a new
feeling of hope and joy, such as he had never had before,
which lasted but a very few hours, being uprooted and cast
out by the announcement of Madeleine's marriage in the
newspaper. When he returned to London his mind was so
far made up, that he contemplated very calmly the possibility of such an existence—without Madeleine, that is to
say—as a few hours previously he had deemed impossible;
and though on first entering on the new life the old ghosts
which "come to trouble joy" would occasionally await him;
and though after that chance meeting with Madeleine and
Lady Muriel in the Park he was for some little time much
disturbed, yet, on the whole, he managed to live his life
quietly, soberly, peacefully, and not unhappily.

The man who, after years of active employment, inherits
or obtains a competency, and straightway lies upon his oars
and looks round him for the remainder of his life, immediately
falls into a sad way, and comes speedily to a bad end. Wilmot was quite sufficient man of the world to be aware of
this; and though he had retired from the active practice of

his profession, indeed from practising in any way, he still
kept up his medical studies, and now became one of the most
sought-after and most influential contributors to the best of
our scientific publications. In this way he found exercise
enough for his mental faculties, which had been somewhat
burdened and overtasked with all the hard work which he
had gone through in his early life ; and as for the rest, he
found he had done society a great injustice in estimating its
resources so meanly as he had been used to do. By degrees
he gave up the rule which he had at first kept so strictly,
never to go into ladies' society ; and the first plunge made,
he felt that he enjoyed himself therein more than in any
other. He found that his reputation, which had been considerably increased by the literary work on which he had
recently engaged, smoothed the way for him on first introduction.; and that the fact of his being a middle-aged
widower secured for him that pleasant license accorded to
fogies, of which only fogies are thoroughly conscious and
appreciative. Instead of losing caste or position, he felt
that he had gained it ; all the best people who had been his
patients in the old days kept up their acquaintance with
him, and asked him to their houses ; and after the publica-
tion of a paper by him on a momentous subject of the day,
containing new and striking views which at once commanded
public attention and attracted public comment, he was placed
on a Royal Commission among some of the first men of the
time, and an intimation was conveyed to him that Government would be glad to avail themselves of his services.

And the old wearing, tearing feeling of love and disappointment and regret which had blighted so many hours
of his life, and which he thought at one time would sap life
itself, was gone, was it ? Well, not entirely. It had been
an era in his life which was never to be forgotten, which was
never to be otherwise renewed. Night after night he saw
pretty charming girls, all of whom would have been pleased

by a flattering word from the celebrated Dr Wilmot, many of whom would have listened more than complacently to anything he might have chosen to say to them,—" he is very rich, my dear, and goes into excellent society." But he never said anything, because he never thought anything of the kind. Sometimes when alone, in the pauses of his work, he would look up from off his book or his paper, and then straightway he would see—although his thoughts had been previously engrossed with something entirely different—a bright flushed face, with blue eyes, and a nimbus of golden hair surrounding it. But for a moment he would see it, and then it would fade away; but in that moment how many memories had it evoked! Sometimes he would take from a special drawer in his desk a small knot of blue ribbon, and a thin letter, frayed in its folds, and bearing traces of having been for some time carried in the pocket. Slight memorials these of the only love of a lifetime which had now extended to some forty years; not much to show in return for an all-absorbing passion which at one time threatened to have dire effect on his health, on his life—yet cherished all the more, perhaps, on account of their insignificance! These were memorials of Miss Kilsyth, be it understood: of Mrs Ramsay Caird Chudleigh always rigidly repeated to himself that he knew nothing—that he never would know anything.

But one morning Chudleigh Wilmot was sitting in his library after his breakfast, his slippered feet resting idly on a chair, he himself in placid enjoyment of the newspaper and a cigar, which, since he had freed himself from professional restraint, he had taken as a pleasant solace, when suddenly, and without being in any way led up to, the subject of his dream of the previous night flashed suddenly across his mind. It was about Madeleine. He remembered that he had seen her lying outstretched on her bed dead; there were Christmas berries in her golden hair, and the robe which covered her was embroidered with the initial letters of his name

twisted into a monogram, such as was engraved on the
binding of a present of books which he had recently received
from one of his great friends, and on the little finger of her
hand, which lay outside the coverlet, was Mabel's signet-ring.
He remembered all this vividly now; remembered too how,
when he had gone forward with the intention of taking off
the ring, a female form, clad in dark sweeping garments, but
with its face shrouded, had risen by the bedside and motioned
him away. He remembered how he felt persuaded, although
the face was hidden, that the form was known to him—was
that of Henrietta Prendergast; how he had persisted in approaching; and how at length the muffled form had spoken,
saying only these words, " It was not to be! " What followed he could not remember: there was a kind of chaos, out
of which rose figures of Whittaker and Colonel Jefferson,
the man whom he had met in Scotland, and Ronald Kilsyth
in full uniform, with his sword drawn and pointed at his
(Chudleigh's) heart; and then he had waked, and the whole
remembrance of the dream had departed from him until that
moment, when simultaneously the door of his room was
thrown open, and Ronald Kilsyth stood before him.

That was no dream. Wilmot thought at first that his
waking fancies were running in the track of his sleeping
thoughts; but there was Ronald Kilsyth, somewhat changed
from the man he remembered—less grim and stoical, a trifle
less cynical, and a trifle more human,—but still Ronald
Kilsyth standing before him.

" You are surprised to see me, Dr Wilmot," said Ronald,
advancing hesitatingly.—" surprised to see me here, after—
after so long an interval."

" On the last occasion of our meeting, Captain Kilsyth,"
replied Wilmot, " you were good enough to tell me that you
objected to the ordinary set phrases of society, and preferred
straightforward answers. I have not forgotten that interview,
or anything that passed therein; and I have every desire, be-

lieve me, to accommodate you—at least so far as that wish is concerned. My straightforward answer to your question is, I *am* surprised to see you in this house."

"I looked for no other reply. You seem to forget that, even so far ago as our last meeting, you were pleased to fall in with my whim, and to answer me with perfect candour, however painful it might have been—it was—to you. That conversation will doubtless be remembered by you, Dr Wilmot."

What did this mean? Was the man come here, in the assurance of his own cold, calm stoicism, to triumph over him? Whence this most indecorous outrage on his privacy, this insult to his feelings? Of all men, this man knew how he had suffered, and how he had borne his sufferings. Why, then, was he here, at such a moment, with such words on his lips?

"I perfectly remember that conversation, Captain Kilsyth," was all Wilmot replied.

"You will spare me, then, a great deal of acute pain in referring to it," said Ronald. "Refer to it I must, but my reference will be of the most general kind. I sought that interview beseeching you "—Wilmot gave a short half-laugh, which Ronald noticed—" Well, you stickle for terms, it appears,—demanding of you to give up a pursuit in which you were then engaged—a pursuit to which you attached the greatest interest, but which I knew would not only be futile in its results to you, but would be fraught with distress and danger to one who was very dear to me. You acquiesced in my reasoning—at great sorrow and disappointment to yourself, I know—and you gave up the pursuit."

"You are very good to make such large allowances for me, Captain Kilsyth," said Wilmot in a hard dry voice. "Yes, I gave it up; at great sorrow and disappointment to myself, as you are good enough to say."

"I can fully understand the feelings which now influence

you, Dr Wilmot," said Ronald, far more gently than was his wont; "and, believe me, I do not quarrel with or take exception at the tone in which they are now expressed. You gave up that pursuit, and you carried out the intention you then expressed to me of leaving England."

"I did. I left England within a fortnight of that conversation. I should not have returned when I did—I should not have returned even now, most probably—had it not been for circumstances then utterly unforeseen, but of which you may have heard, which compelled me to come back at once."

Ronald bowed; he had heard of those circumstances, he said.

"And now, pardon me, Captain Kilsyth, if I just run through what has occurred. It cannot be, you will allow, less unpleasant for me to do so than for you; but since we have met again,—at an interview not of my seeking, recollect,—it is as well that they should be understood. You told me in my consulting-room in Charles-street that you had reason to believe that your sister, Miss Kilsyth, was—let us put it plainly—loved by me. You said that, or at least you implied that, you had reason to believe that she was interested in me. You told me that any question of marriage between us was impossible; first, because I had originally made your sister's acquaintance when I was a married man; secondly, because my station in life—you put it kindly, as a gentleman would, but that was the gist of your argument—because my station in life was inferior to hers. I do not know, Captain Kilsyth," continued Wilmot, whose voice grew harder as he proceeded, "that your reasoning was so subtle in either case as not to admit of controversy, perhaps even of disproof; but I felt that when a young lady's name was in question, when there was, as you assured me there was—and you were much more a man of the world than I—the chance of the slightest slur being cast on her, it was my duty to sacrifice my own feelings, however strong they might have been in the matter.

I did so. To the best of my ability I stamped out my love ; I pocketed my pride ; I gave up the best feelings of my nature, and I did as you and your friends wished. I went abroad, and remained grizzling and feeding on my own heart for months. At length I heard of a stroke of good fortune which had befallen me. I had previously made for myself a name which was respected and honoured ; and you, who know more of these things than your compeers, or people in your 'set,' can appreciate the worth of the renown which a man makes off his own bat by the exercise of his talents ; and by the chance which I have named I had now inherited a fortune—a large fortune for any man not born to wealth. When this news reached me, my first thought was, Now, surely, my coast is clear. I can go back to England ; I can say to Miss Kilsyth's friends, I am renowned ; I am rich ; I am, I hope, a gentleman in the ordinary acceptation of the term. If this young lady will accept my court, why should it not be paid her ? Within twenty-four hours of my learning of my inheritance, of my determination, I heard that Miss Kilsyth was married."

"There was no stipulation, I believe, Dr Wilmot—at least so far as I am concerned—no compact, no given time during which Miss Kilsyth should keep single, in the view of anything that might happen to you ? "

"None in the world ; and so far as Miss Kilsyth is concerned—her name is being bandied between us in the course of conversation, but it is my duty to say that I have not the smallest atom of complaint to make against her. To this hour, so far as I know, she is unacquainted with my feelings towards her, and can consequently be held responsible for no acts of hers at which I may feel aggrieved. But you must let me continue. I will not tell you what effect the intelligence of Miss Kilsyth's marriage had on me. I had been raised to the highest pinnacle of hope, I was cast down into the lowest depths of despair. That concerned no one but myself. I returned to England. Miss Kilsyth was Mrs Ramsay Caird—I had learned that from the public prints—no private announcement, no wedding-cards awaited me. The story of my vast inheritance got wind, as such things do, and all my friends—all my acquaintance, let me say, to use a more fitting word, called on me or sent their congratulations. From your family, from Mrs Ramsay Caird, I had not the slightest notice. The young lady whose life—if you credit her father—I had saved a few months previously, and her family, who professed themselves so grateful, ignored my existence. To this hour I have had no communication with Kilsyth, with Lady Muriel, with the Ramsay Cairds. I met Lady Muriel and her daughter once by the merest accident—an accident entirely unsought by me—and they bowed to me as though I were a tradesman who had been pestering for his bill. What am I to gather from this treatment? One of two things—either that I was regarded merely as the 'doctor' who was called in when his services were needed, but who, when he had fulfilled his functions and saved the patient, was no more to be recognized than the butcher when he had supplied the required joint of meat; or that, by those who knew, or thought they knew, the inner circumstances of the case, my moral character was so highly esteemed that, guessing I had been in love with Miss Kilsyth, it was judged expedient that I should have no opportunity of acquaintance with Mrs Ramsay Caird. I ask you, Captain Kilsyth, which of these suppositions is correct?"

Wilmot spoke with great warmth. Ronald Kilsyth looked on with wonder; he could scarcely imagine that the man who now stood erect before him with flashing eye and curled lips, every one of whose sentences rang with scorn, was the same being who, on the occasion of their last interview, had urged his suit so humbly, and accepted his dismissal with such resignation.

After a short pause Ronald said : " You speak strongly, Dr Wilmot, very strongly; but you have great cause for annoyance ; and the fact that you have borne it so long in silence of course adds to the violence of your expressions now.   I think I could soften your opinion—I think I could show that my father and Lady Muriel have had some excuse for their conduct ; at all events, that they believed they were doing rightly in acting as they did.   But this is not the time for me to enter into that discussion.   I have come to you in the discharge of a mission which is urgent and imperative. You know me to be a cold and a proud man, Dr Wilmot, and will therefore allow I must be convinced of its urgency when I consented to undertake it.   I have come to say to you—leaving all things for the present unexplained, and even in the state in which you have just described them—I have come to say to you my sister is very ill; will you go and see her ? "   He was standing close by Wilmot as he spoke, and saw him change colour, and reel as though he would have fallen.

" Very ill ? " he said, after a moment's pause, with white lips and trembling voice.   " Mad—Mrs Caird, very ill ? "

" Very ill; so ill, that my father is seriously alarmed about her; so ill, that I have obeyed his wishes, and ask you to come to her."

Wilmot was silent for a moment, in thought ; not that he had the smallest doubt as to what he should do ; but the news had come so suddenly upon him, that he could scarcely comprehend its significance.   Then he said, " Where is she ? in town ? "

" She is—at her own house.   I know I am asking you a great deal in begging you to go there, but—you won't refuse us, Wilmot ? "

" I will go at once to your sister, Captain Kilsyth," said Wilmot, pressing Ronald's outstretched hand; "and God grant I may be of service to her ! "

"I won't say any thanks; but you know how g. 'teful we shall all of us be. Perhaps Madeleine had better be a little prepared for your visit; if you were to meet quite unexpectedly, it might agitate her."

Wilmot agreed in this, and promised to come that afternoon.

It was three o'clock—just the hour when Squab-street woke up, and became alive to the fact that day had dawned. The light had indeed penetrated the little street at its usual hour, and the sun had shone; but still Squab-street could not be considered to be fully awake. Tradesmen had come and gone; area-bells had rung out shrilly; grooms on horseback had followed the Amazon daughters of the natives to the morning-ride in the Row; governesses had arrived, and had taken their young charges into the neighbouring square garden for bodily exercise and mental recreation; neat little broughams had deposited neat little foreigners, whose admission into the houses had been immediately followed by the thumping of the piano and the screaming of the female voice; but the cream of Squab-street society had not yet been seen, save by its female attendants. Three o'clock, however, had arrived; luncheon was over, carriages began to rattle up and down, the street resounded with double knocks indefinitely prolonged, and all the little passages were redolent of hair-powder. All society's mummers were acting away at their hardest; and all who passed up and down Squab-street were too much engrossed with themselves or their fellow-performers to notice a very blank and mournful face looking out at them from the drawing-room window of the little house at the corner of the mews. This was Kilsyth's face, which had been planted against the window for the previous half-hour, in anxious expectation of Wilmot's arrival. Sick at heart, and overpowered by anxiety, the old man had taken his position where he could catch the first glimpse of him on whom his life now solely rested; and he scanned every vehicle that approached with eager eyes. At length a brougham, very different from that in which he used to pay his visits in his professional days, perfectly appointed, and drawn by horses which even Clement Penruddock himself could not have designated as "screws," drew up at the door, and Wilmot jumped out. Two minutes afterwards Kilsyth, with his eyes full of tears, was holding both his friend's hands, and murmuring to him his thanks.

"I knew you would come!" he said; "I knew you would come! No matter what had happened in the interval —no matter that, as they told me, you had retired from practice and went nowhere—I said, 'Let him know that Madeleine is very ill, and he'll come! he'll be sure to come!'"

"And you said right, my dear sir," said Wilmot, returning the friendly pressure; "and I only hope to Heaven that my coming now may be as efficacious as it was when you summoned me to Kilsyth—ah, how long ago that seems! Now tell me—for my conversation with Captain Kilsyth was necessarily brief, and admitted of no details concerning the state of his sister—the tendency to weakness on the lungs, which I spoke to you about just before I left Scotland, has increased, I fear?"

"It has been increasing rapidly, we fancy, for the last few months; and she is now never free from a cough, a hollow, dreadful cough, the paroxysms of which are sometimes terrible, and leave her perfectly exhausted. She never complains; on the contrary, she makes light of it, and struggles to hide her pain and weakness from us. But I fear she is very, very ill!" The old man's voice sunk as he said this, and the tears flowed down his cheeks.

"Come, come, you must not give way, my good friend while there's life there's hope, you know; and what is very dreadful and hopeless to an unprofessional eye has a very different aspect frequently to those who have studied these diseases. I think Captain Kilsyth came here to prepare Mrs Caird for my visit?"

"O yes, she expects you. She was greatly excited at first; so much so that we were afraid she would do herself harm; but I think she is calmer now."

"Then perhaps I had better go to her at once. It is always desirable in these cases as much as possible to avoid suspense. Will you show me the way?"

They went upstairs together; and when they arrived at the room, Kilsyth opened the door, and left Wilmot to enter by himself. As the door closed behind him, he looked up, and saw the woman whom he had loved with such devotion and yet with such bitter regret. She was lying on a sofa drawn across the window, propped up by pillows. She turned round at the noise of his entrance; and as soon as she recognized her visitor, her cheeks flushed to the deepest crimson. Wilmot advanced rapidly, with as cheerful a smile as he could assume, and took her hand—her hot, wasted, and trembling hand—within both of his. She was dreadfully changed—he saw that in an instant. There were deep hollows in her cheeks, and round her blue eyes, which were now feverishly bright and lustrous, there were large bistre circles. She wore a white dressing-grown trimmed with blue,—such a one as was associated with his earliest recollections of her; and as he saw her lying back and looking up at him with earnest trusting gaze, he was reminded of the first time he saw her in the fever at Kilsyth, but with oh what a difference in his hope of saving her!

"You see I have come back to you, Mrs Caird," said Wilmot, seating himself by the sofa, but still retaining her hand. "You thought you had got rid of me for ever; but I am like the bottle-imp in the story, impossible to be sent away. Now, own you are surprised to see me!"

"I am not indeed, Dr Wilmot," Madeleine replied, in a

voice the hollow tones of which went to Wilmot's heart. Ah, how unlike the sweet, clear, ringing tones which he so well remembered! "I am not indeed surprised to see you. I had a perfect conviction," she said very calmly, "that I should see you once again. At that time—at Kilsyth, you remember—I thought I was going to die, you know; and when I knew I should recover, as I lay in a dreamy half-conscious state, I recollect having a presentiment that when I did die you would be near me—that you would stand by my bedside, as you used to do, and—"

"My dearest Mrs Caird, I cannot listen to you; my—my child, for God's sake don't talk in that way! I used to have to tell you to calm yourself, you know; but now you must rouse up—you must indeed."

"Oh no, Dr Wilmot; not rouse myself to any action, not wake up again to the dreary struggle of life! Oh no; let me sink quietly into my grave, but—"

His hand trembled with emotion as he laid his finger lightly on her lip, and his voice was choked and husky as he said: "I must insist! You used to obey me implicitly, you recollect; and you must show that you have not forgotten your old ways. And now tell me all about yourself."

Half an hour afterwards, as Wilmot was descending the stairs, he met Kilsyth at the drawing-room door, with haggard looks and trembling hands, waiting for him. They went into the drawing-room together; and the old man, carefully closing the door behind him, turned to his friend, and said in broken accents: "Well, what do you say? what —what do you think?"

Wilmot's face was very grave, graver than Kilsyth had ever seen it, even at the worst time of the fever, as he said: "I think it is a very serious case, my dear friend—a very serious case."

"Has the—the mischief increased much since you detected it—up in Scotland?"

"The disease has spread very rapidly—very rapidly indeed."

"And you—you think that she is—in danger?"

"I think—it would be useless, it would be unmanly in me to withhold the truth from you; I fear that Mrs Caird's state is imminently dangerous, and that—"

Wilmot stopped, for Kilsyth reeled and almost fell. Recovering himself after a moment, he said, in a low hoarse whisper: "Change of climate — Madeira — Egypt—anywhere?"

"No; she has not sufficient strength to bear the journey. If she had spent last winter at Cannes, and had gone on in the spring to Egypt—but it is too late."

"Too late!" shrieked Kilsyth, bursting into an agony of grief; "too late! My darling child! my darling, darling child!"

"My poor friend," said Wilmot, himself deeply affected, "what can I say to comfort you in this awful trial? what can I do?"

"One thing!" said the old man, rising from the sofa on which he had thrown himself, "there is one thing you can do—visit her, watch her, attend her; you'll see her again, won't you, Wilmot?"

"Constantly—and to the end. She knows that. I made her that promise just now;" and he wrung his friend's hand and left him.

"Dr Wilmot, I believe? Will you oblige me by two minutes' conversation? You don't remember me? I am Mr Caird. In this room, if you please."

Wilmot, thus inducted into the dining-room, bowed, and took the chair pointed out to him. He had not recognized Mr Caird at the first glance in the dim little passage; but he knew him again now, albeit Mr Caird's style of dress and general bearing were very different from what they had been

in the old days.   Mr Caird had just come in, and brought a
great quantity of tobacco-smoke in with him ; and a decanter
of brandy, an empty soda-water bottle, and a fizzing tumbler,
were on the table before him.

"I beg your pardon for troubling you, Dr Wilmot ; but
I didn't know you were expected, or I should of course have
been here to meet you.   The people in Brook-street manage
all these matters in—well, to say the least of it, in a curious
way.   You have seen Mrs Caird—what is your opinion of
her ? "

What Wilmot knew of this man was that he was courteous, gentlemanly, and good-tempered—all in his favour.
He had heard the rumours current in society about Caird,
but they had passed unheeded by him ; men of Wilmot's
calibre pay little attention to rumours.   So he said, "Do
you wish me to tell you my real opinion, Mr Caird ? "

"Your real, candid opinion."

Then Wilmot repeated what he had said to Kilsyth.

The young man looked at him earnestly for a moment ;
shook his head as though he had been struck a sudden, stunning blow ; then muttered involuntarily, as it were, "Poor
Maddy ! "

Wilmot rose to go, but Caird stopped him.

"One question more, Dr Wilmot—how long may—may
the end be deferred ? "

"I should fear not more than a few—three or four—
months."

When Wilmot was gone, Ramsay Caird, having lit a
fresh cigar, said "Poor Maddy ! " again ; but this time he
added, "since it was to be, it will be, about the time ; " and
for the next hour he occupied himself with arithmetical calculations in his pocket-book.

CHAPTER XXX.

QUAND MEME!

In years to come it was destined to be a marvel to Wilmot how he lived through the days and the weeks of that time. If they had not been so entirely filled with supreme suffering, with despairing effort—if there had been any interval, any relaxation from the immense task imposed upon him, he might have broken down under it. He might have said, "I will not stay here, and see this woman whom I love die in her youth, in her beauty, in the very springtide of her life. I will go away. I will not see it, at least; I who have not the right to shut out all others, and gather up the last days of her life into a treasury of remembrance, in which no. other shall have a share. No man is called upon to suffer that which he can avoid. I will go!" But there was no time for Wilmot, no chance for him to reach such a conclusion, to take this supreme resolution of despair. The whole weight of the family trouble was thrown upon him; and he, in comparison with whose grief that of all the others, except Kilsyth's, was insignificant, was the one to whom all looked for support and hope. As for Ramsay Caird, he adopted the easy and plausible *rôle* of a sanguine man. He had the greatest possible respect for Dr Wilmot's opinion, the utmost confidence in his ability; but the doctor's talent gave him the very best grounds for security. He was quite sure Wilmot would set Madeleine all right. She had youth on her side—and only just think how Wilmot had "pulled her through" at Kilsyth! And as nobody occupied themselves particularly with what Ramsay thought, he was permitted to indulge his incorrigible *insouciance*, and to render to Dr Wilmot's talent the original homage of believing it superior

to his judgment and his avowed conviction. For the rest,
Ramsay professed himself, and with reason, to be the worst
person in the world in a sick-room—no use, and "awfully
frightened;" and accordingly he seldom made his appearance in Madeleine's room, after the daily visit of a few
minutes, which was *de rigueur*, and during which he invariably received the same answer to his inquiries, that she
was better—a statement which it suited him to receive as
valid, and which he therefore did so receive. Wilmot saw
very little of him; no part of the hardness of his task came
to him from Madeleine's husband. It was at her father's
hands that Wilmot suffered most, and most constantly.
Kilsyth held two articles of faith in connection with Wilmot: the first, that he was infallible in judgment; the
second, that he was inexhaustible in skill and resources.
And now these articles of belief clashed, and Kilsyth was
swayed about between them,—a prey now to helpless grief,
again to groundless and unreasonable hope. Certainly
Madeleine was very ill. Wilmot was right, no doubt; but
then Wilmot would save her: he had saved her before,
when she was also very ill. Then the poor father would
have the difference between fever and consumption, in
point of assured fatality, forced upon his attention, and an
interval of despair would set in. But whether his mood
was hope or despair, an effort to attain resignation, or a
mere stupor of fear and grief, Wilmot had to witness,
Wilmot had to combat them all. The old man clung to
the doctor with piteous eagerness and tenacity on his way
to begin the watch over his patient which he maintained
daily for hours, as he had done in the old time at Kilsyth
—time in reality so lately passed, but seeming like an
entire lifetime ago. When he left her to take the short
and troubled sleep which fell upon her in the afternoon;
in the evening, when he came again; at night, after he had
administered the medicine which was to procure her a tem-

porary reprieve from the cough, which her father could no longer endure to hear, Kilsyth would waylay him, beset him with questions, with entreaties—or, worse still, look speechless into his face with imploring haggard eyes.

This to the man for whom the young life ebbing away, with terrific rapidity indeed, but with merciful ease on the whole, was the one treasure held by the earth, so rich for others, such a wilderness for him! Yes—her life! When he knew she was married, and thus parted from him for ever, he had thought the worst that could have come to him had come. But from the moment he had looked again into the innocent sweet blue eyes, and read, with the unerring glance of the practised physician, that death was looking out at him from them, he learned his error. Then too he learned how much, and with what manner of love, he loved Madeleine Kilsyth.

" Give her life, and not death, O gracious Disposer of both! and I am satisfied—and I am happy! Life, though I never see her face again; life, though she never hears my name spoken, or remembers me in her lightest thought; life, though it be to bless her husband, and to transmit her name to his children; life, though mine be wasted at the ends of the earth!" This was the cry of his soul, the utterance of the strong man's anguish. But he knew it was not to be; the physician's eye had been unerring indeed.

Lady Muriel bore herself on this, as on every other occasion, irreproachably. The first enunciation of the doctor's opinion had startled her. She did not love her step-daughter, but of late she had been on more affectionate terms with her; and it was not possible that she could learn that she was doomed to an early death without terror and grief. Lady Muriel knew well how unspeakably dear to Kilsyth his daughter was; and apart from her keen womanly sympathies all enlisted for the fair young sufferer

she felt with agonizing acuteness for her husband's suffering. The first meeting between Lady Muriel and Wilmot
had been under agitating circumstances; and the appeal
made to him by Kilsyth had at once established him on the
old footing with them—a footing which had not existed
previously in London, having been interrupted by Wilmot's
domestic affliction, and the tacit but resolute opposition of
Ronald. But even then, in that first interview, when
emotion was permissible, when Dr Wilmot was forced by
his position to make a communication to the father and
brother which even a stranger must necessarily have found
painful, and though he imposed superhuman control over
his feelings, Lady Muriel had seen the truth, or as much
of the truth as one human being can ever see of the verities
of the heart of another. She had received him gravely,
but so that, had he cared to interpret her manner, it might
have told him he was welcome in more than the sense of
his value in this dread emergency; and it had been a sensible relief to Ronald to perceive that Lady Muriel had not
suffered the pride and suspicion which had dictated her
remonstrance to him to appear in any word or look of hers
which Wilmot could perceive. But when Lady Muriel
was alone she said to herself bitterly:

"He did love her, then; he does love her! He is awfully changed; and this has changed him—not her illness,
not the fear of her death—the change is the work of months
—but the loss of her. Her marriage—this has made his
life valueless, this has made him what he is." Then she remained for a long time sunk in thought, her dark eyes
shaded by her hand. At length she said, half aloud,

"She is not all to be pitied, even if this be indeed true
and past remedy. She has been well beloved."

There was a whole history of solitude and vain aspiration in the words. Had not she too, Lady Muriel Kilsyth,
been well beloved? True; but all the homage, all the de-

votion of an inferior nature could not satisfy hers. This
woman would be content only with the love of a man her
intellectual superior, her master in strength of purpose
and of will. She had seen him; he had come; and he
loved not her, but the simple girl with blue eyes and golden
hair who was dying, and whom he would love faithfully
when she should be dead. Lady Muriel did not deceive
herself. She had the perfect comprehension of Wilmot
which occult sympathy gives—she knew that he would
never love another woman. She knew, when she recalled
the ineffable mournfulness which sat upon his face, not the
garment of an occasion, but the habitual expression which
it had taken, that the hope which but for her might have
been realized, had been the forlorn hope of his life. It was
over now; and he was beaten by fate, by death, by Lady
Muriel's will. He would lay down his arms; he would
never struggle again.

Knowing this, Lady Muriel Kilsyth dreamed no more.
The vision of a love which, pure and blameless, would have
elevated, fortified, and sweetened her life, faded never to
return. Her gentle step-daughter, who would have been
incapable of such a thought or such a wish, had she known
how Lady Muriel had acted towards her, was at that moment amply avenged.

In vain she had laboured to effect this loveless marriage;
in vain she had placed in the untrustworthy hands of
Ramsay Caird the happiness and the fortune of her husband's beloved daughter; in vain had she been deaf to the
truer, better promptings of her conscience, to the haunting
thought of the responsibility which she had undertaken towards the girl, to the remembrance of Madeleine's dead
mother, which sometimes came to her and troubled her
sorely; in vain had she tempted that dread and inexorable
law of retribution, which might fall upon the heads of her
own children. How mad, how guilty, she had been! She

saw it all now; she understood it all now. How could she, who had learned to comprehend, to appreciate Wilmot,—how could she have imagined for a moment that any sentiment once really entertained by him could be light and passing! She recognized, with respect at least, if with an abiding sense of humiliation, the truth, the strength, the eternal duration of Wilmot's love for Madeleine. Truly, many things, in addition to the beautiful young form, were destined to go down into the grave of Madeleine Kilsyth.

There was so much similarity between the thoughts of Lady Muriel and those of Chudleigh Wilmot, that he too, after that first visit, which had shown him the dying girl and revealed to him how he loved her, pondered also upon an unconscious vengeance fulfilled.

Mabel! She had died in his absence, neglected by him, inflicting upon him an agonizing doubt, almost a certainty, but at least a doubt never to be resolved in this world—a dread never to be set at rest. He did not believe that had he been with her he could have saved her; but no matter; he had stayed away; he had given to another the love, the care, the time, the skill that should have been hers, that were her right by every law human and divine. And now! The woman he had preferred to her, the woman by whose side he had lingered, the woman he loved, was dying, and he had come to her aid too late! He could see her, it was true; he might be with her; it was possible he might hear her last words—might see her draw her last breath; but she was lost to him, lost unwon, lost for ever, as Mabel had been! It was late in the night before Wilmot had sufficiently mastered these thoughts and the emotions which they aroused to be able to apply himself to studying the details of Madeleine's case, and arranging his plan, not indeed of cure, but of alleviation.

Among the letters awaiting his attention there was one from Mrs Prendergast. She requested him to call on her;

she wished to consult him concerning the matter they had talked of. The following morning ho wrote her a line saying he could not attend to anything for the present; and subsequently Henrietta learned from Mrs Charlton, through Mrs M'Diarmid, that Wilmot had consented to act as physician to Mrs Caird, whom he pronounced to be in hopeless consumption.

Henrietta went home grave and pensive, thinking much of her dead friend, Mabel Wilmot.

Time had gone inexorably on since that day, laden every hour of it with grief to Wilmot, with immense and complicated responsibility, with the dread of the rapidly-approaching end. There had been hours—no, not hours, moments —when he almost persuaded himself that he might be wrong, that it was still time, that a warm climate might yet avail. But the delusion was only momentary; and he had told Madeleine's father and brother from the first that she was unfit for a journey, that the most merciful course was to let her die at home in peace, among the people and the things to whom and to which she was accustomed. He understood the attachment of an invalid to the inanimate objects around her; an attachment strongly developed in Madeleine, whose dressing-room, where she lay on the sofa all day, contained all her girlish treasures. She was always awake early in the morning, and anxious to be carried from her bed to her sofa, whence she would wistfully watch the door until it opened and admitted Wilmot. Then she would smile—such a happy smile too! Only a pale reflection in point of brightness, it is true, of the radiant smile of the past, but full of the old trust and happiness and peace. Her father came early too, and received the report of how she had passed the night, and controlled himself wonderfully, poor old man! for agitation and disquiet were very bad for his darling; and he was strengthened by Wilmot's example. It never occurred to Kilsyth to remember that

Wilmot was "only the doctor," and therefore might well
be calm; he never reasoned about Wilmot at all—he only
felt and trusted. The world outside the sick-room went on
as usual. Within it Madeleine Caird lay dying, not poet-
ically, not of the fanciful extinction which consumption becomes in the hands of the poet and the romancer, but of
the genuine, veritable, terrible disease, not to be robbed by
wealth, or even by comfort or skill, of its terrors. Those
who know what is meant when a person is said to be dying
of consumption need no amplification of the awful significance of the phrase. Those who do not—may they remain
in their ignorance !

And Madeleine? Amid the contending emotions, amid
the varied suffering which surrounded her, and had all its
origin in her, how was it with Madeleine? On the whole,
it was well. A strange phrase to apply to a young woman,
a young wife, an idolized daughter, who was dying thus, of
a disease which kills more thoroughly, so to speak, than any
other, doing its dread office with slowness, and marking its
progress day by day. She knew she was dying, though
sometimes she did not feel it very keenly; the idea did not
come to her as relating to herself, but with a sort of outside
meaning. This dulness would last for days, and then she
would be struck by the truth again, and would realize it
with all the strength of mind and body left to her. Realize
it, not to be terrified by it, not to resist it, not to appeal
against it, but to accept it, to acquiesce in it, to be satisfied
and profoundly quiet. Madeleine's notions of God and eternity were vague, like those of most young people. She had
been brought up in a careful observance of the forms of the
Episcopal Church in Scotland, and she had always had a
certain devotional turn, which accompanies good taste and
purity of mind in young girls. But she had never looked
at life or death seriously, in the true sense, at all. Sentimentally she had considered both, extensively of course;

had she not read all the poetry she could lay her hands on, and a vast number of essays? Of late a voice whose tones she had never before heard, still and small, had spoken to her—spoken much and solemnly in her girlish heart, and had taught her, in the silent suffering and doubt, the unseen struggle she had undergone, great things. She kept her own counsel; she listened, and was still; and the chain of earth fell from her fair soul while yet it held her fair form in its coil a little longer. Madeleine had looked into her life to find the meaning of her Creator in it. She had found it, and she was ready for the summons, which was not to tarry long.

One day, when she had told Wilmot that she was wonderfully easy, had had quite a good night, and had hardly coughed at all since morning, he was sitting by her sofa, and she, lying with her face turned towards him, had fallen into a light sleep. He drew a coverlet closely round her, and signed to the nurse that she might leave the room. Then he sat quite still, his face rigid, his hands clasped, looking at her; looking at the thin pale face, with the blazing spots of red upon the cheek-bones, with the darkened eyelids, the sunken temples, the dry red lips, the damp, limp, golden hair. As in a phantasmagoria, the days at Kilsyth passed before him; the day of his arrival, the day the nurse had asked him whether the golden hair must be cut off, the day he had pronounced her out of danger. Outwardly calm and stern, what a storm of anguish he was tossed upon! Words and looks and little incidents—small things, but infinite to him—came up and tormented him. Then came a sense of unreality; it could not be, it was not the same Madeleine; this was not Kilsyth's beautiful daughter. His hands went up to his face, and a groan burst from his lips. The sound frightened him. He looked at her again; and as he looked, her eyes opened, and she began to speak. Then came the frightful, the inevitable cough. He lifted her upon his arm, kneeling by her side, and the paroxysm passed over. Then she looked at him very gently and sweetly, and said:

"Are we quite alone?"

"Yes."

"Do you remember one night at Kilsyth, when I was very ill, I asked you whether I was going to die?"

"I remember," he said, with a desperate effort to keep down a sob.

"And I told you I was very glad when you said, 'No.' Do you remember?"

"Yes—I remember."

She paused and looked at him; her blue eyes were as steady as they were bright. "If I asked you, but I don't— I don't"—she put out her wasted hand. He took the thin fingers in his, and trembled at their touch—"because I know —but if I did, you would not make me the same answer now."

He did not speak, he did not look at her; but her eyes pertinaciously sought his, and he was forced to meet them. She smiled again, and her fingers clasped themselves round his.

"You will always be papa's friend," she said. "Poor papa—he will miss me very much; the girls are too young as yet. And Ronald—I have something to say to you about Ronald. Sit here, close to me, in papa's chair, and listen."

He changed his seat in obedience to her, and listened; his head bent down, and her golden hair almost touching his shoulder.

"Something came between Ronald and me for a little while," she said, her low voice, which had hardly lost its sweetness at all, thrilling the listener with inexpressible pain. "I cannot tell what exactly; but it is all over now, and he is—as he used to be—the best and kindest of brothers. But there is some one—not papa ; I am not talking of poor papa now—better and kinder still. Do you know whom I mean ? " The sweet steady blue eyes looked at him quite innocent and unabashed. " I mean *you*."

" Me ! " he said, looking up hastily ; " me ! "

" Yes ; best and kindest of all to me. And when Ronald will not have me any longer, I want you to promise me to be his friend too. They say he is hard in his disposition and his ways ; he never was to me, but once for a little while ; and I should like him to see you often, and be with you much, that he may be reminded of me. As long as he remembers me he will not be hard to any one ; and he will remember me whenever he sees you."

Thus the sister interpreted the brother's late repentance, and endeavoured to render it a source of blessing to the two men whom she loved.

" When you left Kilsyth," she said, " and came here, and when I heard the dreadful affliction that had befallen you, it made me very unhappy. It seemed, somehow, awful to me that sorrow should have come to you through me."

" It did not," he replied. " Don't think so ; don't say so ! Did any one tell you so ? It would have come all the same—"

" It would not," she said solemnly ; " it would not. If I never felt it before, I must have come to feel it now, that I caused unconsciously a dreadful misfortune. You are here with me ; you make suffering, you make death, light and easy to me. And you were away from *her* when she was dying who had a right to look for you by her side. I hope she has forgiven me where all is forgiven."

There was silence between them for a while. Wilmot's agony was quite beyond description, and almost beyond even his power of self-control. Madeleine was quite calm ; but the bright red spots had faded away from her cheek-bones, and she was deadly pale. His eyes were fixed upon her face

—eagerly, despairingly, as though he would have fixed it before them for ever, a white phantom to beset, of his free will, all his future life. Another racking fit of coughing came on, and then, when it had subsided, Madeleine fell again into one of the sudden short sleeps which had become habitual to her, and which told Wilmot so plainly of the progress of exhaustion. It was only of a few minutes' duration ; and when she again awoke, her cheeks had the red spots on them once more. He watched her more and more eagerly, to see if she would resume the tone in which she had been speaking, and which, while it tortured him to listen to it, he had not the courage to interrupt or interdict. There was a little, a very little more excitement in the voice and in the eyes as she said,

"You are not going to be a doctor any more, they tell me, now that you are a rich man."

"No," he said, in a low but bitter tone. "I am done with doctoring. All my skill and knowledge have availed me nothing, and they are nothing to me any more."

"Nothing! And why?"

"O Madeleine," he said,—and as he spoke he fell on his knees beside the sofa on which she lay—"how can you ask me? What have they done for me? They have not saved you. I asked nothing else—no other reward for all my years of labour and study and poverty and insignificance—nothing but this. Even at Kilsyth, when you had the fever, I asked nothing else. I got it then, for they did save you. Yes, thank God, they did save you then for a little time! But now, now—" And, forgetful of the agitation of his patient, forgetful of everything in the supreme agony, Chudleigh Wilmot hid his face in the coverlet of the sofa and wept— wept the burning and distracting tears it is so dreadful to see a man shed. Madeleine raised herself up, and tried to lift his head in her feeble, wasted hands. Then he recovered himself with a tremendous effort, and was calm.

"I must tell you," he said, "having said what you have heard. Madeleine, there is no sin, no shame in what I am going to tell you. I will tell it to your father and your brother yet; I would tell it to your husband, Madeleine. When I went away from England, I took a vision with me. It was, that I might return some time and ask for your love. It faded, Madeleine; but I claim, as the one solitary consolation which life can ever bring me, to tell you this: you are the only woman I have ever loved."

Madeleine looked at him still; the colour rose higher and brighter on her wasted cheeks; the light blazed up in her blue eyes.

"Did you love me," she said, "because you saved my life?"

"I don't know, child. I loved you—I loved you! That is all I know. I know 1 ought not to say it now; but I must, I must!"

"Hush!" she said; "and don't shiver there, and don't cry. It is not for such as you to do either." He resumed his seat; she gave him her hand again, and lay still looking at him—looking at him with her blue eyes full of the inexplicably awful look which comes into the eyes of the dying. After a while she smiled.

"I am very glad you told me," she said. "People said you never cared for the patient, only for the *case;* but since you have been here I have known that was not true. It is better as it is. If your vision had come true, I must have died all the same, and then it would have been harder. It is easier now."

Another fit of coughing—a frightful paroxysm this time. Wilmot rang for the nurse, and Kilsyth and Lady Murie. entered the room with her.

*   *   *   *   *

Several hours later Madeleine was lying in the same place, still, tranquil, and at ease. She had had a long interval of respite from the cough, and was cheerful, even bright. Her father was there, and Ronald; Lady Muriel also, but sitting at some distance from her, and looking very sad.

When the time came at which Madeleine was to be removed to her bed, Ronald and Wilmot took leave; the first for the night, the second to return an hour later, and give final instructions to the nurse.

Wilmot's left hand hung down by his side as he stood near her, and Madeleine touched a ring upon his little finger.

"What is the motto on that ring?" she asked.

"The untranslateable French phrase, which I always think is like a shrug in words: *Quand même*," he replied.

The ring was the seal-ring which his wife had been used to wear. It struck him with a new and piercing pain, amid all the pains of this dreadful day, that Madeleine should have noticed it, and reminded him of it then.

"*Quand même*," she said softly. "Notwithstanding, even so—ah, it can't be said in English, but it means the same in every tongue." He bent over her, no one was near, her eyes met his; she said, "I am very happy—very happy, *quand même!*"

*   *   *   *   *

Wilmot went home and sat down to think— to think over the words he had spoken and heard. He was overpowered with the fatigue, the excitement, the emotion of the day. A thousand confused images floated before his weary eyes; the room seemed full of phantoms. Was this illness? Could it be possible? No, that must not be; he could not be ill; he had not time. After—yes, after, illness —anything! but not yet. He called for wine and bread, and ate and drank. His thoughts became clearer, and arranged themselves; then he became absorbed in reflection. He had told his servant he should require the carriage in an hour, and, hearing a noise in the hall, he started up, think-

ing the time had come. He opened his study-door, and
called—

"Is that the brougham, Stephen?"

"No, sir," said the man, presenting himself with an air
of having something important to say.

"What is it then?" said Wilmot impatiently.

"A messenger from Brook-street, sir; Captain Kilsyth's
man, sir."

Wilmot went out into the hall. The man was there
looking pale and frightened.

"What is it, Martin? what is it?"

"Captain Kilsyth sent me, sir, to let you know that
Mrs Caird is dead, sir,—a few minutes after you left, sir.
Went off like a lamb. They didn't know it, sir, till the
nurse came to lift her into bed."

CHAPTER XXXI.

FORLORN.

YES, she was dead; had died with a smile upon her lips;
had died at peace and charity with all; had died knowing
that the man whom she had looked up to and reverenced, had
loved with all the pure and guileless love of her young heart,
had loved her also, and had so loved her that he had suffered
in silence, and only spoken when the confession could bring
no remorse to her, even no longing regret for what might
have been. Even no longing regret? No! "Happy,
quand même," were the last words that ever passed her lips;
"happy, *quand même*,"—she had been something to him after
all! In the few short and fleeting hours which she had
passed between hearing Chudleigh Wilmot's confession,
wrung from his heart by the great agony which possessed

him, she had pondered over the words which he had spoken with inexpressible delight. What can we tell, we creatures moulded in coarser clay, creatures of baser passions, soiled in the perpetual contact with earth, its mean fears and gross aspirations, if aspirations they may be called,—what can we tell of the feelings of a young girl like this? Death, which we contemplate as the King of Terrors, threatening us with his uplifted dart, and destined to drag us away from the stage of life, bright with its tawdry tinsel and its garish splendour, came to her in softer and more kindly guise. For months she had been expecting the advent of the " shadow cloaked from head to foot," in whose gentle embrace she knew that she must shortly find herself. Those around her, her loving, doting father, Lady Muriel, Ronald, softened by the silent contemplation of her gradually-decreasing strength, the daily ebbing of physical force, the daily loosening of even the slight hold on life which she possessed, visible even to his unpractised eyes,—none of these had the smallest idea that the frail delicate creature, round whose couch they stood day by day with forced smiles and feigned hope, knew better than any of them, better even than he whose professional skill had never been brought into such play, how swiftly the current of her life was bearing her on to the great rapids of Eternity. And if before she had heard those burning words, intensified by the agony shown in the choking voice in which they found their utterance, she had been able calmly and not unwillingly to contemplate her fate, how much greater had been her resignation, how much more readily did she accept the fiat, when she learned that the one love of her life had been returned ; and that, despite of all that had come between them, despite the interposition of the dread barrier which had apparently so effectually separated them from each other, the man who had been to her far beyond all others had singled her out as the object of his adoration !

In those few last earthly hours the "what might have

been " had passed through her mind, and passed away again, leaving behind it no trace of anguish or remorse. Not only to Wilmot had the time since their first acquaintance at Kilsyth passed in review in phantasmagoric semblance; Madeleine had often gone through such scenes in the short drama, recollecting every detail, remembering much which had been overlooked even in his rapid summary. " What might have been!" Even suppose the dearest, the only real aspiration of her heart had been accomplished, and she had become Chudleigh Wilmot's wife, would not the inevitable end have had additional distress and misery to both of them? The inevitable end! for she must have died—she knew that; not for one instant did she imagine that any combination of circumstances different from what had actually occurred could have averted or postponed the fulfilment of the dread decree. Her married life had not been specially happy; then should she not have less regret in leaving it? Would not the pangs of parting be robbed of half their bitterness by the knowledge that her husband left behind would not sink under the blow? What might have been! Ah, Wilmot would feel her loss acutely, she knew that; the one outburst of grief, of passionate tenderness and heartfelt agony, which had escaped him had told her that; but he would feel it less than if what might have been had been, and she had been taken away from him in the early days of their love and happiness.

A notion that such thoughts as these might have filled the mind of her for whom they mourned occurred to each of those by whom the dead girl was really loved, not indeed at once nor simultaneously, but at divers times, as they pondered over the blank which her loss had left in their lives. Among this number Mr Ramsay Caird was not to be reckoned. The solemn announcement which, at his own request, Dr Wilmot had made to him as to the impossibility of his wife's recovery and the probable short duration of her illness, had had very little effect on the young man. What were the motives which

prompted him were known to himself alone ; but the *insouciance*, to use the mildest term for it, which had prompted him
during the whole of his short married life seemed in no way
diminished even by the dread news which had been communicated to him. He acknowledged that he had seen Dr
Wilmot, and had asked his opinion; that that opinion had
been very serious, and to some persons would have been
alarming, but that he was not easily alarmed, and that he
was utterly and entirely incredulous in the present instance.
Madeleine had a bad cough, and was naturally delicate on
her chest, and that sort of thing ; she did not wrap up enough
when she went out, and sat in draughts ; but as to the way
in which they all went on about her—well, they would find
that he was right, and then they would be sorry they had
listened to any such nonsense. He said this to Lady Muriel ;
for both Kilsyth and Ronald shrunk from any communication
with him. Bitterest among all the bitter feelings which
oppressed these two men, so different in mind and spirit, but
with their love centered on the same object, was the thought
that they had given up the guardianship of their treasure to
one who was utterly unworthy of it, and, as one of them at
least confessed to himself with keen remorse, had blighted
two lives by unreasoning and short-sighted pride.

So, while his young wife had been gradually declining,
Ramsay Caird had made very little alteration in the mode of
life which he had thought fit to pursue since the earliest days
of his marriage. Relying principally on the fact, which he
was constantly urging, that he was of " no use," he absented
himself more and more from his home ; and when " doing
duty " there, as he phrased it, strove in no way to hide the
dislike with which he regarded the irksome task. Companionship was necessary to Ramsay Caird, and was not to
be obtained, he found, among the class with whom since his
arrival in London and his domestication in Brook-street he
had been accustomed to associate. The men who had been

pleasantly familiar with him in those days stood aloof, and seemed by no means anxious to continue the acquaintance. They had come, soon after his marriage, and dined in the little red-flocked tank in Squab-street, but that was principally for Madeleine's sake; and when rumours as to the newly-founded *ménage* grew rife, and more especially after Tommy Toshington's delightful story of seeing Caird at Madame Favorita's door had got wind, the men generally agreed that he was a bad lot, and fought as shy of him as was compatible with common politeness. For it is to be noted that the loose-living Benedick, the married man who glories in his own escapades and talks with unctuous smack of his dissipations, is generally shunned by those men of his own set who are by no means strait-laced, and forced to seek his company in a lower grade.

Ramsay Caird began to be bored and oppressed by his wife's illness, and by the constant presence of her father and brother at his house. It is true that he never saw these unwelcome visitors—on both sides any meeting was studiously avoided—but he could not help knowing of their being constantly with the invalid; and his own conscience, as much of it as he had ever possessed, did not fail to tell him what must be their indubitable opinion of him and his conduct. The companions too with whom he had taken up—for Ramsay Caird was essentially gregarious, and especially during the last few months had found the impossibility of living without excitement—the new companions with whom he consorted, and who were principally half-sporting, half-military, whole raffish adventurers, always well dressed, and retaining a certain hold on society, where they once had been well received,—these men encouraged Caird in his dislike to his home, and assisted him in the invention of plausible excuses to get away from it. The fact that he had "gone on to the turf," which he had at first taken every precaution to prevent his connections in Brook-street from becoming acquainted with, and which, when some kind common friend had told them of it, struck Kilsyth with silent horror, and aroused much burning and outspoken indignation in Ronald, was now put forward on every occasion, just as though it had been a legitimate business on which he was employed. "Meetings" were constantly taking place all over the country at which his attendance was indispensable, and he was soon well known as one of the regular frequenters of the betting-ring. On his return the servants in Squab-street could generally tell what had been the result of his betting speculations; but only to them and to one other person did he ever show his temper. And that one other person was Lady Muriel—the proud Lady Muriel —who in all matters between her husband and this man, who by her instrumentality had become the husband of her husband's daughter, had to be the go-between; to her it was left to soften his irregularities and gloss them over as best she might, and she alone possessed his confidence. To be the *confidante* of a gambler and the apologist for a debauchee was scarcely what Lady Muriel had expected when she gave her pledge to dying Stewart Caird, and when she intrigued and manœuvred so successfully in gaining her step-daughter's hand for Ramsay.

Three days before Madeleine's death Ramsay Caird announced to Lady Muriel, whom he stopped as she was about to ascend the stairs to the invalid's room, that he wanted to speak to her, and, on joining him in the red-flocked tank, told her that he was about to start that night for Paris. There were races at Chantilly in which he was very much interested, having a large sum at stake, and it was absolutely necessary that he should be on the spot to watch and avail himself of the fluctuations in the betting-ring. Then, for the first time during their acquaintance, Lady Muriel spoke out to her quondam protégé. The long-repressed emotions under which she was suffering seemed to have given her eloquence;

she drew a vivid picture of " what might have been " if Ramsay's conduct had been different, and lashed his present life and pursuits, the company he kept, and the general degradation into which he had fallen, with an unsparing tongue. She implored him to give up his intended journey, assuring him that he either would not or could not understand the extreme danger of his wife's position, pointing out to him what scandal must necessarily arise from his absenting himself at such a time, and telling him that his past conduct during his married life, already sufficiently commented upon by the world, might to a certain extent be condoned by his doing his duty and devoting himself to his home for the future. Ramsay listened impatiently, as men of his stamp always listen to such advice, and then he in his turn spoke out. He said that he would be his own master, that he would brook no interference with his plans, that already he was a mere cipher in his own house, which was invaded and occupied by other people at their own pleasure, and that he would stand it no longer; then, after this outburst, he moderated his tone, apologized to Lady Muriel for his violence, and told her that, though the importance of his business arrangements and the largeness of his venture made it absolutely necessary for him to go to Paris on this occasion, yet it should be the last; he would do as her ladyship wished him, as he felt he ought to do, and his enemies should find that he was not so black as by some persons he had been painted.

So Ramsay Caird and a select circle of British turfites took their departure by that night's mail, and enjoyed themselves very much, smoking, drinking, and playing cards whenever it was practicable on the journey. Most of them were men whose acquaintance Caird had made some time previously; but amongst them there was a Frenchman, a M. Leroux, whom Ramsay had never previously seen, although the little gentleman said he had frequently been in England, and seemed perfectly conversant with the English

language, manners, and customs.   He was a lively, viva-
cious, gasconading little fellow ; and any temporary depression of spirits which Ramsay Caird may have felt after
his interview with Lady Muriel quite vanished under the
influence of M. Leroux's conversation.   He and M. Leroux
seemed to have taken a mutual liking to each other ; they
went together to the races, where Caird won a large sum
of money, Leroux not being quite so fortunate ; and on
their return to Paris, Ramsay declined to join his English
friends, and dined with Leroux and some very agreeable
Frenchmen to whom Leroux had introduced him at the
races.   The dinner was excellent ; and after they had done
full justice to it, and to the wines which accompanied it,
they all adjourned to some neighbouring rooms belonging
to one of their number, where cards and dice were speedily
introduced.   Again Ramsay Caird's luck stood by him.
Malheureux en amour, he was destined to be *heureux en jeu*
on this occasion at least.   Nothing could alter or diminish
his flow of success ; no matter what he played, lansquenet,
baccarat, hazard, he won largely at them all ; and when at
a very late hour he left the rooms in company with Leroux
and two of his friends, his pockets were filled with notes
and gold.   They were quite empty when they were examined about noon the next day by the attendants at the
Morgue, whither Ramsay Caird's dead body, found in the
Seine with a deep gash in its breast, had been conveyed.

M. Leroux and his friends did not come so well out of
this little affair as they had expected.   They knew that
Ramsay was a stranger in Paris, known only to the English
sporting-men in whose company he had arrived there, and
who had probably returned to England.   But they did not
make allowance for the fact that of all cities Paris has a
charm for the "English division," who, if they have won
any money, linger for a few days amongst its pleasures, one
of which undoubtedly is a frequent visit to the Morgue.
By one of these late lingerers, no less a person than Cap-

tain Severn, the body of Ramsay Caird was seen and recognized; inquiries were at once set on foot; the waiter
at the restaurant, the *concierge* at the house where the play
had taken place, were examined, and gave their evidence.
M. Leroux and his two friends were apprehended; one of
the friends turned traitor (his share of the spoil had been
too small), and Leroux and the other, being found guilty
of murder under extenuating circumstances, were sen-
tenced to the galleys for life.

The news of this catastrophe was conveyed to the Kilsyth
family in a letter addressed by Captain Severn to Ronald,
which letter lay unopened in Brook-street for several days.
Ronald Kilsyth was far too much crushed and broken by the
blow, which, for all their long expectation of its advent, had
yet fallen suddenly upon them at the last, to attend to anything unconnected, as he imagined, with the dead. He had
indeed carelessly glanced at the cover of this letter, with
several others; but the handwriting was unfamiliar to him,
and he put it aside, to be opened at a later opportunity. It
was not until two or three days afterwards, when Ramsay
Caird had been sought in vain, and when Lady Muriel had
confessed that he had confided to her his intention of going
to Paris, that Ronald recollected the letter in the strange
handwriting with the Paris postmark. He sent for the letter,
and read it through without the smallest sign of emotion.
He was a hard man, Ronald Kilsyth, and the softening effect
of his sister's illness only included her and those who were
fond of her. Ronald knew well enough that Ramsay Caird did
not come within this category, and he felt no pity for his fate.

He communicated the news to his father more as a
matter of form than anything else; for the shock of his
beloved child's death had almost deprived Kilsyth of his
reason. Like Rachel, he refused to be comforted, and
would sit hour after hour in one position on his chair, his
eyes fixed on vacancy, his chin resting on his breast, his
hands idly clasped before him. Nothing seemed to rouse

him,—not even the news which had been conveyed to Ronald
in Captain Severn's letter. He comprehended it, for he said
"Poor Ramsay!" once, and once only; then heaved a deep
sigh, and never alluded to his dead son-in-law again. His
thoughts were filled with reminiscences of his lost darling,
and he had none to bestow on any one else. "My poor
Maddy!" "My bonnie lass!" "My own childie!"—he
would sit and repeat these phrases over and over again; then
steal away down to the house where all that was left of her
still lay, and remain on his knees by the coffin, until Ronald
would come and half forcibly lead him away. He left
London immediately after the funeral, and never could be
persuaded to return to it. After a while, the fresh mountain
air, to which he had been so long accustomed, and away from
which he was never well, had some of its old restorative
effect, and Kilsyth recovered most of his physical strength
and some of his old pleasure in field sports; but his zest for
life was gone, and the gillies mourned the alteration in the
chief whom they loved so much.

The death of Ramsay Caird under such horrible circumstances was a crushing blow to Lady Muriel. This, then,
was the end of all her schemes and plots; this the result of
so much mental agony and remorse endured by herself—of
so much grief and cruel injustice inflicted by her on others.
She had kept the promise she had made to Stewart Caird on
his death-bed, two lives had been sacrificed, two loves had
been blighted—but she had kept her promise. For the first
time in her life "my lady's" courage failed her; and her conscience showed her how recklessly she had availed herself of
the means to gain her ends. For the first time in her life
she dreaded meeting the glances of the world. More than
all men she dreaded Ronald Kilsyth, knowing as she did full
well how she had used him for her own purposes, and with
what lamentable results. She had been seriously affected by
Madeleine's death—like many worldly people, never knowing
how much she had loved the girl until she lost her; and

now the fact of Ramsay's murder under such discreditable circumstances—a story which had been made public in the newspapers, where the world could glean the undeniable truth that the murdered man had left what was actually his wife's death-bed to attend some races—seemed to overwhelm her. The young men who visited at the house had been in the habit of expressing to each other great admiration of Lady Muriel's "pluck"—that quality did not desert her even at her worst. She made head against her troubles, and never gave in; but those intimate enemies who saw her before she left London with her husband declared Lady Muriel to be "quite broken" and a "thorough wreck."

And Chudleigh Wilmot? He lived, of course; lived, and ate and drank, and pursued very much his usual course of life. Well, no; not quite his usual course of life. The effect of the death of the one woman whom in his lifetime he had loved was to him much as are the gunshot wounds of which we sometimes hear officers and army surgeons tell; wounds where the hit man feels a slight concussion at the moment, and does not know until a short time afterwards that he is stunned, paralyzed for ever. While Wilmot had been watching the insidious progress of Madeleine's disease, his mental misery at times was most acute; every variation in her was apparent to his practised eye; and day by day he saw the destroyer creeping stealthily onward in his attack, without the smallest power to resist him. When the bitter tidings of her death were brought by Ronald's servant, the words fell upon Chudleigh Wilmot's ear and smote him as if a sharp cut from a whip had fallen upon him. She whom he had loved so devotedly, so hopelessly, so selflessly, was dead —he realized that. He knew that he should never see the light in her blue eyes, never hear the sweet soft tones of her voice again. He was thankful that, under the impulse of his grief, he had spoken to her out of his overcharged heart and told her how he loved her. He dared not have done it before, he dared not under any other circumstances have confessed the passion for her that had so long been the motive-power of his life ; but then—" Happy, *quand même !* " Her last words—she never had spoken after that—her last words were addressed to him, and told him of her happiness.

It was not until after the funeral that Wilmot experienced the full effect of the blow, experienced it in the dead dull blankness which seemed for the second time to have fallen upon his life. He had had something of the kind before, but nothing equal in intensity to what he now suffered. He felt as though the light had died out, and that henceforward he was to walk in darkness, without care, without hope, without interest in any mortal thing. Previously he had found some relief in hard study; now he found it impossible to fix his attention on his books. The awful sense of something impending was perpetually upon him; the more awful sense of something wanting in his life never left him. The only time that a ray of comfort broke in upon him was when Ronald Kilsyth would come and sit with him, and they would talk of the dead girl for hours together, as Madeleine had predicted they would do. They are very much together now, these two men; Ronald has risen in the service, and he and Wilmot are engaged in ameliorating the condition of the common soldiers and their families. It was a work in which Madeleine at one time took much interest; and this was sufficient to recommend it to Wilmot, who at once took it up.

He is a middle-aged man now, with a grizzled head and a worn grave face. He has wealth and fame, and might have any position; but the world can offer him nothing that arouses in him the slightest interest, unless it be associated with the memory of his lost love.

THE END.

Printed by W. H. Smith & Son, 186, Strand, London.

www.ingramcontent.com/pod-product-compliance
Lightning Source LLC
Chambersburg PA
CBHW021321110726
47900CB00005B/1305